SPINNER

· a novel ·

ABOUT THE AUTHOR

Ron Elliott directed television for the ABC for some years before returning from the east coast to Perth, Western Australia, where he has worked as a freelance script writer and film and television director. He currently lectures in screen writing and production at Curtin University and continues to write for the screen. *Spinner* is his first novel.

SPINNER

· a novel ·

RON ELLIOTT

 FREMANTLE PRESS

To Jill.
And also Vivienne, Leonie and Meredith.
And to Samantha and Frances.

CONTENTS

It was a long time ago, between two wars, when David came and conquered all, not with rifle and bayonet, but with a cricket ball. It was the most astonishing thing you ever saw, but all the more amazing because we needed him so much, not just his family, or his town, but the whole country. We all wore the same dopey grin, blinked through the same shining eyes and gave a collective shake of the head at the crazy, impossible wonder of it all.

Here is his story, the best I can recollect it, from seeing some of it myself, and finding out the rest.

David's favourite place was the dam, and his favourite time was just before sunset, when the midgies came out from wherever they hid during the day. And they hovered, and careered and dived and streaked up, all around the water. Then, as the sun set, the dam water turned golden, and the midgies danced around the liquid gold, themselves turning from grey to silver and then golden. For those fifteen minutes they became fairies, wraiths and sylphs and everything else filled with magic that you could never catch, nor seldom see.

When the sun finally dipped out everything would turn into silhouettes and the magic dancing things would turn back into midgies and mosquitoes, and it really wasn't a good time to be around the dam anymore, because they'd get up your nose, and down the back of your neck and some of them would bite you. Yet, even after the sun went down and the midgies started biting, David would stay a little longer, and think about his mother.

CHAPTER ONE

Just after lunch David's grandad came to the hay shed, where he rested one of his long hands on the torn halter hanging on the nail there.

David looked up, a shimmer of dust filling the air from his frantic sweeping.

He'd been pestering his grandfather all morning for leave to go into town but the old man had just pointed to each of David's unfinished chores then moved off to do his own. On school days David had fewer jobs to do, but Saturday and Sunday were full of them. He'd shifted the hoses, fed the chooks, chopped wood and then attacked the sweeping of the hay with such vigour that Jess the blue heeler had gone to hide under the rain tank.

David set aside the broom and waited, hopeful as his grandfather looked.

'You call this done?'

David tried not to look at the floor, where he knew there was lots of hay still, but the glint of a half covered horseshoe dragged his eyes down. 'Pretty much done.'

'I beg your pardon.'

David swallowed, squinting at the sunlight behind the old man, or maybe at the line he'd crossed. His grandfather was a thin man, long limbed and leathery from work and

the sun. There were a lot of lines around his grandfather's
eyes. And a lot of lines you could cross.

David looked down. 'Sorry, sir. It's not done.'

'Why?'

'Cos it's not done properly.' He could feel the old man still
staring, but didn't look up. He could feel the old man start
to shift to go, and he tried to stay quiet, but it just wouldn't
stay inside him. 'Don't you even want to know the score?'

Australia were playing England. It was the second day of
the first Test being played in Brisbane. It was cricket, the
most wonderful game in the world.

David's grandfather turned back and looked at him with
his closed face.

'The Railway Hotel will have the wireless on,' David offered. 'I can hear it out the window if I stand by the veranda.'

His grandfather looked back out across the yard like he
could just make out the Test match being played all the way
across the country. He took his time. Maybe he was seeing
a ball being bowled or a brilliant dive and catch. Maybe
it was a batsman standing tall and cutting the ball to the
boundary. Maybe it was a spin bowler he could see.

David's grandfather used to be The George Baker once.
He had been an off-spin bowler for The Wheatfields,
and then Country. He had been the coach of a combined
Western Australian team that played Visitors from other
states and other countries. David had seen photographs in
the Railway Hotel. But that was before the war, and before
David was born and ... before. Now George Baker was just
his grandad, and he never talked about who he once was.

David supposed his grandfather must have loved cricket.
He didn't seem to now. Maybe for his grandfather all the
cricket training was like the farm work, an eternal wrestle

against a stronger competitor who just wouldn't quit.

His grandfather finally answered. 'They brought over a pretty good team this time.'

The English had brought out a fearsome team. George Proctor was said to be the fastest bowler who had ever lived. Tudor was the most fierce, Windsor was cruel and gifted, and Longford a talented bat and a winning captain. They had a very strong batting line-up and it was difficult to see how Australia would manage to bowl them out especially with so few quality spin bowlers in the current game. That's what the newspapers said.

'Can I go then?'

'They will have finished for the day.'

'Then I can get the final score, for the day's play.'

'You can get that tomorrow.'

'But tomorrow, there'll be another score.'

Grandad nodded.

'You mean I can go?'

'Finish your work.' The old man turned and walked towards the work shed.

David went back to sweeping up the hay. He pulled up the horseshoe and put it with others on the wood frame of the wall. He picked up the fallen bale and restacked it. He swept up the chaff and hay bits into a pile and sifted out the dirt so they could use it as feed for the few sheep they still had.

As David swept he also played cricket. He called the game aloud like a wireless report and sometimes he swung the broom, making the stroke. 'Proctor turns having reached the start of his run-up. David Donald takes guard, having played majestically to ninety-six. Proctor is running in, fiercely. Donald is ready. Proctor like a steam train. He bowls. And a cracking stroke to the boundary for four runs. What a show. What a wonderful hundred against the most fearsome bowling in the world today.'

At around three o'clock, while David was mucking out the stables, his grandfather came to the fence holding a badly bent shaft bolt. This joined the horse traces to the plough. He placed the bolt on a fence post. 'When you've finished that, go and see if you can get another of these from Pringle's.'

David cycled madly, his long fingers a bunch of eager snakes riding on the handlebars.

Dungarin, like many country towns, kept some places open for business on Sunday afternoons. The pub, the blacksmith's and a back door of Pringle's Westralian Farmers Hardware and Stock Feed allowed for some extra farming needs and gossip.

David rode down the main street of Dungarin at full pelt, his eyes fixed on the Railway Hotel, his ears already straining to hear a cricket report from the wireless by the front window. As he neared Pringle's, a motorbike backfired with the sudden charge of a rifle shot. David wobbled on the bike just regaining control, but a horse, waiting outside the blacksmith's, baulked and danced back, its rope snapping. Wide eyed, the horse spun into the street in front of David, who tried to turn his bike the other way, only to whack his right handlebar into a veranda post. The bike stopped and David somersaulted as he let go.

As the world turned violently upside down, David watched the horse continuing its mad dash up the street. His bike was sliding still. He needed to protect his wrist. There was a big spider web on the underneath side of the tin roof of the veranda. Some sacks of feed were coming towards his back.

David pushed his right wrist under his left arm and hugged it as his head cracked against something hard and his back collapsed into the sacks.

Silence. The end.

David became aware of his own raspy breathing and a slight dampness at the back of his head before he made out the voice.

'What do you think you're doing now, Donald?'

David opened his eyes to see Mr Pringle's red face glaring down at him.

'He fell, Mr Pringle.'

David, still lying on his back on the meal sacks, looked over to see Nell Parker, the blacksmith's eleven year old daughter, coming towards him.

'I can see that,' said Mr Pringle. This was the oldest Mr Pringle. Dungarin had three Mr Pringles. There was a middle Mr Pringle, who ran the butcher's, the baker's and the pub, and a younger Mr Pringle who managed the wheat operations. This Mr Pringle was the stoutest, most usually angry Mr Pringle, who ran the Westralian Farmers and the bank. None of the Mr Pringles liked David very much. 'You should stop dreaming and concentrate on what you are doing.'

'But it wasn't his fault, Mr Pringle,' pleaded Nell. 'The car backfired and that spooked the horse. Dad was going to shoe it this afternoon for the Kellerways, only he had to look at Taylor's flat-bed first, on account of him needing it to go into Geraldton tomorrow.'

David watched an upside down Nell look brightly at a blinking Mr Pringle, whose whole capacity for anger seemed to just go out of him right then. He seemed thinner when the anger was gone.

Nell looked up the street, before adding, 'Dad's gone after the horse.'

'Well, be careful,' said Mr Pringle, going back inside.

Nell looked down at David, who began to unwind himself. His wrist was fine. 'Do you know the cricket score?'

'Haven't you heard? Australia is in all sorts of trouble.' Nell said 'trouble' like other people might say 'fine weather' or 'jolly good swim.'

'Already? But it's just the second day.'

'The Poms are six hundred and twenty-three runs.'

'In just two days. Are you sure?'

'I've been going over to the Railway to listen. I knew you'd want to know. It's just as your grandad said. We don't have a good spinner.' She took a dramatic swallow before going on. 'It's worse than that. Australia are two out for eleven runs at stumps.'

'Who's out?'

'Johnson and Bardsley.'

David was relieved. Johnson was in poor form, so no real loss there, and they were trying out Bardsley so he'd learn from this Test. It meant John Richardson, the Australian captain, was still in. He could hold things together, and rebuild the innings. But letting the other team get six hundred runs in the first innings was always going to put your batsmen under pressure.

'Some boys are playing at the oval,' said Nell.

David started to flex his fingers. He winkled them, keeping them straight, then bent and straightened, keeping them tense. He flicked them out, loose, like he was trying to shake off water. He started to bend his wrist, and turn it clockwise, then anticlockwise.

'They won't let you play.'

Nell was smiling but when she saw David looking at her she changed her face to a sympathetic look. She had a smudge of grease on her cheek, and quite a lot on her dress. David noticed she had a scab on one knee. The scab had split and two flies were fighting to get at the blood welling there.

David picked up his bike. One handlebar was badly bent but everything seemed to work.

Nell said, 'Are you going to go and watch?'

'Yep. Who scored all the runs for England?'

As Nell recounted all she could remember of the cricket score, David wheeled his bike. They passed the new Anzac memorial on the way. The town had built a kind of tower out of granite that was a memorial to the Anzac soldiers who'd died in the war. It was sometimes called The Great War and sometimes called The War To End All Wars, which was worth it, some said, to end war. Mostly, it was just called The War, and people didn't want to talk about it. Australia had lost a lot of men to The War. So had Dungarin. Some men came back with an arm gone, or a leg or an eye. Lots of men didn't come back at all. One of the men who didn't come back was David's father.

There were ten older youths playing in the centre of the school oval. A motorbike was parked along with a farm flat-bed and a couple of horses under the trees. They were playing tip and run. If the bat made contact with the ball, you had to run. Whoever got you out, be it the bowler or the catcher or the fieldsman, became the next batsman.

A lad, whom David didn't recognise, danced down the wicket to hit a drive. Judging from the slumped shoulders of the bowler and the fieldsman who was trotting over the far boundary to retrieve the ball, they were having trouble getting this fellow out.

'Geez, Eddie, hit us a catch,' yelled Billy Clarke from cover.

'That was a catch,' said the older youth, 'you just weren't standing in the right place.'

From his accent, you could tell Eddie wasn't from around here.

Bob Pringle sprinted in and bowled a beam ball straight at Eddie's head. David heard Nell gasp, just before the youth stepped neatly aside and helped the ball over his shoulder to the fence near the school.

'He's got good technique,' said David. He and Nell had edged onto the field now.

'That one fair nearly took my block off, Bobby,' smiled the batsman.

'Yeah, well maybe you wanna think about retiring,' growled Bob.

'Before you're hurt,' yelled Fred Calligan from down near the boundary.

There were mutters of agreement from the field. It was hot and dusty. The school oval hadn't seen grass since last May when it rained for a single day. When the men got tackled at football they got gravel rash.

Eddie pointed grandly towards the stumps. 'There they are, boys. Just hit the wood.'

Bob Pringle bowled again, and again Eddie stepped forward, but this time he cut and the ball raced towards where David and Nell were standing. As Nell bent to try to field it, David said quietly, 'He uses his feet really well. So he's turning the length into a half-volley all the time. Here. Give it here, Nell.'

Nell threw David the ball. He caught it and stepped a few more paces towards the cricketers before throwing the ball. It was a poor throw. It fell between two boys without even much dust jumping.

That's when Eddie turned and winked to David. No one else had even looked, but that was what David had been waiting for. 'Can I play?'

'No.'

'Not likely.'

'Rack off, Donald.'

It was instant, practised and said without feeling.

Eddie said, 'Why not let them field near the boundary? You could use the help.'

'He'll want to bowl,' spat Billy.

David was watching Bob Pringle. He'd picked up the ball and looked from it to David, thinking. Now Bob was smiling a nasty smile. He looked at David then tossed him the cricket ball. 'Come on.' He looked back at Eddie. 'We'll let the young lad have a bowl at you, Eddie.' He looked around at the other youths who started nodding suddenly.

David rubbed the ball in his palms. It was well worn, some stitching loose with lots of tears in the leather. It was a very good ball—for a spin bowler. He spun it gently from hand to hand, as he walked to the bowler's mark. The feel of the rough ball made his hand tingle.

Bob yelled, 'Come on, you fellas, come in.'

Eddie looked suspicious. 'What you blokes up to?'

Bob said, 'I'm just setting my field.'

Fred yelled, 'Hey, you're about twelve, aren't ya, David?'

David nodded, but was not really interested in talking. He looked down the pitch to the batsman.

Jimmy Drake yelled, 'Geez, I'd hate to be bowled out by a

twelve year old kid. Crikey.'

They were all in on the joke except Eddie, who could not figure out what was going on. There was clearly some trick.

Bob set his field. It was most unorthodox for a game of tip and run. There was a wicketkeeper, and fly, two slips, two leg glances, two silly mid-ons and two silly mid-offs. David was the only fieldsman more than two paces in front of the batsman.

David stood, spinning the ball from his right hand into his left. He'd then put it back in his right hand and do it again.

Bob finally looked at David properly, eye to eye and really looking. 'You happy with that field?'

David nodded.

Eddie looked at David and then around. 'I'm gunna clobber you blokes.'

Jimmy said, 'No, you gunna get out.'

Bob said, 'I'll tell you what, Eddie, if you can hit David over the fence, you don't have to buy a beer all night.'

'You're on.'

Eddie took guard, and David walked in to bowl. The ball didn't come out of David's hand very fast. It seemed to float. But just as Eddie took his two steps down the wicket to smash the delivery to the boundary, the ball dipped in the air, and when it hit the rough flax weave of the pitch, it spun left. It didn't spin a lot but just enough to evade the swinging bat. Eddie staggered forward then twisted to look back at the wicketkeeper who held the cricket ball. He smiled at Eddie then pushed the ball into the wickets.

'You're out, stumped,' yelled Fred gleefully.

'Time for the pub,' said Bob Pringle already heading

towards the horses.

'It was a lucky ball,' exclaimed Eddie. He looked up at David. 'Give me another.'

David nodded eagerly. 'All right.'

'Rack off, Donald. You got your bowl,' said Jimmy, gathering up the stumps and heading after the others.

Eddie ruffled David's head. 'Lucky ball kid, but Bob couldn't try that trick twice.'

'It wasn't a lucky ball,' said David.

Eddie had already gone.

'It was the right ball at the right time to the right batsman. And it went how I wanted it to, so it wasn't luck,' said David to the empty pitch.

'It was great, David. You got him,' said Nell, coming up. 'You got that fellow out.'

It was like David woke from the dream of bowling to the older youth. The sky was darkening and it was ten miles to home.

'I better go.'

David headed for his bike, and replayed the ball as he rode home. He had some difficulty steering because of the bent handlebar. He thought he could have got Eddie out with a completely different ball. That one had beaten Eddie in flight, but had spun away, just enough for the stumping. David could have spun it less, he thought, and drawn the edge of the bat, but you could never be sure if a batsman would be good enough to get a nick, and as for catching, David knew the youths of Dungarin were not very good fieldsmen.

There were a lot of parts to the leaving of a day. There was late afternoon, when the sun finally stopped burning. Then there was the golden time. And then sunset, as it went down and sometimes turned the sky into pinks and purples all mixed with light and shade. Then came dusk. Even dusk had parts to it. When the sun first went down, there still seemed to be light, all around on the things of the ground, just dimmer than the day. Things would start to look grey. Then, after that, everything on earth would go dark, with the land, and the buildings and trees and windmills all black. But the sky stayed lit for quite some time. And it would still be warm for a while. After that, finally, after all the parts of the sun going, it was night and the sky went dark too. Just after that the world would snap into its black coldness and you'd give a shiver. Then the stars came out, and they covered the sky with their dots of light, like a grapevine over a trellis bursting with fruit everywhere you looked until you felt it was close enough to pluck one, and pop the star into your mouth.

CHAPTER TWO

The ground was grey but the sky still light when David got home. Jess barked at his approach until he hushed her.

'Grandad,' he yelled, 'they let me bowl, and I got this fellow, Eddie, from the city. One ball and I took his wicket. Out stumped.' David stopped.

His grandad was looking at the bike handlebars. 'How long have you been gone.'

It was a statement not a question. David tried to remember, and he tried to remember whether there was an actual time that had been agreed on for his return.

'What happened to your bike?'

'Um, I ... a horse,' said David, 'oh, and I've got the cricket score. Terrible news Grandad.'

'Where's the new shaft bolt?'

'Shaft bolt?' David grabbed for his pocket, feeling the old bent bolt, safe but not new.

The old man stood looking at him.

'I'm sorry, Grandad. I forgot.' He brightened. 'I'll get it tomorrow, before school.'

'No.' Grandad was shaking his head. 'You said you'd get it. Get it now.' He turned and walked back inside. The back door led right into the kitchen. David could smell dinner. It smelled cooked. 'But Westralian will be shut.' The door closed.

David looked around. The farm was dark now but the sky still grey. It was time to have his dinner, then to practise his bowling by the tool shed. 'But Mr Pringle will have gone home.'

He got back onto his wobbly bike and cycled towards town. The back of his head hurt and he was hungry but soon he stopped thinking about that and started to think again about how he'd bowled out Eddie from the city. Stumped.

The Westralian Farmers was closed. David rattled on the window by the front door, but knew it was useless. He looked across the street where he could hear a piano at the Railway Hotel and some laughter. David stood outside Westralian Farmers trying to work out what to do. Mr Pringle would not be in the hotel so late on a Sunday. Only the youths from the oval would be there. And Old Jack. Old Jack was always there.

David went on to the other end of town to Mr Pringle's house. The Pringles had mowed grass and roses and a carriageway that had been covered in gravel and turned into a neat track for their motor car. David went around to the back door and knocked. Nothing happened, so he knocked again more loudly.

Mrs Doolan opened the door. Mrs Doolan did some cooking for the Pringles, and looked like she did some eating too. 'David Donald, what is it? What's wrong?'

'Can I see Mr Pringle please?'

'Is your grandfather all right? Has there been an accident?'

'No. He's good. I'm here to buy a bolt for our plough trace.' David pulled the bent bolt from his pocket and held it forward into the light of the kitchen.

Mrs Doolan's face changed. 'At half past seven on a

Sunday evening?'

'Yes,' said David. He supposed the time must be half past seven.

Mrs Doolan shook her head patiently, which meant she was having trouble being patient with him. She lowered her voice. 'David, you can't go bothering people this late in their homes. Go to the store tomorrow, before school.'

'That's what I said to Grandad, Mrs Doolan, but he said now.' David went on quickly so he could explain that it wasn't as odd as it sounded, and not his grandfather's fault, but very fairly thought out. 'I should have got it this afternoon, but I forgot, so I have to get it now, because Grandad's making me responsible, instead of a dreamer, which, in the end, is mostly dangerous.'

David thought over what he'd just said, and was pretty happy with it as an accurate summary of his grandfather's view, but when he looked at Mrs Doolan, she was shaking her head. Nonetheless, she did go in to the Pringles.

David saw her wiping her hands on her apron as she opened the other door of the kitchen. He could see in, past the hall and into the dining room. The Pringles were eating dinner. It smelled like roast chicken. And pumpkin. He could see two of the Pringle children sitting at the table, but not anyone else. They looked to where Mrs Doolan had gone, then suddenly turned and looked towards David, who looked at his boots, which were dusty.

Mrs Doolan returned to the back door. 'Just as I thought, David. It's much better if you go to the store tomorrow before school. These people are having their dinner, child.'

David shook his head.

'How would it be if Mr Pringle had to open up his store at all hours whenever people felt like it? He's the bank manager. He's the mayor. The poor man would get no sleep at all. Now you can stop being so selfish and go home and explain to your grandfather that Mr Pringle said no. All right? And, look, here's an apple for you. To eat on the way home.' Mrs Doolan took an apple from the sink and gave it to David. She closed the back door.

David spun the apple up in a nice arc in the air and caught it in his left hand. He tossed it over to his right and repeated the process. It smelled good. He ate the apple, first in big bites, but in the end, nibbling along the core and around the pips. When he finished, only pips were left. He knocked on the back door of the Pringle house.

When Mrs Doolan opened the door, he offered her the pips. 'Thank you, Mrs Doolan, for the apple. I know it's not fair on Mr Pringle and I'll say sorry, but I have to get the bolt.'

Mrs Doolan took the pips. Her lips went tight, as though she were sucking at a sore tooth. She didn't say anything this time but just went to the other door and opened it and went through to the dining room again. This time Diane Pringle, who was David's age, looked straight at him before he could look away. She looked with hatred.

Mrs Pringle came to the back door. David didn't like Mrs Pringle. She always sounded too nice. She often gave David barley sugar when he was in the shop, for no reason and no charge. She always smelled of flowers and honey. He'd get tongue-tied around her, and never be able to answer her questions, which were about how he was doing at school or what he'd had for lunch. Mrs Pringle was always so very nice and all the other Pringles were so very mean.

But that wasn't why David didn't like to talk to Mrs Pringle. It was the look he'd catch, just at the edges of her niceness. She looked sad. Seeing David made Mrs Pringle feel sad, and seeing Mrs Pringle made David feel sad, in spite of all the barley sugar. Mrs Pringle had been a friend of David's mother.

'Good evening, Mrs Pringle,' said David.

'Hello, David. This horse thingie. If we go down to the store, will you know what it looks like?'

'Yes, Mrs Pringle.' David stood, aghast, as he watched Mrs Pringle get a shawl and light a lantern and take a big key from a hook by the back door. The whole while, he moved from foot to foot, and all he could manage to say, in all that time was, 'You.'

'And why not me?' said Mrs Pringle. 'I think I can unlock a door. And the rest of my family seem too worn out by their luxurious Sunday to manage it. What do you think?'

David didn't know what to think. He thought she shouldn't. He thought she spoke in a funny way, that wasn't poetry or anything like that, but that had a little music to it.

'Come on then,' she said, as she led the way around to the front of the house, the lamp lighting up a circle of roses, then the front fence, as David grabbed up his bike and wheeled it after her, not saying a word, and hoping that she wouldn't say anything either. But she did. As they walked down the main street of Dungarin, with the lamplight moving out ahead of them like a tide, Mrs Pringle told a story.

'I'm from Carlton. Carlton is part of the city of Melbourne which makes even Perth seem small. So when I first came to Dungarin, as the young bride of the oldest son of a gentleman farmer named Mr Reginald Edward Pringle, I was all at sea. Well, all at sea, but all at desert really, and I didn't know how I would cope, as I knew nothing about farming, and nothing about country folk, and I had very little I could share in the way of my interests or the interests of others. Then I met your mother.'

Mrs Pringle looked at David to see if he was listening. Of course he was. He was holding his breath he was listening so hard. He was caught between wanting to hear with all his heart and not wanting to hear another word. But he was locked in the light of the lamp. It was beyond his power to leave the centre of the circle of light that was held by Mrs Pringle.

'And, in spite of her growing up on your farm we found common ground. She'd been down to Perth with your grandfather, you see, on his cricket duties, and became quite the belle. There are a lot of dinners and dances and social occasions surrounding cricket, apparently.'

'That's where she met my father.'

'Yes,' said Mrs Pringle flatly as though David were spoiling something. Then she smiled again, continuing with her remembering. 'Mary loved to dance. She loved music and she loved dancing, and so did I. And she loved to laugh.'

Mrs Pringle went quiet for some moments as she smiled. 'You know, she was a good listener, I think. I had stories from things in Melbourne and parties and anecdotes, as one does, and she, your mother, would drink them in, and laugh in exactly all the right places. She was a joy to talk to you know.'

David nodded. He didn't know, because he could not remember her in any real way. He'd been too young.

They'd reached the store. Mrs Pringle handed David the lamp and unlocked the door.

David's mother was not an actual memory because she'd died when he was three. His mother was a scatter of ideas, and left over objects and some photographs. She was stories, like the one Mrs Pringle was telling; stories about incidents, like the ones Grandad told, although all of his were of his daughter as a child. So David's concept of his own dead mother was more about someone his own age, like a ghost sister, rather than a mother.

Mrs Pringle pushed open the door of the store, took back the lantern and stepped in. The light made lumps turn into tools, and grain sacks, and hardware, with long shadows reaching greedily as she swept the light around the store.

She stood silent, lost in thought, so David took the bolt from his pocket and went to where hostelry items were kept. There were smaller boxes kept on a shelf there and David held up the bolt, as he went from box to box until he found the matching size.

Mrs Pringle started talking again. 'Even after she met your father, we were still friends. Even after he went away. After you were born. David ... I ... I never knew that she ...'

'I've got it,' said David, edging towards the door. He didn't want any more. Not too much all at once. Mrs Pringle had a tear dribbling down her cheek. It was shiny in the lantern light.

'I wanted to tell you ... I wanted to explain ...'

'Please don't, Mrs Pringle.'

'What?' Mrs Pringle looked at him where he retreated to the door.

'Please don't explain. It's making you sad. And I'm not. They were gone before I can remember, so I guess I don't know any better.'

Mrs Pringle looked at him deeply, and it made David look down at the bolt in his hand. 'The bolt was a ha'penny.'

'What?'

'The bolt, when you write it down on our account. It was a ha'penny.'

'Good night, David.'

'Good night, Mrs Pringle.'

David backed out fast. He put the new bolt in his shirt pocket and grabbed up his bike and cycled away from her as fast as he could. When he looked back over his shoulder she was still in the store.

Mrs Pringle made him feel like fainting, he decided. Like fainting, but you don't fall over, but you feel like it, and you can only just breathe, and you've nearly got a headache, but you haven't fallen all the way over yet.

People never seemed to be able to leave David alone. Some had to practise patience on him. Others teased. Some just looked away. He used to think it was because he was an orphan. They were wondering about his bad luck. Then he started to think it was because he was such a dreamer, and didn't seem to understand lots of things that were obvious to others. But this talk with Mrs Pringle had him convinced he was going to die. He was going to die of consumption like a returned soldier, and everyone knew it except David, and only Mrs Pringle wanted to tell him the bad news.

A mile out of town, David had to get off the bike and wheel it because it was so dark he couldn't see the road.

CHAPTER THREE

David headed down towards the river to turn on the irrigation before the sun came up. He had a thick piece of bread dangling from his mouth and Jess watched the bread rather than him as she trailed him on his morning jobs.

The irrigation was a clever system of pipes and taps, which came up from the river to water a couple of paddocks where they grew fruit trees and some melons. If things got dry, and they were already very dry this year, they could move some of the hoses and pipes to keep some feed going on higher paddocks. If the river held. His grandfather said, 'If the river goes, and it does every twenty years or so, there's no good pumping dirt.'

To save as much water as they could there were taps at virtually every juncture of pipe. It was David's job of a morning to turn every single tap on, then half an hour later, turn them off. Each tap was big and hard to turn. He liked to think of it as part of his bowling practice, for the years of turning and turning back had considerably strengthened his wrist and fingers. David crouched by a tap. 'Donald to Windsor ... and he bowls.' He turned the tap sharply. 'Bowled middle stump.'

Jess came up and prodded him with her snout and David gave her a bit of crust. He knew he shouldn't. 'Don't pet the dogs. They're working dogs. You want a pet, move to town.' His mother had ruined a good working dog when she was young. She kept giving it biscuits and petting it and playing and mothering. The dog took to sneaking off to her in the day when it should have been working sheep. 'What did you do, Grandad?' David had asked. He half expected his grandfather to say he'd shot the dog or locked his mother in the tool shed or something like that, but the old man had simply coughed and spat before confessing, 'I wasn't tough enough on her and she kept the dog. It was already spoiled by then.'

David turned angrily on Jess, 'Go on, git. Git out of it. I got work to do.'

Jess's ears dropped and she skulked off, but she didn't go far.

David reached another tap down by the river. He tugged before it gave, but then turned, allowing the canvas hose to fill, like a huge snake breathing in. As David went to the second tap, some twenty yards on, he returned to his commentary. 'And Mr Donald moves in to the English captain, and he bowls. The ball is spinning viciously in the air. One can see it spin from the stands. It bites on the pitch and spins. Longford is reaching. No. It's past him. He's out. Longford has been bowled, out for forty-nine.'

David waved his hands in the air, making a scratchy crowing sound, like the crowd cheering when it's heard down a telephone line and into the wireless.

Jess joined in, barking with the crowd noise.

David was now approaching the next tap. 'Windsor, imperious as ever, regards young Donald as he comes in to bowl.'

David's grandfather felt that Windsor was susceptible to

spin because of his open stance.

Jess had moved now. She'd taken up her position at the next tap along the line. As David came forward, she shuffled back low on all fours seeming to wait for the next dismissal.

'He bowls. It's the skidder.'

Jess barked.

David made the crowd cheer as he moved to the next sprinkler.

David and his grandfather had been working on strategies to bowl at all the great batsmen in the world, especially the English. David's grandfather said there were few quality spinners in the world today and so batsmen were not practised at playing them. David wondered if the war had killed all the old spinners as it had his father.

David bowled out Proctor and continued spinning his way across the paddocks, bowling out batting line-ups from around the world to the adoring barks of Jess.

Breakfast was at six and usually quiet, as Grandad thought through his own chores for the day. Today though, he was more talkative, as he swallowed bread and egg with a gulp of strong tea.

'You got the linchpin all right then.' Grandad nodded at the bolt lying on the kitchen table.

'Yes, sir.'

'No trouble?'

'No, sir,' said David, thinking that maybe his grandfather didn't need to know about Mrs Pringle. It was likely to upset him too. His grandfather was studying David hard, and so David smiled to let him know he was fine about it all and knew he'd deserved what happened and there were no grumbles from him.

'You didn't do your bowling practice last night.'

'But I couldn't, sir, because I had to get the bolt.'

'If you're ready for school, we can do five minutes now.'

'Can we? Oh, I'm right. Ready as rain. Beauty, Grandad.'

The old man followed his grandson out to where they practised. There was a concrete pad exactly the size of a wicket set along the side of the work shed across the yard from the house. There was matting laid across the top of half the slab, just like they did on non-grassed wickets down in Perth and in India.

When his grandad was The George Baker, he had built it to practise on in the off-season. David practised on it now. At the far end was a metal contraption resembling the three stumps, but which would not fall over when hit by the ball. Three yards behind the wickets was half a corrugated rain tank, set in a semi-circle to stop any balls from rolling too far away.

David went to a box of old cricket balls at the bowler's end, grabbed one and started spinning it up into the air, to catch it and start it spinning again.

'Show me your new one,' said Grandad, taking a position halfway down and next to the pitch so he was looking back at David.

'The skidder?'

His grandad nodded.

David could feel him watching closely as David concentrated on getting the grip right. He extended his forefinger and index finger across the seam, with his thumb bent under. The thumb was the key to this one.

David moved in normally and bowled with his usual loop. But, as he was about to let it go, he ripped his thumb backwards rather than spinning his fingers forwards. It was like clicking his fingers to make a noise, as he squeezed out the ball. The ball hit the mat and instead of turning away from the wicket like normal leg spin or towards the wicket like a googly or wrong-un, it went straight, skidding forwards and low. When the ball hit the metal wickets it clanged and David leapt into the air. 'Yes.'

'No.'

David thought through everything. Good grip. Same flight and action. It was a good straight ball. Might have got an lbw if the batsman was defensive. And it did go lower for the backspin. David didn't know what he'd done wrong.

'Show me your grip again.'

David got another ball from the box, and extended his three longest fingers across the seam once again. He bent his thumb under and checked his other fingers.

'Now show me your grip for the googly.'

David moved his thumb up toward the other fingers just a little.

His grandfather pointed to his hand. 'Your thumb's come up closer to your other fingers.'

'Yes, sir,' said David, turning his hand to see. 'It lets me spin it more.'

'No problem with the googly or your leggie, but when you're running in to bowl your skidder, what's the batsman doing?'

'Taking guard?'

'After that?'

'Deciding on the shot?'

'Before that.'

'Watching the flight?'

'Before that?'

'Looking at the ball in my hand!'

'Yes.'

David moved his thumb backwards and forwards. 'He might see I'm going to bowl the skidder, because I've moved my thumb.'

'Find a way to get your hand positions closer to your other deliveries.'

'Yes sir.'

'Fifty or so, then get off to school.'

'Yes, sir.'

His grandfather nodded before leaving. David looked down at his hand around the ball moving his thumb backwards and forwards while feeling it push into the leather. Happy that he had a similar grip to his leggie, he stepped in to bowl. The ball was straight but it didn't back spin at all. In fact, it simply bounced up and would have been hit into the grandstand. 'Maybe even out of the ground,' said David as he grabbed another old ball out of the box. He practised for another ten minutes before having to hurry for school.

David wasn't much interested in school and it didn't seem to have much interest in him. When confronted with pen and chalk, his long fingers behaved with the sureness of the legs of a newborn calf. He wasn't bad at 'rithmatic but just couldn't make the spelling of words stick at all. His reading was awful. Even in a farming school, where most kids would be working at thirteen, David was a poor scholar. His dreaming didn't help, said his teacher Mr Wallace.

At lunchtime, Mr Wallace came up to where David was sitting on the edge of the oval watching the other kids play cricket. 'Not good news, I'm afraid, David.'

'Worse than this morning sir?'

'All out for one hundred and twenty-three. And four for forty-nine.'

'Us or them?'

'They enforced the follow-on.'

'We're getting killed sir.'

'They haven't beaten us since 1912.'

'Until now.'

'You never know. Read on,' said Mr Wallace with a half smile. He was offering the paper. It wouldn't have today's figures but the back pages were full of the first two days play. It was Mr Wallace's way of getting David to read.

David tried to read the story down the bottom because the word 'Spinner' had caught his eye. 'Spinner Cause?'

Mr Wallace must have already read it all because he nodded. 'Spinner Curse. There's a sports reporter named O'Toole who believes there is a curse on Australian spin bowlers. Hobbs fell off a horse and broke his arm.'

'Hobbs! He had a sore foot. He was nearly better wasn't he?'

'Read the story and find out.'

David sighed and pretended to read the news report while he considered Hobbs' accident. Hobbs was past his prime but a clever and talented spin bowler. Australia could sure use him now as England seemed to fancy the fast bowlers.

'If you didn't try so hard they'd let you play, you know?'

When David looked up confused, his teacher pointed out to his classmates, including Nell, who were playing cricket during their lunch break. 'It's no fun for any of them if you just get them out with every ball.'

'Don't try, sir?'

'Not so hard. Just with them. For the fun of the game.'

'I can't, sir.'

'Of course you can. Toss some up so they can hit them.'

'Even if I want to, Mr Wallace, my fingers won't let me. I've tried. When I come in to bowl my fingers take over and bowl properly no matter what I tell them.'

David watched Mr Wallace looking at him with the kind of look he gave when he thought someone was lying about the spit ball on the blackboard. 'Then you can't blame them if they won't let you play.'

'No, sir.' David didn't blame them, certainly not for the ban on him bowling and probably not for any lack of friendship either.

'You can keep that,' said Mr Wallace, pointing at the newspaper. 'Practise your reading. You might want to look at the falling wheat prices too.'

'Thank you, Mr Wallace,' said David, watching his teacher mop the back of his neck under his hat as he went back inside. Mr Wallace was one of the people who David made especially irritable, like hot muggy weather or a fly that won't stop going at your eyes. David would like not to annoy Mr Wallace. He quite liked him. But David did not know how to get people to like him.

School ended at two p.m., which was four p.m. in Brisbane because it was across the other side of the country. Even so there should have been some hours of cricket play to listen to from the wireless in the window of the Railway Hotel. By the time David got there, it was already over.

'In what has been one of the most comprehensive victories from a touring side, England has given Australia a lesson in all aspects of the game. It is a lesson that Australia needs to take to heart forthwith if they are to have any hope in the remaining four Tests. It's very difficult to see any possibility of improvement by the next Test in Melbourne.'

Australia had been bowled out for just eighty-four in the second innings. They'd been beaten by an innings and four hundred and sixteen runs. It seemed they needed batsmen as well as bowlers. They'd been thrashed in all areas of the game.

Mr Pringle's motor car was parked in the yard when David got home. The engine ticked slowly like a one-winged cicada. Even though his grandfather never said a word, David was pretty sure that the Pringles rarely visited without taking some of the farm with them when they left.

Two of the Mr Pringles were in the kitchen with Grandad when David went in. The oldest Mr Pringle, who owned the Westralian and the bank and the dancing Mrs Pringle, was standing. The youngest Mr Pringle, who ran the silos, was sitting at the table with papers out in front of Grandad.

'I told Mrs Pringle to put the shaft bolt on the account,' said David quickly.

'That's good, David,' said Mr Pringle without looking at him.

'Good afternoon, young Donald. School, eh?' said the youngest Mr Pringle with a grimace.

It was as if David had come across a painting of the kitchen. His grandfather never looked up from the papers and the other two men stayed frozen where they'd been when he came in, looking at the papers as though they might try to fly away.

David felt like he had to rescue his grandfather from something. 'Did you hear the result? It's over already.'

'Not now David. Get some food and do your jobs.'

David went to the meat safe for apricot preserve and

bread. He didn't get butter because he could feel the men waiting for him to leave. His grandfather just kept reading one of the papers, his forefinger tracing the numbers on the page, with his lips moving ever so slightly as if in prayer.

David did his afternoon chores. He put the chooks back in the coop and fed them. He raked out the stockyard, wiped down the horses and topped up their trough. He dug the horse manure into the vegetable patch and watered. Each chore entailed a trip to the well where he'd wind up the bucket. It wasn't a deep well because they were so close to the river, but Grandad had always said all that winding was strengthening his bowling shoulder.

David chopped some wood and some kindling but he didn't take it in because the Pringles were still in the kitchen. David thought of the way his grandfather had told him to get his food and do his chores. He thought of it in different ways, trying to find if there were some reproach, but he could not find any. It was simply a matter not for children David finally decided, and he was glad of it.

It was nearly sunset so he went down to the dam. The dam was about a hundred and fifty yards from the yard and down towards the river, overlooked by a small hill. His grandfather had hired a special kind of road-making tractor during the war, and had the tractor push the dirt and gravel up and out, to make the hole for the dam and the sides. It was topped up by the rains each winter, catching run-off down the hill, so the sheep could water all summer. It had never been empty since David could remember, but he'd never seen it as low as it was now. His mother had drowned in the dam when David was little.

David sat a little way up the hill above the dam. He closed his eyes a moment and felt the warmth coming from the ground. He watched the light become gentle then golden and turn the midgies into dancers. He watched the water in the dam turn silver then black. He thought about what Mrs Pringle had told him about his mother being a laugher and listener and mostly a dancer. He wondered why no one ever said things about what kind of person his father was.

When the Pringles had driven away, David came in and served out rabbit stew and cut bread while his grandfather read the newspaper Mr Wallace had given him. David knew not to ask after the Pringles or the important papers.

'The English batsmen had a particular appetite for Turner's bowling. If ever a player were misnamed, it's Frederick Turner.'

'What do they mean?' asked David.

'He's a spin bowler, a turner of the ball.'

'That's unfair.'

'But accurate. He took one wicket for a hundred and fifty-three. Did you hear about Hobbs?'

'Yes, sir.'

'Lawrence with consumption. Moffit drowning. And Brand with malaria.'

'From the India tour.'

'And now Hobbs to a horse riding accident. Strange times.'

David pushed his grandfather's plate across the table and sat down. 'So how did our fast bowlers go?'

As they ate their dinner, Grandad and David checked the scores and dissected the game as they guessed at what might have gone on behind the cold facts of the newspaper report. After they'd washed up, David was sent to practise his bowling alone because his grandfather said he had more bookkeeping to do.

David lit the lantern by the tool shed so it lit his practice wicket. He carefully got the old plough horse halter out of the hay shed, and placed it on a good length, right in front of the wickets. The hole, in the centre of the halter, where it fitted around the horse's neck, faced forward, so there was a gap of about one foot high by four inches wide.

Moths dashed themselves against the lantern, some so hard that their wings shattered to drift away in pieces as they fell to the ground. There was a goanna who lived in a small burrow under the cricket pitch; in the morning, when the sun warmed things, the goanna feasted on the dead and dying moths of the night before.

David got the box of cricket balls and began to practise. First he bowled some off spin, around the left edge of the halter and into the stumps. Then some more off breaks that held their line a little more so they clattered noisily into the corrugated iron behind the stumps. Then he switched to leg spin. He bowled some balls to the right of the halter, spinning them in towards the wicket. He really let his fingers rip on these balls, making a humming sound he liked, spinning them back around and into the stumps from a long way out. He bowled some more leggies towards the halter, but spinning away to the left and an imaginary slips line. Next David bowled a loopy. This had his usual leg-spinner grip, but used more of his third finger and a lot of overspin so that the ball dipped a little in the air and then bounced higher over the halter and the stumps beyond. Then, still checking his grip, he started to work on bowling the skidder, so the ball would go through the gap in the halter and into the stumps.

And all the while, he kept up an imaginary commentary. 'O'Malley, the English opener, is well set. His tight defence and patient attacks have thwarted Australia. He's on forty-eight. David Donald comes in to bowl.' David bowled, and the ball skidded through the hole to hit the wickets in the middle stump. David leaped in the air. 'Yes, he's bowled him.'

There was clapping. David turned.

A man's voice came from the darkness, 'Well bowled, but I don't think you would have bowled O'Malley with that ball. He's defensive. He would have played back. Leg before wicket, I would have said, low on his back pad.'

The man stepped into the light by the edge of the shed. He smiled a big, open smile with lots of teeth. He had good teeth and bright eyes that seemed to sparkle with his smile. David found himself smiling too, but stopped.

'We haven't got any work. Not that we could pay for.'

'Glad to hear that. I can't say I like work much.' The man kept smiling. He looked down the wicket.

'Are you here to see Grandad?'

'Directly. I got caught up watching you bowl. Neat trick with the halter.'

'My skidder.'

The man nodded seriously. It was a proper conversation.

'They call that ball a flipper, over in Melbourne.'

'Oh,' said David, disappointed that he hadn't invented it.

'Don't worry,' said the man, 'you get it right, you're still going to surprise most batsmen in the world whatever you call it.' The man smiled again, and so did David, knowing straight away this must be right.

'I've got one that doesn't hold up so much. It goes straight on, but faster than the skidder.'

'Do you call it a "shooter"?'

David nodded, pleased that the man knew the right things about cricket. He got shy then, and looked down, but he could feel the man still looking at him.

'Your thumb's more under than with the other balls.'

David looked up, surprised. 'You know a lot of bowling?'

'A bit. I was a batsman. Once. I used to know enough about bowling to stay in sometimes.'

David looked at the man. He had a jacket and good shirt and hat but wore no tie. Now that he looked more closely he thought he was dressed too well to be a swagman. His shoes were good, but dusty. His hat was pushed forward in a cheeky way. He started to roll a cigarette as he talked, holding the paper easily in one hand, as he dropped in the tobacco without wasting any.

'My grandfather was a spin bowler down in Perth.'

'The inimitable George Baker. Yes,' said the man, taking his eye off the cigarette making for a moment to look straight into David's eyes. 'That's where I met him. He was a coach. Hard but fair, they always said of him.'

'They still say it now when he sells a cow.'

The man licked along the edge of the paper, and rolled the cigarette. 'Me, I always found him hard, but—just plain hard.' The man laughed, and David did too for a moment, before he checked for his grandfather.

The man lit his cigarette, then jiggled some coins in his pocket. He suddenly moved down the pitch making David step back. But he moved past and grabbed up the horse halter, moving it off the pitch. He took some pennies from his pocket and started placing them on the pitch about a yard in front of the wickets. His clothes were loose on him, like they didn't quite fit. He stepped and bent and weaved, placing the coins. He had a limp.

'The name of the game, David Donald, is to land the ball on the coin and thereby knock the penny off the pitch. Every penny off the pitch is yours.'

'There's sixpence there!'

'Looks like you're going to be a rich man. If you're any good.'

The man flicked the brim of his hat and winked.

'How did you know my name?'

'Well I listened to your wireless commentary for a start. But also Donald is your father's surname ... and mine.'

David held his breath, standing in the middle of the pitch, in the middle of the lamplight in the dark.

'I'm your father's brother. Michael James Thurstan Donald at your service.'

David blinked. He didn't even know his father had a brother.

'Well there's no James Thurstan in the middle. I just made that up. I suppose you should call me Uncle Mike.'

The man smiled again and tipped the brim of his fedora.

No one had ever said anything about an uncle.

The man nodded as though he could see into David's head. 'No one's mentioned me, eh,' said the man, gathering up more cricket balls. 'I'm one of the black sheep kind of brothers, and as I recollect, your grandfather never did like me too much, so the feathers might fly a bit tonight, or perhaps some wool, me being a black sheep. Wool flying doesn't quite have the same feel to it as feathers. Not quite so much stuff floating in the air, or squawking either, come to think of it. Think quick, live grenade!'

At that, David's Uncle Mike tossed up one of the cricket balls. David woke from all the news and all the words with a cricket ball nearly on him. He grabbed his hands at it, but only succeeded in knocking it away.

'Not much good at the return catches then, are you Davey?' Then he laughed. It was a big open laugh, laughing at David.

David grabbed up the ball, and hugged it to his chest.

Uncle Mike kept laughing.

Only David didn't mind this man laughing because he wasn't laughing meanly. It was like he was joining in. Joining in at David's surprise and panic and confusion and enjoying it with him. It made David laugh too. A little bit embarrassed at first, but then they laughed together.

The laughter brought Grandad.

'Look, Grandad,' said David, 'It's my Uncle Mike.'

His grandfather stood still, his face hard, his eyes harder still.

David stopped laughing.

'Gidday George,' said his uncle, looking sly.

David looked from his grandfather to his uncle and back. They weren't friends, he knew straight away.

'I thought it was time. Time I came and had a talk to you about the boy.'

David's grandfather looked a little afraid, then angry, then nothing. David had seen the second two looks on his grandfather, but never the first.

CHAPTER FOUR

David woke again. It was still night, with just a little light coming from the kitchen lamp. Someone was at his wardrobe.

The men had talked late. David had strained to hear but couldn't make much of the urgent murmur. He could half remember waking to shouts. 'You have no right. No right at all.' His grandfather. He was sure he'd heard his uncle yell too. 'A promise to a dying man.'

David watched the person stealing his clothes. He turned and saw David watching. He smiled his electric smile and David saw it was his Uncle Mike taking clothes from the cupboard and putting them in a bag.

'Gidday Davey. We're going on a trip.'

David got out of bed dragging half his blankets with him. He pulled his pants on as he went into the kitchen. His grandfather was sitting at the kitchen table still in the clothes of the day before.

'What trip?'

His grandfather turned with dark, sleepless eyes.

'What's wrong?' David asked.

'Nothing's wrong at all,' said his uncle, coming from behind carrying the bag of clothes. 'David, how would you like to go down to Perth and bowl for the Western

Australian team?'

David couldn't think of anything for a moment. He had trouble focusing on what was said.

'Sure hope you don't freeze like that in front of a batsman, matey. You know that's what rabbits and roos do on the road when a motor car comes along at night. It's the headlamps. They're halfway across the road and they look up and see this light. They're so confused that such a thing as the sun or moon could be coming at them, they just sit there. Mighty easy way to get rabbit for dinner. Come on, lad. We got a train to catch.'

David looked back to his grandfather. 'What trip?'

'I'll take your rig,' his uncle said, 'if that's all right. Leave it for you at the station.'

David watched his grandfather who sat at the table looking at an empty tea mug. He'd never seen him like this; like he was soft, empty of his woodiness.

The back door opened and Uncle Michael stood looking at the grey light of pre-dawn. 'Will you look at that? Not a cloud in the sky. It's gunna be a hot one. Any particular horse you'd rather I took, George?'

His grandfather shrugged. His uncle did too as he went out towards the sheds.

'Grandad, what's happening?'

David watched his grandfather suck in the air in one long, strong breath until he filled and became himself, full of tree once again. 'Just as your uncle said. You're going down to Perth so you can improve your cricket.'

'But ... now?'

David and his grandfather had talked of Perth, and of eventually going down there to the city to play for a team. When David was older, and a better bowler, it would be time to try out for Western Districts or Fremantle and show what he could do. That's what his grandfather had done when he was a young man.

'I'm not ready.'

His grandfather got up from the table but stayed a moment holding it, before he took another big breath and went over to the stove to prod the embers. 'Maybe. And maybe not. I think your technique is very strong. No, it is better than very strong. You are the best spin bowler I have ever seen. Technically. But I don't know whether your game is strong. It's what's between the ears that makes the bowler.' He turned from the fire and looked at David. 'You've got a very young head on young shoulders even for twelve, so that's why you might not be ready. On the other hand, there is only one way to get experience and that is to get it.'

'Grandad, I don't know him.'

'He knows his way around the city and he knows the game. He knows cricket people so they'll take a look. It's about time you bowled to real batsmen.'

'Can't you come?'

'Course I can't come. I have to look after the farm.'

'But I help you. What about the animals? Who will turn the taps on the pump by the river? The eggs. Who'll get the eggs?' David was panting, and he had to blink a sting in his eyes.

'Don't you cry, boy.' It was an order, his grandfather's voice all hard again. 'You think you can stay here forever?'

David gulped, but he couldn't stop the first gasp coming up, loud and pained. He was going to cry and he knew it, so he ran.

Outside the sun was coming up. His uncle was hitching up the rig. David ran out past the other shed, Jess chasing him and barking. David growled at her, but she kept at him as he tried to outrun her. When she nipped his leg he stopped, not far from the dam.

'Ow, you bloody dog.'

Jess crouched, her ears down and tail still, confused that the game had turned out wrong.

He pulled up his pants leg and saw that she'd drawn blood. 'You bloody dog. I'll fix you.' David grabbed up a lump of quartz ready to throw, but she got all excited again thinking he had something for her to catch and she danced back and forward and then turned around ready for the throw. She was not afraid of the rock because he'd never thrown anything at her. He wanted to pat her and didn't care if he spoiled her because he was going. It would serve his grandfather right to have a spoiled dog.

David took a piss, watching it steam and burrow into the dry ground. Jess inched forward until she could smell where he'd been. He went down to the dam, and looked at the water. It was black.

'You gunna go for a swim?' His uncle limped down towards him.

David didn't say anything. He kept looking into the dam.

'It's all a bit sudden, eh?' he said gently. 'It's always sudden, when it's time to grow up. Well, so they say. Wouldn't know myself. I seem to be growing down rather than up. So they say. Bloody opinionated they are, aren't they?' David's uncle sniffed at the air or the day, looking out over the farm.

David realised he was watching him out of the corner of his eye. He seemed to find everything so much fun, even the air.

'See, here's the thing, David. I saw you bowl last night. I think you are good enough to bowl for Australia. Right now. I mean even if there were any other bowlers not on death's door.'

David looked up at him. He couldn't help it.

'Insane, yes? Of course it is. Won't happen. Can't. You have no idea how good a bowler you are. The control. I saw it straight away. And your grandfather knows it.'

David started to shake his head.

'He knows it and he knows it's time. So I've convinced him to let us try to make it happen. Now.'

David looked at his uncle closely. He needed a shave, and some sleep, but his smile was still such a dazzling thing, David had trouble looking away.

But he did. He looked away and said, 'I don't want to.'

'I think my brother would have wanted you to do that. I think it would have made him the proudest man in the world.'

David felt like he was up a tree; as though the branch he'd just grabbed had snapped and he was about to come away.

'See David, here's the other thing. Your grandad can't afford you. The farm can't afford you.'

The branch gave way. Snap. David was falling.

'But that's okay. If we get you bowling down in Perth, then I think I know a way we can make enough money for you to send some to him, to help him on the farm. Would you like that?'

What David would have liked was to be asleep again and to wake up not in this day. But he wasn't falling now. He checked the sun. It was higher and shining on all the ground. He sniffed the air too and found the faint stirrings of sheep dung and earth mixing with something else he couldn't quite place. Yes. The fetid water of the dam had a musty smell that the sun stirred up.

'My mother drowned here.'

'Here?' His uncle blew a long, slow sigh until there surely couldn't be any air left in him. He took a step forward and skidded slightly on the dusty incline.

David watched his uncle searching about in the dam as though he might see her floating there. He took another step forward as though to dive and retrieve her. 'Well I'm here now, all right,' he said into the water before turning straight away and scrambling up the slope and limping back towards the house.

Grandad was waiting for them by the wagon. David got up on the seat and sat silently. His uncle climbed up beside and grabbed the reins.

His grandfather said, 'If anything happens to him, I will find you and I will kill you.'

'Fair enough, George. But what if what happens is fame and fortune and wonderful things for everyone? Any room for that in your perspicacity?'

'Not so's I've seen.'

David made himself not look at either man or at the farm. He watched a bag of bread get pushed by his grandfather's long fingers into the well by his feet. Then came a Gladstone bag.

'Bowl well, boy.'

David made himself hold still. He didn't even nod, but just looked at the bags in the footwell. His uncle shook the reins and the horse stepped. They were going. He watched his knees swaying in time to the horse's steps until he knew they were off the farm and onto the main road, and that's when he finally let himself look around at the paddocks and other farms on the way to Dungarin.

'How will Grandad get the rig back?' asked David, after a mile or so.

'Come in on a horse, I expect, and lead it home.'

'How did you get out to the farm last night?'

'Maybe I borrowed a horse.'

David looked at the man but couldn't tell if he was lying or not until he winked. 'What if everyone just took any horse or bicycle they fancied and took it wherever they had to go?'

'That would be stealing.'

'Aye. But what if everyone did it, so's there were horses everywhere, cos someone else took them there too. If everyone just picked up a bicycle or horse wherever they found it and went wherever they wanted to go, and they left it there. Plenty enough then to go around. And the next fellow to come along could take it too.'

David thought on that a little. 'But then it would be no one's to look after.'

'Or everyone's. In a place called Russia, they're doing that. Letting everyone own everything. Sharing it all out, so everyone is as free as bird, instead of getting weighted down with all their things.'

David nodded and thought some more. Finally he said, 'I guess that's what heaven's like too.'

'Maybe,' said his uncle in a way that David suspected meant the opposite. Leastways, his uncle had no more to say and David was thankful to ride in quiet.

They were in town early, but there were a few carts and some flat-bed trucks waiting on account of the train, which would deliver newspapers and some fresh goods, and take away some items for fixing down in Northam or over in Geraldton.

David tried to look for Nell in the blacksmith's when he put the horse in, but she wasn't around. His Uncle Michael made him hurry, saying they were late, but they had to wait a good half-hour in a corner of the station. David wanted to wait out front so he could tell someone he was going.

'You ever been to Northam?' his uncle asked.

David shook his head. 'I went to Geraldton once with the school and saw the ocean.'

'Pretty big eh?'

'Oh, I reckon Geraldton's not too big. Lot of shops.'

'I was thinking of the ocean,' said his uncle with one of his smiles that was laughing at you.

David didn't smile back.

'Did you like the smell of that seaweed?'

'No sir.'

'Pretty pongy stuff that.'

'Too right.' David laughed.

And his uncle started laughing too. He put his head back, and he opened his mouth and his lungs and he laughed loudly for all he was worth. He laughed so much, there were little tears coming out of his eyes.

It made David stop laughing as it didn't feel right.

When the train came, David put his bag next to him on the seat.

His uncle said, 'Righteo, old bean. See you on the other side then, what?' in an English accent. Then he left him alone.

David couldn't decide about what had just happened to him or what it meant. It seemed too big to be grasped. He supposed it was because he was just too dimwitted to be able to understand. He began to wonder if he was a black sheep too, like his uncle. He wondered if he was the black sheep of Dungarin.

He thought about his grandfather and how he'd allowed him to go with his uncle so easily. He started to consider whether he was a black sheep, not just in the town, but back on the farm with his grandfather too. He did not know how or in what ways his grandfather had feelings for him because he had never said. But he realised now he had counted on it. He assumed it was there under his feet even if no special time was taken to point that out. David thought about this and was suddenly unsure if it was true.

Then David stopped thinking and just looked. He mostly looked at the country he didn't recognise going past the train. It was not yet harvest time but most paddocks had poor crops. A willy-willy sprang up and danced down a hill kicking up the dust before disappearing suddenly midair. There were dead trees on each hill, and white fallen ones too that made you squint at their brightness. Swagmen and rouseabouts and itinerants watched or waved from roads and bridges looking hot and tired and not much good for the work they begged. A mob of Abos looked up from a river and were gone. There were rocks that were sometimes piled and sometimes scattered. The rocks got bigger and more interesting as the train moved into the hills. There were more trees too, bigger gums and others that David didn't know. Soon the trees got so thick you couldn't see the farms any more.

Some ladies sat in the carriage, dressed up and knitting

as they talked in murmurs that David couldn't make out over the noise of the train. A man in a suit read a book the whole way, his hat sitting on the seat next to him. David guessed they must travel on trains so much that they didn't care what was outside, nor about the coal smoke and grease smells coming into the carriage.

David got up and went back to another carriage. He stood in the doorway where he could see his uncle playing cards with two rouseabouts and a man in a suit. There was money piled on the fold-down table between them. David watched his uncle drink from a hipflask and offer it round. He told jokes and laughed. David noticed his eyes lose their laughter each time he looked at his cards. It was like a blink of seriousness before turning his smiles back on, like an electric light. He laid down his cards and scooped some pennies, making more jokes. Then he looked at David, and he winked, before going back to shuffling the cards and talking and talking. He talked all the time while he laughed and played the cards. There was just that blink every now and then when he didn't.

David went back to his seat to watch the rocks, the wandering jobless and the big trees as they neared Toodyay. He wished they weren't going to Perth.

In the end they didn't.

They got off in Northam and Uncle Mike carried his bag up to one of the Northam hotels. They went in the main door and down a passage. The bar was noisy with harsh laughter and men's voices as they passed and went up some stairs. His uncle took a key out of his pocket and unlocked the door to a room.

Inside was a lumpy double bed, with an old quilt and a

big chipped wardrobe. 'Home sweet home,' said his uncle as he opened the wardrobe doors to put David's Gladstone in. There were clothes hung up and some cricket bats lying on the bottom.

'There's a farm show here, David. It's like the Royal Show in Perth, with rides and animals and vegetables. There's a show at the side. What the Americans call a sideshow which is full of games of skill and chance, where a man with a bit of blather and a good trick can make some money.'

David didn't say anything. He sat on the bed and smelled the coldness of the room.

His uncle went on, 'So, I'll go get us some food, and tomorrow we'll go to the Northam Regional Show, and show you off.'

Before David could ask what he meant his uncle yelled, 'Think quick. Live grenade.' A cricket ball was coming towards him and he just caught it before it hit his chest. 'Much better,' smiled his uncle before leaving the room.

David looked down at the ball. It was new and all leather.

David went to the double doors that led out onto the veranda to look through the curtains. There was a man further along, leaning over the rail and looking at the street. David could hear a motorbike coughing up the road. It went past and away. Things got quiet again.

David put the cricket ball up to his nose and smelled its newness. He went over to the wardrobe and looked in, seeing that there were five cricket bats and some more, older cricket balls. He cupped the new cricket ball in his hands, squeezing gently to feel its firmness. He tossed it from hand to hand, spinning it in gentle arcs. Then he lay down on the bed, rested the ball under his chin, and thought about nothing.

It was late, and the sun's light was already at the veranda doors. Uncle Mike was asleep next to him on the bed. With his eyes closed and his mouth open his magic was gone. He had a puffy face, with little lines of blood on his nose and at the top of his cheeks. He had a small scar near the temple of his right eye.

David eased off the bed and sat at the small table where his uncle had left a cold pork pie on a plate. David bit into the pie, looking at his uncle's back. On the floor next to the bed were his boots and socks.

David needed to go to the toilet, but finished the pie first as he thought about his uncle's limp. He eased forward on the floorboards and across the mat to the side of the bed. He looked down at his uncle's feet. He only had four toes on his right foot. The little one was gone and so was a big piece of foot, leaving a dip in the sole there and a smooth but lumpy pink scar.

David looked under the bed but there was no chamber pot. He put on his boots, tucked in his shirt and took his brand new cricket ball from his pillow.

The corridor was quiet. The rooms had numbers except on the door of one near the stairs. That sign read Bathroom. But when he turned the knob the door wouldn't open. A deep voice grunted, 'Oi, I'm 'ere.'

David went down the stairs of the sleeping hotel. He looked into the bar. It was empty. Stools were upside down on the bar and on some other tables. It smelt of old beer and cigarette smoke. He heard a pot bang further down the corridor towards the back of the hotel and he went down there. He smelt stove smoke and heard a cook or someone in the kitchen, getting things going he supposed. Back on the farm, he would have done his chores by now. He'd be just sitting down to breakfast before riding to school.

By the kitchen door was the open back door of the pub. There was a large cleared area behind, where horses could be watered and bullock teams turned. There were empty hitching rails and troughs by the back of the hotel. Some trucks and a motor car were parked out there so David went over between two of the trucks to piss on the wheel, which was the right thing to do under the circumstances of being caught short. He looked around as he stood there.

He was not only at the back of the hotel but at the back of the town, it seemed. Up past the hotel, were the backs of some shops and then the backyards of some houses. Not much was moving. The river was just down the slope a little and he could see some smoke there, which he supposed was where the town Abo camp was. Dungarin used to have a mob of Abos every winter, but they'd been moved on, Nell had said. David's grandad gave them some salt and sugar for chopping wood just as he tried to give some food and water to anyone else who was passing through.

He did up his pants feeling the weight of the cricket ball in his pocket. He looked over to behind the hotel again. There were some packing cases by the back steps. David looked at the cricket ball. There was nothing so beautiful as a new cricket ball. It was shiny and round and precious ... and usually no good at all to a spin bowler. A ball spun much more easily off the pitch when it was scuffed and battered. It swung and drifted and dipped in the air as its rough and torn edges dragged it this way and that. An old ball was a good ball for a spin bowler. But to David, a new ball was a precious ball; he wanted to keep it new forever and yet, at the same time, he couldn't wait to bowl it and see it spinning, bright and red and glinting through the air.

David found an apple box, which was just about the right size for some wickets, and dragged it up near the back of the hotel, so the foundations would act as wicketkeeper. He turned and he paced out the twenty-two yards for a pitch and dragged the toe of his boot across the dirt to make the line of the crease. He stepped on from that to the couple of paces of his run-up and turned to look at the packing case. He looked at the ball, and started to spin it from hand to hand.

'A murmur has run through the crowd here at the Melbourne Cricket Ground,' said David in his smoothest wireless voice. 'Richardson has tossed David Donald the new ball. Longford seems to be licking his lips at the prospect of spin in the first over of the second Test.' David stepped in and bowled a flattish delivery which hit the dust in front of the box and went straight on, clipping the edge of the makeshift wicket.

David grunted. If he'd bowled that ball in that way to Longford it would have disappeared back over his head and probably over the boundary. David kicked away some of the dust so the ball could grip on more solid ground, and then he started experimenting with his fingers and flight, so he could get some movement and variation from the new ball. Finally, he started to get the ball to spin and dive and dart to the left and right of the wicket. He even got a couple to make the whirring noise as the ball spun in the air before it bounced.

Giggling made him turn. There were a couple of Abo kids near the trucks.

'What?' said David.

'You keep missin',' said one.

'I'm trying to,' said David.

The kids looked at each other with secret smiles, then started giggling again, before the bolder one turned finally and said, 'Well, you bin pretty good den.'

David smiled too. 'You wanna bat?'

And so the little game started.

By breaking off a board from one of the other cases they made a manageable bat. One of the kids batted while the other retrieved the ball and tossed it back to David.

David's first ball dipped under the wildly swung 'bat' and hit the stumps in the middle. His second was a shooter that jumped off the pitch and over the bat to hit the top of the stumps. There was giggling from the fieldsman and wonder from the batsman. David's next ball spun down leg. The fourth spun past the edge towards slips.

The fieldsman picked up the ball, turning it to see if there was some visible trick before throwing it back to David. 'Let 'im hit it?' said the fieldsman.

'I can't,' said David.

Both boys looked a little sulky. David thought of an idea. 'Okay.' David bowled a top-spinning loopy. This ball landed short but climbed quickly. The batter raised his bat, but nearly too slowly, and only just managed to snick the ball, which continued on to hit the wall behind on the full. It would have been an easy wicketkeeper catch.

The batsman looked disappointed.

'It touched your bat,' explained David.

The fieldsman grabbed up the ball and smiled past David before launching the ball over his head. David turned. Another Abo kid was now there and he caught it.

David held out his hand.

The new kid looked at the ball. Then threw it over David's head towards the batter. David turned in time to see the batter hit the ball off through extra cover. The fieldsman ran off towards the ball, laughing. And then the kid who'd thrown it to the batter started to race him to the ball too.

David smiled and looked back to the batter to share that smile, but he was running off past him and around the trucks. David looked back to the kids who'd nearly reached the cricket ball with a bad feeling growing. One of them picked the ball up and held it towards the other boy. The batter ran up to them, and all three boys turned and ran off towards the river.

'Hey, that's my ball!' yelled David. He was just about to set off after them, when his uncle's voice stopped him.

'You won't catch 'em,' said Uncle Mike from the top veranda. 'And even if you do, you won't get it back if you go down there.'

'Thievin' Abos.'

'Don't say that around me, David.'

'Everyone says it. They stole my ball.'

'If you ever fall through the bottom of the world, the Abos will look after you. It's one of their failings, never judging nor refusing someone in trouble.'

David looked up at his uncle, then off to the river, completely confused again. It was true that his grandfather was always polite. But no one else in Dungarin was. And here was his Uncle Mike speaking up for them.

'You should have let him have a hit.'

'No.'

His uncle looked at him a moment, then shrugged. 'Come on then. Seeing as we're up at sparrow's fart, we might as well get up to the show. There'll be free eggs and milk and we need to get about twenty or thirty cricket balls.'

'Twenty or thirty! What for?'

But his uncle had gone, and David had to hurry inside.

CHAPTER FIVE

David had never seen so many people. He carried Uncle Mike's cricket bag into Northam's football and cricket ground. There were tents. There were brand new tractors with their spiked metal wheels bigger than a man. There was livestock: chooks and cows and horses, sheep and dogs. He saw a bull with a chest as wide as a cow was long.

David closed his eyes. He could smell bread baking and cow dung and horse sweat and wheat dust and smoke all mixed together. There was hammering. And quiet talk. Ladies' voices. Bits of laughter. He heard ducks. There was a cow somewhere across the other side of the oval complaining that it was long past milking time.

He got a fright when a hand was suddenly shaking his shoulder.

'You part horse or something, boy? Sleep standing up.'

'I was listening.'

'Keep moving is my motto. Here. Get this into ya.'

Uncle Mike had a battered tin cup of milk. He took the cricket bag, and handed David the still-warm milk. He had a half-loaf of bread, and David took that too and bit into it.

'Come on,' his uncle ordered, as he turned and started through the stalls and tents. 'I've got an idea for a spot in sideshow alley.'

'Why?' called David, hurrying after. His uncle didn't say. He moved through, nodding to people and calling greetings as he went.

'I know where I need to be at lunchtime, love,' he said to an old lady setting out cups, and she giggled.

'So, this looks like about the best little nag in here. She running in the race this arvo?' he called to a farmer pulling a pregnant cow.

People laughed and smiled and nodded to him. David noticed that you could barely see the limp when his uncle strode through in this way, carrying the cricket bag over his shoulder, being everyone's friend. And then the people's eyes would drift to David and he'd have to look down to not see them.

When they left the produce area things began to change. At a little outside bar, a man was shovelling sawdust off a wheelbarrow and spreading it around the rough wood plank tables. There was a big tent with colourful paintings of boxers. There were stalls where you threw hoops over things to win a doll, and others where you threw darts and lots of shooting galleries with little pellet rifles and little metal planes and the shapes of helmeted German soldiers' heads.

The people began to change too. There were no women here. The men hadn't shaved. Their clothes were older and unwashed. And their eyes looked more careful, like when his uncle looked at his cards on the train. They were like the men you passed on the road to town, the men who came to the farm looking for work at the farm. There was something hungry and hurt about them.

Uncle Mike changed too. He didn't call out here. He whistled something tuneless and nodded and winked, but he didn't say anything, and David soon stopped looking around, just watching his uncle's back as they moved through.

Until they came to the coconut shy. There was a man with one arm, setting things up.

Uncle Mike nodded to the man's arm, and said, 'At least you brought your nuts back all right, eh?'

'An' I still got a good fist on this arm too, you bastard,' said the man, stepping up as though about to hit him.

'That's the ticket, cobber,' said his uncle, as if the man had said 'top of the morning.'

They looked at each other a moment, the one-armed man glaring and Michael smiling.

'I had a bit of a holiday in Egypt, then played up in France,' said Uncle Mike.

'Gallipoli,' said the man without any emotion at all.

'Gotta laugh.'

Neither man did laugh but they both nodded to each other. His uncle said, 'I got a business proposition. Flat rate or percentage?'

The men started whispering seriously.

David noticed a little hessian bag on the ground. It was not much bigger than a man's wallet. It weighed about as much as a cricket ball but had the feel of a loosely packed sack of gravel.

'Throw it.'

David looked up. His uncle was pointing at a coconut resting on a bench.

He put on a caller's voice. 'Step right up and have a go. Knock off the coconut and win a prize. Come on sir, let's have a look at that throwing arm.'

David aimed at the coconut and threw, missing by a good few yards.

'So out of fielding and bowling, what would be your best thing, you reckon?'

'I'm not very good at fielding.'

'Too right. Well, we won't put fielding into the equation then.'

Michael paced out twenty-two good strides, dragging his boot across the dust. Then he went to the cricket bag and got three stumps and knocked them in near the back of the tent. He stood in front of the stumps and played some invisible shots and David realised if you played most shots except the drive, you'd hit the sides of tents on either side and behind, just like cricket nets.

Then he got the side of a tea-chest and some paint from behind the next stall and came to David. 'Time for you to draw up our sign.'

'Me?'

'Yep. Gotta have a sign. Um, let's see. Win a pound. That oughta get them in. I reckon we'll charge a sixpence for three balls. Once they see that it's a kid bowling, they'll be lickin' their chops. Sixpence is a fair bit, but ... well, we'll see how it goes.'

David looked at the wood and the paint brush then back at his uncle. 'Win a pound?'

'Yep. I'll go see if I can find some old cricket balls.' He

looked at the ground. 'And a mat. Gotta give you a fightin' chance.'

So David worked carefully on his sign trying to get the letters to come out right, as he considered his uncle's plan, which he guessed had him bowling at people and them giving his uncle money. No matter how long David thought about the plan he could not find the sin in it.

When Uncle Mike came back he had two big strips of coir matting over his shoulder and a hessian bag. He dropped the bag and old cricket balls came spilling out like overripe apples. He laid them in front of the wicket, 'To give you something to spin on.'

David said, 'The thing is, Uncle Mike, I don't think this is going to work.'

'Is that what you been thinking?'

'Yes, sir. I figure you're thinking if I don't get them out, you have to give them their pound.'

'Whoa, boy. That's makin' it a bit hard on us. No. I was thinkin' that if they hit you back over your head, that'd be tempting enough for them. It's a pretty big gap here. Fancy their chances and put in their sixpence. They get three chances at ya.'

'But I won't have seen them bat before.'

'You think any of them will be able to bat worth a damn?'

'But I have to see someone bat, to work out what their weaknesses are.'

'Not this time, David.' His uncle came over to him and went down on one knee. 'You see we know what they're going to do. If they block you or just keep you out or pad up then they've wasted their sixpence. The money is in the slog. They want to hit you and they want to hit you in that direction there.' He pointed to a big tent about fifty feet away. 'Most of them are going to see a little kid—you—and they're going to see that juicy slow cricket ball floating through the air, like an apple ripe for the eating, and they're going to plant their front foot, and close their eyes, and swing the bat like an axe. Their weakness is you because they've never a seen a bowler so good. And their weakness is themselves because they're hicks and they won't be able to bat. And there's all their mates giving them the "oh aye". And there's that pound making 'em lick their chops. The only thing you gotta remember is to keep varying your deliveries, because some will watch you for a while and take a punt on where the ball might land.'

That was exactly how it went, except that David had much more fun than he thought he would. Part of the fun was the way Uncle Mike talked to the crowd.

'Let's see how this fella is going to go. Anyone reckon he's even going to get near it?'

And the crowd, which had grown to over forty, would cheer and groan and boo along with Michael.

'Come on now. What's your name, son?'

'Frederick,' replied the beefy farm youth defiantly, as he took a couple of loosening swings with the bat.

'Frederick, huh. Now that's a king's name that. Not Fred, mind.'

There were spirited calls from Frederick's friends. Good-natured cheers from the crowd.

'Okay, then. Quiet now. Give King Frederick a chance. This is for a pound. Bit of concentration here.'

The crowd settled.

'Belt it Fred,' yelled someone.

'Don't let him hit you, David,' yelled someone else.

There was some more cheering then, and some mutters and talk.

David stood waiting, trying to ignore the talk a little. In the beginning he had listened and gotten caught up with the jokes and cheering and the like. And it had put him off. He'd been lucky, because as his uncle had predicted, the batters swung so wildly that it didn't seem to matter where he pitched the ball. He'd bowled a few wide though, and his uncle had insisted he bowl those again, 'With no extra charge, good folk of Northam.'

Also in the beginning, David had looked at the people. A man had a big round nose, like a pig's. A lady had ears that squashed out under her hat. An old man had a sore on his face that was weeping some nasty looking water. There was hair growing out of noses and ears and into eyes.

And the people looked back. Some had smiled. Others had glared. There were some who gave him even odder looks. A farm boy yelled, 'Gawd will ya look at the kid's fingers. Like he's holding a couple of dead chooks.' They'd all laughed loud at that. David bowled the next ball without even thinking about it at all and the ball had sailed over his head and way out near the big tent.

That's when Uncle Mike had started talking to him as much as the crowd. He whispered to David, 'Good. That's the pound we wanted to give away, so everyone thinks they've got a chance. You sly old devil you. But you concentrate now, all right. Not them. You got that?'

Now David was concentrating on each ball as though it were practice at home. He started to pretend he was by the shed, with nothing but a few chooks clucking after dinner. He had tried a skidder a couple of times and a shooter, but

Uncle Mike had whispered to leave them out today. He'd explained that they were too straight and could be mis-hit with a bit of luck. So David concentrated on his leggies and wrong-uns and his off breaks. Although he only had to make sure the batters didn't hit his bowling at all, David still hit the stumps with regularity, which seemed to please the crowd more than anything. As did the wild swings.

David looked at Uncle Mike who tapped his forehead. This was his uncle's sign that Frederick was a wild swinger. They had settled on some calls by mid morning. The wild swinger. The dancer, who'd try to advance down the wicket. The sideswiper. The prodder. Uncle Mike privately called them punters and seemed to know what they would do.

David decided on the perfect ball for a wild swinger. He tossed it up slow, with a good arc, watching Frederick open his eyes, not believing his luck with such a slow thing. The lad took the bat back way past his shoulder, then started to bring it forward just as the ball dipped suddenly in the air. David watched Frederick realise. He tried to speed up his stroke, to bring the bat forward faster than he had first intended, but he never quite got there. The ball hit the mat, a good six inches in front of where Frederick could possibly reach it, and bounced high. Frederick's bat flashed uselessly, but also kept going, dragging the lad forward with his own momentum. His front foot went too far forward then, and Frederick fell over on his back.

The crowd cheered hugely, and David couldn't help turning to them.

Amidst the laughing, jeering faces, David saw a serious man who wasn't looking at fallen Frederick but at David. He was a big man with a full, browned face. He wore a checked suit and a derby hat. He looked at David and then tapped his nose, knowingly.

David looked away.

Uncle Mike was helping Frederick up and making a big show of dusting him off. The young lad was blushing red, and trying to shrug David's uncle off.

'Let's have a big hand for Frederick, please folks. And I'll tell you something. If this bloke here goes into the boxing tent, I'd put a couple of shillings on him.' The crowd cheered again, especially Frederick's mates, and the lad settled down. 'Can't bat for nuts, but good shoulders.' And the crowd laughed again, and Frederick found himself grinning too, as his uncle gently pushed him back towards the crowd.

Uncle Mike stopped smiling.

David looked where he was looking, and it was the big man in the derby moving forward. People were patting him on the back.

David looked back to his uncle, who had made the smile come back to his mouth but not his eyes. He looked at David and made his eyebrows go up and down.

'You get 'em, Jack,' yelled someone from the crowd.

'That's Jack Tanner,' David heard someone nearby say.

'Jack, how are you?' asked Michael flatly.

'So this is where you've been hiding,' said the big man, without any humour at all. Tanner took his coat off and flexed his shoulders. He was tall and well fed, with massive forearms. He had a yellow silk vest that caught the light and shimmered.

'Not hidin', Jack. I been waiting for you, so I can take your sixpence.'

There was a look in the man's eyes that David did not like. It was clear Jack Tanner did not like his uncle, and David felt compelled not to like Jack Tanner on that account alone.

'Well, then, will you take a pound worth,' said Jack loudly, bringing out the note. 'Thirty or fifty balls ought to do it, eh?'

Uncle Mike's shoulders slumped, ever so slightly, before he spoke loud enough for everyone to hear. 'Come on now, Jack. A state cricketer like you trying to take money off a kid of twelve years old.'

Jack turned to the crowd with his pound note still raised high. 'Seems to me this kid's been taking plenty of pounds out of Northam. Just want to get a little back for my home town.'

They cheered.

Uncle Mike licked his lips, then shrugged. 'Suits us then doesn't it, David. We'll take the great Jack Tanner's money. I'll make sure I spend it at the Colonial here in town tonight.'

Another cheer.

Jack Tanner smiled, as he handed his coat and hat and fob watch to a pretty lady in a bright yellow dress. He strode to Michael's cricket bag and took out the heaviest bat in there before taking his time to flex his shoulders again, and roll his big neck. He went to the wicket and finally took his guard. 'Nothing personal, lad. You bowl pretty good for a nipper.'

David wasn't sure what to say. He'd heard of Jack Tanner. He was a batsman for the Western Australian combined side who played visiting teams from the other states and from overseas. He looked to his uncle, who gave the 'dancer' signal, but he wasn't smiling his usual smile.

David took a moment to think. What would Grandad say now? Probably that this was a good thing. If David was going to learn to bowl better, he should bowl against better batsmen. Learn. The crowd started muttering a little at the delay. David decided to bowl a high bouncing leg break, to avoid the dancing down the wicket. He bowled.

Jack Tanner didn't move. He didn't raise his bat. He simply stood before the wicket and watched the ball hit the mat and spin a long way to the off side.

The crowd groaned.

'Nice overspin there, lad,' said Tanner.

'He's having a look at you, David,' said his uncle.

David next bowled a ball on the other side of the pitch. He gave it everything, ripping his fingers across the stitching as he let go of the ball. It sang in the air like a little car motor. It was another leggie and it pitched perfectly outside leg stump where it spun behind Jack's legs, knocking over the wickets with a lovely woody sound.

Some of the crowd cheered. Some gasped.

Jack stood smiling and nodding towards David. He still hadn't played a shot. 'That was a beautiful ball, boy. Just about impossible, it was so good.' Jack Tanner went and retrieved the cricket ball, examining it.

'No tricks, Jack. Just good bowling,' said his uncle.

'I'm sure there's a trick, Michael. Just can't see it yet.' Then to David, 'You got a googly?'

'Don't bowl him one, David,' urged Michael, as he put the wickets back in position.

'If you bowl me a googly next ball, I promise I won't hit it.'

'He's going to start playing little guessing games in your head,' said Uncle Mike.

'Unlike Michael Donald, I don't tell lies, boy. I don't know where he found you, but I hope he's paying you your bloody share in advance.'

'Oi, no call for that in front of the ladies now, Jack.'

'Apologies ladies. David. Uncalled for, I grant. How much money you got in the kitty there, Michael?'

'Just try to hit the ball, Jack.'

Jack nodded. Waited. David bowled another leg break, but it never landed. Jack Tanner took a huge step down the mat and caught the ball on the full. There was a gasp from the crowd, and maybe from David, as they ducked. They didn't need to. The cricket ball flew high and far, crashing into the tent near the central arena. There was applause.

When David looked back to the wicket, his uncle was handing Jack Tanner the pound note they'd been showing everyone as the prize. Michael applauded too. 'Ladies and gentlemen, the great Jack Tanner, famous son of Northam, takes the prize. Congratulations Jack. Now who else wants a turn? Come on folks. See, no tricks. It can be done.'

Jack shook his head. 'By my figuring I've got twenty-seven balls left.'

A cheer. Jack grinned at the crowd.

'Come on, Jack,' said Michael quietly. 'You've taken me.'

'Not yet. Not while you've got all those coins in the can there and not while you're still in Northam.'

So Jack Tanner proceeded to hit David's bowling everywhere. When David tried to land shorter, so he couldn't hit the ball on the full, the batsman let it bounce and collected it on the half-volley, before it could spin far. For the next ball he stood so far forward, David mixed up where he was going to land it. David took his wicket on the third ball but it didn't seem to matter. Tanner chuckled, and muttered, 'Nice nut. Now that was a googly,' before blasting the next ball, which didn't spin at all, out over the big tent.

David looked from where the ball had disappeared to his

fingers, which seemed to have lost all feeling. He couldn't account for why the last ball hadn't spun at all. This had never happened. The crowd were laughing and jeering. Many had moved to the side, peering round the side of the tent and from behind each other, in fear of injury. A fat man, with white whiskers and a red runny nose, yelled, 'That one got hit to Perth.'

Jack Tanner stood over Michael, watching him count sixpences and shillings into piles, as the crowd edged closer. Finally, Michael handed Tanner the can and turned out his pockets.

'That's it. Six quid. The lot.'

'But you still owe me a lot of deliveries.'

'And I can't pay you if you hit them, Jack. I'm flat.'

Jack Tanner turned to the crowd and raised the tin. They cheered.

'That's it then,' said Jack. And it was. A man came from the Northam Show and made them pack up because it was too dangerous. One of the cricket balls had hit a prize melon and smashed it.

Uncle Mike giggled. 'I would have liked to have seen that. Must have been pretty hairy down in the main arena with all those cricket balls raining down on the Agrarians of Northam.'

They worked quietly, putting the coconut shy back together. The one-armed man seemed pretty happy himself because he'd been paid in advance and would get a half a day of coconutting in as well.

'Could ya spare a broke digger the price of a drink,' Uncle Mike asked him.

'You bet big, you lose big, mate.'

'Yep,' said Uncle Michael with a smile, 'but it's a bigger

laugh along the way.'

As they made their way out through the crowds who were all still enjoying the day, David said, 'My fingers wouldn't do what I told them.'

His uncle walked a few more paces, nodding, before he finally said, 'Well, that's a good thing to find out now I guess, rather than in front of the Western Australian team.'

CHAPTER SIX

Just after dark Uncle Michael returned to the hotel room to tell David they had a ride waiting downstairs. He pushed his own clothes into the cricket bag and grabbed up David's Gladstone.

'I'll just toss them both over the veranda side mate. Much quicker. Meet ya down at the truck. Down the stairs and out the front. Last one there's a dead Kraut.' He was already opening the door to the veranda when he prodded David towards the hall door.

David went down the stairs and out past the rowdy bar to find a truck idling out in the street. A man with a huge beard and only one eye sat next to the wheel. Uncle Mike was already sitting next to him.

'Come on mate,' his uncle called. 'We can't keep the captain waiting. We got deliveries to make.'

David climbed into the back amongst lots of sacks and

packages. The truck lurched with a crunch of gears as it left Northam. They stopped every now and then at towns and houses along the road and David passed parcels and boxes down for his uncle to put on verandas and in little tin sheds by the road while the captain sat rolling cigarettes in the cab, watching Michael wordlessly.

The truck finally came off the road and backed into a shed behind a hotel, near some railway lines. Michael nodded to the driver who nodded back again wordlessly before he went into the hotel.

Michael came back to where David stood ready to jump down. 'So how were things back here in steerage eh? Looks warm enough to me.' His uncle climbed up and arranged some empty sacks and some of their clothes into a makeshift bed.

David looked out at the hotel and back again, before he finally said, 'We've got no money?'

'Jack Tanner got most of it. I got a little for the old cricket balls and matting.'

David started to take his boots off.

Uncle Mike said, 'The second Test starts soon.'

'In Melbourne,' said David, brightening. 'How do you think we'll go?'

'We're gunna get killed.'

'Grandad says they are formidable.'

'Yep. And we don't have a spinner worth a damn.'

David smiled and looked at his uncle, but he was lying down, with his back to him. David thought of grabbing a bit of his uncle's coat over him, but the night was hot with barely a breeze.

'Don't we just need better batsmen?'

'The Australian team's paltry scores of a hundred and

twenty-three and eighty-four contributing to your thinking there?'

'If paltry means bad.'

'Hmm. But what did England make in their first knock?'

'Six hundred and twenty-three.'

'Seems to me there are two ways of looking at that particular problem. It would be good to turn up a couple of brilliant batsmen just lying around the country. But it would be pretty useful to the existing team to keep England from scoring such a whopping big total too.'

'Yes.'

Up in the rafters of the shed were mice. David watched their silhouettes scamper and chase. He thought maybe city mice were the same as country mice in their habit of playing about in the dark.

In the morning, they took their bags and caught the train to the city. David looked out from the station at the crowds of people dodging cars, trucks and trams on the street in Perth. There was a man in rolled-up shirt sleeves, standing outside the station holding up a sign which said 'Out of work.' The men in suits passed without stopping to read it. Ladies in bright dresses looked away as they pushed their wicker baby carriages. A taxicab driver was trying to crank his car engine into life, but it didn't seem to want to go. Car horns squawked, brakes squeaked, gear boxes groaned and engines coughed. Perth was noisy and smelt of petrol fumes and smoke.

'Come on Davey,' said Uncle Mike, 'we gotta get down to the WACA.'

'I'm hungry.'

'I know one or two men down at the cricket ground.

They'll spot us for a feed.'

David felt jostled by yet another passenger and pushed himself back against the station wall. Other passengers coming up from the trains didn't seem to mind all the pushing and bumping.

Uncle Mike looked like he might get angry but then fished in his pocket. His hand came up with a few coins which he looked at without much enthusiasm. 'Let's see. Four bob, and ... not much more.' Michael looked at David a moment. 'Well, you're right. Can't bowl on an empty stomach. Come on. We'll get breakfast here at the station. They say, in England, that breakfast is the most important meal of the day. In France they eat sweet buns and chocolate for their breakfast, which seems to go on most of the day.'

David followed his uncle back into the station.

'You ever thought about that word? Breakfast. It breaks the fast of the night, you see. A fast is a period of non-eating. In some places around the world, they fast for days. Not cos they're poor. Believe it's good for the soul. Other places of course, they fast for longer and die. That's cos there's nothin' to eat, because the czars eat it all, but we won't go into that this morning.'

When they were seated with a pot of tea and toast and a bun at the railway station cafeteria, David asked, 'Are you a teacher?'

'A teacher?'

'Sometimes you talk like a teacher.'

'Oh dear. Sorry.' His uncle was smiling with his eyes and not sorry at all.

'Other times you talk like a swagman, I suppose. Rough. And other times you talk like ...' David struggled to place what he meant, but then found it. 'Like someone on the wireless. A wireless person being funny.'

'You think altogether way too much. If you think too much your head breaks in half. Did you know that?'

'Yes, sir, I do. Then I just stop thinking and look at things.'

David saw surprise on his uncle's face. It was the first time he'd seen such an expression on Uncle Mike. Perhaps he'd given the wrong kind of answer. He stopped looking at the man and concentrated on the good taste of the bun. A bit of jam would have been good if they'd had the money.

'That's a good trick that,' said Michael. 'I do the same but it takes a fair amount of grog to get there.'

David looked up, ready to smile, but his uncle was not looking at him.

They finished their breakfast in silence. David thought of his grandfather. It was easy to make him angry because he had high standards and was a hard taskmaster. But the rules were there, plain and clear. You could predict what would please and displease the old man. Every time he thought he had worked out how his uncle wanted things, it would all go sideways again. Like a leggie on a dusty pitch, thought David, smiling at his own joke.

After breakfast, they walked to the WACA ground, seeing as David 'had eaten their tram fare.'

Just inside a back gate, Uncle Mike stopped and took a couple of cricket balls from his cricket bag. He then stowed both their bags behind the empty gatekeeper's box.

David looked around with pleasure. 'This is where Grandad used to play.'

Michael led David past a grandstand and around the ground towards the scoreboard. The ground was green and grassy. It looked even and flat, watered and cut. David wanted to go out to the middle just to touch the turf wicket. The grass was rolled and cut and rolled again so that it was as nearly as hard as cement, but also soft enough to take spin.

David heard a bat hitting a cricket ball. Down past the scoreboard, behind some seating, there was another grassed area. Nets had been suspended from big poles, surrounding two coir-matted pitches and two turf pitches. A bowler was bowling to a batsman, while two older men watched and talked.

Michael handed David the cricket balls. 'Bowl these down on that spare wicket there, matey. Make sure you hit the wickets every time. All right?'

'Yes, sir.'

'I'm just going to talk to Dunny there.'

'Dunny?'

'Bob Dunne. You heard of him?'

'Yes. He's the West Australian Combined coach. Like Grandad was.'

'Yeah, well, maybe nothing like Grandad was. He's also a bit of an unofficial national talent scout. Tells 'em who's worth a look from the bush.'

David had more questions, but his uncle was already walking on ahead to greet the older man in the loose grey suit. Bob Dunne looked to Michael in a wary kind of way, then over to David for a moment. Michael talked into his ear.

David went to the near vacant nets and started to loosen his shoulders and wrist, spinning one of the balls in nice little arcs over his little finger. The ball was torn and weathered and easy to grip.

In the next nets the bowler ran in fast and bowled. The

batsman brought his bat down hard and neat on the rising ball, and hit it back down into the pitch. 'Nice nut, Cracker.' The batsman used his bat to flick the ball back to Cracker, then caught sight of David watching, and winked.

David nodded, then turned to bowl a ball at the wickets at the other end of his nets. He bowled a bad ball. It was flat and spun uselessly away down leg side. David closed his eyes. He hadn't thought about the delivery at all. He had not thought about what he would bowl, had not considered the pitch or imagined who he might be bowling to.

He took off his cap and pullover and made himself prepare to bowl properly. He made himself think out loud. 'Okay, so what kind of pitch is this? The ball spun, so there's something in the wicket. Looks like there's some bounce too.'

David went to retrieve the ball he'd just bowled. He looked down at the wicket where a batsman would stand. These were nets, so there were no foot holes down this end where a bowler would run through on a real pitch. But there were worn patches where batsmen had stood, and it was greener in some places and drier in others. The grass smelled of water and good dirt.

'Davey. David.'

David looked up. His uncle was standing at the open end of the nets with Bob Dunne and the young man who had been batting in the next net. 'Come on. Mr Dunne wants you to bowl at young Hasluck here.'

The batsman headed down to take his guard, saying, 'Come on chappie, can you be quick about it? I really need to practise.'

Other players had begun to arrive on the other side of the nets.

David noticed the derby hat first. It was Jack Tanner from Northam. Before David had time to think more about that his uncle touched him on the shoulder.

'Davey, it's time to concentrate, mate.'

'Yes, sir.'

'Now it'd be good if you could get this young bloke out. I haven't seen him bat.'

'I have. He was batting when we got here.'

'All right. I've used up my last favours in all of Perth for this, so we probably don't have many goes.'

David wasn't sure what his uncle meant or what the goes were for. Michael must have seen the confusion because he said, 'Naw, just have some fun and get him out. All right?'

'Yes sir.'

'What's this, boss?' Jack Tanner called out. 'Haven't we got training this morning?'

Bob Dunne held up a quieting hand.

'David,' warned Uncle Michael, and just pointed to the batsman.

David stood at the top of his mark. Hasluck had been batting quite well against speed. He seemed to like to cut and play on the off side. David decided on off spin, but with a little flight to entice him into a shot. He stepped in and bowled.

The batsman saw the ball well in the air, but was very casual with his footwork, and merely dangled the bat outside the line. The ball spun inwards and took middle and off stumps. He looked back at his stumps, then angrily at his own feet. Some jeers came from the other men. Tanner yelled, 'Hit him out of the park, Lucky.' Hasluck righted his wickets and tossed the ball back, scowling at his team mates. Bob Dunne and Michael said nothing.

SPINNER · *a novel*

David stood at the top of his mark watching Hasluck take guard. He was hitting the bat down on the crease, solidly and repeatedly. 'He's angry,' said David to himself, 'really angry, and really ready to hit me as hard as he can.' David knew exactly what to do.

David ran in and bowled a looping delivery, with some back spin. Hasluck saw it early, and hit early too. The ball dipped in the air and then held up a little when it hit the wicket so that Hasluck was partly through his shot as the ball arrived. It took the bat high, ballooning easily back to David. He caught it with both hands against his chest.

'Live grenade,' said David, not quite believing he'd caught the ball.

'Good ball, David,' said Uncle Michael.

Hasluck was looking at his bat as though it had a crack in it. Dunne was scratching his chin.

'Bowl me another one. I got it now,' yelled Hasluck.

But Dunne called out to one of the other players. 'Derrick, would you mind having a look at this young fella here?'

Michael said, 'Derrick Jarvis.'

David said, 'Opening batsman for Guildford and Western Australia. Tight defence. Scores on the on side mainly.'

Michael opened his eyes, in his pleased surprise look. 'Yes, that's the one. You sleep with a radio next to your ear or something?'

'The newspaper,' said David. 'Grandad and me always read the sporting results and discuss the players.'

Jarvis nodded a smile to David as he entered the nets. Other players cuffed and pushed Hasluck as he came out. An older player had moved behind the rear of the nets, directly behind the batsman, to get a better look at the bowling from there. He pulled a cigarette paper from a packet and started to sprinkle tobacco onto it as he watched.

Jack Tanner said loudly, 'Last time I saw this kid, he was taking pennies off folk at a county fair. That was a sideshow too.'

Jarvis took his guard. 'All right then, son.'

Michael stood with David at the top of his run. 'He's not the sort of player who will go after you, so don't think you have to get him out straight away.'

'Yes, sir.' David decided on trying to set up a trap for Jarvis.

The comfortable silence of concentrated attention fell over the nets.

David's first ball was flatter than usual and pitched outside off stump, spinning in towards the wicket. Jarvis stepped back, and straightened, the bat held steady to keep the ball off his wicket. Jarvis blocked it, saying nothing, but nodding at what he'd seen.

David's next delivery was a leg break. It pitched on-line with leg stump where Jarvis liked it, but moved swiftly towards his off stump. He didn't get his bat there in time. The ball sailed over the wicket.

'What did you reckon about that one then, Wally?' said Jarvis to the man behind the nets.

'That was a leggie. Nice variation. I didn't see it coming. Seems to be a leg spinner who can bowl offies. What was that last one he gave you, Lucky?'

'Dunno. Held up on me, sudden. Maybe a flipper.'

Jack Tanner spat a decent sized chunk of chewing tobacco onto the ground.

David was now ready to spring his trap. If it looked the same as the first, the batsman would think he recognised it, only it would really be much faster. When Jarvis saw it land, he started to go back again, ready to hit it on the off side. But this time it beat the bat and crashed into the stumps, the perfect wrong-un.

'There you go Bob. I told you the kid could bowl. A prodigy. George Baker trained him.'

'George Baker. Wow.'

The man behind the nets called out to David, 'So how is old George?'

'He's good. He's my grandad.'

'George Baker's grandson!'

'There's pedigree for you.'

Bob Dunne turned to David too. 'That means your dad was Ernie Donald.'

Jarvis chimed in, arriving at the bowler's end, 'Now that man could bat a bit.'

David held himself still, waiting for them to talk about his father.

Jack Tanner spoke from the cricket bags. 'He's proved nothing 'cept there's some soft-hearted dills want to make a kid happy. This lad might be the grandson of George Baker but he's the nephew of Michael Donald. You forgotten why Michael left the WA team?'

Michael spoke to Dunne and Jarvis. 'It's personal with Jack. Nothing was ever proved and it cost me my cricket.'

Tanner grabbed his bat and strode towards them as though he might hit Michael with it. 'He got thrown out of the side for taking bets ... against his own team.'

Michael continued to talk more quietly to Dunne. 'Suspected, not proved. But this isn't about me. It's about the kid, and what he can do for your cricket side. Come on Bob, since Sean O'Leary did his shoulder, you got no spinner worth twopence.'

'No team in the whole country has a spinner worth a zack,' called the man from behind the nets.

Jack Tanner stood with Michael, Dunne and Jarvis. 'He's got the coward's wound.'

'Now he's going to attack my war record.'

'Enough of that, thank you, Jack,' said Jarvis.

Tanner turned and went to the wicket where David was bowling, talking all the way. 'When will you blokes learn? He doesn't want me facing the boy cos I know how to play him. Part of the trick, I reckon, is how he looks. You see this gormless little scarecrow with those long arms and longer fingers, and you feel sorry for him. And you get yourself out. If you act like a batsman facing a real bowler then he's easy.'

'Now he's cruelly insulting the poor lad just to put him off,' appealed Michael. 'I don't have to stand for this. We'll come back later Bob and you can have a look at him when things aren't so ... heated.'

'Uncle Mike,' said David quietly, 'I can bowl him.'

'What?'

'I've seen him bat. A lot. I thought about what I did wrong at the show.'

Michael led David off a little. 'You sure? He smacked you a fair bit.'

'I was thinking about all the people. They ... all the looks. All the poppy eyes and ... I started thinking about the people and what they were calling, and what he was calling.'

'What's different now?'

'It's cricket nets. Cricket players who I've read about and ... It's cricket nets.'

'Well, we'll have to sort that out some time, but for now ...'

Uncle Mike looked at Tanner then over at the other cricketers and to Dunne. He shrugged. 'You're right. Just cricket nets. Just some chaps from the paper.'

'Just practice.'

Michael patted David's shoulder. He stood and called, 'All right Jack. If it'll shut up ya whingeing.'

David went to the top of his mark. He decided that a dipping, well-flighted ball should beat Tanner in the air. He ran in. Tanner suddenly stepped away from the crease, not taking his guard, as though not ready to bat. David had to pull up and not let go of the ball. Tanner smiled then waved at the air. 'Flies are bad.' There was laughter.

'You afraid to face him are ya, Jack?' said Michael.

David ignored them. He just thought about Jack Tanner in his batting stance. The same ball would do. He ran in to bowl. Again Tanner started to step away, but it was later in David's delivery. He bowled the ball, but dragged his arm down too far. As the ball came out, Tanner stepped back in. He'd just been pretending. He leaned back and launched the bat with his powerful shoulders, catching the ball on the full. Whack. It flew back over David's head and over some sheds towards the wall surrounding the ground. Tanner started bowing. There were cheers from his team mates. 'Like shellin' peas, gentlemen.'

David yelled, 'That wasn't fair.'

'Fair game, I reckon,' said Tanner. 'Now are we done?'

'That wasn't fair, Mr Dunne,' repeated David.

'Things aren't always fair, son,' replied Dunne.

'Yes it is. It's cricket. It has to be fair.'

'I bet ya twenty quid that David gets you out next ball,' yelled Michael suddenly.

'Twenty quid?'

'Twenty quid. And if he doesn't, we'll leave.'

Tanner smiled as he exaggerated taking his guard.

David looked at his uncle with growing alarm. David wasn't so sure any more that he could bowl at the unreadable Tanner. Uncle Mike was coming towards him, holding out a cricket ball.

'Do you have twenty pounds?'

'Will soon, I reckon.' He smiled the good smile, his best smile, the one with all the sparkling in his eyes.

David tried to resist it. 'That's not right, Uncle Mike.'

'This Tanner bloke deserves to get his comeuppance, wouldn't you say?'

David turned to look at Jack Tanner. The big man was looking at the tightly wound string around his bat handle as though David and his uncle weren't even there.

Uncle Mike talked quietly. 'I reckon he's going to just block you.'

'What? But he always hits me way over. That's how he shows off.'

'But he hates me more. So, my thinking is this. He knows you've seen him go for you. But here's the picture I think he's starting to get in his mind. Tanner will just block the ball back, with nothing on it, then look at me, and hold his hand out to get the twenty pounds. He won't even smile. Take the money, and show me that he'll never think about me for a moment ever again. I'm nothing to him, and this next shot is going to show everyone, but mostly me, that that's what he thinks. Not even worth the energy of hitting hard.'

David looked at his uncle. He had just told a whole story about what was going to happen inside Jack Tanner's mind. David looked down to his hands. He had the cricket ball there. It was scuffed and torn with a frayed stitch, but the leather was still firm.

Michael took the ball from him. 'Do you understand, David?'

'No, sir.'

'Let me put it this way. He is going to block you. He is absolutely definitely one hundred per cent going to block you. Do you believe that?'

David looked at his uncle. He was trying to believe him.

'Now get him out.' Michael gave him the ball and walked back to the others.

Tanner stood tall and loose like he was going to smash the ball out of the ground. He did not look like he was going to block it. But he often changed his stance late. He often tricked David into thinking the wrong thing. From where he was standing, it would be very difficult to get down to block one kind of ball.

'David Donald prepares to bowl. Jack Tanner, on ninety-nine, looks set. Donald comes in.' David ran in and bowled a shooter. The shooter was like the skidder, but did not hold up when it hit the wicket. The ball flew in a temptingly slow arc through the air but when it hit the pitch it sped up, also keeping low. Tanner was caught by surprise. Just as his uncle had predicted, Tanner had moved back to block the ball, but didn't bring his bat down low enough or quickly enough to block the ball. It spun forwards fast and hit his pads, directly in front of the wickets.

'Not out,' yelled Tanner.

Dunne's finger was up in the umpire's sign for out.

The man behind the stumps had his finger up too. 'He's got a shooter. Lad's got a shooter. Takes ten years to work up a decent shooter, I thought. Old George musta had him practising before he was born.'

Dunne was nodding.

Tanner stayed in the crease. 'Hit a crack. Give us another ball.'

'We done, Dunny?' said Michael quietly.

Dunne nodded, with a bright smile. 'By my calculation, young Michael, that boy just took four wickets in six balls.'

'Yeah,' said Michael, 'he'll do better tomorrow when he's had a decent feed.'

Both men laughed.

The man from behind the nets was suddenly next to David, rubbing his hair. 'Nice work lad. Wally Grimmet.' He held out his hand.

'The wicketkeeper, yes sir, pleased to meet you, sir.'

'I seen your grandad bowl you know, when I was a nipper.'

'He doesn't bowl now, Mr Grimmet. His hands are too tough from the farm.'

'Can you bat?'

'No, sir. Shocking.'

Grimmet laughed. 'Your dad could bat.' He smiled, then remembered, 'That's right. That's the story. Your dad married George's girl. Ahh. How is she, your mum? She was a grand beauty that one.'

'Come on David. Time to go.' His uncle was tugging at his shoulder. 'Will you get our bags, mate? I got to get our money off Tanner. Nice ball that one. Come on. Shake a leg.'

CHAPTER SEVEN

David stood at the scoreboard waiting for his uncle. He was not thinking about what he had just done, but on some of the things that had been said.

Wally Grimmet had talked about his mother and father as though they lived in an ordinary world where people could bat a bit or someone could ask how your mum was. It seemed possible for a moment to grasp their lives, past childhood, to see them doing things in a world that was not surrounded by a strange and threatening darkness. David thought about how he felt and he found he wasn't breathless at the image of his mother. Then he thought about having that thought, about how it was like feeling whether you were cold or hot, and deciding on that—feeling it and thinking about it and thinking about thinking about it all at once.

If his mother was, as Mr Grimmet had said, a real beauty, then how could David be a little scarecrow? David smiled.

He had got Jack Tanner out. And Derrick Jarvis. He wondered whether this would please his grandfather, or if his pleasure in getting Tanner was childish and would lead to poor bowling.

David turned and looked at the oval. It was so green, the green of month-grown wheat. He went down the slope past row after row of wooden benches to the picket fence. It had even, well-watered grass all the way out to the middle. There was a grandstand over the other side that looked like a kind of palace. The Test that had just finished in Brisbane at the Exhibition Ground was the first ever played in Queensland. It was hard to imagine that happening here. David would settle for being able to play for WA one day right here and never leaving.

There was a gate in the fence. It was nearly closed but not quite latched. David pushed it open with his knee. He stepped onto the ground. There was a patch of uneven grass a few yards ahead. He bent and looked at it. It was greener and higher than the grass around it. Just one patch that looked different. He imagined Jack Tanner running towards a ball hit along the ground. He imagined the ball reaching this patch. It would twist and bounce away in a different direction. 'Oh no. Rotten luck for Tanner. The ball has evaded him and it crashes into the boundary. Four runs to Windsor in this first-ever Test match for the Ashes at the Western Australian Cricket Association ground. Oh look, it's young Donald coming on to bowl.'

David was at the end of the wicket. It was beautiful. He knelt and touched the grass. He thumped the pitch gently with his fist. It was very hard, but not like coir matting and nothing like cement. He stood and looked down the other end. Twenty-two yards. It was always the same. Always the same distance, the right distance, the same wherever he bowled. Twenty-two yards.

David became aware of the rest of the ground again: the grandstand and seats, the scoreboard. He slowly looked around the ground, following the fence all the way. From here, from the centre, it seemed vast. Strange. It must have been much smaller than the paddocks on the farm. Yet, it seemed bigger.

He looked back to the other end of the pitch. He felt the weight of a ball in his pocket pressing against his leg. His uncle must have given him one to take back to the bags. He took it out. It was the other old ball that he'd got Jarvis out with. He spun it up and watched it hang in the air before dropping to his other hand, spinning all the way.

There was a breeze. David felt it for the first time. A hot easterly, blowing late. It blew across the wicket. A bowler could toss the ball up and let it drift a little in that breeze before it landed and spun. From this end, David could drift the ball left and away from a batsman, then spin it even further away or suddenly back at him.

David bowled. He watched the ball float and drop. When it hit the wicket it suddenly bounced high, much higher than David had expected. He carefully walked around the wicket as he went down to the other end to get the ball. The extra bounce was good. With some overspin he could make the ball seem as if it was jumping at the batsman. He could use that. If a batsman reached out for the ball they might mistime the hit. The batsmen would have to worry about movement up and down as well as side to side. David thought he would try a loopy and see how fast he could make the ball bounce up. And then a shooter to make sure it didn't bounce too high. He bent to pick up the ball.

A policeman grabbed him by the arm. 'What do you think you're doing, lad?' The policeman was in full uniform with heavy blue jacket and helmet.

'If you've damaged this wicket in any way, I'll 'ave yer bloody guts for garters, you little urchin.' This was from a man in a white coat and broad hat. He was moving along the edge of the wicket as though searching.

'How'd you get in here?' said the policeman, still holding David's arm.

David had an urge to run. He hadn't formed an idea of where he'd run to, or why he should, but he just knew he wanted to.

'Well, cat got your tongue?'

'I know a fellow—we call him Captain—that if you said that to him, Constable, you'd get no answer. Bullet went up through his chin, took off his tongue and went out through his left eye. And he lived, although admittedly not to tell the tale. Does deliveries round Northam. Good listener though.' It was Uncle Mike.

'Is this lad yours?' said the policeman, not joining in on Michael's smiling.

'He bowled on the wicket,' said the man in the white hat.

'Ah, well for that you have our sincerest apologies, gentlemen. David here has just been asked to join the WA combined team. He did not realise that the centre wicket is off limits.'

'Poppycock,' said the man in the white coat.

'How old are you?' said the policeman.

David couldn't answer. He was speechless. Asked to join the Western Australian team?

'He's twelve.' Uncle Mike was bringing things out of his

pocket. There was money and papers and finally a card with writing on the back. 'This is from Bob Dunne. Our grounds pass.' He handed the pass to the policeman.

'Well, you need to have this on you at all times, you know.'

David nodded.

'Twelve! Twelve years old,' said the man in the white coat, walking away and shaking his head.

'Very good spin bowler,' said Uncle Mike. 'You seen better around here?'

But the man was too far away now.

Uncle Mike said to the policeman, 'Do you know a decent spin bowler in all West Australia right now?'

'I wouldn't know,' said the policeman, handing back the pass. 'I don't like cricket.'

'Fair enough too. Boring game. Huge waste of time. Come on, David. Time to find a hotel.' Michael grabbed David's arm and steered him towards the other side of the ground.

'Is it true?' asked David.

'Which part?'

'That I'm joining the team.'

'Ah. Well, yes. It is true. You've been asked to join the team. But I didn't mention you were joining the team—at practice.'

'Just practice.'

'Well that's just a start. You'll be in the team in no time if you keep getting them all out.'

David was relieved, not disappointed.

'With Wally Grimmet?'

'He was particularly keen.'

David nodded.

'Say what you like about Jack, he likes to travel in style.

Fancy walking around with twenty quid in your pocket.'
Michael still had a small wad of pounds in his hand. 'Time
for a treat, I reckon. Want to go to the motion pictures? How
about a swim in the river?'

'I want to sleep.'

'Sleep?'

David thought some more. 'And a wireless. Can we stay at
a place that has a wireless?'

'You never know your luck in the big city.'

So Uncle Mike got them a room in the Royal Hotel which
was back down near the railway station. The room had a
radiogram which was a wireless in a little wooden cupboard.
Uncle Mike turned a knob and the radiogram came on with
a hum and glow.

'Is the Test on?'

'No. It starts tomorrow.'

There was music. It would sometimes fade away but then
would get louder, like the wind was blowing the sound. The
room had polished boards with rugs on the floor and a big
soft bed. There was a bureau and wash stand. There was
an electric light on the wall. The wallpaper had so many
little yellow flowers David couldn't count them, but when
he closed his eyes just a little bit they'd seem to slide and
join and dance to the music.

He wondered if Nell would listen to the cricket too. He
wasn't sure what day it was. If it was a school day she might
be able to hear a little after school. Would Grandad have
told Mr Wallace that he wouldn't be in school? Would Nell
know? She would have gone out to the farm after the first
day, David supposed. She would have ridden out and said,
'Hello, Mr Baker. Where's David?' Would Nell ask why he

was gone? Would she ask when he was coming back? David couldn't imagine what his grandfather's reply would be. He couldn't see past the old man standing in the kitchen and ordering, 'Don't you cry, boy.'

David woke in the dark. He lay there trying to recall where he was. Some music was playing and he remembered the radiogram. Tomorrow the second Test would start. Lights flashed across the ceiling. There was noise outside somewhere, like a constant clatter, but with no detail to it. The man on the radio said, 'That was King Oliver's Dixie Syncopators with "Showboat Shuffle."' Some more music came on then.

David was hungry. There was light coming under the door of the hotel room. He went out into the hall which was well lit and then halfway down the big jarrah stairs that led to the main entrance. There was carpet and flowers on tables, but he couldn't see his uncle. The front doors were open and people walked past. In the street were cars with their night lamps turned on.

A lady came in. She wasn't dressed up like lots of the people passing. David thought she looked like an ordinary lady in a print frock. She was unhappy. She went to the door of the main bar, and pushed open the swing door.

David went down the steps to see past her into the huge, smoky bar filled with noisy men.

The lady yelled, 'Frank Reilly. Frank Reilly.'

There was laughter in the bar. A man yelled, 'Frank, better run.'

Another man yelled, 'He's not here, missus.' More laughs.

But the lady didn't move. She yelled louder, 'Frank Reilly,

you come home now and feed your kids.'

The bar went quiet a bit then.

'Frank Reilly, don't you drink any more of our money.'

The men seemed to decide then, as though they'd taken a silent vote. Someone said, 'Go on then, Frank.' 'Go an' get some dinner there, Mr Reilly.' It was Uncle Mike. There were mutters and yeahs, and then the men nudged him forward. He had no hat or tie. The men rippled the Frank Reilly man towards his missus. He looked drunk and subdued, but as he reached the lady he gave her an angry look. She turned and walked out. His shoulders slumped and he followed her.

The men in the bar were quiet for a moment.

'All right then,' said Uncle Mike. 'Mr Reilly won't be getting a chance at this authentic Terry Brown bat. Might get the rolling pin.' The men laughed.

One of the swing doors to the public bar had stayed open when Mr Reilly had left and David edged up to see further inside. Some men were in work suits, but most wore the loose shirts and trousers of working men. Each man was holding a glass of beer. Some gulped and slammed their glasses down; others sipped; one or two stroked the glass as though feeling for blemishes.

'This is the bat he used to score his double century against England in 1893.' David's uncle was using the voice he'd used at the Northam show.

'Bullshit,' yelled someone.

'Oi,' laughed Michael, 'careful of your language around young Alice there.'

There was more laughter, and the barmaid, who didn't look young to David, yelled, 'Yeah, youse kin all watch ya bloody language.'

More laughter. David looked at her through the smoke. She was moving up and down the bar, pouring beers and taking money. The top buttons of her blouse weren't done up and when she bent you could see a little bit of her breasts.

'I'll prove to you that it's not bulldust. I'll pass the bat around. Have a look. If nothing else tonight, you can say for the rest of your life, that you've held the bat that belted the Poms.'

Someone yelled, 'Yeah, that's not gunna happen again soon.'

'Yeah, we're bloody useless.'

The bat was passed and men touched and turned and studied.

'While you're lookin', let me just tell how I come into the possession of this amazing piece of cricket legend.'

David noticed that his uncle's voice had changed a little. He was sounding more like a farm labourer or a normal person now. He didn't sound like a teacher at all. 'Now you might have heard about a little fracas over in Europe a few years ago now.'

There was a cheer. There were grumbles too.

'Well, I was there.'

'Is that when you shot your toe off?'

There was a sudden big silence. Men looked from Michael to the man who called.

Michael suddenly smiled. 'You wanna find out how much of a coward I might be?'

All the men in the bar waited a moment with eager, hungry smiles.

But David's uncle suddenly shrugged and smiled and called, 'I notice you waited until I didn't have Mr Brown's cricket bat in my hand when you slagged me, mate.'

Laughter. Someone called, 'Yeah, get over it.'

'Tell us the bat story.'

The man who had called, scowled and looked down into his beer, saying nothing more.

'Well, on the way to France, where I stepped on something sharp, I met a man in Egypt. No, he didn't have a hump and wasn't called a camel, and he wasn't wearing a tea towel.'

More laughter. David was laughing too in the warmth of watching his uncle tell his story and making the men smile and laugh while he did it.

'Well, I did a bit of a good turn for the fella, and chased off a couple of Pommie sailors, and we got to visiting some ... um, close your ears now Alice ... one of those harems, shall I say ... Anyway, pissed as newts, I find out he's Terry bloody Brown's bloody son. And he's luggin' around ... yes, you guessed it. He's luggin' around his dad's bat, all over a beach in Turkey and Egypt and wants to take it to France. He sleeps with the bloody thing. Mostly, he gets it through by tying it to his rifle and no one's the wiser. Not too good if he has to see a bit of action, mind, trying to get to the trigger past two stocks.'

More laughter. Laughter at each of the jokes. Laughter at all sorts of things that David didn't understand.

Then Michael stopped smiling. He looked sad. 'Well, I don't want to go into the particulars of what happened to Stan. Suffice it to say, like many a good mate, he copped it soon after we got to France. And ... well ... here I am, all these years later with the bat. The bat that Stan's dad, the great Terry Brown got two hundred with.'

The men had gone quiet as they listened to the story, just sipping beer now.

'Anyway,' continued Michael, 'I've kept this bat through thick and thin. And now it's just thin. I'm outta work and I'm ... To cut a long story short, this bat has to be worth forty or fifty quid. But I'm short. Skint, like a lot of you. But, now wait for this idea I've had. I'm not going to sell it. Who's got that kind of money but some toff. No. Terry Brown was just a simple bloke by all accounts even when he was a champion. So ... I'm going to raffle it. One shilling is all I ask to get yourself a chance at history. Keep passing the bat round. That's his signature and date right there, plain as day. This is your chance to own a piece of history. For only one lousy shilling. You couldn't buy a new bat for that. Now I got these bits of paper here I've written numbers on.'

Alice the barmaid came over to Michael and gave him a beer. He winked to her, and she smiled. 'And Alice here, as honest and trustworthy a lass as I've ever met, can draw the winner.'

Hurrays, laughter.

David rubbed his cheek feeling a tear. His own father had died in France and he had never met him. He turned and went back up the stairs to his room. There was news on the radiogram about banks closing. He turned it off and lay back down on the bed.

He thought he might ask his uncle what he remembered about his father. He'd ask Wally Grimmet too. Maybe they shouldn't be staying in such a grand hotel if they didn't have much money. David had lost all their money when Jack Tanner had belted his bowling all around the Northam showground. He'd won some back today, but he supposed it must be expensive to do all this travelling and feeding and trying to get David some bowling experience.

David woke to giggling. A woman. He lay listening, thinking for a moment that he might be dreaming. Sometimes he would dream of women he liked, but in the dream, they would be his mother.

There was a sigh and a rustle outside. He could see shadows in the gap of light under the door. Another giggle. 'Shhh, you'll wake him,' whispered his uncle.

'Easy for you to say. Stop pawing.'

David said, 'Who's there?'

'Ah, damn, see. You just had to be quiet.'

'Yeah, with your hand down me top.'

The door opened, and David saw his uncle swaying in the light of the hall. There was Alice the barmaid, with her top open. She saw David and started to button her blouse.

'Hello there, laddie. Saw you watchin' Michael's bat lottery.'

Uncle Mike turned, mostly hidden in the dark behind the door. 'You should have come in, mate. I would have got you something to eat.'

David watched them both standing in the doorway.

'Doesn't say much. Is he right?' said Alice.

'Out you go, Alice. You're a little too rude, I fancy,' said his uncle, suddenly unkind.

'Not what you thought, when you couldn't keep your hands off.' She was angry too.

'Out.' Uncle Mike took her by the shoulders and turned her away. 'And shh, or you'll lose your job.'

'You lying bastard,' Alice called, as Michael shut the door.

It was dark in the bedroom once again.

'All too true, in every sense,' said Michael. Then he must have banged into the chair by the door, because there was a scrape of wood and the sound of lots of coins clattering and rolling onto the floor. Shillings, thought David, from the bat lottery. He could hear his uncle crawling on the floor, as he tried to find the coins, in the dark.

David got up and turned on the electric light on the wall. His uncle was on all fours gathering the shillings.

David bent and started to help. He said, 'I'm sorry, Uncle Mike.'

'Plenty more where she came from.'

'I meant the bat. I'm sorry you had to sell the bat.'

Michael laughed, but not with pleasure. 'Plenty more of those too, in my bag of tricks.' He got up with difficulty, grabbing onto the back of the chair for help. He looked towards the bed from there, still holding the chair. He pushed off and staggered to the bed where he sat. 'You can only do one per city though. You'd be surprised how likely it is for someone to turn up in more than one pub.' Michael let himself fall back in bed. 'Not going to talk your way out of that. Front bar full of cheated punters. That is a shit-kicking. You can take it from me.'

'What do you mean?'

His uncle rolled over. 'Newcastle once. A right shit-kicking.'

David collected all the coins and put them back in the hat. His uncle was snoring on the bed, his shoes still on.

David went to the wardrobe. He opened the sports bag, pushing aside the cricket balls and some batting gloves. Under some newish bats were two older ones. David took them out. Both were signed. Both were dated. Terry Brown. 1893.

David looked from the bats to his sleeping uncle. He wondered suddenly if the man really was his uncle at all.

He never said anything about his father or mother. He told lies to all kinds of people. Even the barmaid Alice had called him a liar, and she was a floozy. Michael told stories about sad things just so he could trick people into giving him money. David thought back to the night and then the morning he had been driven away from the farm. He wondered if it were possible that Michael had tricked his grandad into letting him go.

David looked down at the sleeping man. His mouth was open and ugly, his eyes closed. David hurried to put on his shoes and coat. He needed to talk to his grandfather. He needed to check with him to see if Michael had told lies. He needed to tell his grandfather what his uncle was really like. He needed to ask his grandad about why Michael made him scared.

David took a cricket ball from his uncle's bag and two shillings from the hat.

Outside the Royal Hotel, it was still night. Two night carts clopped up the road, lanterns swinging. Apart from them, it was quiet, the city asleep. Nearly deserted.

The train station across the road was dark. That was a start though, reasoned David. The train tracks would take him to Guildford, and from Guildford, he could follow more train tracks, or maybe even find the highway that would take him home.

He started walking, figuring that daybreak wasn't too far off.

It took David three days to get to Toodyay. He had walked along the line past miles and miles of dark houses. At six the trains had started and he caught one to Midland, then a mail truck, going further. But after that, David decided not to spend any more money, so he walked and only used what he had left for food. It felt good to be walking in the country again. There were magpies and crows. There were cockies and twenty-eights and honeyeaters and finches and cockatiels. Some birds were bright and loud. Others had dull feathers and hid amongst the bushes. They all darted, and called and chatted and chided and screamed and squealed.

David didn't so much walk, as bowl. 'David Donald has the ball. O'Malley crouches forward, waiting. Defensive. Donald steps in, and bowls.' The ball arced, and bounced. There was little sideways movement to be got from the road, but some overspin. 'O'Malley steps forward, bat out and angled down. The ball hits the bat. It's up. Bardsley's diving. Catch!' David danced around on the gravel, his hands raised. 'England, one down already for only ten runs.'

David walked along the road, to gather up the ball, ready to bowl again. He'd pick out a smooth spot on the road some twenty yards ahead. He didn't want to hit a stone. He was trying to nurse the cricket ball for as long as he could. He stood a moment, at the beginning of his run-up, deciding who he'd like to bowl at. O'Malley again. He bowled at O'Malley for four miles straight that afternoon, and had England one wicket down for less than twenty runs every time.

The real cricket score was not nearly so encouraging. At around 4 p.m. on the second day of walking, David bought some cheese from a store along the Toodyay road, and he asked.

England had declared four overs before the end of play at eight down for four hundred and fifty. Australia had already lost a wicket. They could play for a draw by equalling or nearing the English first innings score. They'd have to dig in, but surely could. They had a very experienced opener in Johnson. John Richardson, the captain, was the best bat in the country. Ken Hall was handy and McLeod, the all-rounder, was a real goer. They had the makings of a good batting line-up. Everyone said that, including Grandad. They just had to get a good start.

It was hot. David slept under a bridge on the first night, after wolfing down some bread and tomatoes. Mostly he was thirsty, as the creeks were dry. He'd only occasionally come across a water tank. There were others about on the road too. There seemed to be a lot of men tramping and looking for work. David kept a wide berth, uneasy in their unshaven, desperate-eyed presence.

They found him on the road just out of Toodyay. David had been glad to be walking downhill for a bit, and the thicker trees here gave him a lot of shade. The heat of the day was making him a little giddy. When he heard the car coming up behind, he'd stepped off the road, but the car's gears strained down ready to stop. He already had his little story ready. 'Just going to the farm up there, Mister. No worries. Got any water? Heard any cricket?' But when David turned, there was Michael smiling lazily from a roadster driven by Mr Dunne.

Mr Dunne laughed. 'Well, you're a sight for sore eyes, young David.'

'Hello, Mr Dunne.' David didn't look at his uncle.

Mr Dunne turned off the engine and pulled out a canteen. 'You look thirsty.'

'Yes sir. Thank you.' David went up onto the road and took it. It was one of the ones left over from the war, made of metal but wrapped in a thin blanket to keep the water cold.

'That ball looks a bit easy to spin,' said Michael.

David looked down at the ball. It was a mess. There was no leather left. It was fluffy and not even round.

'You sure that's not some run-over pigeon you're trying to bowl there?'

David smiled, but made himself turn to Mr Dunne. 'I don't suppose you know the cricket score, Mr Dunne.'

''Fraid I do, lad. We lost.'

'Already?'

'All out for two hundred and eighty-seven and then one hundred and twenty-two. A few retired hurts, mind.'

Michael was reaching into his jacket and pulling out some bits of coloured cardboard. 'On the other hand, every cloud has a silver lining.'

Mr Dunne looked darkly to the other man, then to David. 'They want you to come over. The Australian team want to have a look at you.'

David went blank a moment. Maybe it was the heat. He had to shake his head to see things again. 'What?'

Michael got out of the car and showed the bits of cardboard. They were train tickets. 'Their fast bowler, Tudor, is turning out to be a bit of a menace. He's bowled a short ball and it's collected Freddie Turner in the face. Broken nose. Shattered teeth. He's in hospital.'

'The spinner's curse!' said David.

'Wally Grimmet telephoned Anthony Crowley,' explained Mr Dunne, 'and kept on about you. They telephoned Sir Livingston, the chairman of the board. Poor fellow will try anything at the moment. Anyway, Biggins, the Cricket Board's money fellow, sent the tickets. You see Wally's seen some spinners in his time, and they trust his opinion. They wired me. I don't think you are ready, David. But I don't think it will hurt you or the team to see you bowl. It might just lift their spirits.'

Michael interrupted. 'Grimmet saw how good you are. Mr Dunne knows that too.'

'I figure what will happen is that they'll ask you to bowl to them in the nets. Just like I was planning to do. David, they are much better batsmen than young Hasluck, and Jarvis is not as good as he used to be. But it will give them some practice against a quality spinner, and you'll get to meet them all. That'd be pretty good eh?'

David smiled. To meet the Australian team. He blinked the sweat out of his eyes. Mr Dunne and Michael were still standing in front of him on the road.

'Anyway, they want to see you and Jack Tanner in Adelaide. As soon as you get there.'

'I got to go home first.'

'There's no time. We're on tomorrow's train,' said Michael.

'No, I'm going home.' David turned and started walking.

His uncle caught up, limping a little. 'It's the Australian team. It's what you're meant for.'

David kept walking.

'When they see you bowl they won't be able to say no.'

David stopped and turned on the man. 'So you can make money.'

Michael grinned. 'Yeah. Where else we going to get it?'

'You're a cheat. That bat wasn't special. You just signed it and told lies about it.'

'Ahh. The bat.'

'It's not even his. You lied.'

'David, it was just a bit of fun. Everyone in that pub got a cracking good yarn, and for a spare shilling they got a chance at a score. And back in Perth a fella is carrying round that old bat and bragging to anyone who'll listen about the wonderful thing he's got in his possession. Are you really telling me that many of those blokes believed me? They were all in on the blarney of it. That's half the pleasure.'

David said, 'And what about Alice. You lied to her.'

'Alice. Alice who?'

'The floozy.' David had been thinking about the barmaid angrily doing up her blouse. 'What lie did you tell her?'

'Ah, right. Well, sometimes a man, when ... No. No, you're right. I didn't handle that night very well, mate. Been just me for too long, and I wasn't thinking. How about this then? I'll be better. No more floozies. No more lies. Okay?'

David looked at him closely.

Michael smiled. It was one of his big, bright, shining smiles, and it made David angry again. 'I don't want to go with you.' David started walking again.

He heard Michael hurrying after him. 'You got to.'

'No I don't.'

'I'm all you've got.'

'I've got Grandad.'

'He can't look after you.'

'You don't know anything.'

'Of course I do. He told me.'

David stopped. He looked at Michael. 'You're lying.'

'You think I just turned up out of the blue one dark night? He telephoned. He knows how good you are. He knows you're better than anyone who's ever been. He can't leave the farm and he can't afford to look after you.'

'He can,' said David weakly.

'Can you imagine The George Baker letting me take you if it wasn't what he wanted?'

David was having trouble getting enough air into his lungs.

'He couldn't face you. He couldn't say it himself.'

David was trying to concentrate on his breathing and not hear Michael's words.

'Anyway, when he asked, I couldn't say no. You see, I promised your father in a hole in the French mud that I'd look after you.'

There were no birds. No trees. No road. Nor even any sky. Maybe there wasn't even any David. There was just Michael's voice.

'Now will you just get in the bloody car so we can go play cricket against the Poms?'

CHAPTER EIGHT

The train went under a bridge and everything was a scream in the dark until it burst out the other side. David let his head rock, like he had no neck muscles, allowing the train to flop him as it would, sometimes forward and sometimes back against the seat.

They were on their way to Kalgoorlie. They would change trains there and go across the desert, before changing again to another train which would take them to Adelaide. The second Test in Melbourne had finished early and the Australian team were going to use the extra time to practise, things being so calamitous. David had got the word calamitous from Mr Dunne and rather liked it.

Mr Dunne had seen them off at the station. The Australian Cricket Board had paid for their tickets. They would also pay for their hotels and meals. Mr Dunne never lost his doubtful look though, even when he shook hands with David and said, 'Make your grandad proud, son.'

When they had stowed their bags in their sleeper David asked his uncle, 'If we do make money, can we send it to Grandad?'

His uncle looked away a moment, then straight back with the smile that David was beginning to distrust. 'What a nice idea. Super. Does that mean you willing to try to get into the

Australian team?'

'But we're just going to practise.'

'No. In the team. If you're willing to start getting serious?'

'Yes, sir.'

Michael smiled an easier smile. 'You know, of course, the best course when getting serious is not to be serious at all. Part of being serious is relaxing and enjoying. A batsman does not concentrate all day at the crease. A batsman who is good enough to spend some time in the middle relaxes between deliveries. As the bowler turns and starts to run in, the batsman starts to concentrate again, and his concentration increases, so it is at its maximum, with eyes wide open and feet about to move, just as the bowler releases the ball. Once the batsman plays the delivery, and then makes a series of decisions about running, he relaxes again, relaxing his body and resting his mind—seriously.'

'I know.'

His uncle nodded as if he'd been corrected, and went to leave.

Even though David had wanted him to go, and looking a little hurt, just as he was, he couldn't help adding, 'But when a batsman is facing a quality spin bowler, you can do all sorts of things to not let him relax. You can move the field. You can put doubt in his mind about what ball he might bowl next. You can hurry him too by stepping up to bowl your next delivery sooner and sooner, or you can keep him waiting as though you're thinking of a clever delivery that is going to be his downfall. You can tell that, because he'll look around the field frowning, or prod the wicket where he thinks there's a funny spot, or he might practise the shot he just mistimed. And so he doesn't relax between balls, and he worries more and more.'

Michael smiled clean and laughed his bright laugh. 'You're like a kind of genius aren't you?'

David felt some slight in the comment. 'Grandad told me.'

'But it's all in there somewhere, isn't it?'

'It's just training. And hard work.'

'Dear to me shall be the lyre and bow, and in oracles I shall reveal to men the inexorable will of Zeus. No, Davey boy. It's not just training. It's all kinds of gifts and curses. You know you have to watch out, don't you? When the gods give a gift there is always some hidden catch, some huge price that goes with it.'

David watched his uncle's eyes. He seemed to have become serious himself, even though his words sounded joking. He thought he detected something else. Somewhere, below all that smiling and teasing, there was anger.

David thought of Gruff. Gruff had been a magpie that lived on the farm and mostly just chased other magpies and occasionally sang in the late afternoon. But every mating season, Gruff got protective and started swooping the dogs and David. Gruff would hide in the big tree down near the pumps, and he'd wait for David. If David watched the tree and never took his eyes off, Gruff wouldn't swoop. But eventually David would forget and he would turn his back. And suddenly, there was that noise, the last flap of wing before a beak clacked close to David's ear and he'd be diving into the paddock dirt. David didn't know why his uncle made him think of Gruff. He had never done anything like an attack. Maybe it was just the feeling you shouldn't take your eyes off him.

When David came back from the memory of Gruff he

found his uncle had gone. David thought about the end of Gruff. One year, during the magpie breeding time, his grandad had come back to the house, bleeding from his head. He had got his rifle and gone back out and shot Gruff. After, over tea, his grandad said he felt badly, as he had succumbed to a disgraceful show of anger, and that the bird was only following its instincts. Grandad's anger was easy to see if you were alert to it, and mostly earned. Poor old Gruff had badly misjudged his man that day.

Some hours later David went to find his uncle to see about food. He came upon a carriage called 'Buffet' and opened the door. There was Jack Tanner. He was sitting at the table just inside the door drinking a cup of tea. He looked up at David and glared. David stopped, and backed out instantly.

All through the morning, David rechecked. Jack Tanner would sometimes be playing cards, sometimes eating and sometimes just talking. And the people with him, both ladies and gentlemen and less gentle men, would change, but not Jack Tanner. This became his place on the train, between David and his uncle who he guessed was somewhere beyond, and also between David and food. Yet each time, when David willed himself to go to that carriage, he couldn't bring himself to pass the batsman who he knew would continue to be unkind. And it seemed to David, as the morning dragged, and lunchtime came and went, that Jack Tanner was taking delight in keeping David out.

So David sat in the day carriage and watched the country go flat and dry. It didn't seem like a desert, as there was so much scrub and bush, but the colours were white like bone and grey like dead leaves, and even though every window of the train was open, and they sped fast enough to make a breeze, he could feel the heat coming off the land and pulling at his face as his head bobbed and swayed.

At dusk the sky turned orange and the kangaroos and rabbits came, and later the foxes and dingos. Inside the train, people went past dressed for dinner. And still Uncle Mike had not returned and still Jack Tanner sat, this time eating his dinner. David's stomach howled at him.

When they lit the lights inside the buffet David noticed that if he leaned forward, he could see the glass window at the place where the carriages joined. Every time someone came and went, and they opened the buffet door, there was a flash of Jack Tanner, reflected in the door window. David waited. Half an hour after Tanner had eaten he got up and left the table.

David went to the buffet door, in time to see Tanner heave himself out the other end of the carriage. David went in. They had tables, with tablecloths and a servery, but they were clearing up now. People drank beer and wine, but had finished eating it seemed. David would have to find his uncle to get some money for a meal.

He went to the other end of the buffet in time to see Tanner disappear into a toilet room. David entered that carriage, passing a little kitchen room and through another sit up. He went through another carriage filled with curtained sleepers and into yet another carriage. This one was filled with smoke and laughter and shouts. It was a bar, like a hotel on the train.

David came up behind his uncle who was playing cards for money. A woman was sitting next to him, laughing. She seemed old. Older than Mrs Pringle. But she was quite well dressed, with lots of pearls. David supposed she was not a floozy like Alice the barmaid.

'Now that, Mrs Miller, is why you should be wary of bluffing with a pair of twos,' explained his uncle to the lady. 'If anyone has anything at all, you're ... down the gurgler. Which is why I never bluff.'

'Yeah, right. An' pigs might fly,' grumbled one of the men on the other side of the table.

'What about on their way to pig heaven?' said Michael, fast.

The lady looked shocked a moment, before pushing against Michael, with her shoulder. 'Oh, you. You have an answer for everything.'

'Gidday, laddie,' said the other man, looking up at David. 'Let me give yer a tip. Never gamble. With your own money, that is.'

They all laughed, loud and harshly. They were drunk.

Michael turned and saw him. 'David. Where ya been?'

'I'm hungry.'

'Hello there, David,' said the lady. She had thin eyebrows and soft eyes. Her mouth had lipstick on. Her earrings were black, like three little black grapes that peaked out from her cloche hat. When David didn't say anything, she turned and asked Michael, 'Yours?'

'No,' said David, loud and sudden.

'My brother's son. David, let me introduce you. Ned is in sales. Fred is a bushy going home. And last, but not last at all, let me introduce you to Mrs Elizabeth Miller who is recently widowed and travelling to Melbourne to see her sister and family. Mrs Miller likes whist but not poker and she is proving of inestimable assistance in my eternal search for both convivial conversation and paltry riches.'

The lady giggled. The Ned man winked at David. The Fred man said, 'You a bullshit artist too? Your uncle can talk the leg off a chair.'

'Fellow travellers, this is David Donald, the greatest spin bowler that has ever been born. He's about to play for the Australian team and prove it to the entire world.'

They laughed. Fred sounded like he would choke. Ned slapped his leg, spit coming from his open mouth. Mrs Miller nodded her head into Michael's shoulder. They laughed, all except Uncle Mike, who watched them laughing without a smile.

David felt his face go hot.

'Stop your teasing now.' It was Mrs Miller. She had stopped and was looking kindly. She had powder on her face, quite a lot of powder.

'I'm hungry.'

'Well, get something to eat, mate,' said his uncle.

'I haven't got any money.'

'What?'

'I haven't got any money.'

'Yeah, an' I won't in a tick the way I'm going either,' said the Ned man.

'Come on,' said Fred. 'We playin' cards or what?'

'Just a sec,' said his uncle. 'You just show your ticket, David. The food's included.'

David thought about this. He had his ticket in his pocket. Maybe he should have read it. Found out the rules of the train ride. He'd do that when he got back to their sleeper.

'Do you want me to come with you, David?' It was Mrs Miller. 'I can help you get your dinner if you like?'

'No way, Lizzie,' said one of the men. 'You're the only one I'm winnin' off.'

'He'll be right,' said Michael.

She smiled at David, and did a twitchy thing with her nose,

before turning back to the men. 'You bunch of brutes.'

They all laughed.

David went back to the buffet car. Jack Tanner was back in his seat, but with his back to David now. No one was eating, but they all looked like passengers and not train workers. He went back to the kitchen room, where a man dressed in white clothes was washing dishes.

David stood at the door until the man noticed him.

'Eh, boy. What you want?' The man was an Italian like Mr Buralli, who had a farm further up river in Dungarin.

'I want some dinner, sir.' David took out his ticket and showed it.

'Dinner finish. No more.'

'I can have dinner because of my ticket.'

'No, no. Five-thirty sitting. Seven o'clock sitting. Dinner finish.' The man gestured with both hands to all the dishes in the sink.

David looked at all the dishes. He saw one that hadn't been scraped. There was a half bread roll and some gravy. David pointed. The man threw down his washcloth and said lots of angry Italian words. David looked back towards the card game end of the train, and wondered if he should go back and ask for the kind Mrs Miller's help. But the Italian man came out of another door, carrying a plate with a metal lid on it. He pointed at David, and said, 'Breadfast sitting. Lunch sitting. Yes?'

'Yes, sir,' said David.

The man gave him the plate, and smiled and slapped David on the cheek. It was not so much a slap, as a hard pat. Then before David could react, the Italian man pushed David towards the buffet carriage, saying, 'Eat.'

David went, knowing that in spite of all the slapping and

yelling and pushing it had been friendly, and that the man had broken some rules so that David could have his dinner.

Jack Tanner was back in his seat at the other end of the buffet car, so David stood in the alcove between the kitchen car and the buffet car. It swayed violently and he could see the tracks rushing past, but he felt he could eat in peace. He lifted the metal lid to find a chicken leg and some salad and two bread rolls with butter. David tried to make himself eat slowly but was soon sucking on the fleshless chicken bone.

He wondered whether he should take the plate back to the Italian man, but didn't want to. So he edged into the buffet car, and put the plate on the first table, and then crept along until he was just a few feet behind Tanner. Then he ran to the door.

As he grabbed the handle to turn it, he could hear, 'What are you doing, skulking around?'

But David didn't turn and didn't stop. He ran straight out, leaving the door flap unlatched, as he made it to the other door and went through, slamming that shut tight, before running on, all the way to his sleeper number seven.

David panted as he lay on the small bed behind the curtain. His heart was beating fast and he listened to it until it slowed and he wasn't aware of it any more. The train swayed. He listened to the regular click of wheel on rail.

David woke as he was pulled forward by the force of the train suddenly stopping. It was night. There were people calling in urgent voices, the sound of running feet. David pulled aside his sleeping curtain to see stewards scrambling. Someone was yelling for water.

Below him, his uncle's bed was empty and unused. There was an odd sound somewhere, like screaming, but not like any screaming David knew.

He put on his boots and moved up towards the end of the carriage, pushing past other passengers who asked, 'What's happened?', 'What's wrong?' The door at the end was open, revealing an orange glow outside. And still the distant screaming, low and pained and fearful.

Lanterns were moving outside. More shouts. David jumped down onto the rough ground next to the tracks.

There was a cattle train with half its carriages overturned. A fire. Cows were wandering and calling. Some limped. Some were down. Most were bleeding. Men ran, lanterns swaying and shuddering. The fire was billowing halfway down the carriages, like a big yellow flower. A driver from David's train had attached a canvas hose behind the steam engine. Men were filling buckets with water from it. Everyone was shouting.

Jack Tanner reared up out of the smashed wood of the guard's van with a man over his shoulders and staggered over wreckage. 'Doctor! We need medics here.'

Then David saw where the screams were coming from. There were cows trapped in the shattered cattle trucks. The wooden planking had splintered in places, stabbing and spearing them. Many looked dead. Others were gashed or had stakes of wood sticking out from their stomachs, their flanks, their faces. Other cows, David saw, were not dead, nor even wounded, but still trapped and struggling. Their eyes were huge and open, reflecting the approaching fire.

David thought he saw his uncle on the other side of that carriage, pulling down a broken piece of wood so the cows could escape. A lantern swayed.

'Dynamite!' someone called.

Up ahead some of the cattle train was still on the tracks,

including the engines. Men were trying to unshackle the fallen carriages to get the upright ones away. Men were throwing buckets of water on the fire, then running back to the passenger train to refill them. A man came out of a wagon with a wooden box. 'Get out, there's dynamite.' Men backed away. 'Get it out of there.' Jack Tanner, his derby gone, jumped up into the dynamite wagon.

David saw another carriage near the fire. The cattle in there were stomping their hooves in puddles of blood as they tried to back away. They whimpered. They called. David grabbed onto the side of the wagon and hauled himself up at the gate. The metal pin holding it closed was already warm.

'Get out. Get out,' yelled someone.

David was trying to pull the pin up, but his long fingers were awkward with this kind of fiddly work and the pin kept falling back down into the slot.

'The dynamite's gunna go.'

'Run!'

David pulled the pin out and threw it to the ground. But the gate stayed closed. He grabbed it with both hands, and pushed hard against the side with his feet. The gate swung out and he held on, riding it away. Then just as it reached the end of its arc, he let go. But one of those long stupid fingers of his caught on something. The third finger of his right hand jammed, and took the whole weight of David's body for a moment before it came free.

He fell to the ground as the cattle poured out of the wagon. The first hit the ground, breaking its forelegs. It floundered and collapsed, as others jumped down on top running off into the night.

A hand grabbed his shoulder. It was Jack Tanner. 'This is

no place for a boy.'

'The cattle. Got to get them away.'

'You get back. Now!' He shoved David hard towards their train.

David staggered a few steps but looked back to see Tanner go to the cow that had jumped first. It struggled uselessly. Jack Tanner had a pistol. He fired into its head.

Then the dynamite exploded. The wagon holding it disappeared in white light, followed by a dull, short whumph. It and half the next wagon were gone. The air shook and puffed alive for a moment. Burning bits of wood fell from the sky.

David was on his knees. He could see Mrs Miller, standing in a white nightgown off to the other side of the track. It was darker there but the firelight showed her trying to pull at a sitting man. David climbed between two carriages and went to them.

'Michael please,' said the lady, dragging at his uncle's shoulder.

Michael sat in the dirt, with a cow, its head in his lap. 'And by his smile, I knew that sullen hall. By his dead smile I knew we stood in Hell.' Michael stroked the cow's cheek. It lay, unmoving, but with an eye open, carefully watching the man. Michael looked off at one of the rifle shots. 'Shoot straight and kill them all,' he said without emotion.

Mrs Miller looked to David. She was frightened.

'Shh, shh, matey. Let it go. Just let it go, and slip into the warm water. Like a swim, they say. Like swimming in a warm bit of river, floating.' Michael talked gently, soothing. 'Good news, mate. You're all here. All your bits and pieces all together. In heaven, you'll be you. That's a comfort, surely.'

David could see blood covering the cow's stomach. Its

chest moved slowly. Barely.

'Please,' said Mrs Miller, 'he's talking crazy.'

Michael ignored her, talking only to the dying cow. 'Bugger the poetry, buddy. That's what the yanks call their mates. Buddy. I'll find your hands, Ernie. I promise, I'll look around in the mud here and I'll find them sure. Be somewhere near my toe, I reckon. I'll tell 'em you went easy. I'll tell them, you died quick, with no pain. They'll like that, won't they. Clean it up to make them feel better. Be a medal in this. Someone better send a bloody medal home.'

'Please Michael, come away. You're frightening me.'

David couldn't speak. He stood with Mrs Miller watching.

'I can see down into your eyes, all the way, to the other side. Pain. It's like hot, melting metal being pushed into the smithy's water, like lightning frozen into the sky. Watch. Watch. There. It's going now, mate. I can see it going. I'm not lying. I'm watching the pain go. It's already miles away and flying. Just drift, mate. Just relax and let go and float away. Good lad.'

David looked down into the cow's eye as the pain seeped away. A moment later, you could see the life go too, just as his uncle had described it. Like a match blown out.

Michael started to laugh. It was happy and light and awful in the gore and fire by the train tracks.

Jack Tanner stepped from nowhere, his pistol in his hand.

'No,' called David, thinking in that instant that Tanner might actually use the gun on Michael.

But Tanner stepped forward, slapping Michael hard with an open hand.

Mrs Miller gave a small gasp. Michael's head jolted back

from the blow. He seemed to wake and look around.

'Pull yourself together, man.'

Tanner walked off, as Michael looked down at the dead cow a moment. He seemed confused and surprised and stupid all at once, as though trying to remember something. Then he looked around at David and Mrs Miller. 'Don't need to pull myself anywhere, man. I have Liz here.' He reached up towards her, trying to smile. His nose was bleeding a little from Tanner's blow. His cheeks were wet. 'Oh, Lizzie, I need to lie on those wonderful breasts and forget about this head I've got on.'

He grabbed at her nightgown, and she jumped back. 'No,' she gasped. 'No, Michael. Not now.' There was a smudge of blood on the nightgown where Michael had grabbed. She turned to David. 'We only just met. Fun like. I can't ... No.' Then she got angry with Michael. 'And you have no right to expect it.' She started to walk back towards their train, but then she ran. There were other women gathered back there, watching her with fear.

David looked back the other way. There was only one carriage still burning. Men with buckets ran dark against the fire. The dynamite had exploded a gap in the train. There was less moaning from the cows, and fewer gun shots. The accident had taken on a calm and order.

'Stupid old cow,' said Michael, as he patted the dead thing on his lap. 'Help us up would you old bean? My leg seems to have gone to sleep.'

David pulled at his uncle to get up.

'You know,' said Michael, 'you look a lot like your father sometimes.'

He limped badly as David led him back towards the train. Someone gasped as they saw how much blood was on him.

A voice said, 'Was it bad?'

'Is anyone hurt?' said another.

David helped his uncle lie down in the sleeper and stayed with him.

He looked at his finger, which hurt, and saw it swelling. He could barely wriggle any of his fingers on his bowling hand. He pushed it under his left armpit where the warmth settled the pain a little.

He looked to his uncle who was laying in his bloody clothes with his eyes closed. 'Is that the war you were talking about? Out there, Uncle Mike?'

'Did I have a bit of a turn, mate?'

David didn't answer.

'Say some silly things?'

'Yes, sir.'

'Scary things?'

'I don't know.'

'But we had a train crash and there was fire and hurt cattle?'

David waited. His uncle wasn't smiling. He still had his eyes closed. 'Yes, sir.'

'Well, that must mean I scared off Mrs Miller then eh.'

David didn't answer, but he did smile just a little.

'But not you.'

'You said things about Ernie—my dad.'

'Naw, couldn't have. Wasn't there.'

'Where?'

'Where he was. Forget it. That's the best bet. Forget everything. The only way.'

His uncle lay there eyes still closed. David waited with him, intending to go out and watch the fire again, but he fell asleep.

In the morning, his uncle begged for brandy, and pushed some money at David.

David was hungry. Always hungry. He hoped there'd be a breakfast sitting. The train was still. No rocking. No click click click. There seemed less voices too. David hoped that Jack Tanner would be out looking over the wreck or still sleeping, from a long hard night of fire fighting and rescuing, but there he was in his spot at the first table of the buffet car, sitting in the seat, with his jacket off, his derby gone, and his face smudged in soot. He looked up to see David looking at him through the glass.

David opened the buffet door, and said, 'I have to get brandy for my uncle.' David hoped his voice sounded fearless.

'No one's stopping you, lad,' said Tanner. He looked down at his breakfast and speared some bacon.

David found a man in the bar car and explained about his uncle and was given a bottle of brandy in a paper bag. He took it back without looking at Tanner. Then he returned to the buffet car, going past Jack Tanner again without even looking at him. He went to a table at the other end of the car and asked a man in white who wasn't the Italian man for breakfast. When David asked for another breakfast, the man said, 'Certainly, sir.' David ate that too.

After that, David came and went whenever he wanted, and he and Jack Tanner began to nod to each other. Sometimes Tanner would say, 'Morning.' And David would reply the same. And it went like that: 'Afternoon. Evening. Night.' There was no more glaring.

Apart from going for food, David stayed back with his Uncle Mike, who nursed the brandy, and ate a little himself. He eventually changed out of the stiff bloody clothes when the flies came. He was like a man who had the flu and was waiting to feel better.

David asked him questions, and sometimes he answered them.

'How did you hurt your foot?'

'In the war.'

'Why do people see it and call you names?'

'Because, when some men couldn't take it any more, they took their .303s and aimed it at their toe and shot it off. Then they were injured, so they were allowed to go home. So, after a while the officers caught on and they thought a foot wound was a bit suspect. Some men called it a coward's ticket.'

After thinking about his uncle's answer for quite some time, David asked, 'How did yours happen?'

'What do you reckon?'

'I don't know.'

'Then I won't tell you.'

'I reckon you didn't do it that way.'

'You're just saying that, to see what I'll say.'

David lost track of time, one day often blending into another, and some seeming to disappear altogether. A bridge had been washed out hundreds of miles ahead so they couldn't be transferred on. Other trains from Perth were being held at Kalgoorlie until things were sorted here. They were stuck in between. They would be spending Christmas in the middle of the desert in the middle of Australia.

The track was being cleared, and repairs were being made where the dynamite had blown a hole in the tracks. Everyone explained that they were lucky only one box had blown and they'd got the rest out, or who knew what would have been left of any of them. They ate a lot of beef in those first days, but had to bury the rest because of the stink. It was always hot and people tried to stay in the carriages. Mostly they got drunk.

David's finger turned blue and green, then black, but he still couldn't wriggle it.

Then it was Christmas Day, and they had roast for lunch and pudding which was brought in by a fixing crew on a little hand-pedalled rail car. There was a tree and people sang carols around a camp fire made of broken carriages. The days were searing and the nights freezing.

David's grandad didn't make much of a fuss about Christmas back on the farm. He said he'd lost the habit of it once David's mum was no longer organising. Besides, the farm jobs weren't going to take the time off.

David borrowed a knife from the train kitchen and made his uncle a letter opener out of some of the wood planking from the blown up dynamite wagon. He sharpened it on a huge flat rock back near the guard van. It had taken some time as he'd only had the use of one hand. His finger was being slow to get better. He'd keep forgetting to protect it and go and grab the rail to get back onto the train or catch it in his jacket and start it hurting all over.

Uncle Mike took the present out of the paper bag and looked at it suspiciously.

'It's a letter opener,' David explained.

'Christmas, eh? Well, blow me down. I'll have to owe you the gold, frankincense and myrrh, King David. Just have to settle for the *merde*.'

Michael lay back down on the bed.

'Tell me about my dad.'

There was a long silence. Finally, Michael said, 'He was

a bloody hero. True believer. Not a bad cricketer. A prince and a golden boy who everyone loved. Even more so when he died.'

'Why don't you like him?'

'Maybe I'm jealous.'

'You didn't like him?'

'Maybe I loved him. Maybe I didn't think about it.'

'Tell me something about him.'

'I have.'

'Something I don't know.'

'When he was young, he was so smart, he got a scholarship to a private school with ivy growing up the walls, and he was a house captain.'

David thought about that for a long time, imagining his father in that kind of school, like the ones in books about England.

On the day after Christmas, the train people came and took their luggage and moved everyone to a new train on the other side of the accident. It was like the train they'd been on, but had clean water and fresh salad and breezes that blew the flies and stink of other people away. They were on their way to Adelaide again.

'Did you know my mother?'

Michael lay most of the day in his new bed in the new train, as if they were still trapped in the desert. Sometimes, he'd answer David's questions. 'Most beautiful woman I ever saw in my life. From another world, Aphrodite, come to visit. For such a short time.'

'Who's Aphrodite?'

'A goddess from Ancient Greek myth.'

'Why don't you like her?'

'Who says that?'

'You're making jokes.'

'She liked jokes. She liked laughing. She had long fingers. Not as long as yours. But long, and they helped her play the piano. She played all the happy songs. She would have loved this jazz music they got now. She must have been dropped from the gods, or how else could your grandfather have ended up with her?'

'Don't say anything about Grandad.'

His uncle didn't. Just lay there like he was never going to move.

'Did you like my mother?'

'No more questions. I'm sick of it. Truth is tawdry.'

He wasn't sleeping, David knew. He was drunk and it made him like an old dog, lying in the sun, not asleep but not awake either. He just lay there, like he was never going to move.

CHAPTER NINE

Hours before the train was due to arrive in Adelaide, Michael sat up in his bunk, put his feet on the floor and stretched his neck, rolling his head around one way, then the other. Finally he looked up at David. His eyes were clear. 'I gather from the smell around here that it's time one of us had a bath, and judging that part of that smell would seem to be brandy sweat, I have to conclude it's me. Unless you picked up a habit along this trip that has, until now, escaped me.'

'Um, yes, sir. I mean no, sir. Do you mean drinking brandy?'

'Joke, my friend. Joking.' He stood and patted David on the cheek, then gathered up his bag and went to the bathroom.

David stayed sitting on his top bunk, feeling the touch of the man's hand on his cheek.

He studied his injured finger. The blue had turned to green and yellow. It was still swollen and it still hurt. He'd been hoping that it would get better. He'd had plenty of spills and scrapes on the farm. His grandfather had observed that his natural dreaminess seemed to leave him standing in the path of just about everything that was moving somewhere else. This had included his grandad when David was really small. If there was a horse it would kick him, a hole he'd fall in it, a plough he'd trip over it or a post he'd bang into it. The thing was he didn't usually hurt himself much. He was like a cricket ball, said Grandad. He always bounced.

He had expected his finger to be right by now. He had thought to tell his uncle, but Michael's strange sickness after the train crash had not invited that kind of bad news. Besides, David had not wished to break the spell of having his uncle lying quiet on the bunk and sometimes ready to answer questions about his mother and father.

When Michael came back, he was showered and shaved and had changed into his city clothes. 'Come on, Davey boy. Look lively. Adelaide, the city of churches. Let's pray we can get you into this team.'

As they got off the train, Jack Tanner was talking to a newspaperman, who was taking notes on a small pad, while a photographer set up his camera. David moved slowly, so he could hear.

'Tell me about the accident, Jack. By all accounts you were a hero.'

'Don't you want to talk about the cricket?'

'But surely, with the delay of your train, you don't have time to try out or train for the team? The Test is tomorrow!'

'I'm always ready, Mr O'Toole. Ready for a bat and ready for a middy.' Jack winked at the people who had gathered round to listen to his comments. 'Or do they call 'em schooners in Adelaide?'

'Who's this other fellow from Western Australia, Jack?' asked O'Toole. 'I can't find any record of him. David Donald?'

David felt a hand tighten on his elbow. It was his uncle, who winked and started to lead him away, but not before

David saw Tanner fix a look at him for a moment, before he said, 'Simple game, cricket, for a batsman anyway. My job is to hit the ball some fellow tosses up. I like hitting the ball.'

David couldn't hear him anymore, and his uncle said, 'Don't want to become a news story too early.'

'Why?'

'Well, my thought is this: if you become a paper story now, before you get in the team, lots of people with lots of opinions about cricket and maybe outside of cricket, might want to stop you. Mostly because of your age. All because of your age. Whereas once you're in, then they can write and comment and say what they want, because you'll already be in. Just like cricket, you'll be in and they'll have to get you out. Get it?'

'No, sir.'

'Well,' laughed his uncle, 'that's okay, because I could be wrong.'

'I've hurt my hand.'

His uncle stopped walking. 'When?'

'When I was letting the cattle out. To get them away from the fire. It swoll up later.'

Michael put down their bags, and grabbed up the hand.

'It's gone down a lot.'

'Wiggle it.'

David did, but the hurt finger was slower than the others and still ached at the knuckle joint.

'Bugger,' his uncle said mildly.

David watched him thinking.

Michael suddenly raised his arm, and yelled, 'Taxi.' As a taxi pulled in, Michael added, 'Seeing as we've got a little seed money from the ACB, we might as well use it, eh?'

David climbed in the cab after his uncle and waited for

him to reveal a plan of action. He didn't, but merely started talking to the driver about some pubs he seemed to know. 'How about the Richmond? Is that still a good place for a bet? What about the Victoria Park? Good crowd for cricket or just the nags?' David stopped listening, and started to look for churches. There didn't seem to be as many as he'd thought, but the ones he could see had high spires and looked old.

Michael hustled David to the nets next to the University of Adelaide ground. The sun was well up and the grass here also had a brown tinge. It crackled when you walked on it.

Out in the middle of the oval a solitary sprinkler watered the wicket. The sunlight was caught in the water spray, shining bright silver. The buildings across the way looked important. There was ivy growing and lots of windows. They looked like the kind of buildings David imagined his father going to and being house captain of.

David turned to see Michael putting stumps in at the batters end of the nets.

'Is this where I was supposed to bowl?'

'Where you will bowl, yes.'

'I don't think I can.'

'Here,' said Uncle Mike, rolling a cricket ball along the pitch to David. 'Bowl a couple of balls, and we'll take a look.'

'I can't grip it.'

'Course you can. Use the first two fingers spread for off spin.'

'But I'm a leg spinner. And Grandad and I have been working on my grip looking the same for most of my deliveries. With all three fingers.'

David put the ball in his hand, arranging his thumb and index and middle finger spread. He had to gently push his hurt third finger to try to bend it back behind the ball. 'Much more variety and with the same grip, but it's using all the fingers and thumb that give it so much spin when I need to give it extra.'

Michael was at the bowling end of the nets with his hand on David's shoulder, and looked steadily at him. 'I know, mate. I know what you can do and you will do once the finger's right. But today, you haven't got three fingers, and off spin uses the two fingers you have got working, so let's use that to come up with something that will get you in the team. Until your bad finger's better.'

'But I thought we were just here to help them practise.'

'Why don't you want to get into the Australian cricket team?'

'I do. But not yet.'

'Why not yet?'

'I'm too little. I'm not ready.'

'How do you know you're not ready?'

David didn't know the answer to this.

'We can find out the answer. This morning. It's wonderfully simple. You bowl as well as you can and get these men out, and that will be your answer.'

'But my hand is hurt.'

'Well let's see if you're still not better than anybody else going around with a sore hand an' all.'

'Yes, sir,' said David without any conviction.

'Look,' said Michael gently, 'you can still flight it and drift it, so find a grip that doesn't hurt and send a few down to me.'

David looked doubtfully at the ball in his hand while

his uncle went down to the stumps again. His uncle was right. The off spin grip mainly used his two healthy fingers. He had used the grip before and knew it worked well for some types of balls, but certainly not the variety he had been working on lately. Nor would he get as much bounce. Michael stood behind the stumps without a bat.

David bowled. The ball went low and straight, but spun in towards the wicket, where his uncle caught it. 'Good offie. Some more of those, but get a bit more height or they won't be tempted. You can still flight it and land it on a penny, you know.'

David bowled more. His finger hurt a little, because he'd still put his natural flick into the movement to work the ball, but it wasn't impossible.

David bowled some more off breaks, and found he could land them quite well.

'Good,' said his uncle, 'now try your shooter with that grip.'

David bowled, and the ball landed in his uncle's hands like a full toss. 'Sorry,' yelled David.

'Nice six there. Very well. We'll come back to that one. We better work on your arm ball. See if you can control how much side spin you get.'

David bowled. He bowled for an hour in his street clothes and shoes. He was sweating, and the webbing between his two longest fingers was starting to hurt, as he was spreading them more than he ever had before to try to get extra purchase for the spin. Finally, David threw the ball down in disgust. 'It's useless.'

'It's not useless,' said Michael coming to the bowler's end.

'But I'm only using a couple of fingers. Even for offies, I

could do heaps better, if I used all my fingers.'

'Can we do that?'

David looked at his hurt finger. It was starting to swell again. 'No, sir.'

'Line and length, David. You're flighting it. You're landing it mostly in the area. You know you don't always have to spin the ball a foot sideways. You just have to make the batsman think—'

'That the ball will spin.' David finished the mantra. 'And by how much,' he added, feeling a little better.

Voices were approaching. Michael looked that way, then patted David on the shoulder. 'Okay, you take a break. Go and find a tap and put your hand under the cold water.'

David found a small fountain dribbling under a weeping willow in the shade by the nets. It was cool there and had a comforting smell of dead plants turning to compost. He put his hand in the water of the fountain and kept it there while he watched, hidden, as his idols began to arrive.

The Australian cricket team.

He already knew all their names and how they played their cricket. He knew some by the photographs he'd seen, in the newspaper and an almanac that his teacher Mr Wallace kept in a bookcase behind his desk. Yet they didn't arrive like the confident warriors David had expected. They trudged in, dragging their feet and tossing down their cricket bags.

Terry Johnson was a redhead who still had freckles even though he was older. He said nothing, but bent over his bag, messing with the buckles and looking hurriedly over his shoulder every now and then as if he thought he was being pursued by something.

A younger man edged up near him kind of furtively and

nodded. 'Gidday, Mr Johnson.'

'Ah, young Bardsley,' said Johnson, not looking at him.

David looked at Andrew Bardsley, the Victorian opener who had just joined the team in their last Test.

Paul Hampton, the big-chested fast bowler, arrived sucking hard on a cigarette and looking worried. Geoffrey Calligan, the other fast bowler, marched in, speaking to no one. He stood alone looking out at the oval, rather than his team mates. He was a lawyer when not playing, so perhaps he had a big case, thought David.

The older man who came in next, as though his back hurt and his knees were about to collapse, had to be the Australian wicketkeeper, Bill Baker. The reports said he looked more as if he needed hospitalisation than sport.

Maud McLeod was with him, all straw hair and country spit. Even he was subdued and distant.

The men did not look proud. They did not even look like a team. They looked more like strangers waiting for a late train.

'Well, this'd bloody be right wouldn't it? Another training session before we get thrown to the wolves.' It was a chubby man, with big arms and a checked jacket.

'Oi, Ken,' said Baker, 'don't you start in on us.'

This must be Ken Hall, the middle-order batsman. He was famous for standing up to the opposition, but not so far in this series. His face looked nearly as red as some of the checks in his jacket.

'Someone bloody should. The Poms sure do. Where's the boss?'

No one answered. The men all seemed to be looking at some different part of the nets, or the ground or their own gear.

'Well bugger me,' yelled Hall angrily. 'I coulda finished me breakfast.'

'Ken, can you spare us your personal thoughts on life's unfairness, just for this morning?' It was the lawyer, Calligan.

'What's up your nose?'

'You're up my nose, Ken. And I don't appear to have a handkerchief large enough to dislodge you.'

David watched, aghast.

The men stood glaring at each other. Hall was shorter, but with the body of a bull. Calligan might have been a lawyer, but he was a tall, strong-looking man. None of their team mates stepped in to stop them. Some weren't even looking.

Michael was. He was standing on the other side of the nets, leaning against one of the poles that supported them. His hat was pushed down over his eyes, but you could see him watching.

Another group arrived. There was John Richardson, the Australian captain. His eyes looked sad, his shoulders slightly stooped, as he listened to two men in suits. One of them was big and round and old. He smoked a cigar. The other was smaller and walked with his eyes darting all about him.

Behind them was Jack Tanner, looking as confident and comfortable as ever, walking with two other players. One was a youth and the other much older.

'Morning gentlemen,' said Richardson.

'What's the deal, Gov?' said Hall.

The man with the cigar took it out of his mouth, and used it as a pointer. 'Gentlemen, I think it's fair to say we are in trouble.'

Richardson said nothing.

'And,' continued the man, 'I'm not going to stand for it. We are two Tests down. We haven't just lost. We've been routed. Killed. Humiliated.'

'Yeah, righto, Mr Livingston. We know,' said Ken Hall.

'And it wouldn't hurt the cause if you got a few more runs, Mr Hall.'

Richardson stepped in then. 'Yes, all true, Mr Livingston, but I don't think it does any good to start pointing the finger.'

'Something has got to be done. People need to see some spirit out there. They have enough problems in their daily lives without our cricket team contributing to them.'

The cricketers bowed their heads. All except Ken Hall who just looked back at the man who was clearly Sir Bartholomew Livingston, chairman of the Australian Cricket Board.

'We expect changes,' said Richardson levelly to Sir Bartholomew.

'Gentlemen.' It was the little man in the suit. He spoke quietly with a faintly embarrassed smile. 'For some of the new chaps who don't know me, my name is Steven Biggins. I'm the ACB treasurer. Mr Richardson and the selectors have spent the last few days looking at batsmen. John?' He turned with great politeness to Richardson.

'Andrew Bardsley is going to open with Chalkie.'

Bardsley looked up warily.

'We've also brought back George Jackson.' He pointed to the older player next to Tanner, who nodded. 'As some of you might know, George has been playing in the counties for the last few years. He's faced these fellows a bit more, and he's got a pretty good defence.'

Richardson turned to Tanner. 'We're also going to have

a look at Jack Tanner from WA this morning. He couldn't make it earlier because he was pulling people out of fires and chewing dynamite, if the press is to be believed.'

Jack flexed his shoulders as he nodded. 'Oi boys. Bit of a hit with you, if that's all right?'

'Hey, Jack,' said Maud McLeod. There were nods.

'So that's three new batsmen. And we need a spinner.' It was Livingston again, pushing his cigar at each of them.

'So, we'll be taking a look at a couple of spinners this morning,' went on Richardson more calmly.

'We got any left?' said Hall grimly.

The blond-haired youth with Tanner grinned and nodded, lifting his chin.

'This is young Ashleigh Hobbs. He's been doing all right for Mosman.'

'How are you fellows?' said Hobbs, still smiling.

The players looked back at him, not giving much away.

Mr Biggins spoke again quietly. 'And we have another spinner who comes very highly recommended. David Donald.' The men looked up and around and finally towards Michael.

Jack Tanner folded his arms and waited.

Then Michael said, 'David. Come and meet the team.'

David stepped out from behind the leaves of the weeping willow, and into the sunlight, as the men turned. They looked at him with a kind blossoming scorn. David's heart was thumping as their faces closed to him and became blurs. He could hear words only dimly, and in pieces.

'Joke.'

Richardson saying, 'Most unfair, Steven.'

'Not funny.'

Then David saw his uncle coming through them. When

he reached David he was saying, 'You didn't think it was going to be easy did you? What, they'd just meet you, and the fellows would give you their spot? They don't know how good you are, do they?'

David looked at the Australian team. They had already turned from him. Some were at Livingston, arguing. Others were going about the business of getting ready to train.

'David.'

David looked to his uncle.

'How's the finger?'

David looked down at his finger. It was throbbing. 'It hurts.'

'That's going to make it interesting.' Michael was smiling.

'But ...'

'Who would have thought we'd both be here on a day like this, standing in the grounds of one of the country's oldest universities, just about to bowl at the Australian team, eh? Lucky we're not the sort to be overawed by an occasion, eh? You wouldn't be dead for quids would you?' He patted David on the shoulder, and turned with him to watch what was happening.

Livingston was defending David, but a little weakly. 'And I trust Grimmet's opinion. And if Dunne thinks so highly, I have to be willing to take a look.'

Mr Biggins, the treasurer, was not listening to the argument. He stood, turning his hat in his hands as he looked at David curiously.

Richardson seemed furious. 'When you said he was a lad, I assumed you meant sixteen or seventeen like Hobbs here.'

'But I'm not a little kid,' said Hobbs derisively.

Mr Biggins said, 'Can't we take a look, John? Wally Grimmet was extremely keen. I have never heard him speak so glowingly of anyone.'

Richardson turned to Tanner, 'Have you seen him bowl, Jack?'

Jack Tanner nodded, but said nothing.

'What do you reckon?'

Jack opened his mouth, but seemed to think about it more carefully, before he finally said, 'I think he's very, very good. But this is a man's game, and he should come back when he's older.'

There were mutters of agreement.

Tanner then added, 'But you are asking for my advice, Captain: give him a bowl and belt him out of the park. I want to try and get into this team too.'

Ashleigh Hobbs stepped forward, 'You are giving me a bowl too, I hope. I mean just because there's this to-do, does not mean I'm going to be overlooked, surely.'

'Hardly, Asheigh,' said the fast bowler Calligan. 'It suddenly looks as though you're a shoo-in, doesn't it?'

Hobbs smiled. 'Yes. I see.' He stood nodding.

'Do we actually have to have a spin bowler?' asked Maud McLeod.

'Yes!' yelled Livingston, which caused Hobbs to nod even faster. 'Now can we please get a move on. There's a Test tomorrow and Mr Biggins here would rather appreciate it if the game lasted more than three days.'

Mr Biggins nodded, but only once and very politely.

Richardson had stood for some time, looking at David. Finally he said, 'I'll take the look.' He moved towards his cricket bag and selected a well worn bat. 'Bill, stand behind. Ashleigh, bowl in the next nets and we'll rotate through our two spinners. And you blokes ...' He pointed to his fast bowlers. 'How about you do a bit of warming up. We're not scoring many runs but we're not getting them out very promptly either.'

Hampton and Calligan exchanged a look. Ken Hall shook his head and kicked his cricket bag.

Richardson headed down to the wicket end of the nets. 'What's he bowl, Jack?'

'He's a leggie. Bowls some trick balls too.'

David looked down the other end of the net wicket and he smiled. Here was John Richardson, jumping into action and organising his team. He was fast on his feet and a good tactician. He'd been an officer in the war.

Michael turned David to face him. 'Your first ball has to be a ripping leggie, mate.'

'But my hurt finger.'

'Just that ball. If you bowl something that lands say just outside his leg stump, but turns way across him, he'll remember that ball for the rest of his time at the crease. He'll be waiting for another, for as long as you bowl. Jack's told him. It doesn't have to be a great ball. He'll have a look. It just has to convince him that there's plenty more where that came from. Got it?'

'Yes, sir.'

Richardson was waiting. The wicketkeeper had taken the position behind the batsman. Others stretched and also put pads on, but they were all watching.

Ken Hall said something that David couldn't quite hear, and someone laughed.

Michael was by his side. 'David, concentrate. There's the batsman. Bowl. I got a good ball here.'

David took the ball. It was the one they'd been practising

with, well scuffed and old. He pushed it painfully into his normal grip. It was time to bowl. He did know Richardson's game. He saw in his mind the way he would bowl, then stepped in and bowled it. It was a looping leg break that drew Richardson forward, but then spun across the face of his bat. If he wasn't just looking, but was trying to hit it, it may have got an edge, although it didn't spin nearly as far as David had intended. David hid his hand under his arm, squeezing it against his body. Pain shot through his finger like a burn.

Bill Baker said, 'Nice ball, son. He can turn it, Cap.'

Ashleigh Hobbs said, 'But a back-foot player would have driven that to the boundary.'

Richardson said, 'Possibly. But it would be an uppish shot.'

Tanner had set up in the nets next door. He was ignoring David completely. 'Come on Ashleigh. Let me have a bat too.'

The young spin bowler nodded and ran in and bowled. Jack Tanner watched it bounce, spin a little then had time to lean into a strong cut on the off side.

Michael was next to David again. 'Hurt?'

'Yes.'

'All right. Now go for the other grip. You know how Richardson bats don't you?'

'He's a stroke player. Good cutter. Likes to use his feet.'

Hall yelled, 'Is this bloke in the fedora going to come out and coach him between every delivery?'

Hobbs bowled again. Jack Tanner stepped forward, hitting the ball on the rise and back over the young bowler's head. The crack of wood on ball was clean and loud everyone turned to watch it go.

Richardson said, 'Jack, how about you move down to the next net and have a go at the fast bowlers. Chalkie, you have a look at Ashleigh.'

'Don't show them you're hurt,' whispered Michael, 'or the jig's up, matey. And I hate it when the jig's up.'

'I'm ready son,' said Richardson.

'He wants to hit you,' said Michael quietly.

David noticed Richardson tapping his bat against the ground as he waited for David to bowl. He knew the ball. Hoped for flight. He bowled the off break. It was flatter than he wanted, but came in suddenly and surprised Richardson who was expecting it to go the other way. He was a good enough batsman to scramble back and jam his bat down in front of his wicket. The ball ballooned in front a little, but would have been safe if the fieldsman at silly mid-off wasn't close enough for the catch. David felt disappointed.

'Bloody hell,' said Hall, still watching.

'Well, those two were pretty different, eh Cap,' said Baker from behind the stumps. 'I think I might have gone the wrong way too, eh?'

Richardson merely nodded, taking his guard for the new ball.

Michael was there again. 'Notice how he's edged forward. He wants to come to the pitch.'

'Yes, sir.'

'He's going to go after you.'

'I hope so.'

'Be a bloody long day's cricket,' grumbled Hall, 'if this bloke's gunna trot out to the middle between every ball.'

'He's changed his grip, Mr Richardson, from the first ball,' called Hobbs.

'How about you concentrate on bowling a ball that doesn't

get hit to the boundary,' said Johnson, now replacing Tanner in the next net.

David imagined the ball he would bowl. He stepped in and bowled a topspinner, but with his off-break grip. Even though his first two fingers did most of the work with this ball, there wasn't much spin, but luckily there was enough flight to tempt Richardson towards it before it dipped. Richardson jammed his bat down to smother it before it could bounce high, shooting it out sideways along the ground.

'Four runs!' yelled Hobbs.

'Not likely,' called Baker from behind.

'Clever ball,' nodded Richardson.

David felt a mixture of pride at Richardson's words and disappointment at his bowling.

Richardson turned back to the Australian wicketkeeper, saying, 'I didn't have much idea, Tinker.'

The wicketkeeper looked from David to the men in suits, and scratched the stubble on his chin. 'That Wally Grimmet always was a good judge of a horse. Maybe he's sent us a thoroughbred Shetland.'

'Maybe we should also put your position on the table, John.' It was Livingston.

'No,' said David. 'He's a great captain and good batsman.'

There was silence a moment, before laughter.

'Looks like you still have one fan, John.'

'Best captain he's seen since the under tens.'

David blushed. He shouldn't have spoken. It wasn't his place and now they were laughing. He tried not to look at his finger.

Michael touched him on the shoulder. He was grinning

too. 'David. It's all right mate. It's funny. They're laughing at the situation and not you. It's funny.'

David tried to smile, but he didn't feel like it.

Ashleigh Hobbs ran in and bowled. From his grip, David judged that he was looking to spin it away from the right-handed Johnson, but it was over pitched and went too far in the air. Johnson drove it straight back at Hobbs with such power that the ball passed his ear and was gone before he had time to react.

'Careful there, Chalkie,' yelled Hall. 'Don't kill the only spinner left in the country. I mean who's over the age of ten.'

Michael pushed the ball into David's chest, and made him reach up for it. 'David, you have to bowl one more leggie.'

'I can't.'

'He's picked you. He worked you out last ball, but only halfway through the shot, I reckon. You bowl another off spinner without your usual spin, he'll drive or cut you. Probably all the way to where young Hobbs has gone to get his last delivery.'

'But my finger is already starting to swell up again, Uncle Mike.'

'Very well,' said Michael nodding. 'All right. This is the last ball you have to bowl today, so give it everything.'

'The last ball?'

'All or nothing. Death or glory. And woops no legs.' Michael turned to Richardson. 'He's going to bowl you out now, Mr Richardson.'

'I beg your pardon?'

'Watch his bluffs, John,' said Tanner. 'This bloke here likes to talk the batsman out.'

'I'm just saying that David is going to bowl you out next delivery.'

Mutters of excitement rippled around David as Michael turned and whispered, 'Bowl him around his legs.'

'Well, we'll see about that,' said Richardson, none too happily.

Tanner had stood aside so he could watch. Johnson did the same on the other side. The men in suits came in next to Baker behind the net.

David pushed the ball into his fingers. His hurt finger throbbed, but he wouldn't think about that, just where the ball would land.

Hobbs yelled, 'He's changed his grip back. It's going to be a leggie.'

David was already stepping in. He let it rip. He didn't even see it land, because the pain in his finger took over all his thoughts. He grabbed at it, and held it tight so that the grabbing would take his mind off the deeper ache within. Finally, he found that by pushing the thumb of his left hand into the pad below his third finger, he could concentrate.

Richardson was still standing in front of his wickets, only they were askew, and he was still replaying the ball flight in his own mind, looking out at David, and then around behind his legs, to work out what he should have done.

'Go and put your hand under the tap again, mate. That's you done for the day,' said Michael, patting him on the back. Michael turned towards the Australian captain. 'So, Mr Richardson, what do you think?'

'I'd like to see a couple more,' said Richardson.

'No matter how good he is, he's not playing,' said Livingston. 'We'd be a laughing stock.'

'On the other hand,' said Mr Biggins, to no one in

particular, 'this could prove to be a most interesting business opportunity.'

'Anyway, you've seen some of his balls,' said Uncle Michael. 'We're off. Prior engagement.'

'Off!' said Baker.

'Got to get David some cricket clothes, I'm afraid. Can't have him representing his country in his civvies can we?'

David looked back, at that. He couldn't help it. Michael was smiling. He was going to talk to them in the way David had seen before, through spinning his words this way and that, so that they wouldn't quite know which way the conversation was going.

Then Paul Hampton, the giant fast bowler with the enormous moustache, stepped in front of him. David gasped. But Hampton smiled and said, 'Nice bowling, little man.'

'Thank you, Mr Hampton,' said David, completely forgetting about his finger. 'Nice bowling to you too, Mr Hampton. Especially in South Africa.'

Hampton laughed. 'You sure got a good memory.' He shook his head and walked off, laughing again.

David moved into the shade of the weeping willow and rested his hand in the water once more, waiting for it to go numb. Whatever happened now, he'd tried his best. And he'd met Paul Hampton who'd said nice bowling, and he'd bowled to John Richardson and bowled him out. Apparently. He had only seen it in his mind, but not when it had actually happened.

'What are you doing?'

David turned to see Mr Biggins standing just outside the weeping willow branches.

'Nothing, Mr Biggins. The water cools my hand.'

Mr Biggins peered at the nearest willow branch as though

looking for spiders, before reaching up with his left hand and raising it so he could step through without it touching his suit. His clothes seemed brand new. He carried his homburg in his right hand.

David took his hand from the fountain and made it look like he was scratching the back of his leg.

'They are picking Ashleigh Hobbs, I'm afraid. I know it may seem unfair, as you are clearly a better bowler.'

David noticed that Mr Biggins was not looking exactly at him, but at someone who seemed to be standing next to him. David checked and there was no one behind him.

'It is sensible really. The team is already in turmoil. Their confidence is frail, you see. It would be cruel to add a player so young and at the same time suggest they believe in themselves.' He flicked his eyes to David's.

'Yes, sir.'

'I wanted to say, David, that it was a pleasure seeing you bowl. Your time will come, I have no doubt. So you keep up the good work, and I hope to meet you again soon.'

'Yes, sir. Thank you, um, Mr Biggins, sir.'

Mr Biggins nodded to the invisible person next to David and then let himself out of the weeping willow as if it were a fine, curtained tent.

Michael took the news badly. He paced in their hotel room, his limp making the pacing look like an angry jig. David sat with his hand in a bucket of ice that his uncle had got from downstairs with a bottle of brandy for himself. The ice made his whole hand ache and not just the finger.

'Oh, my dear chap, it's the rules, old bean.' He was putting on an English accent, a little like Mr Livingston. 'We don't actually have a rule to cover this, but now that you mention it, we really should. Let's say no lads under fifteen. Sensible, what? So, that's now the rule, I'd say. Rules old chap. Must have rules. Simply not cricket otherwise.'

Michael paused to spill some brandy into his tumbler. He'd found it on the little sink in their bathroom. Their room had its own bathroom which included a toilet. There were lots of lamps and they were all electric.

'Fairness and rules. Except for the other times. Called a codicil, old bean.' Michael had gone back to his own voice. 'As soon as you agree to abide by their rules, that's when they've got you. Duty and honour and ... that's how they use you, while they break every one themselves, every time it suits them.'

David had seen his uncle in lots of moods, but never like this. His anger was bitter and obvious.

'It doesn't matter, Uncle Mike. My finger is hurt.'

'And you got Richardson out a couple of times.'

'But ...'

'But nothing. You still bowled four excellent balls. You are the best bowler I've ever seen and you deserve to be in that team. Hobbs! They actually picked Hobbs. The only chance that fellow has of getting a wicket is a catch on the boundary. In Melbourne.'

David made himself wriggle his fingers in the ice and water in the metal bucket on the bed beside him while he hoped his uncle's anger would wear itself out.

'The world is going to see you bowl at the best there is. And no one is going to stop that. No one.' He started emptying his pockets on a little table by the door, and separating bits of paper and tickets from the coins and pounds he had.

'I can work my way up through the other teams, so everyone can see me. Learn my trade.'

'No. Now. Australia needs you now. You're ready now. Now.' Michael grabbed up his little pile of money and the bottle of brandy, a fair bit of which was now gone. He put on his hat and left the room without saying goodbye.

David wiggled his fingers again in the ice bucket, making the ice clink. He wondered for the first time if his uncle was a bit mad. Not just hurt and sad, like at the rail crash, but ... David found himself hoping that his uncle would find a lady, even if she were a floozy. He seemed happiest when he had a lady he was joking with.

He thought of Nell Parker. She was a girl. His best friend. She and Grandad were his only friends, until Uncle Mike came along. Seeing as it was school holidays, Nell would be helping her dad in the workshop. It would have been brilliant if Nell had turned on the radio, and heard the Australian team being called out. David Donald. 'Dad, Dad, Dad.' She'd scream it. 'He's in the team. He is.' She'd probably run around the town yelling it. Run all the way out to Grandad and tell him, and then they could jump around the kitchen at the amazing news.

No, David thought. That was too far for Nell to run. David sat with his hand in the ice bucket imagining how the word would eventually get to his grandad if Nell didn't bring it. He didn't want any of the Mr Pringles to tell him. That would ruin it, and besides, whenever they drove out to the farm it was to take something. Maybe Mrs Pringle could do it. Seeing as this was David's daydream, he decided that Mrs Pringle would tell Grandad. She'd ride a horse out there, and Nell would ride with her.

David woke to a fist banging on the hotel room door. It was day, and his uncle was asleep in the bed beside him. When he opened the door, he found Mr Biggins standing in the hall. His collar wasn't done properly, one corner up too far at the front.

'Good,' he said, 'you haven't left. Something terrible has happened. Ashleigh Hobbs got into a fight last night. He's hurt his hand. Someone stepped on his bowling hand. Every finger broken.'

'So, a bit of an emergency, then?' said Michael from the bed, as though he was ordering jam and toast for breakfast.

'Can you get David to the ground in time for play today?'

'No problem. How about that rule? That rule is going to be a problem.'

'Ah, well perhaps it won't be.' He nodded sadly to Michael, like an apology, then turned to speak to David's ear. 'Chances are you will come as no more than a guest. I think Sir Bartholomew and I are taking a rather big chance. Betting the bank, so to speak.' He waggled his head back and forward, his shoulders going side to side with the invisible weighing up. 'We will see. Desperate times and all that. But this will not be easy, David. Not easy at all. I hope you're up to it.' Mr Biggins looked encouragingly to the invisible person by David's shoulder.

'Course he is,' said Michael, putting his feet on the floor, but still not rising.

Mr Biggins looked a moment, perhaps embarrassed. 'Bowl like you did yesterday, and we'll all do splendidly.' He nodded, then backed out into the hall, closing the door gently as he left.

David turned to his uncle. 'What happened?'

'Sounds like you got in the team.'

'What did you do? To Ashleigh Hobbs.'

Uncle Michael looked at him, bleary-eyed.

David could see no clue in him. 'Mr Biggins said he got in a fight last night.'

'You've met him. A Mosman boy with a plum in his mouth. Wouldn't you say he's a fellow quite likely to get in fights?'

David didn't know about this. It seemed to him that most men, and boys for that matter, wanted to get into some kind of fight.

'Manifest destiny, son. Ever hear of that? Westward ho, and there it is, all laid out by the Good Lord. Eat, drink and don't mind the incumbents. Lo, the lilies of the field, they toil not at sparrow's fart.'

David kept looking at him but still could not see any sign that he had done anything wrong.

'What you've got, how you play, is a God-given gift. It's so special that it's not the work of man. All the planets must have been in exactly the right place and all the witches looking on. When the hurlyburly's done, when the battle's lost and won.'

'Stop it,' said David.

'And who's to say that these same deities or planets or crazy bits of dumb good luck haven't conspired to clear your way once again, eh? Other spinners had accidents. Now Hobbs. These things happen. Why is bad luck the only thing that runs in packs? Ask my missing toe.' His uncle wiggled his scarred foot at David. 'And still you're a better bowler than all of them.'

'Did you do anything to Ashleigh Hobbs?'

His uncle looked at him, unblinking, put his hand on his heart, said unsmiling, 'I swear.'

David stared. He did not know if the man was lying to him. He never knew.

'Come on,' said Uncle Mike. 'A big breakfast, then we better get you some cricket gear. The Australian Cricket Team. Let me see, I think you're playing England today. You're allowed to say bonzer, you know.'

CHAPTER TEN

The river seemed to turn right outside Adelaide Oval. David waited as his uncle tried to talk their way into the players' entrance, his brand new cricket gear at his feet. He felt scared. He felt like he was living outside his own dream, watching the man in the grey jacket looking dubiously at them both, and continuing to deny admittance. Yet he had faith in his uncle's ability to talk his way in, just as he'd talked his way to their free cricket gear earlier in the day.

At exactly 8.30 a.m., as Mr Gould of Gould's Sporting Goods was winding up the canvas awning outside his shop, Michael had marched up.

'Are you the proprietor?'

'I am.'

'Mr Gould? I can't be talking to someone who doesn't have the complete authority of the entire firm,' said Michael very seriously.

'I'm Mr Gould,' said the man, looking back at his small store and seeming to appraise whether it could be called an entire firm.

'Good. This fellow here is David Donald, and he's about to play his first match for Australia in this morning's Test. He needs a full kit.'

David watched the man turn to look at him. He nodded to Mr Gould, whose eyes seemed about to pop out of his head a moment before he blinked, then nodded. He turned back to Michael with an 'Ah, I think I see. Yes. Good.' Then he winked.

Michael was patient, even though he continued to talk rapidly. 'No, Mr Gould. I'm not indulging the fantasy of a young nephew. What I'm telling you is the absolute truth. David is to play for Australia in approximately two hours, and because he has been rushed here by train all the way from Perth, Western Australia, and because that train was delayed due to a rail accident in the middle of the Nullarbor Plain, we ... he finds himself without any cricket gear. None at all.'

Mr Gould's left eyebrow went up and down, twice, then he indicated his store. 'I've got all the cricket gear you could possibly want. And in the lad's size too, I'd wager.'

'That's exactly what I was hoping to hear, Mr Gould. The term "wager" is a most suggestive one. Do you like a punt, Mr Gould?'

Mr Gould folded his arm across his chest. Both eyebrows rose just a little.

'We want pads, bats, gloves and creams. We want shoes. Balls. A cricket bag. Do you have a cricket bag with Gould's Sporting Goods on it, Mr Gould?'

'Of course I don't. You'd put your club there.' Mr Gould was becoming impatient.

David too. He wanted to get to the ground. He wanted time to warm up. He wanted time to get used to the idea of what was happening to him. He wanted his finger, which had only gone down a little, to settle.

'You might want to consider rethinking that, Mr Gould,

because in exchange for you giving us all this clobber, we'd want to tell all of Australia, and very often, that the great David Donald is kitted exclusively by ... Gould's of North Adelaide.'

Mr Gould's eyebrows collapsed back toward his eyes. 'You're barking mad,' said Mr Gould, as he tried to retreat into his shop.

Michael followed him. 'Come in, David. Start picking out some gear.'

'He's not going to, Uncle Mike.'

'Of course he is.' His uncle smiled the brightest smile and David knew that of course the man would.

The previous day's newspaper was dragged out and David's name read as someone being considered. Turner's injury was noted. Hobbs' accident was explained. Finally, Mr Gould was persuaded to telephone the ACB and talk to the Chairman, Sir Bartholomew Livingston. Even then Mr Gould's eyebrows continued their dance around his narrowed eyes. It was a big outlay of goods in the troubled times, and all based on the flimsiest of promises and the most preposterous of stories.

At that point Michael laughed. He even clapped his hands a couple of times. 'Isn't it wonderful though. You are right, Mr Gould. It does you credit to be suspicious and circumspect and a little cynical. It would be prudent and entirely sensible to wish us luck and say no. I do not believe this and I will not be part of it. Twelve years old. Please, you have gone too far. You ask too much.'

Mr Gould was nodding.

'On the other hand, think of the rewards. And I don't just mean in the potential good word and publicity. I don't just mean the chance for financial gain, which is virtually guaranteed. I mean the pleasure of joining. Here's this most unlikely story you are being told ... and it is about to come off. David is going to play for Australia. It is like a fairy story and you can be part of it. Part of the wondrous ... History of David Donald: the Early Years. Let's just take a moment to think about what this means? Have you got children, Mr Gould?'

Mr Gould blinked yes.

That was when David wandered the sports store and began to choose his cricket gear. He had not touched cricket gloves before. No one in Dungarin owned a pair. They were stiff. He didn't even try to put the right glove over his hurt finger. He wasn't sure any of the gloves would fit over his fingers. The pads were stiff and shiny white. Mr Gould stopped bargaining long enough to suggest a smaller pair so that David could run more easily between the wickets. His uncle had stopped his convincing long enough to suggest a lighter bat, rather than the one David had first taken up. David didn't tell either man that he was not a very good batsman, and had seldom had occasion to run to the other end of a wicket, even at school.

The cream pants and shirt were very smart. The shoes were much more comfortable than his farm boots, but he found it difficult to clatter along the linoleum floor on the short spikes that were attached to the soles. He took some steps to bowl an imaginary ball and skidded immediately.

'No spikes in the shop, please,' called Mr Gould.

David looked into a full-length mirror where he saw a little kid, small even for his age which, as everyone kept pointing out, was twelve. He stood there looking at the boy in the brand new creams. His arms were too long, his fingers longer still. He looked like some tree—like the weeping willow at the university with its branches hanging down to the ground. He needed a haircut. His nose was sunburned, which seemed strange, given all the time he'd spent inside these last weeks. David tried to pull his shoulders back, to make his arms somehow not seem to hang there so floppily. He tried them over his stomach, but they were just a tangle. He put them on his hips, but looked like a teapot. He finally found a position that seemed to somehow not call attention to them. By pretending to scratch the back of his neck, with the arm bent, and the hand hidden behind his head, and with the other hand pushed up under his chin, as though he was thinking deeply about things, David decided his arms looked quite normal.

'So,' said Mr Gould into his telephone, 'you're actually telling me, Mr Biggins, that the Australian team is playing a boy in the Test today?'

And that's what the man at the gate of the Adelaide Oval was saying to Mr Scully, a short, lean old man who was apparently the Australian team manager. 'This boy is playing in the Test?'

Mr Scully spat on the ground. 'He's named. We'll see about the playing. Just let 'em in mate, and leave the team selection to us.'

The man stood shaking his head. Michael grabbed up David's brand new cricket bag and they followed Scully towards the back of the grandstand. 'Thought you buggers weren't gunna make it.'

'Yep,' said Michael in his working man's accent, 'all a bit last minute, eh.'

'Well you've missed the cap presentation, so that'll have to wait.' Mr Scully pushed a door under the back of the stand, but then suddenly turned and looked at Michael, not two feet from his face. 'Funny what happened to Ashleigh Hobbs.'

'Laughed so much, I thought I was gunna cry,' said Michael with no smile.

'Just like that.'

'Funny ol' world.'

Mr Scully spat towards the ground, and seemed as if he'd like to say more, but he turned and led them in.

David followed the men into the darkness. There was a corridor with many rooms under the grandstand. Their footsteps echoed on the floorboards. They went towards the front. David could see the ground out an open door at the end of the corridor. It was like a shining green motion picture showing on a tall skinny-shaped screen.

'I'll take the lad's bag,' said Mr Scully, at the players' door. 'Players only.'

David turned to his uncle in alarm.

Michael bent down to him. 'This is it, mate. I'll be in the stands.'

'But Uncle Mike, what do I do?'

'Well, what the captain tells you. Always. Um, and maybe you should bowl them all out.'

His uncle winked, then turned and walked back down the corridor the way they'd come. David watched him until Mr Scully tapped him on the shoulder.

'You comin' or what, boy?'

Just inside the door there were four men in creams, smoking and playing cards: Bill Baker, the wicketkeeper, Maud McLeod, the young all-rounder, George Jackson, the older player who had come back from the counties, and big, red Ken Hall all turned and looked at David. They didn't say a word.

David felt he should nod or say good morning, but couldn't make his mouth work. It felt dry.

'It's bloody come to this,' said Hall, turning back to his cards.

'Through here, lad,' said Mr Scully, in a not unkind tone.

David looked out a huge window as he followed. There were some bench seats out the front. Geoffrey Calligan, the lawyer and fast bowler, was sitting out there, reading a book. Paul Hampton sat nearby, talking to Jack Tanner. They looked relaxed, enjoying the sun. Beyond, John Richardson was walking out to the middle, where the umpires waited, and the groundsmen pulled the roller.

'Wakey, wakey lad. Yer a bloody dreamer.' Mr Scully had opened another door which led to the lockers.

A variety of street clothes, shoes and cricket gear was tossed on bench seats and in the shelves and large pigeon holes. There were nicely written name tags. The room smelled of leather and old sweat which made David's nose wrinkle at its unpleasantness.

Terry Johnson was sitting at one end of the room near a floor fan. He had a hand on each knee, staring at the floor some two feet in front of himself.

At the other end of the room, young Andrew Bardsley, who was playing in his first game, was practising some strokes. He had on an Australian cap that looked a new dark green. He turned to Mr Scully. 'We batting or bowling?'

'Captain's just gone out for the toss.'

'Right,' said Bardsley. He caught sight of David, and hurriedly left the room, his cricket spikes clattering.

'This is yours, Nipper.'

David looked to an empty shelf. His name was there,

printed on cardboard. Master Donald.

'Don't talk to Mr Johnson. He doesn't like talking, right now, in case he's batting. You better get changed.'

'Thanks, Mr Scully.'

'Yeah, well, most of the boys just call me Scully.' He looked down and thought. 'But I suppose you and I can stick to Mr Scully then.'

'Yes, sir.'

David opened his sports bag. He looked at Mr Johnson again. He was still staring at the floor, the fan pushing his fringe like he was in a motor car. David started to get changed, checking every now and then that Mr Johnson wasn't watching. He looked at the lockers again.

Each name was famous but their clothes seemed so ordinary, even though there were different styles of dress. Some clothes were neatly hung up. Some were fine, but a little haphazard. Others were piled into their lockers or simply dropped onto the seat in a heap. David realised that the batsmen had laid out their batting gear on top of their bags. There was a pile of huge cricket shoes of different ages tumbling out below a seat which must have belonged to the big fast bowler, Hampton. A photograph of a lady and child was tacked to the side of the shelf above. In Jack Tanner's locker his derby was propped against an unopened bottle of champagne.

Andrew Bardsley came in. 'Batting.'

'We're batting,' said Mr Johnson grimly.

'Yep. Has John won a toss yet?'

Mr Johnson didn't reply. He'd begun to put on his pads.

David said, 'No.'

Bardsley looked at him, but said nothing.

David said, 'Not this series. That's the third toss that

Henry Longford's won in a row.'

Bardsley ignored David and started to put his pads on. He talked towards Johnson. 'You reckon they'll open with Tudor or Proctor? Proctor's faster, I reckon, but Tudor's smarter. Both bloody fast. Who would you rather face, Mr Johnson?'

'Scully,' yelled Johnson, dragging out the ee sound at the end like a cooee bush call.

Mr Scully raced into the room, looking worried.

'Get these two kids to shut up and get out of here, will you?'

Scully looked at the other two and jerked his head to indicate they should leave. He winked at them, and David understood that they should not take too much offence.

'Just asking,' grumbled Bardsley. 'Got a right to get ready too, you know.'

As they came out of the locker room they met John Richardson coming back in. 'Morning chaps. Right, we'll just have to see off the new ball, Andrew. That'd be the ticket. Don't play at anything you don't have to.'

Bardsley nodded. David thought he looked terrified.

'Cometh the hour, cometh the man, Beardie,' added Richardson, in a gentler tone.

Bardsley nodded again as he wandered to the door which led out to the ground. He stood looking out at the oval.

'Mr Richardson,' said David, 'where should I go?'

Richardson looked down. He seemed surprised and mildly annoyed to see David. He called, 'Maud!' Maud McLeod stepped into the doorway from the card room.

'Look after David here, will you? Seeing as you're both from the country and all.'

'I'm from the country, boss, but I'm no bloody wet nurse.'

Ken Hall yelled, 'Watch out Maud. Likely to get your hand stepped on, you get too close to this kid. That's what happened to Hobbs.'

'I'll take him.' It was the giant, Paul Hampton, who was leaning in from outside. 'Come on out here, David. Best seats in the house.'

Outside the players' rooms were two rows of bench seats which were under cover, but which had a complete view of the ground. Jack Tanner looked over at him as he stepped out into the light. David made himself look back. 'Morning, Mr Tanner.'

'Morning, Mr Donald.'

'Push yourself along the bench there, David,' said Hampton.

'Yes, sir.' David sat on the empty bench seat, and Hampton plonked himself next to him.

'Call me Paul. Or Ten Ton if ya like.'

'Ten Ton?'

'Hamp-ton. Ton. Ten Ton on account of I'm a big bloke.'

'Ha. That's clever,' said David, smiling at the word play.

'Not very clever. But it's stuck. Like the Christmas pudding.' He patted his stomach.

People started clapping, and David turned to see Bardsley and Johnson walking down between the seats to the gate that led onto the field.

Geoffrey Calligan looked up from his book and yelled, 'See you fellows at lunchtime.'

The English team were out on the field, some jumping and others swinging their arms. A bowler was bowling practice balls to another fieldsman, but David couldn't make out who most were. They were all a lot further away than he expected. The English team stopped their warm-ups to watch the Australian openers coming towards them. Looking at it from this perspective, it seemed unfair, as though two had to play against eleven.

Calligan called quietly to Tanner, 'You might want to get padded up there, Jack.'

Jack Tanner turned to look at Calligan, then up at the doorway. David looked there too, in time to see Richardson in his pads looking anxiously out to the middle.

'That's all right,' said Tanner loudly. 'I don't want to sit around in me pads all morning.'

Bardsley waved his arms and trotted up and down on the spot, still all nervous energy. Johnson trudged. David didn't like the look of that. He knew they'd describe it as a bad sign on the radio. He looked to the bowler.

'Who's that warming up with the ball?'

'Proctor. Big bloke, eh?'

David nodded, squinting out towards the middle.

'So, your first Test,' said Hampton.

'Yes,' said David, 'I've never seen one before.'

'Seen one. Ha. I meant first yer played in. So you've never even seen a Test match?'

David saw Calligan was watching too. He just nodded, embarrassed. Then he noticed the crowd. They were hemmed in around them. There were a lot of empty seats, but thousands had gathered to see Australia and England play. Some people were looking his way. A man looked angry, his hat pulled low. A boy stuck his tongue out.

'So,' said Hampton, 'yer mum and dad out there?'

'No sir, I'm an orphan.'

Johnson was taking guard. He would ask for leg stump from the umpire, David thought, recalling radio and newspaper reports.

David noticed Mr Hampton was looking at him. Mr Calligan and Tanner were too. He thought about what he'd said and tried to put them at their ease. 'My grandad looks after me. He's in Dungarin. My Uncle Mike brought me. He's here.' David looked away from them, in case they were still unhappy with his answer.

Proctor was at the top of his mark.

'Not much of a crowd, boys,' said Tanner.

David was glad for the change of subject.

'Not much pleasure in spending three and six to watch your country getting walloped,' said Calligan.

'Not much pleasure in being walloped for that matter,' added Hampton.

David couldn't even see Proctor's first ball. He ran in and performed a bowling action, and down the other end Johnson seemed to bend and duck, while his bat waved a little, and then the wicketkeeper acted as if he caught the ball. It was like a mime of cricket-playing. There were some ahs from the crowd, but evidently Johnson hadn't hit it, because the umpires had not moved. 'Was that fast?' asked David.

'That was fast,' said Calligan.

Johnson jammed down on the next ball, but was very rushed in his action.

'Yorker,' said Hampton next to him.

The crowd made little noise. Things were tense.

It was quiet enough for them all to hear the nick Johnson got on the third ball. All six men who had been standing in a semicircle in slips jumped up shouting, 'Howwwwww's that!' Johnson turned and walked from the field, not bothering to wait for any umpiring decision.

'Oh no!' yelled David with the rest of the crowd.

Hampton nudged David in the side. 'As a player, we try not to barrack so much.'

'Considered bad form,' added Calligan. 'Not like the hardened professionals we are.'

'So, don't go telling him it's his third duck in a row, either, right.' Paul Hampton winked at him.

David nodded.

Tanner got up from his seat, stretching casually, and strolled back into the change rooms. Richardson passed him going the other way, whistling 'Waltzing Matilda'. He passed Johnson who was still on the ground coming in.

Someone from the crowd yelled, 'And don't come back, yer useless mongrel.' Other jeers came too, as Johnson walked back through the gate and up the steps between their seats. He didn't look at anyone, just where he was putting his feet.

The jeers continued and David looked to the crowd again. Angry faces. There were ladies yelling too. A lady in a coat and pillbox hat with one yellow flower was screaming so much it seemed to David she would have killed Johnson right there and then, had she had him in her hands. An old man was yelling, and David saw that he had no teeth. His mouth was a black growling hole. Some people raised fists. The boy that David had seen before was looking back at him, and again he poked his tongue out.

David looked away, and focused on the white painted wood of the seats in front of him. But he could feel the crowd still, feel their angry cries finally ebb, as the Australian captain John Richardson reached the wicket. The silence was tense, like the air in a thunderstorm charged with the power of the thunderclaps.

David felt for the first time the excitement of seeing the Test. Each ball bowled at the Australian batsmen brought gasps from the crowd, gasps David felt as his own.

Richardson was surviving rather than playing shots. Bardsley jumped and ducked and weaved as though dealing with a swarm of bees. Bardsley was having the worst time because he was facing the English fast bowler named Tudor. Proctor was very fast and very accurate, but Tudor was meaner. Many of his balls would follow Bardsley. He was hit on the chest and on the leg. The crowd gasped and winced, as though under attack themselves. When Bardsley skied one to mid-on, fending off another rising delivery, the crowd groaned in disappointment. Although he'd only scored fifteen runs, he had occupied the crease, and taken the shine off the new ball. Hampton said, 'Got some guts, that boy.' Bardsley walked back to the players' area to scattered clapping.

Tanner strode to the gate, swinging the bat like a windmill. 'Who the bloody hell are you?' yelled someone from the crowd. There was a roar of laughter David found very disrespectful. But Jack Tanner walked back to the fence, with his hand held out, and a big smile, 'Name's Jack Tanner, from WA. How ya going?' There was a roar of laughter and approval. Jack doffed his Australian cap, to another cheer, then jogged out into the middle.

'Jack knows how to get a crowd onside,' laughed Hampton.

'Let's hope he can bat,' said Calligan.

David followed the example of the bowlers and clapped as Bardsley came back into the pavilion. 'That Tudor is a right bastard,' he said through gritted teeth, 'right at me.' David thought he seemed to be about to cry. Bardsley thumped the side of a bench seat with his bat, making David jump.

Richardson and Tanner withstood the English fast-bowling attack. They had their moments of discomfort, but Richardson's tight defence and Tanner's more bludgeoning approach began to work. Once they saw off the tiring Tudor and Proctor, they started to score some runs.

Mr Johnson came out to sit in a corner of the players' area. Occasionally someone from the crowd would yell out to him that he should get a job. David wanted to explain that he had one. He was a mathematics teacher when not playing cricket. Someone else in the crowd knew this too because they yelled, 'Hey Johnson, what's nought plus nought plus nought equal?' There was laughter from the crowd accompanied with quacking noises, and the Australian opener soon went back inside.

Hampton, or Ten Ton as David was learning to call him, talked about his family. He had two girls and a baby on the way. They were buying a house in Fitzroy, a suburb of Melbourne. 'You see, the brewery likes having a bloke who is in the public eye, who looks like they like a drink. That's me. You'd think a brewery would survive hard times, wouldn't you? Nope. Half the blokes in the despatch area are for the chop.'

'But you've got your cricket, Ten Ton?'

'Yeah,' laughed the big man. When Hampton saw David looking he added gently, 'I will just have to make sure I start taking some wickets then, shan't I?'

Towards noon, Maud McLeod and Ken Hall came out, both with their pads on. Hall looked around at the crowd. 'Not much faith in us then, eh?'

'Seen better,' said Hampton.

Tanner hit a four from an Ostler delivery and the crowd applauded enthusiastically.

'He goes all right, doesn't he,' said McLeod.

Hall glanced at the crowd, then shot a sly look back towards David. 'Yer know what the crowd are gunna do when the kid goes out. They're gunna laugh for a bit, but then they're gunna tear the place apart. We're gunna be the biggest joke since New Broom cleaned up at Flemington.'

'Leave it alone,' said Hampton. 'Didn't pick himself, did he?'

'As I understand it, maybe 'e did? With a bunch of burly helpers.'

David didn't know what to say about this. He had no proof that his uncle didn't have a hand in Ashleigh Hobbs' accident.

Hall wasn't finished. 'And what the bloody hell's going on, picking a kid who no one's ever bloody heard of?'

'Language,' warned Hampton.

'It's a bloody man's game and I'll bloody use a man's bloody language.'

David was thinking about a speech about doing his best, or something about not minding swearing, but none of it came. 'I'll just go inside,' he said instead.

'An' don't stop there,' yelled Hall at his back.

'I'll bloody dong you if you talk to him like that again,' said Hampton.

'An' I'll help him,' added Calligan, 'just for the pleasure of it.'

'Just sayin' what we all think.'

There were more chairs inside the players' room with the big window and a large electric ceiling fan that made it cool. Johnson sat at a table writing a letter, and occasionally looking at the cricket. In the card room, a radio was on. Bill Baker and Bardsley were listening to the cricket as they played whist. They both looked up at him. Bardsley looked down straight away, but Baker stared as though David was a two-headed lamb.

David got a wooden chair from the card room and moved it into the room where Mr Johnson was. He put it against the wall near the card room door so that he could hear the radio but not be seen by the card players. Or the crowd outside. He closed his eyes and listened to the game.

The radio man thought that Tanner's fearlessness was a hopeful addition to the side. At lunch, Australia was two for a hundred and four. It was the best start they'd had in the Test series. Richardson was on thirty-two and Tanner on forty-three when they came in.

Someone had brought down trays of cold meats and salads, and the card table was turned into a dining table. Mr Scully arranged plates and put out bottles of barley water for the batsmen.

David sat in his chair outside the lunchroom door with his plate of cold meats and salad and listened to the men.

There was a lot of talk about the English bowlers and how Richo and Two Bob (as McLeod had nicknamed Tanner) were handling them. It was clear that both Proctor and Tudor were very dangerous, but that if they were seen off things could get reasonable.

'Ostler's no mug, mind,' said Richardson.

Jack Tanner said, 'Maybe we can go after the spinner.'

'Better find someone we can hit,' said Baker.

'Speakin' of spinners, Skip.' It was Ken Hall.

'Oh, leave off Ned,' Hampton replied. Ned was Hall's nickname.

Maud McLeod chimed in. 'You read the paper this morning? They still think Hobbs is playing. Even the radio is only talking about the surprise inclusion of another spinner. They don't know. They all think the kid is Ten Ton's nephew or something sitting out there.'

'What's your point?' asked Richardson, testily.

'Wouldn't want to be out there in the players' area when the public find out,' said Hall.

'Is this what the card game's decided, eh?' commented Calligan.

'How does it look? What does it say about us?' said McLeod.

'This was not entirely my decision,' said Richardson. 'It was made at the last minute and as a bit of an emergency. I'm sure we can get another spinner for the next Test or bring in our twelfth man. Anyway, how I handle it is my call. Isn't it? Ned? Maud? You too Tinker. I don't want all this bickering. Not now. How about we get a decent score for once, and give the big lads something to bowl at. Then we won't have to bowl the kid anyway. So—enough?'

David left his plate on his chair and went into the dressing room. He sat on the bench in front of his locker where the sign said Master Donald. He wished he had some photograph or letter or anything from home that he could put up there.

Terry Johnson came in. Before David could get up and get out of his way, Johnson spoke. 'Are you tough enough to do this, son?'

'I don't know.'

'We'll find out, I suppose. Think about this though. You can't do worse in here with them, or out there, against the Poms, than I'm doing right now. We're all secretly scared, and each of us is alone. So, suck it up, do the business and don't wear your heart on your sleeve.'

David nodded.

Johnson left the change room.

It was exactly what his grandad would have said. No one's going to do you any favours. Stop snivelling. Just bowl well, and everything else will look after itself. David nodded again. He wished he could be bowling instead of sitting in these rooms with nothing to do. If he could bowl, then he could forget everything else. He could disappear into the world of bowling where everything was big, and clear and possible.

David saw dusk on the farm. He saw the grey light fading in the sky by the shed. He began to conjure a setting sun, the first glimmers of midgies gathering to dance. He shook the picture in his mind away. He patted his hands on his knees, just as his grandad always did after lunch. It was time to get back to work.

Richardson and Tanner were on their way out to the middle and David's plate was gone when he sat back down on his seat near the card room door. Mr Johnson looked around from his letter and David nodded to him. Hampton came out with another plate of food.

'You all right there, Davey?'

'Yes, sir. Right as rain.'

'Thought you might have the runs, but not the kind they put on the score book.'

'No. Um, no?'

'Happens to the best batsmen. Not me, mind, cos I can't

bat worth a farthing.'

'Me neither,' said David.

'Me neither, apparently,' said Johnson.

Hampton burst out laughing. 'He's back. Hey, Chalkie's back.'

A little while after lunch they all went out in the players' area to watch and applaud Tanner's fifty. He was out soon after, when he skied one from Proctor and was caught for fifty-four runs.

When Hall got out for seven, David felt guilty about being secretly glad. Richardson got his fifty, then McLeod got out for eighteen. George Jackson hung around without scoring much, but supporting Richardson to eighty before he was bowled by Tudor. When Baker went out to bat, Calligan came in to get his pads on.

There was a huge gasp from the crowd, and David followed the others to look out on the ground. Baker was lying at one end of the pitch surrounded by English players. Richardson was signalling the dressing room. Scully and the twelfth man, Don Bidman, ran out. The radio said that Tudor had bowled a lifter, which had caught the Australian wicketkeeper in the face, much like the delivery in the previous Test that had put Turner in hospital.

'That Tudor's a right bloody killer,' growled Maud McLeod.

Baker was being helped from the ground, retired hurt. Calligan headed out. Hampton already had his pads on. There was shouting and muttering and movement all round.

David went in the dressing room to put his pads on, but had to sit on the toilet first. He hoped the chicken was not off, as he also felt a bit sick. When he came out to put his pads on, they had Mr Baker lying on a bench, and were wiping at his face. There was a lot of blood. David had difficulty tying his pads behind his legs.

Mr Scully leaned over Baker, saying, 'The doc's on 'is way, Tinker. 'Aven't I told you that little secret about ducking?'

Baker gave a half-hearted groan.

Mr Scully suddenly turned to David. 'Hand us a couple more towels will ya, Nipper? And then better get out of here, eh?'

David handed over the towels and looked down at Mr Baker. He had a gash high on his cheek, but the bleeding was slow. His cheek was already swelling around the wound.

'I can't tie my pads on, and I can't get this glove over my sore finger, Mr Scully.'

Mr Scully's laughter was birdlike, coming through his nose in a kind of high pitching snort. 'Hear that, Tink. Kid can't put his own pads on. And apparently, he has a sore finger. On the first day of his first Test. You think you got problems, eh.'

'I'm sorry, Mr Scully.'

A well-dressed man came in carrying a doctor's bag.

Richardson came in too. The doctor turned to him. 'Nice knock, Mr Richardson.'

'Thank you. How is Bill?'

'Just about to look now.' The doctor bent over the wicketkeeper.

'How'd you go then, Gov?' Scully asked the captain.

'Got bowled. Ten Ton and Legal are out there now. Tudor's got his tail feathers up again.'

'Like's the smell o' blood, that one,' said Scully.

'Cracked cheekbone I'd say,' said the doctor. 'Better get

you to hospital, Mr Baker.'

Scully said, 'Ah, Gov ...'

When Richardson looked, Scully nodded towards David.

David stood, one glove on his left hand and one of his pads hanging untied from below his knee. He bent quickly and grabbed up his new bat.

'No,' said the captain. 'You're here for your bowling, son. I'm not going to send you out.'

'I'll bat, Mr Richardson,' said David.

Richardson looked at the doctor, who was no longer looking at his patient. He stood with his mouth hanging open, looking at David. He sat down on Baker's legs.

'Ooii,' mumbled Baker.

The doctor jumped back up. 'Sorry.'

Richardson pointed at the doctor. 'What do you reckon, Doc?'

'Oh, he'll be right tomorrow if we get the swelling down.'

'The boy. I notice you looking a little bewildered at our tenth drop.'

'He's on your team?'

'That's right.'

David felt like he was the patient, being examined but otherwise ignored.

The doctor looked back to Richardson. 'I don't know what to think.'

'Hmm,' said Richardson.

McLeod stuck his head in the door and said, 'Ten Ton's out.' He looked to David, who started to move again.

'No,' said Richardson. 'Let's have a bowl. I declare our first innings closed.' He moved past David and headed for the door.

'Eight for a hundred and ninety-eight!' said McLeod.

'Nice round figure,' said Richardson, pushing past.

David sat back down again and took off his glove and his pads and changed his shoes.

The other players came in and they changed shoes too. Hampton and Calligan took off their pads, Hampton throwing his bat into the corner with a loud crash of wood on wood. Mr Baker was taken out on a stretcher and received lots of digs and compliments. 'Just a flesh wound, Bill,' said Tanner. 'Get up a couple nurses, Tinker,' said Hall.

No one spoke to David. Even Paul Hampton didn't look his way.

Richardson came back, dusting his hands. 'George, you've kept a bit, haven't you?'

'Just in the counties, Gov,' said the older man.

'Right. Until tomorrow, when Bill gets back. Very well. If we get a couple of wickets tonight, we might be able to put a bit of pressure on them—for a change. See how they like it.'

'Sounds like a plan, boss,' said Hampton rolling his neck.

'Last thing though,' said Richardson, before anyone had a chance to move. He looked to David, and everyone else did too. 'When David comes out we're all going to cop a bit of stick.'

'You got that right,' said Hall.

'Not David's fault. He can bowl. And much better than Hobbs or Freddy Turner, in my estimation. That aside, choosing someone so young looks desperate. Yes, Ned, which it bloody is, I grant. We can't do much about what the crowd does. Just be ready for it and take it on the chin. But here's what I'm thinking. The Poms don't know yet. They'll start trying to hop into us. Get under our skin like they've been doing all tour.' Richardson looked round at each man, and tapped his nose in the sign of knowing something. 'We grin a secret grin, lads. We never answer back. We act like he's our secret weapon. Up our sleeve. You just wait, boyo. I'm holding a straight, but you are going to have to pay to see my cards. Got it?'

They were nodding. Some, like Calligan and Mr Johnson, liked the idea. Others weren't sure, but shrugged.

'Let's go lads,' yelled Scully, clapping his hands. 'This one's for the Tinker.'

They clomped out, David walking with them. He stayed in the middle, taking care where he put his feet, but keeping in step and within the mass of the men, until they filed through the gate onto the field. That's when players ran off in different directions and speeds to get themselves ready for the fielding part of the game. David started to trot after Paul Hampton, but realised that the big fast bowler needed to get ready too. He thought for a moment he might find Mr Johnson, but couldn't see him.

He stopped as the group of men separated to different parts of the field and he was alone. The ground was huge and the noises from the crowd became inescapable. It was as though the biggest flock of black cockatoos had just landed in the trees. Each bird made its own screaming call, but it was somehow understandable as a whole. The cheering and clapping had given way to a sudden silence, short but definite. Then came a ripple of consternation. There were clearly questions, even though David couldn't make out a single one. It was the tone of the hum around the ground. Pockets of laughter broke out, but there were angry calls, these over the top of the continuing bewildered murmur.

George Jackson came past, walking slowly in his pads and slapping together his recently acquired wicketkeeper's gloves. 'Come on lad. Don't you pay them no mind.'

'What are they saying?'

'What you have to remember is they've paid their two bob, so they think they own you for the day. You might be trying to win a game of cricket, but they expect a lot more for their money. See.'

'No, sir.'

'That's the shot. Stay out near the middle if you can.' He patted David on the back and moved off behind the stumps.

The crowd noise changed to polite clapping, and David turned to see the English openers making their way onto the field.

'David, come here,' called Mr Richardson. When David went over, Richard explained, 'Stand next to me and don't say anything to them. Not a word, do you understand. You're my secret weapon.'

David liked that idea and he stood next to Mr Richardson as the English opening batsmen, Dorrington and O'Malley, reached the pitch. David was anxious to see them. They were already legends of the game. Dorrington was a left-hander and free scoring. O'Malley scored very slowly but was hard to get out.

'What's this then, John?' said one.

'New player, William.'

'New is right. Barely weaned,' said O'Malley. O'Malley turned his back and went to set his guard, but Dorrington seemed upset. 'You can't play a lad. It's not right.'

Richardson smiled. Dorrington turned to Jackson behind the stumps. 'This is some Australian joke, is it?' Jackson just smiled. David thought it was a very good sneaky smile.

Dorrington turned to the umpires who David realised were also watching him closely. 'Mr Wisden, surely this is some tactic of disrespect.'

Mr Wisden, David recalled, had umpired a number of Tests and other series. He'd even gone to England once. 'Mr Fitzmorris and I have consulted on this since the team was announced this morning, Anthony. There is no age bar in the rules.'

'They're desperate, Anthony. Let it go,' called O'Malley.

But Dorrington could not. Richardson placed David at silly mid-off, which David knew was one of the most dangerous positions in the field. It was called 'silly' for a reason. He thought he saw Bardsley in slips giving a wink to Mr Richardson, but he couldn't be sure. He wondered if he should explain to his captain that he was not a very good catch.

Calligan had the new ball. Everyone took their positions in the field. There were five slips. David watched Dorrington take his guard. He was standing not six feet away from the English batsman who had scored five centuries against Australia and more than three thousand runs. David made himself take a deep breath, as if he were at the top of his own run, and forced himself to remember that everyone had their job to do and often a new player was sent to silly mid-off.

Dorrington suddenly backed away from his batting stance. 'He's not even crouching down,' called Dorrington pointing at David. 'He's likely to lose his block, if I get one on the on side.'

Calligan had pulled up halfway through his run in. He stood smiling at his captain.

'You're quite right,' he called. 'Can't have you injuring my bowler. Maud, get into David's position would you? David go over there to leg gully.'

David ran to the fielding position the other side of the pitch.

'He's on the pitch!' yelled Dorrington.

David realised he'd stepped on the pitch. He should have gone around.

'Warning, Mr Donald. Mr Richardson, that's a warning,' said the umpire, Mr Fitzmorris.

'Sorry, Mr Fitzmorris. Sorry. I forgot.'

Dorrington was watching him, with his hand out, gesturing in protest. David took up his position, and only then became aware of the ripples of laughter coming across the ground.

'Right circus, this is.'

O'Malley came down to talk to Dorrington. David was right there, behind the batsman, but close enough to hear. 'Settle, Anthony. It must be gamesmanship. Don't be drawn in.'

Dorrington turned to look at David one more time. 'Right. Right. I'm with you. Righteo,' he said to O'Malley, but he looked confused.

McLeod took a step closer to him from his new silly mid-off position. 'You all right there Andrew?'

Dorrington took his guard, but David could see that he was shaping to favour the off side. This was not how he usually played. It was obvious he wanted to hit the ball at Maud McLeod, right where David had been fielding. Calligan must have seen it too, because he bowled a fast yorker which went under a wildly swinging bat to hit the base of Dorrington's leg stump. He was out.

But Dorrington was not done. He pointed a finger at Richardson. 'I will protest this. It's not cricket.'

'Oh get off, ya whinger,' yelled Hall.

David turned to see all the fieldsmen crowding around Calligan, and patting him on the back. He ran to join them, but couldn't find a way in past the big backs of the men.

'Well Gov,' said Jackson, 'that's used up that trick, I reckon.'

David saw it then. It had been a trick, putting him at silly mid-off. Dorington had been upset because he had not wanted to injure a boy.

Calligan turned to David. 'I wouldn't have bowled with you there, David.'

David turned to Richardson to see if he agreed, but he was in conversation with the other players.

Only Jack Tanner was looking at him. He stood with his arms folded. 'Playing with men, Master Donald.' He turned to join the other men's conversation without waiting for a reply from David.

Henry Longford, the English captain, was the next to the crease. His voice was quiet. 'Good afternoon gentlemen.'

'Afternoon, Henry,' said Richardson.

'And welcome to the game, young Donald, is it?'

'Yes, sir. Very pleased to meet you, Mr Longford.'

Longford laughed, but gently. 'I bet you are, lad. And I'll tell you what. At the end of this Test, I'll give you my autograph if you like?'

Before David had a chance to say yes please, Richardson interrupted. 'The collection of memorabilia can wait I think, David. Now, I might put you at mid-off.'

David ran to that position but didn't stay there for very long. Henry Longford proceeded to hunt him. O'Malley maintained his tight defence and scored with occasional ones and twos, but Longford, after a few careful overs against Calligan and Hampton, started to hit the ball to wherever David was fielding. David would hear the crack and look to see this speeding red thing coming at him. He'd try diving and he'd try sliding, but to no avail. When Richardson moved David to different fielding positions, Longford would contrive to hit the ball at and near him again.

The laughter came like a hot wind, and then the jeers. It grew worse when David was moved near the boundary because he could hear the actual words that the people were yelling.

'Dive kid.'

'Get ya body behind the ball.'

'Who'd you pay to get in here?'

'Disgrace.'

'Stupid.'

'Ugly duckling.'

'You are an outrage.'

'Disgrace.'

'Disgrace.'

David finally managed to stop a ball. He got to it, and heard cheers, although they were the slow, low kind. When Mr Johnson ran towards him to take his weak throw and throw it on to Mr Jackson behind the stumps, actual booing broke out, even though the relay throw made O'Malley have to dive to make his ground.

The sun was hot and the field shadeless. David ran many miles and mostly to retrieve Longford's hits from the boundary fence. He was constantly thirsty and the drink breaks came infrequently, even though they served barley water when they did. He was sweating and flies kept finding his eyes to drink there or bite the back of his neck. His left heel felt like it was being rubbed by his new shoe, and the top of the spikes were starting to feel lumpy all along his soles.

Still the crowd jeered every time a ball came past him.

Calligan was taken out of the attack and replaced by McLeod, who bowled medium pace. David was finally moved to field just behind the bowler. It seemed an odd field placement to David as the bowler got most of the balls before they came to him. David hoped he could bowl soon, as he had lots of good ideas about bowling both O'Malley and Longford.

Longford brought up his fifty before stumps with a lofted drive over David's head to the boundary.

David turned to go and retrieve it, thankful that he could run slowly. As he got closer, the noise of the crowd got louder and their faces got bigger. He tried to focus only on the ball.

'Get off, ya mug.'

'Waste o' space.'

'My ten year old can play better than you.'

The last one brought laughter, and it made David look up as he ran towards the ball. There were so many people laughing and pointing. They had hats. Most had drinks. Ladies had fans. Someone leaned down over the fence and picked up the ball. David held his hand out for it, but the teenager leaned back and tossed it towards the centre.

'That's how ya throw,' yelled a man in a white shirt with red tie.

'Hey mate, put on some whites and get out there.' More laughter.

'Get back to the game, dopey,' yelled a blond-haired man in a blue shirt.

'Dopey, that's a good one.'

'Dopey Donald, yeah.'

A lady in a green and white floral dress said, 'Only a mother could love that one.'

There was more laughter, and David finally turned back to the game. Richardson was clapping over his head. They'd been waiting for him. He trotted back, his mouth dry and his stomach like a hole in the world where there was nothing, just things falling through to China.

Finally, the day's play was over. England were one for sixty-eight, a good start. David looked up at the scoreboard. Longford had made fifty-five and O'Malley ten. Calligan, Hampton, McLeod had all bowled. Richardson had bowled a few overs of medium pace. Even Hall had bowled an over of his own part-time leg spin, although David couldn't really remember him doing it. He looked at the name Donald on the scoreboard, where nothing was recorded.

He tried to move closer to his team so he could go off with them, but Longford came over. 'Nothing personal, lad. If your team choose to sacrifice a pawn for novelty, then so be it.'

'I don't understand, Mr Longford.'

The English captain turned back to look into David's eyes. The look was so deep and searching that it made David look down. The English captain crouched to meet David's eyes again.

'Why are you here?'

'I'm a really good bowler, sir.'

'It's not some trick?'

'I don't know, Mr Longford. If it is, I don't know what the

trick is.' David took moment before he added, 'I believe I can bowl you out.'

Longford smiled, and nodded ever so slightly. He stood but bent forward, offering his hand. 'Well good luck in that, David, and I hope you'll wish me good luck in trying to belt you out of the park.'

'Yes, sir,' said David. 'Of course. That's the game.'

'Indeed it is, Mr Donald. Exactly that. I look forward to our contest.' Longford joined O'Malley, who was waiting near the fence for his captain.

'What did he say to you?' asked Paul Hampton coming up.

'Sorry, I think, for making me run so much.'

'Too bloody right. Made your life a misery. Mind you, if we'd bowled better, maybe he couldn't hit it wherever he liked.'

'He's nice. I like him.'

'Steady on lad. He's the enemy. I'm only half joking too.'

'Do you think Mr Richardson will give me a bowl, Ten Ton?'

'You can ask.'

David did, as they were nearing the gate into their rooms. It was a good time to, as he could already start to hear 'Dopey Donald' and 'Disgrace' amongst the clapping, and 'Good start lads.'

'I know how to get those two out, Mr Richardson.'

'Good.'

'Can I have a bowl tomorrow?'

'We'll see. When the ball is older.'

'It doesn't need to be old.'

'We'll see.'

David's Uncle Michael was waiting in the rooms with Mr Scully when they came up. David felt a rush of relief to see him there.

Tanner said, 'Players only I thought.'

Mr Scully looked serious. 'Just this once, Mr Tanner.' He looked over to Richardson, 'Mr Donald here has suggested a discreet exit might be the go, boss. Lotta press. An' a lot of ... um ... iffy punters, if you take my meaning.'

'Of course,' said Richardson. 'Tomorrow, David.'

David saw that his uncle had his street clothes and bag. He turned to say goodbye to the team, but they'd already gone into the change rooms to take their showers and change their clothes. Mr Scully had some bottles of beer that he grabbed up and took in.

The viewing room and the card room were empty.

'So matey, your first Test,' said his Uncle Mike.

David looked at his uncle's smile, but didn't share it. He felt like crying.

CHAPTER ELEVEN

Michael grabbed David around the shoulder and took him outside the players' rooms. They went down the corridor towards the back of the pavilion. David could hear the thuds and scrapes of people leaving the grandstand above.

Where the corridor met the other passage they went left, instead of right towards the door out of the pavilion. Michael opened a green door and looked around before guiding David in. He turned on an electric light to reveal a table with a thin mattress on top. There were old bottles on a shelf and an empty bathtub. Their bags sat by the table.

'New digs. A storeroom that they are going to turn into a players' aches and pains room, I'd say. Or maybe make it a doctor's room on game days.'

'Why can't we go back to the hotel?'

Michael checked outside once more before closing the door. 'Maybe later, when everyone has gone.'

David nodded. 'They don't like me do they?'

Michael turned serious, almost angry. 'They have no idea. They know nothing. Tomorrow, you can show them just how good you are, mate. Show the whole world what you can do. Then we can bore it up 'em. Bore it up all of 'em.'

David didn't share his uncle's anger. But ... what if Mr

Richardson never let him bowl?

Michael opened his bag and started bringing things out. 'I got a couple of pork pies. Some brandy for me. Some water. They give you lunch?'

'Meat and salad. As much as you wanted. Cups of tea too with lots of sugar.'

'Livin' it up then. Best seats in the place too, sitting out there with Paul Hampton.'

'He looks after me. He's got a wife and two girls and another baby coming.'

'How's your finger?'

'Gone down a bit. But not right.' David bit into one of the pies and started chewing.

His uncle took a gulp of his brandy, then smiled. Something new was coming. David could tell by the smile. David kept eating, and waited.

'Do you think you can bowl out Longford first ball?'

'First ball!'

His uncle nodded.

David thought. He and Grandad had discussed many plans for Longford. Before now, before today, he might have said yes, but now he thought no. 'No, sir. I think after our talk today, he'll have a look at me for a few balls. Maybe longer.'

'What talk? It looked like he was punishing you in the field.'

'He came up after. He wasn't angry like Dorrington. I think the way to get Longford out is to have him caught behind, playing across the line, if I can cramp him up a bit, but I think he'll wait to see what kinds of balls I've got.'

'You can't trap him leg before.'

'Not first ball.'

His uncle grunted and looked around the room, searching. David waited. If his uncle wanted to tell him more he would, and in the meantime, the pork pie was delicious.

Michael reached into his pocket and brought out a pound note. He laid it on the table, flat and looked down on it, as if it were a Bible and he were about to do a nightly prayer. Perhaps he was going to perform a magic trick. 'That's it. That's all I got left. We're broke.'

'Is that really why we're sleeping here?'

His uncle looked caught out, then a little hurt. 'One day of fame and you've already become distrustful.' He smiled and waited to see if David would too, but when David didn't, he went on. 'One of the reasons, but only one. The others are still good reasons.'

'They gave you lots of money. The Australian Cricket Board. You showed me.'

'Expenses, David. Business expenses.' He looked uncomfortable enough for David to wonder again about Ashleigh Hobbs' accident, and then, as though Michael could see what he was thinking, he said, 'Last night I took Mr Livingston and Mr Biggins to supper, and while they ate fine food and drank expensive drinks, I put your case. Talked the leg off a couple of chairs and spent most of our money doing it.'

David was relieved. He reasoned that this meant his Uncle Mike couldn't have been off fighting Hobbs. Not if he were with the Australian Cricket Board men.

'We won a little bit this afternoon when you walked on the field, then lost most of the rest when you didn't bowl.' He looked down at the pound again, a little sadly. David wondered whether the sad look was pretended.

'They are going to let you bowl, aren't they?'

'I don't know, sir.'

'You can lead a horse to water, but you can't make him think.'

'Drink,' said David.

'Don't mind if I do,' said Michael, and winked as he raised his bottle.

David smiled.

Michael smiled with him, but turned back to the pound. 'This isn't a bad amount for a juicy bet. A crazy long shot, name-your-odds kind of one-off. I'm pretty sure I could get a few blokes to give me a hundred to one on you bowling Longford out first ball. You see?'

David nodded. He wasn't sure how he felt about the betting. It seemed to lead them to win lots, then lose it all again, so was proving rather a short-term kind of a way of making ends meet.

Michael added, 'It would have made a difference to your grandad. More of a stake to send something back.' Michael was looking at the pound, but not really. David could see that he was watching him with his eyes twisted up in a way David didn't like. 'Can we work out a way of getting him out first ball, because I don't think I can get great odds for just getting him out some time? Got to be first ball—to make it sound like I'm being ridiculous. Then someone will want to teach me a lesson, and show everyone else just how ridiculous I'm being. There's no more desire to be instructive than in the Australian front bar. Or with a bookie in front of punters.'

'I think I can get O'Malley out first ball.'

'Oh.' Michael thought some. 'That could work. Yeah. In some ways that might even be better, seeing as he's so famous for his defence. Yep. Good.'

David asked, 'Can I have this pie too?'

Michael gestured around the dingy room. 'David, for you—anything.'

David ate the other pie. Michael went to the bath and tried the tap. Water gurgled out, rusty at first, but then clear. He watched the water as he sipped some more of his brandy.

Finally David said, 'What if I don't get O'Malley out?'

'What if the sun doesn't come up? Have a bath and get some sleep. Big day today, bigger one tomorrow.'

Michael left the little room and David took off his cricket clothes and climbed into the cold water of the bath. It felt good on his sore feet. He looked at his injured finger. It didn't seem too bad given all the fielding he'd had to do. His shoulders felt stiff. His neck too. David eased himself all the way into the bath until the cold water was up to his chin, and lay panting shallowly as he tried to find some part of his body that was not aching.

He dried himself on his dirty cricket shirt and lay on the mattress on the table, dragging one of his uncle's coats over him. He thought about the kind of field he should set for O'Malley. It would have to be very different for a first-baller. And he'd have to be able to let it really rip. Maybe he should be putting his finger in ice again.

David woke stiff. Uncle Mike was coming through the green door with a parcel and a cup of tea. He winked as David sat up on the table.

'I can fix up your spleen for you, while I've got you on the table, son. Seeing as you're already open. Field hospital humour, that. Breakfast is served.'

He handed David the tea. It was warm and sweet. He undid the parcel. There was a cold sausage, and two boiled eggs and a thick sandwich of butter and jam.

'Gotta keep your strength up.'

David got down from the table and started to dress.

Michael took up his own bag. 'Now I have to get going, mate. Things to see and people to do. In about an hour, you have to go to the players' rooms. Have a wash and get ready for the cricket. Right?'

'Yes, sir.'

'O'Malley with your first ball?'

'Yes, sir.'

Michael left, without a backward glance.

David began to crack and peel the eggs. He knew better than to ask where his uncle had gotten the breakfast. He would have talked someone into giving them. It might have been in the cricket ground and in the kitchen there, but it was just as likely that his Uncle Mike would go into the surrounding streets and knock on doors and introduce himself and tell some stories about the war and then ask for breakfast.

He was as likely to say, as far as David had seen, that he needed the food for a cricket player who was playing his first game for Australia. Then he'd make them nearly believe it, and go too far with something completely unlikely, but they would so enjoy the way that Michael told it that they'd give him the food anyway.

David thought about truth. Some folk, like his grandad, put a great store in the truth of a thing, its fact-ness. Nell Parker too. Other people seemed not to care. Not deep down. They'd make a show of fighting for the facts, of making someone stick to the rules of truth, but really they loved it being pushed further and further into ... what was the word? One of the Mr Pringles used to use it a lot. Preposterous. David had been watching the faces of the people his uncle told his lies to. When Michael's story moved to the preposterous, they'd fix him with a look, and they would both stop a moment while they looked each other in the eye. It was like a secret dare between Michael and his listener. Then Michael would nod and talk some more, and wrap the preposterous in more little details and kinds of facts. A beaming delight would come into their eyes and from then they'd all laugh and nod, as though it were all completely true and had been all along.

David didn't think he could live his life like that. You did need to count on some things. 'What killed these chooks, Grandad?' 'A fox.' 'If you don't water these seedlings they will die.' 'We need a bolt like this to fix the plough.' Good clean, knowable answers that did you some good. 'How did my mother die, Grandad?' 'I've told you. She drowned in the dam. Stop asking.'

David's father had died in the war. Everyone knew that. And his mother had drowned in the dam. But David saw now, while eating his jam sandwich, that there was something more to that too. It was the way people's eyes slid away when they mentioned it. Grandad. Mrs Pringle. Uncle Mike. He had not realised before what this look meant. Or maybe he didn't want to know more then, but he had his suspicions now. A truth could be a truth, but only because you didn't look at it closely enough. Or a fact is just a fact, whereas a truth is a bigger thing that makes facts look puny and stupid and beside the point.

Bardsley's innings, for instance. It was a fact that Bardsley got out for fifteen runs. On the scoresheet fifteen runs would look like he failed. It's such a small number, especially held against say one hundred. Yet that fact of the fifteen didn't tell the true story—that he'd been hit and pummelled and struggled for a long time, and took the shine off the ball and helped get Australia off to the best start all series. Bardsley hadn't failed at all. He had done really well. That was the truth.

Then David thought about Dorrington's dismissal. The trick of putting David in danger at silly mid-off still bothered him. It seemed not so much an allowed misdirection or bait, like setting a certain kind of field or bowling certain kinds of deliveries to set up the batsman for the ball they never expected, as something that was unfair. Only David and Dorrington seemed to see it that way, and although David was uncomfortable about it, he was still uncertain whether it was a cheat.

Which made David think about his uncle.

'I think my head is going to pop. Like a ripe melon,' he said to the empty little room. He resolved to think about cricket and how to get O'Malley out with his first ball, rather than all the other things in the world which he didn't understand and could do nothing about.

Scully was in the players' rooms reading the morning paper when David arrived carrying his bag. He immediately folded it up when he saw David.

'You're early then?'

'Yes, Mr Scully. Good morning.'

Mr Scully stood there, tapping the paper against his leg, and looking like he couldn't remember what his next job was.

'Can I read the paper when you've finished, Mr Scully?'

'No.' Mr Scully looked embarrassed. 'Best not to read the papers, lad. Good or bad, it can affect a player's confidence. Lots of captains have said that. Why don't you go and get changed, and let me finish tidying up after you messy buggers.'

Mr Johnson was the first of the players to arrive, but had barely said hello to David, when Paul Hampton came in. 'Where'd you get to last night?'

'Me?'

'Yes, you. I came round to your hotel to go out to dinner, but they said you'd checked out.'

'Oh. Um ... moved.'

Calligan and McLeod came in together.

McLeod said, 'Don't worry about it, David. Pressmen are bastards.'

David looked to McLeod, who was looking at Hampton, who was touching his lips with his finger.

'I di'n mean nothing. Specially after Richo's talk last night. Good luck kid. Let's all get these Poms out.' He looked around to show willing.

Bill Baker came in with George Jackson and Ken Hall. His cheek was swollen and he had a couple of stitches.

'Look what the cat dragged in,' said Jackson.

'Bloody Les Darcy here wants another few rounds with Tudor,' said Hall, shaping as though he was going to punch Baker.

Jack Tanner came in looking as though he was about to go to a dance, he was so well dressed and his derby pushed down over one eye.

'Two Bob. Swashbuckling, I hear.'

'Amazing what nice things a journalist will say if you buy him a few drinks after a day's play,' said Tanner.

There were chuckles and grins.

'Lot better than being an affront to the memory of cricketers all over the world,' said Hall.

Hall didn't look at David, but because everyone else did, he knew this had something to do with him.

'Ken,' warned Hampton.

'One big happy family, like the cap'n says. I didn't write it.'

David was dressed and decided to leave the dressing room.

Mr Richardson was arguing with Mr Livingston and Mr Biggins in the card room.

'Unless you give him a bowl, you will make us all look ridiculous,' said Livingston.

'I think you've already done that when you picked him in the side,' retorted Richardson. 'I'm merely trying to win a Test match.'

David moved away from the door. He thought he might go outside, to get away from the arguments. It seemed that today was to be no easier than the day before.

He saw the newspaper on the seat outside. He sat near it, but didn't intend to read. He looked out to the gathering crowd, then instantly away again. The cartoon caught his eye. It had a picture of a giant, with a helmet and armour and weapons. A caption at the top read: *David and Goliath?* There was a Union Jack flag, so David knew that this Goliath was England. Standing in front of the Goliath was a baby in a nappy. The bottom caption read: '*Oh dear. I forgot my sling.*'

David thought it was amusing. He opened the paper and found a photograph of Henry Longford bending down and talking to David Donald. The caption read, 'Longford consoles Donald, or tells bedtime story.'

A headline said 'Insult'. It was an article by Charlie O'Toole, the newsman who had been at the rail station. David found his name but was having trouble with the smaller print.

'That O'Toole's article, Mr Donald?' It was Calligan.

'Yes, Mr Calligan.'

'I believe our Mr O'Toole has dreams of his own fame, and turning you into a national insult might be the way he believes he might achieve that. So don't be hurt about it. It's actually not personal, in a way.'

'No, sir. I'm not.'

'Good. Then might I have my paper back?' Mr Calligan was smiling.

The crowd had clearly read and agreed with the newspaper because they continued to yell insults as the team took the field. David ignored the distant noise and went to Mr Richardson. 'Can I bowl, Mr Richardson?'

'Not yet, David.'

'I think I can bowl O'Malley out.'

'Good. Keep thinking that way. But it's a new day and the ball is not very old and I want to use my main bowlers. Do you understand?'

'But I don't need an old ball.'

'No. Go and field behind Legal.'

David now knew he'd been consigned to his hidden position on the field, behind Mr Calligan. His sole task here was to retrieve any straight drives that had reached the boundary.

He got into position and clapped with the rest of the team as Longford and O'Malley came out to resume their innings. Longford was on fifty-five, O'Malley on ten. David had an awful thought. If either Hampton or Calligan got O'Malley out before David could bowl at him, what would happen to his uncle's big bet?

Longford defended against a few balls as he got his eye in, before hitting his first boundary for the day. David was pleased to see that it was hit square and nowhere near him. Mr Longford was not going to embarrass him again this morning. The sun was high already, but not as hot as the day before.

O'Malley blocked solidly too, after a Longford single, protecting his stumps as though they were his life. David had to field behind Hampton next over. Longford struck the ball solidly on the off side and McLeod dived sideways to stop it. The crowd applauded until McLeod tossed the ball to David, who dropped it. The crowd jeered loudly, as David gathered it up and concentrated on rubbing the polished side.

'Yer gunna give me that ball, David, or wear it out?' said Hampton. He was smiling.

David trotted over to give the fast bowler the ball.

'Sorry I missed you for dinner, Ten Ton. Did you call your wife last night?'

'Yes mate. And this morning. Janey, my oldest, has a bit of a cough on, you see. We think she's allergic to the grass seeds.'

'I hope she's all right,' said David.

Then Paul Hampton did a big mime act. He suddenly nodded, then looked around at Longford, then looked back to David and pointed at him nodding again.

'What are you doing?' said David.

'Want them all to think you've just given me advice on

how to get him out.'

Longford's smile suggested no one was being fooled, but it gave David an idea. A couple of overs later, when David next had the chance to hand Hampton the ball, he said, 'The top of his off stump. The only time he's got a gap is when he fancies a drive. He moves forward, to give himself room and plays just a little bit away from his body. Off the pitch, with slight inswing, and you could knock over off stump I reckon.'

'You're a funny bugger,' laughed Hampton.

'You'd probably have to move McLeod away from mid-off to leave a big gap there to encourage him to go for it.'

'Are you blokes right?' yelled Richardson. He gestured for Hampton to hurry it up.

Hampton bowled normally at the stumps and Longford cut him to the fence. After some more overs, as Longford fairly raced to eighty runs, Hampton went to Richardson and they had a brief discussion.

Calligan was taken off, and McLeod brought on to bowl. David went to Richardson. 'Can I bowl, Mr Richardson?'

'Let the child bowl, for goodness sake,' said O'Malley. 'We don't want tears before bedtime.'

'Thanks, Bill,' said Richardson to the batsman. 'Not now, David.'

'But ...'

'Not now,' said Richardson.

Next Hampton over, McLeod did not go back to mid-off after he'd bowled, but moved to the on side. Paul winked at David as he turned at the beginning of his run. He bowled, and Longford drove the ball for four through the newly vacant mid-off area.

The crowd groaned. Richardson looked concerned. David

said quietly, 'Nice set-up ball, Ten Ton.' When Longford also hit the next delivery for four, David was worried that Richardson would lose his patience, or Hampton his nerve. He did have to bowl the ball just right.

Paul Hampton bowled Longford out on the next ball. Longford hung his bat out a little, and got a slight inside edge which sent the ball into his stumps. The English captain was out for eighty-eight runs. Everyone was running to Ten Ton and congratulating him.

'Nice nut, big bloke,' yelled Hall.

'Very clever,' nodded Richardson.

'Can I bowl now, Mr Richardson?'

'No!'

England were two for one hundred and twenty-one when Windsor strode imperiously to the wicket. Windsor was considered to be England's most damaging batsman. He could turn a game in a session, and could play shots all over the ground. He took no prisoners, they used to say on the radio, and David studied him closely. He had no chin, and small lips and blossoms of blond curls that reminded David of a statue of a Roman leader he'd seen in a school art book.

Windsor stroked Hampton's first ball to the boundary. He drove and pulled and hooked. He was particularly vicious against McLeod. With only a few overs to go until lunch Windsor had already raced to forty-three runs. O'Malley had crawled to twenty-one.

As David was changing ends he heard Baker saying, 'I saw him bowl to you, Skip. Maybe buy a wicket.'

'David,' said Richardson, tossing him the ball, 'you're bowling.'

David flexed his fingers. It was O'Malley who would be

facing. He figured that he had a couple of good overs in him before his finger swelled again.

The noise in the Adelaide Oval rose considerably, applause and laughter competing with anger and yells.

Richardson started pointing and calling. 'Chalkie, you can stay in slip. Maud, out on that boundary. Ten Ton can you go down to deep gully. Ned, further back.'

'No,' said David, going up to his captain. 'Mr Richardson, that's not how I'll get him out.'

'I'm giving you some protection, David.'

'I don't need it. It's O'Malley. He's going to block me.'

'Then those players won't be a problem.'

'No, I want them in a catching position, so we can get him out.'

Richardson put his hands on his hips and took some deep breaths. 'David, O'Malley has been blocking balls all morning. Why is he suddenly going to give a catch to you?'

David looked at him, trying to understand the question. 'But that's my bowling. To get him out. I've been planning it and working him out.'

'Gentlemen,' called Mr Wisden, 'shall I call lunch now, or are we going to play some cricket?'

'Just bowl to the field I set. We'll contain them, and then maybe take a catch or two after lunch.'

'No.'

'What!' Richardson looked like he'd just been struck.

Baker came forward. 'Oi, lad. None of that.'

'If you won't give me the field I need, then I won't bowl,' said David. The field placements were part of the bowling. They were part of the tactics, but also part of why he'd be bowling how he would. To bowl to the field that Richardson wanted to set would say to the batsman that the team had no faith in the bowler's ability. And taking wickets would be a matter of chance. Why do that, when he could get the fellow out?

'Are you refusing to do what I ask?' said Richardson.

Other players were coming in.

Windsor was close enough to hear some of it. 'Complete disarray,' he said with contempt.

Ken Hall smiled and said, 'There ya go, Cap'n. Disobeying and all that. You got your wish. Out of the team.'

'What's going on?' said Hampton arriving from the boundary.

'Won't bowl to the captain's field,' said Baker.

'He told me how to get Longford out, boss,' said Hampton.

'Oh right,' said McLeod.

'Taking Maud out of mid-off was his idea.'

'Time for just one over before lunch, gentlemen,' called Mr Wisden calmly.

The noise around the ground had dropped to a rumble. Booing could be heard.

Windsor chimed in again. 'Is it your intention to talk your way to a draw?'

'Put a cork in it,' shot back Hall.

'Jack,' said Richardson, 'can you persuade your compatriot to follow my instructions?'

Jack Tanner looked at David. David looked back. He was not going to bowl badly. People had been trying to make him do that all his life, and he would not do it. Not then and not now. 'I can get O'Malley out.'

Tanner finally said, 'Give him his field, then we'll know, eh?'

David tried not to smile. Tanner was only looking to the

captain.

Calligan spoke up too. 'Point is, John, this could be your out clause, with Biggins and Livingston. Just following orders yourself.'

'Oh, right. Backside covered and that's all that matters. I'm trying to win a Test. Just one.' He stopped and pointed at David, 'David, you are driving me insane. Do you understand that?'

'No, sir.'

They laughed. Even Hall.

'Look, Gov,' said Jackson, eyeing the booing crowd, 'seeing as we may not even get out of here alive, why don't we put on the full show? Place the field, turn the screws and do what you did with Dorrington. Scare O'Malley out.'

'Or bore 'im out,' said Maud.

'Very well, Master Donald, where would you like my team?'

'But Mr Richardson, a captain always sets the field with his bowler,' pleaded David.

'Don't push it, son,' said Johnson.

And so they set the field as O'Malley and Windsor stood together in the middle of the pitch watching.

David set two slips and another player on the off-side. There was a backward point and an extra cover. He set two players on the on side, one at mid wicket and one at square leg. Most of these were decoys. David was planning a catch to Maud McLeod at silly point.

Maud looked uncomfortable, but smiled as he said, 'For the sake of my children's children, don't bowl a lollipop kid, or I'll lose me head.'

The cries from the outer were getting louder. There were lots of boos and calling. There was also a banging that may have been feet stamping in a grandstand.

'They're not the only ones getting impatient,' called Mr Fitzmorris from square leg.

'My theory,' said Windsor, projecting his voice without shouting, 'is they are too scared to bowl to us. I think the crowd has "cottoned on" as you say.'

O'Malley wandered back to his crease and reset his guard. 'Mr Wisden, could I have middle stump thank you.'

Mr Wisden signalled where his bat needed to be.

Windsor called down the wicket, 'Hit the little stinker for a single will you, William? I'd like a good crack at him.' Then Windsor turned to look at David. David nodded and smiled. Windsor poked his tongue out. David stared, blinking. The great Edward Windsor, soon to run for parliament in Britain, had poked his tongue out. David swung to his team mates to see whether they'd seen. No one was looking. David looked back to the fearsome British batsman, who was casually surveying the field.

'David,' yelled Richardson, 'before lunch, please.'

The crowd finally went quiet. Silent.

David focused. He stood at the start of his run. He put the ball in his normal leggie grip and imagined the ball he would bowl, with fingers and wrist spinning the ball straight towards the batsman. He whispered to himself, 'Donald is ready to bowl. O'Malley waits, thinking about defence.' David bowled flat, but with a lot of top spin. O'Malley came forward a full stride, offering the dead face of the bat. But the ball gripped the wicket as it was supposed to, and it kicked up more than most batsmen would expect. It hit the bat hard and on the rise. The angle of O'Malley's bat was downward, so when the ball struck it headed forward but down. Maud McLeod dived full length and got a hand under it. He held up the ball. Wisden put up his finger.

The crowd seemed to gasp, then laugh as one. Then the chatter of a thousand arguments began, like rain on the shed roof at home.

William O'Malley was out caught for twenty-one runs, bowled David Donald.

Mr Wisden looked at the clock over the scoreboard and nodded to his fellow umpire, Mr Fitzmorris. 'I think we will gather our collective minds, and finish this over after lunch, gentlemen.'

Paul Hampton ran to David and lifted him in the air and turned him round so fast he felt dizzy. When Ten Ton put him down, some of the other players came up. Calligan and Bardsley patted him on the back. Mr Johnson looked him in the eye and shook his hand, 'Good ball, son.' Mr Baker patted him on the head. 'Some more o' those, thanks.'

The rest of the team were going off with Maud, clapping him on the back for his catch. Richardson was in an animated discussion with the umpires. He appeared to be in some trouble.

The crowd clapped the team off, but David heard someone call, 'Fluke.' There were calls of 'Gamesmanship' amongst the 'Good on yer David's.

David moved his chair to the same spot outside the card room. He didn't like the smell of the cigarette smoke. They had sandwiches today, and David had corn beef with lettuce. He thought about the ball that got O'Malley. His grandad would nod at that one. Grandad had thought some kind of bat pad or blocked catch would be the go for O'Malley. If you could put enough work on the ball to generate some pace off a dead bat. David found himself hoping the bet had been made because he would insist his Uncle Mike use some of the money to cable Grandad.

Lunch seemed to take no time at all. There was an eagerness to the murmurs as they went out now. David looked to the scoreboard. Bishop was in next.

'Ten Ton, who's Bishop?'

'New kid. Like you. His first game.'

'But I don't know how he bats.'

'Join the club, mate. We'll soon find out, or are you gunna get him out first ball too?'

Richardson joined them. 'Well Master Donald, where can I place your field?'

'I don't know.'

Richardson's shoulders slumped.

'I know for Windsor, but I don't know for Bishop.'

'Well, let us just make it up as we go along, shall we. Start with the field you had for O'Malley?'

'I don't think that will work, Mr Richardson.'

'Might not, but let's start somewhere. Yes?'

'Yes, sir.'

Bishop played back to the first one and knocked it down easily. He moved forward to David's second and edged it down to fine leg for two runs. He stepped forward to David's off spinner, but then didn't play a shot. He got to the pitch of the next ball and hit it back over David's head for four. Richardson moved some players back to more conventional positions.

David started to feel his finger. It hurt a little at the knuckle. Richardson was scratching his chin.

Windsor called out, 'See, Timothy. Take the circus element out, and it is like batting against a child.'

David over-pitched his next delivery and Bishop stepped inside it, cross batting it on the full to hit a six over the square leg boundary. There was some clapping for the English, but some of the booing had started up again. Bishop scored three runs to deep mid-on on the second last ball of David's over. His finger was starting to swell again. He had one ball at Windsor.

David started to wave to players to come in. Richardson came to his end of the pitch, and asked quietly, 'What are you doing?'

'I don't want anyone on the boundary, Mr Richardson.'

'After being hit for two, four, six and three?'

'But not by him. Windsor will try to go over the top.'

'Yes he will. But he can go over the top virtually anywhere around the ground.'

'I want him to try, sir. I'm going to bowl a shooter.'

'A what?'

'My shooter. It is like halfway between my skidder and my loopy.'

'Your what?'

'It has top spin, but it keeps lower than the loopy. Good for lbw or bowled. Maybe even a slips catch.'

Mr Wisden came over to them. 'Mr Richardson, we've discussed these unnecessary delays.'

'Certainly, Mr Wisden. I can only repeat my word of honour that I am not intentionally causing delays.'

And so David had two slips and an otherwise defensive looking field. It was the kind of field you might set if you were saving a single, which is what David's grandfather had suggested was what you wanted the batsman to think. Grandad's reasoning had been that Windsor would see these fieldsmen as a kind of fence, a fence he would immediately try to break down. There was always the possibility of a miscued catch, but the field positions were really bait.

Grandad felt Windsor would not be able to resist going over the field to all that lush green space beyond.

Windsor stood, surveying the field, with his bat planted like a hussar's sword. After making a point of keeping David waiting longer, he took his guard. David imagined the ball he would bowl. He whispered, 'And finally the moment we have been waiting for. The great Windsor meets the great Donald.' David imagined where the ball would land and how. He stepped forward and sent it flat through the air. Windsor's eyes widened and he stepped forward to drive it. The ball hit the pitch, speeding up and keeping low. Windsor flashed his bat, but over a ball that crashed into off stump.

Windsor looked back at his stumps. Then he patted a spot on the wicket with his bat. 'Hit a crack,' he said as he walked off.

Windsor bowled Donald for forty-three. England were four for one hundred and eighty-six, only ten behind Australia. But their four best batsmen were out.

'How'd he bloody miss that?' said McLeod as he came in. 'Nice ball, kid.'

'That was David's shooter, apparently,' said Richardson.

'Shooter, flipper, my aunt Mary … call it what he likes as far as I'm concerned,' said Baker.

Then all the men stopped and went quiet. David looked at their faces to find them looking at him differently.

'Well here's a bloody go then,' said Johnson.

'Did you just swear then, Chalkie?' smirked Calligan.

'Too bloody right. Let's have at 'em, I reckon,' said Johnson.

Richardson tossed the ball to Calligan. 'Legal, how about you knock over this new fellow, now that David's made him over-confident?'

The men laughed. David noticed that they trotted back to their positions with their shoulders back. There was clapping from the players now, and calls of encouragement to Calligan.

The crowd's single voice had broken now; there was just noise, but none of it with common mood.

David looked at his finger. It was starting to swell. He'd have to change his grip.

Calligan bowled a terrifying over of short-pitched deliveries that moved off the seam. Bishop flashed at one and missed. He stepped back at the next one blocking it dangerously off his chest. The batsmen scampered for a single.

Morgan was a left-hander and took his guard, saying in his dry Yorkshire accent, 'Glad to be facing up to the adults, like.' Calligan bowled a yorker to the Yorkshireman, and it struck him on the foot. Everyone jumped up to yell their appeal. Mr Fitzmorris raised his finger. Five down for one hundred and ninety-one.

David's next over was to Bishop again. He changed his grip to try to relieve the pressure on his sore finger, just as Uncle Mike had shown him to do at his trials. The first ball surprised Bishop and he only just got back to keep it off his stumps. He was more wary of David now. But the ball didn't carry as far when David bowled with this grip, and Johnson and Baker had to edge up closer to the stumps. Bishop flashed at the next ball, which caught the high edge of his bat only to fly past Johnson and down towards the boundary for two runs.

That's how it went for some overs. David kept getting Bishop to bowl to, while Calligan kept getting the English all-rounder, Peter Ostler. Both batsmen seemed to fancy their respective bowlers. David resented that he couldn't get as much variety with his alternate grip. He thought he might try an offie that behaved like a leg break. He and Grandad had been working on a ball that came out of the back of the hand, with lots of top spin, so that instead of spinning in towards the stumps, it would behave like a leggie and spin away. He thought he might fool Bishop. But it was so slow that Bishop had plenty of time to pick the spin and lean back to cut it to the boundary.

Richardson came to David before his new over. 'Why have you changed your grip? Enough of these experimental balls, David. Bowl the leggies.'

David held his hand out.

Richardson looked at the finger. 'Did I say you were going to drive me mad, David?'

'Yes, sir. Insane you said.'

'That's you for the day.'

'It might settle down after a couple of overs.'

There was encouraging clapping around the ground when David went to his usual position behind the bowler. He stood for a moment, looking around and relaxing for the first time. He marvelled that he did not feel particularly hot, or thirsty. There seemed to be a breeze about somewhere that cooled him.

Hampton was brought on for David. He pinned Ostler down a little, slowing the scoring. Then Calligan got a chance at Bishop. He played at a rising delivery that came on to him faster than he expected. He skied it and Tanner took a catch at short fine leg.

Darby was caught behind a few overs later, and they went to tea with England at seven for two hundred and thirty-six. There was respectful clapping for the whole team this time, and David noticed that many more people seemed to have found their way to the cricket ground. It was fuller than it had been all match.

Scully came to David. 'Mr Richardson says for me to look at your sore finger.'

When David held it up, Scully shook his head in disgust. 'We were going to look at this before, weren't we?'

'Yes, Mr Scully, but Mr Baker got hurt. Then my uncle took me before I could get changed.'

'Well, he should know better. You're going to have to rest it.'

'Yes, sir.'

'Yeah right. Yes sir, no sir, three bags full sir. Turn it. Wriggle. Bend. Hmm. I think you got a torn ligament. Which is bad. I can't do any tricks for you. You gotta rest it. You got to put it in ice at least. Promise me you'll do that tonight.'

'Yes, sir.'

'Yeah, sure. You players are all the same. No respect for your own bodies.'

'Sorry, Mr Scully.'

Scully harrumphed, but then smiled. 'Any time you want to get that Windsor prat out, you go ahead.'

It was Australia's afternoon. Although Ostler made forty, the bowlers finally mastered the English tail enders. David even managed to field a strongly hit ball that went past McLeod, and received some applause.

David had a good plan for bowling at Tudor, but Richardson gave him a firm no. Besides, all the other bowlers wanted to have a go at Tudor, because of his mean streak.

There was little polite chat while he was at the crease. Even Hall made no jokes.

With only half an hour to go until stumps, Ostler was caught behind off Hampton, and England's first innings was complete for only two hundred and eighty. It had been Australia's best show all tour.

The crowd gave them generous applause as they left the field, and David felt confident enough to look at their faces for the first time all day. An old man in a striped shirt doffed his hat. A young boy ran forward to the fence and waved. But then a man behind with a large grey moustache and big eyebrows gestured for David to get off. His face was angry. Two men behind pointed at David and laughed. Mr Jackson mumbled, 'Might get the blighters off our backs for a session or two.'

Mr Livingston and Mr Biggins were dressed in tails and carrying top hats as they waited for them in the rooms when they came in. Mr Livingston waved his cigar like a conductor as they passed. 'Good show fellows. Fine day.'

'Not over yet, Mr Livingston,' replied Richardson.

'A very good crowd too,' said Mr Biggins with a twinkle in his eye.

Ten Ton, Legal and Mopsey McLeod were very bouncy in the change rooms. Bardsley and Johnson had gone quiet however. Richardson turned to everyone and said, 'Good day in the field, lads. Now can you fellows hold off your showers for a tick, and let the openers and I get ourselves focused?'

Outside the dressing room, Ten Ton stopped and patted David on the chest, nearly knocking him into the wall. 'Good job.' Then he wandered into the card room, yelling, 'I suppose it's too soon for a beer, eh?'

'Don't you dare, Ten Ton,' yelled Scully, 'or I'll fine you. Don't you think I won't. Oi, you blokes, what yer doin'? Ned, you put me down. I'll 'ave you.'

When Mr Johnson and Bardsley came out of the change room, David started clapping. It made them both turn and look at him oddly. He said, 'Good luck.' Bardsley shook it off, but Mr Johnson looked at David a moment longer, before deciding to nod.

Unfortunately luck wasn't what Mr Johnson got. He was given out leg before wicket in the third over, in spite of the fact that everyone thought it had struck him both high and outside the line. Mr Johnson wasn't jeered off this time, so clearly the crowd also thought he was having awful luck. Or they may have been so buoyed by the rest of the day's play that they were in a forgiving mood.

Richardson stuck around with Bardsley, and Australia were one for twelve at stumps. The man on the radio said the game was finely poised. It was anyone's.

CHAPTER TWELVE

Uncle Mike appeared early again at the players' room door. The team members were either in the showers or outside near the players' race having a glass of beer in the shade. Michael too smelled of beer.

'Did you see my wickets?' David asked as they headed down the corridor.

'Sure did. Windsor was my favourite.'

'I can do much better.'

'Good.'

'Has Grandad called?'

'He doesn't know where you are, mate. Here, put these on.' Uncle Michael took a grey school shirt out of his bag and a cap. When David looked at them, his uncle explained, 'Disguise.'

David changed in the corridor, looking at the school cap a moment before he put it on.

'Perfect. Just another lad at the cricket with his dad.'

David looked at his uncle and smiled, but Michael was already moving towards the door.

'Do you think they will give me an Australian cap?'

'Why didn't you bowl more overs?'

'My finger. It swole up again. Mr Scully said we have to look after it. Rest and ice.'

'Yep.'

'He said it's a ligament.'

As they came out the players' door, some people turned, but his uncle said loudly, 'This way, Freddy,' and the people lost interest. They caught a taxi outside the ground.

'Can I cable Grandad?'

'Soon as we get back to the hotel. We have to go somewhere first.'

David hid his disappointment. He was tired and hungry too. He was always hungry. It seemed to him, as the taxi tooted and grumbled into the other traffic, that only half an hour after he ate, he was ready to do it again. The players' lunch was good, but afternoon tea was cakes rather than a real meal. They never ate flash food on the farm but there was always bread and lots of meat.

There were people at Gould's Sporting Goods, and they all turned to watch the taxi pull up. David crouched low at the back window.

'There's not too many. Think of it as a kind of training. For when you're famous and lots of people want to say hello.'

'I don't want to be famous.'

'Oh dear.' His uncle put on an English drawing-room voice. 'Then you have begun to excel in entirely the wrong kind of work. You didn't think about being a child genius at library book filing? Or a whiz at shoe fitting? How about the greatest coal miner the world did never see?'

Finally, David had to smile.

Mr Gould bustled forward, his eyebrows dancing about in delight. He opened the door, saying, 'My dear David Donald, I'm so glad you could drop in and see your old friend, which is me, here today at your favourite store, which is here. Here too, in Adelaide.'

'Hello, Mr Gould,' said David. The closer people gasped.

'Mr Gould, old friend,' said Uncle Mike, loudly.

Mr Gould breathed through his nose, like a dog sniffing something, and with as much pleasure.

'David Donald, may I present my son and daughter, John Gould and Mary Gould.' He turned to show David to a teenage boy who looked him up and down as though he were a cow well past milking age, and a girl who had definitely inherited her father's eyebrows. 'Oh my,' she gasped looking only at David's hands and grinning.

David met Mr Gould's wife, his brother-in-law and family, his sporting good suppliers, store neighbours and a number of presidents of local cricket clubs.

Most complimented him, then told him what he was doing wrong.

'Good bowling today son. Got to practise that fielding.'

'Can you bat?'

'Lucky ball, I think. You won't have Windsor falling for that one again.'

'It's a gimmick, isn't it? To get more people to go to the cricket to see what all the fuss is about? You can tell me.'

David found he was not actually called on to reply. He had tried at first, but had not had a chance to get more than a word or two out, before the questioner either supplied their own answer, or he was taken to someone new. At the counter he saw Uncle Mike being given another sports bag and some money.

Finally David was presented with a sticky bun, but before he could bite it his uncle took it away, because the photographer was there. All the people were cleared away as the man set up his tripod and arranged a bun-less David and a sniffing Mr Gould in front of the shop awning. Mr Gould's eyebrows were up near his fringe. The flash of bright light stayed in front of David even when his eyes closed. When his vision finally cleared, people were swarming in again. Uncle Mike dragged him towards the taxi.

All the voices called on top of each other. 'Good luck tomorrow, David. Hope you bat. Work on that fielding. Give it more flight. Have to do better next time—to stay in the side. He touched this bun, you know.'

David sat silent in the taxi, seeing the people again in his mind, while Michael opened the cricket bag. More cricket clothes and gear.

'Are there batting gloves with longer fingers?'

'Yes. I asked.'

The hotel had thick carpets rather than floorboards or linoleum. There were electric lights and red chairs with brass ashtrays on stands and little tables with gas lamps. There were fresh roses in huge glass vases. It smelled of leather and something nice, rather than soap and cigarettes and old beer.

The man behind the counter, who got their key down from a row of hooks, wore a black uniform and said, 'Welcome, Mr Donald. Welcome, Mr Donald. I hope you had a good Test today.' The man had a black beard trimmed close, and slicked down hair.

'Yes, sir. We took it to them today, I think.'

'You certainly did, sir.'

They went to a door marked 'Lift' and a man in a red suit with a funny brimless hat opened two doors sideways and David and Michael got into a small room.

Uncle Mike said, 'Five please.'

The other man said, 'Very good, sir.' He slid the doors

closed and turned a winding lever. The room moved.

David grabbed for the wall. The room was rocking.

'First time in a lift, David?' smiled Uncle Mike.

David said nothing, just leaned against the wall.

'A system of pulleys and cables that pull us up and down, sir. An electric motor and two sets of brakes. Very safe,' said the man in red.

'Saves on the stairs. Very posh.'

The lift room crunched to a halt. The man put the lever flat, and then pulled open the doors. They were no longer at the lounge room of the hotel, but were now facing a corridor with lots of doors like any hotel. There was more carpet and more little lights.

'I do hope you'll try the lift again, sir. You do get used to it,' offered the elevator man.

'Not likely,' said David, who tested the corridor floor for firmness.

The room was no bigger than some of the pubs they'd stayed in, but had lots more furniture. There were little tables and chairs that matched each other and the sheets on the bed looked brand new. Michael opened a door and David saw that they had their own bathroom. There was a toilet and a bath and mirror. There were shiny tiles with a pink rose on each one.

Michael looked at what appeared to be a new pocket watch, and said, 'You have a wash mate, then we'll go down stairs to eat.' He turned on two different taps and the bath started to fill with warm water. 'Tomorrow, we better get you some city clothes.'

After his bath, Michael suggested David get dressed in his new cricket clothes, to see if they fitted. 'Don't think those workboots of yours will go well on these rugs here.'

'No disguise?'

'Not in here, mate. A bit of knowing who you are will take us a fair way.'

David looked at him warily.

'What?' said his uncle.

'Don't sell any of those fake bats, Uncle Mike.'

'No need to. When you're on your uppers, it all comes to you.'

David didn't like the sound of that, but was fairly sure Michael wouldn't sell the bats.

On their way out again, David insisted on the stairs, although by the time they got down to the lobby area, he noticed his uncle's limp was a little worse.

In the dining room, which was a big restaurant, there were round tables with white tablecloths and their own little gas lamps in the middle. Each table had lots of knives and forks and spoons already laid out. A man in black coat-tails and a blue velvet vest looked at them, and Uncle Mike said, 'O'Toole.'

As they followed the man, David was trying to remember why this name meant something. At a table next to a wall sat the reporter who had been at the railway station. This was the Mr O'Toole who had written in his newspaper that David was a disgrace.

He still wore his coat, but his tie was loose and he seemed crouched over his whisky as though he thought someone might try to take it. 'Michael. I've ordered the lobster and some prawns. Always eat the seafood in Adelaide, if you can't go into the Barossa valley for the Kraut stuff. Hope you don't mind, but I have to shoot off after dinner. Deadlines, print runs, bevies of typists to debauch.'

David sat watching the newsman watching him.

He smiled but not with his eyes, then suddenly turned and called to a man in white, 'Another two scotches and what, David, lemonade or you on the hoochie cooch too now you're in the team?' He turned to Michael. 'Imagine living in the States now. What were they thinking?'

'Lemonade thanks,' said Michael to the waiter.

'So, David, how's the Australian team treating you?'

'Very well, sir.'

'Call me Charlie. Didn't look like anyone was too pleased by your selection in the team.'

David said nothing.

Their food and drinks arrived.

'That was fast,' said Michael.

'Yeah, chop-chop, chin-chin. Like I said ...'

David had never eaten lobster, although it looked like crayfish which he'd seen but not eaten in Geraldton. It was in a cream with lots of greens on the side. The prawns were done in something smelly, but tasted good.

'I'm guessing two things, David. One is you're bloody hungry.'

'Hollow legs,' said Michael.

'Still growing,' said O'Toole. 'And the second thing is you read my article this morning.'

David looked up from his eating a moment. Mr O'Toole was looking at David's hands. 'No, Mr O'Toole. I only saw the headlines. They wouldn't let me.'

'Ah, I see. Many of the players choose not to read the newspapers while they're playing. Puts them off. Unless they're doin' well of course. Then they can't get enough. Okay, as the Americans say, would you like to put the record straight?'

'What?'

'Do you want to tell your side of it, David?' said his uncle through a mouthful of lobster.

David thought for a moment. 'We're doing our best and we're in this game. One good session is, um, good, but we need more to beat them.'

'Yes, very true,' said O'Toole without interest. He downed his scotch, and glanced at his watch which lay open on the table next to his cigarette packet and lighter.

'You bowled some great leg breaks today to get your wickets, then changed to off breaks and mystery balls. Why?'

'Trade secret,' said Michael before David could answer.

David was conscious of his finger, but didn't stop eating.

'Do you think that once the novelty or shock value of you being in the side wears off, you'll take no more wickets?'

'I'll take more.'

'These are the best batsmen in the world today. Won't they learn to pick you?'

'I'll have to vary my bowling enough so they won't be able to.'

'Your whole inclusion and Richardson's tactics of holding up play for interminable discussion is just shameless gamesmanship isn't it?'

'I don't understand.'

'Yes, I can see that's likely.'

'Oi,' warned Michael. 'You're the only journalist talking to the biggest story in cricket.'

'And paying for the privilege. But never mind. You're in the team to trick the batsmen out. You're insultingly young and, well, let's say it. You look strange. You don't bowl them out like a man, you trick them out. Care to comment?'

Michael started to stand. 'Right, O'Toole, that's enough.'

SPINNER • *a novel*

'It's all right, Uncle Mike.' David turned to O'Toole. 'Tricking batsmen is what spin bowlers do. They make the batsmen think the ball will go one way, and make it go another. Instead of speed they use variation. All bowling is mostly mental, unless you've got just the out-and-out speed of a Proctor. You place the field in such a way as to get wickets or slow down the runs, but you also use it to put ideas in their heads.'

'Well, here's someone new. Who told you all that?'

'My grandad. We've been training. He's George Baker. He was coach of Western Australia Rural.'

David gave a big burp. His plate was empty.

Michael said, 'David grew up on a farm and trained every day under his grandfather's expert tuition. He was a state-level spin bowler and coach. David's father played for Guildford Grammar on a sports scholarship. So he hasn't come out of nowhere.'

'Why's your uncle touting you around then, and not your dad?'

'My father died in the war.'

O'Toole suddenly looked interested again, lighting a cigarette. 'How old are you?'

'Twelve.'

'So you don't remember him.'

'No, sir.'

'So your uncle and your grandfather have been helping you with your game.'

'No, sir, just my grandfather. And Nell Parker.'

'Nell?'

'She's my friend from school. We listen to all the games on the radio and work out ...' David burped again. He felt a pain in his guts, but it passed.

Michael said, 'David, why don't you go up to the room and rest?'

David stood. He didn't feel so good.

O'Toole said, 'So is Johnson going to keep his place?'

'He shouldn't have been out today. It was a mistake.'

O'Toole smiled. 'So many headlines, so few column inches.'

David left, glad to get away from O'Toole. He felt hot and took his cricket vest off as he walked up the stairs. His legs felt light and weak. He had to stop a moment at the fourth floor to rest before going up to the room on the fifth. He was sweating by the time he went down their corridor. He was trying to remember the room number. He didn't have a key. He sat down to wait for his uncle. The walls were dark and heavy.

David woke in the corner of the players' rooms. He was in a wicker chair with a blanket over him. There was a metal bowl on his lap that was clean but gave off the faintest smell of vomit. He remembered he had vomited a lot. He blinked and looked towards the glass viewing window. From where he was sitting all he could see was sky. Sky and Mr Johnson's back.

'What's the score, Mr Johnson?'

'Ah, back with us. Good. We're doing fairly well I think, although Richo is out. We were two for seventy-eight at lunch—young Bardsley and Two Bob are going along nicely.'

'Good.' David thought he might have another nap.

'Thank you for your support in the newspaper, by the way.'

Yes, thought David. There had been a meal with Mr

O'Toole. That's when David had started to feel sick. He remembered now.

Uncle Mike was in the hotel room. With towels. 'Better out than in matey,' he'd said more than once. There was ice too. David was shivering and sweating, his hand was in the ice bucket, his face panting into towels.

He recalled waking another time when his uncle was carrying him from a taxi. 'You'll be right, you'll be right, you'll be right,' over and over in a strange tight voice. Maybe this memory was a dream because his uncle had said, 'Don't you bloody go, Ernie,' which can't have been right.

Mr Scully had been in the rooms. No one else. Scully and Michael had talked about crayfish and field hospitals, and Michael made jokes about Private Simpson and his donkey. 'A tent is a bloody lousy battlement; the cloth doesn't keep the bombs out very well at all. Skin isn't much better, mind, for keeping the bombs out.' Mr Scully had spoken in an unusually gentle voice. 'Hey, boyo, you got to leave that stuff over there. If you keep it with you, you'll go under.' David thought he was referring to the vomiting and promptly obliged.

His stomach ached now, but not with the stabbing pain he'd felt before. Now they were just sore. He felt thirsty. He opened his eyes and was about to call his uncle for water, but he was in the players' room again.

Mr Richardson dragged a chair over and sat next to him. 'Right there, David?'

'Yes sir. Much better. How we going?'

'Jack Tanner's out and Ken's gone in. Young Bardsley is gutsing it out.'

David nodded, feeling at his own guts once again.

'Your talk to Charlie O'Toole last night.'

'Yes.'

'Did he pay you?'

'I don't know. I think he paid Uncle Mike. And the dinner.'

'I'll talk to your uncle. It's not on, old chap. We give interviews for free.'

There was a groan and then applause. Richardson stood and looked out the window.

Mr Johnson turned. 'Caught at gully.'

'Damn.' Richardson walked to the door leading out and called, 'You look after yourself Bill. Don't be a hero with that cheek.'

Mr Scully came in from the card room with some barley water. 'See if you can keep that down.'

David took it and drank.

'You remember what the doc said?'

David shook his head. 'Thinks you got an allergy. To the crayfish or the prawns or to the bloody garlic. So don't eat 'em again.'

David nodded, handing back the empty glass.

'Might want to stay away from that garlic stuff anyway, if you want to keep any mates. It's got a pong.'

'Good show, Beardie,' called Johnson from his chair, as Andrew Bardsley came back in.

'Short of me fifty,' he said, but he seemed happy. Richardson patted him on the back, and he smiled at David on his way past, saying, 'Right there, cobber?'

'Thanks, Mr Bardsley.'

Richardson came back. 'Now about this interview. I've got to sort out some of the things you've said.'

'What kind of things?'

'Well, firstly, you really shouldn't wear your cricket gear

around in public. Kind of bad manners, really, at this level of the game.'

'They were my best clothes. We were going to buy some street clothes this morning, but I got sick. I only had farm clothes.'

'Oh, I see.' Richardson looked down. He blushed slightly.

'The bastards,' yelled McLeod in through the door. 'They've brought Tudor on against Bill.'

'That's to scare him,' said David, 'so he'll be worried that Tudor will hit his cheek again.'

'Yes. Look, I have hurry up this talk we're having, and I shouldn't, but ... Now that I'm beginning to know you David, I think you're a stand-up sort of chap. But you're young. So, here is a rule for you. You can't just say what you think. Especially to a newspaperman. You mustn't. The umpires are angry with us, and Proctor's livid.'

'Why?'

'Well, you said Proctor was stupid.'

'No I didn't.' David thought about it some more. No, he was sure he didn't say that, because he didn't think it was true. 'I wouldn't.'

The crowd was starting to sound concerned, and Richardson got up and moved to the window again. He watched the rest of the over before he came back to David.

'Did you accuse the umpires of making mistakes?'

'No, sir,' said David, then he added, 'well, kind of yes, maybe. I said that I thought Mr Johnson wasn't out.'

'You must not do that. We don't criticise the umpiring. Well, only in private, but never on the field and never in public. That is a rule.'

'But that's not how I said it. Not like that. He was being mean.'

'O'Toole?'

'He's twisted things.'

'Hmm. That's what I suspected. Good. I will explain and apologise to Mr Proctor, and to the umpires.'

'I will.'

'Not at all. My job. No more talk to any newsmen, even if your uncle says.'

There was a big groan out around the ground, then applause. 'Baker's out,' said Johnson.

'What's the score?' asked David.

'Five for a hundred and forty something. Ken Hall looks like he's got his eye in though. Touch of Jack Tanner about him today.'

At lunch Australia were five for one hundred and fifty-seven. Their lead was less than eighty.

David went into the change rooms and had a shower while things were quiet. He felt sweaty and a little weak and wanted to wash the oniony smell from his skin.

He dressed in his cricket clothes. He put on his pads as he'd been shown. He found his new, longer-fingered gloves and his bat, then went outside to sit with the other players. The sun was so bright it made his eyes water and his forehead start sweating. He took some little breaths while he waited for it all to come back into focus.

He heard someone from the crowd yell, 'Hey David, how stupid is Proctor?' There was a burst of laughter.

Someone else yelled, 'Hey, Babe, how stupid are you?' More laughter, but some shushing.

David looked as people turned to look at him and the wave of chattering noise got louder.

A boy yelled, 'Good on ya, Dave. Stick it up 'em all.'

A man, sweating awfully in a football jumper, yelled, 'You think you're too good to talk to us for free do ya Donald?'

Ten Ton stood up and pointed at the man. 'You can leave off, right? And Norwood couldn't play footy if they tried.' There was laughter around the man with the football jumper and he sat back down into the other people again.

Calligan said, 'And that is the Members Stand. You certainly polarise opinions, Babe.'

Ten Ton sat back down.

'Babe?' asked David.

'O'Toole's headline was "Out of the mouth of babes."'

'"The wit and wisdom of David Donald, aged twelve," was the subtitle,' added Tanner who was sitting near the back. David wasn't sure whether he heard pleasure in Tanner's voice.

'He's sure taken a shine to you,' added Calligan.

There was applause as Hall scored a boundary. He was batting with McLeod. David looked to the scoreboard. Hall was fifty-eight. Jackson had made thirty-five before getting out to Proctor. David noticed that Proctor had taken most of the wickets.

Mr Calligan and Ten Ton seemed tense. His own legs started jiggling up and down too, as he looked out across the ground and thought about batting. When McLeod edged one of Proctor's deliveries to slip, Richardson called David inside.

Richardson had a cricket ball in his hand. 'Show me your guard?'

David grabbed for his bat, dropping his gloves in the process. He bent for the gloves and managed to stick the handle of the bat into his stomach.

'Gloves first,' said Johnson, who'd turned in his usual

seat. Tanner had moved to the door to look in. Bardsley and Jackson came to the card room door, fags hanging from their mouths.

David put his gloves on. Bardsley came out and bent down, and pulled David's gloves hard, back towards his elbows.

'You don't want them loose.' He pulled the little belt at the wrist. 'And no flaps or buckles out either, or the ball might hit them.' He tucked the flaps back behind David's hands.

David sneezed as the smoke from Bardsley's cigarette went up his nose.

Bardsley stepped back, not much happy with what he saw. He shrugged.

David took his guard stance, bat down, facing Richardson.

'Grip the bat tighter,' said Johnson.

'My finger hurts.'

'Turn your body to face Chalkie,' said Richardson.

'But keep your bat facing Richo,' said Bardsley.

'Feet further apart,' said Jackson.

'Not that far,' said Richardson. 'Here it comes.'

David was so busy twisting and getting his feet in position that he didn't actually see the ball get thrown. Even so, it was so slow, that David suddenly lifted his bat, managing to scoop it up at the ceiling, where it came down right at him. He threw his arms up just in time to ward off the ball, sending that bat towards the card room door. Jackson ducked back in as David's bat hit the door jam with a woody crack. It fell to the wooden floor with more thuds and bangs.

David stood looking at the men. Tanner was the first to

laugh. The other men joined in. Even Mr Johnson.

'I wasn't ready,' said David, blushing and angry.

'Strewth,' said Jackson, 'thought I was gunna lose an eye.'

'So, out of fielding and batting, fielding would be your strength then,' said Richardson with a grin.

Tanner shook his head. Jackson bent down to find his cigarette.

David glared at Mr Richardson and he stopped smiling. 'Beardie, toss the kid a couple of balls. Help him get his eye in.'

'You can't send him out there. He'll get killed.' It was Jack Tanner.

'This isn't the time, Jack,' said Richardson. Then he looked around at the other men and finally David. 'If he can just hang around for a few balls, just maybe Ned can farm the strike and get his hundred. If we can get up to near two hundred and fifty ahead, we can put some pressure on these blokes. For the first time.'

David nodded.

Richardson turned to look at Jack Tanner. Tanner said, 'My mistake, John. I spoke out of turn.'

They both nodded.

Richardson said, 'David, if the ball is bowled anywhere short of halfway, you just hit the deck. Don't even try.'

Bardsley threw a couple of balls to David and gave him some pointers, until Calligan was bowled for eleven. 'Better sit outside and get your eyes used to the sunlight, mate.'

David went outside to watch Ten Ton. Slowly all the seats outside began to fill. David looked around. The whole team was outside watching Ten Ton and Hall bat. Even Mr Johnson had come outside.

'You just have to block it, David,' said Bardsley.

'Just do what Ned says,' said McLeod.

'If you're not sure, duck away,' said Baker.

Ken Hall had reached ninety-two runs when Ten Ton fended a ball off his throat to silly mid-on. It was the fifth ball of Tudor's over.

David remained sitting on his bench until someone pushed him up. He went out the small white picket gate, aware of the distant noise of a million bees. He walked out towards Ten Ton who smiled and said something but David still couldn't hear past the buzz. He got halfway to the wicket, then stopped. The English team had gathered in a group after dismissing Ten Ton. They'd all turned and were looking at him. David couldn't move. They were big men, all dressed in white, with unreadable faces. Tudor pounded the cricket ball from hand to hand like it was dough. Ostler whispered to Proctor who nodded. Windsor smiled with nothing like welcome. And still the buzzing in his ears. Hall was coming towards him, speaking. David made himself breathe. He took some slower breaths and finally the buzzing started to fade.

Hall reached him. 'So you came out eh, mate?'

'Yes, Mr Hall.'

'Right. Good on ya. Now if you can last out the over, I'll have a real crack next one, and try and keep them off ya. Right?'

'Yes, sir.'

Hall turned and David followed. Hall turned back to see him, and pointed. 'That end.'

The Englishmen started to go back to their fielding positions, but talked loud enough for David to hear.

'There he is, Mr Proctor. That's the genius who said you

SPINNER · *a novel*

were nothing but raw speed with no skill.'

'Oh aye,' said Proctor and grimly watched David pass.

Morgan got back behind his stumps and called, 'Personally, Mr Wisden, I think you've been doing a first class job.'

'Let's see how many tricks he's got with a bat,' called someone else.

Windsor stood in slips, with his hands on his hips, scowling. He called, 'Knock his little head off, Douglas.'

Longford stepped forward, 'All right, enough of that. Good afternoon, Mr Donald.'

'Good afternoon, Mr Longford.'

David took his place at the crease. The sun was too hot, too white. It made the ground and all the people around him too bright. He was already sweating from the walk out. His throat was dry.

'Take your guard.' It was Hall calling.

Mr Fitzmorris called, 'Which stump would you like, David?'

When David said nothing, Hall said, 'He'll take middle.'

All the while Tudor stood at the top of his run, watching. He was so far away that David couldn't make out his features. With the sun, he seemed to shimmer a moment, like some white bird across the river. Then he started to run in, at first slowly, but then faster and faster until he reached the crease. He bowled.

David felt movement in the air near his face and heard the sound of a whack as the ball hit the wicketkeeper's leather gloves. He played a shot, even though he assumed the ball had been bowled. Then he ran.

Hall was in front of him, yelling, 'No. No. No.' He was waving David back like he was sheep coming the wrong way.

David turned. He was quite a few steps down the pitch. The wicketkeeper had the ball. David started running back. Morgan underarmed the throw with his glove still on. David got back to his crease. The crowd were screaming and cheering all at once. Morgan had missed.

David looked down at the crease, listening to the crowd noise wash around him from all directions. At his feet, the wicket was scuffed and lots of lines had been drawn across. There were juicy footmarks too. There was a tap on his shoulder. It was Hall.

'Don't run. Just stay in.'

'Yes, sir.'

'Cripes, what kinda shit shot was that?'

'I didn't see it. I didn't see the ball.'

'Bloody lucky then. Nearly took yer nose off. Two more balls.'

Longford had stepped in. 'Let's not waste time here, Mr Tudor. I want the wicket.'

Tudor had the ball again. He was standing at the top of his mark.

David took his guard. He made his eyes open wider as Tudor got closer. David tried to start his shot as Tudor let the ball go. He saw it, at the last minute, near his legs. There was a woody sound, but not of ball on bat. He turned. One of the wickets was missing. Then he saw it, still in the air, cartwheeling past second slip.

David groaned, and turned to say sorry to Hall, but the Australian batsman was already striding towards the boundary, raising his bat like it was a flag.

The English players were leaving too. David looked at the scoreboard. They'd got two hundred and eighty-two. The same as England had in their first innings. It didn't seem like enough. They needed to get England out for less than two hundred.

He turned back to the pitch and bent down to look more closely at the surface. There were some very nice footmarks to bowl at the left-handers. There were cracks too starting to open in the turf, splitting as the sun dried it out.

David saw Proctor, and hurried up to catch him. 'Mr Proctor,' he called.

The English fast bowler stopped. When he turned, he did not look angry. He didn't look anything, but just stood above David waiting with an unreadable face that put David off. He'd wanted to say sorry about the newspaper, and to explain, but he didn't have those things straight in his head, and Proctor's dead look made his mind go even blanker.

David said, 'Um, nice bowling.'

'Thank you.'

He still looked at David, still waiting. And David could think of nothing.

'Good day then,' said Proctor and walked off the field.

But he twisted it, thought David, thinking of O'Toole. Only he couldn't be sure because he couldn't remember when and how he'd mentioned Proctor during the meal.

Proctor followed the English team to the gate leading to their rooms. David went into the Australian rooms where they were already getting ready to field.

Mr Calligan was patting Hall on the back. 'Good knock, Ned.'

'Blimey, comin' from you, I musta done something wrong.'

'Well, good knock and I owe you a beer for not sticking with you.'

'Wake me up, I must be dreaming,' whooped Hall, even

though his voice stayed sarcastic and teasing.

'Let's just get a wicket or maybe two in this half-hour, and we can finally put the wind up them,' yelled Richardson, clapping his hands together.

They didn't however. Although both Ten Ton and Calligan bowled with pace and movement, England were none for ten at stumps.

CHAPTER THIRTEEN

Uncle Michael wasn't in the rooms after stumps. David checked through his bag and locker but found no clothes. Apparently he'd been delivered that morning in his cricket whites.

Most of the team had already showered before they took the field, and didn't stay long. Ten Ton was going back to the hotel so he could telephone his wife before she bathed the kids. Bardsley, Johnson and Tanner were going out to dinner at the old Exchange hotel. Mr Calligan and Mr Hall shared a glass of beer in the card room.

When Mr Scully came to tidy up the change rooms, David hid in the toilet at the end of the showers, crouching behind the half-closed door. Mr Scully might feel he had to stay, or had to take David somewhere, and David didn't want that. He would feel like he was putting him out. So he just listened to Mr Scully mutter about messy buggers and the sound of the broom swishing. When Scully turned the light off, David waited longer, until he couldn't hear anything except the faint drip of the toilet.

Out in the players' viewing room it was still light. David looked out the window. In the centre of the oval, groundsmen were working on the edges of the wicket, filling foot holes with sand. Others were dragging a roller up and down, firming up the wicket. There were still some people in the outer, sitting and talking as though the cricket were still on.

David sat in Mr Johnson's seat and watched things around the ground. The front awning of a pie van was put down. The light went out in one of the bars. David wondered whether his uncle might have been there, whether he would be coming soon. He knew the name of the hotel, but didn't think he could get there without a taxi. He was used to taxis now, but had no money. You paid the driver when you got to where you asked them to take you. If they were bright and chatty, like Uncle Mike, you said keep the change, mate. Men with hessian bags moved along the seats picking up people's rubbish. All the spectators were gone.

David went into the card room. He searched the side table, where Mr Scully often left extra bits of bread and left-over sandwiches during the day, but he'd tidied all the food away. Otherwise the mice would get it, David supposed. He sat at the card table for a moment. The cards were well worn, but it was already getting too dark to see their faces clearly. David didn't want to risk turning on the light. He thought he might go to find Uncle Mike, or at least the room with the mattress on the table down the corridor, where he could sleep, but the door leading out of the players' rooms was locked.

He went to the door leading to the players' outside seats. It was bolted, but from the inside. He pulled back the bolt and opened the door. The air smelt of grass and distant smoke. He went out, pulling the door closed, then walked down a couple of rows of seats, then across to where another low picket fence joined the members' area. He climbed over and made his way along the face of the grandstand towards its end, where he could hear people talking and the clink of glasses somewhere above.

'Oi, what you doing?' There was a man with a hessian sack standing in the nearby shadows.

David jumped over some benches and out over the picketed area to the side of the grandstand. He ran around towards the back.

'Oi, you,' yelled the man from behind.

There were stairs round the side that led up to another part of the grandstand. Some men in black evening dress turned. One peered down. 'Should you be here?'

David kept running. At the back of the stand, there was a horse and cart. A dark-skinned man and boy were unloading metal trays. They both looked up at him a moment, but then went back to their work. The lights were brighter here. Another man was sweeping with a huge broom, by the players' entrance.

'Hey,' he called as David ran past him.

David headed right along the road behind the grandstand to come around its other side, where there were more shadows. He edged along the side and moved towards the front. At this end of the grandstand there was a higher wire fence separating the members' from the grassed area.

David looked across the ground. The sky was cloudless still and going grey. A man with a kerosene lamp in a wheelbarrow was heading towards the wicket from the other side of the cricket ground. Two other figures were dragging the roller off. Someone else was moving a sprinkler in the gloom.

David jumped over the picket fence and onto the ground, ducking down.

'He was round this way,' he heard a gruff voice say. There

were footsteps. 'A kid in white.'

'The ghost of Babe Donald,' said another voice, laughing.

David crawled along the shadow of the fence. He could see lights up high in the grandstand—a party. Laughter and light and glass tinkles carried out into the dusk. He crawled to the players' gate, and reached over to unlatch it. He thought he could see movement down where he'd jumped the fence, but looking the other way couldn't see the man who'd been picking up rubbish. He crawled up the steps and pushed at the bottom of the door into the players' viewing area. It was still open.

He closed and latched the door, panting. His knees were wet and probably grass stained. He raised himself carefully and took another look out the big window. The figures in the centre of the oval continued to work by lamplight, moving in purposeful but slow diagonals. They'd pause and bend, then move again. More lanterns wobbled about like drunken moths.

David found a little bit of barley water syrup in a bottle and filled it in the change room. When he'd drunk that, he found enough gear to make a little nest in the chair he'd slept in during the day. 'My kingdom for a horse,' he said aloud in the empty room then smiled, as his uncle would fancy such a quote. He thought that if he had a horse he'd probably eat it all, he was so hungry.

He'd eat a big breakfast in the morning, then go out and bowl. He wiggled his sore finger. Not too bad. Those footmarks looked very useful. He could do a lot against the left-handers. He'd have to convince Mr Richardson to let him bowl early, before the English put on too many runs. Otherwise they'd have their eye in and their tails up. They might approach him differently now. Windsor wouldn't.

Grandad had said that. Windsor would try to dominate you, no matter what. Bishop was a different matter. David had no idea how to bowl to the new batsman.

David woke early with the light. He felt stiff and hungry. He went into the change rooms and washed, then changed into a fresh set of cricket creams from his cricket bag. He got his bat and tried to hit a cricket ball against the brick wall, but it made his finger hurt too much, so he bowled the length of the change rooms, finally finding the spot where the ball would hit the wall on the full and come back to him without having to move his feet. He did that until he heard Scully calling, 'What's that bleeding racket?'

Scully put his head in the door. 'What the 'ell are you doing in here?'

'Got locked in.' David bit his lip. Thought maybe he should have said something else.

'All night?'

'Yes.'

'Why didn't you hammer on the door? Or go out the players' race and tell someone?'

David looked down at his feet. He only half knew the answer to this and didn't want to explain.

'Geez, David. Use ya noggin for cryin' out loud. Maybe O'Toole's right and ya are touched. I don't know. Geez. It's not right. I'm not your ... I shouldn't have to be looking after a kid, not an' the team as well.'

'Don't tell anyone,' said David.

'Tell?'

'They'll think the same as you. That I should have done something different. Like someone else would.'

Scully stood staring so long, that even though David

wanted to keep looking him in the eye, he couldn't.

Finally Scully spat on the floor, which was as much a relief to David as it must have been for Scully. 'Yeah, well, all right. I got to tell some day though.'

David looked up.

Mr Scully was smiling. 'Too good a story. All night in the rooms. An' bloody bowling in the morning. In 'ere.' He shook his head, smiling a dreamy smile, in the way people did.

David decided the dreamy smile was better than them staring. 'Have you got any tucker?'

'What?'

'I'm pretty hungry.'

'Yeah. An' all. Where's yer bloody uncle?'

Uncle Michael came to the door as soon as the Adelaide Oval gates opened. David went out into the hall to talk to him.

'I couldn't get in, mate. They'd locked the gates when I got back from the ... um ... and they wouldn't listen to me or let me in. They said you musta gone with the rest of the team. Anyway here're some clothes.'

He had a bag with pants and shorts and jackets and shirts. They looked quite smart, although not new.

Michael was unshaven and his eyes were murky. His hands shook slightly. 'Have to get shoes when you're with me. Not sure about those big feet of yours.' He kept looking up and down the hall while he spoke, and caught David looking to see too. 'I better be off. Richardson wants a chat, so Tanner's probably been in his ear. And now Livingston wants a confab too. Not just yet, eh?'

'You're not allowed to take money for interviews.'

'That bloody O'Toole. Stitched us. Take some wickets. That will shut him up. Lots of folk are starting get on your side anyway, mate, if only on account of him being so mean-spirited. Which reminds me, I better show you some batting too. If just so you can get a knick on it. Anyway, I'll be bright an' early after play today, don't worry about that.' He stood to attention and did a silly salute, saying in a funny voice, 'Reporting as ordered, Sarrr.' When David smiled, he said, 'Well, go get 'em, tiger. You couldn't take five wickets today, could you?'

'Five!'

'Not to worry. Be a good bet is all.'

'Um, I don't know about that, Uncle Mike,' said David, feeling like he was letting him down. But he couldn't help it. He was less sure now because of his finger, and he couldn't be sure how they'd bat now they'd seen him bowl. And there were the other bowlers. They could take more. No one could know. Even Grandad couldn't know that.

'Forget it. Enjoy, matey. Enjoy.'

His uncle limped down the hall, leaving David feeling flat, as though he'd just received bad news, even though he hadn't.

After an hour of play, when Ten Ton and Calligan had failed to take a wicket, Richardson finally gave in to David's begging and let him bowl. Dorrington and O'Malley seemed well set with England no wickets down for forty-eight runs.

'So same field against O'Malley?'

'Yes, sir.'

'You think he'll fall for it twice?'

'No sir, but I want him to think that's what I might try.'

'And this you also discussed with your grandad back on

the farm long before you got here?'

'Yes, sir. We'd talk about the different ways to get them out, and then if you'd bowled one way, what they might do next.'

'Like a bit of chess, really.'

'No, sir. I don't play chess.'

'Let's not make this our habit again please, Mr Richardson,' called Mr Wisden.

Richardson set the field to O'Malley as he had in the first innings.

McLeod went into silly mid-off again. 'How ya goin', all right there, Bill?' he said to O'Malley as he took up his position.

David stood at the start of his run-up, and held the ball in his leg-spinner grip. He whispered, 'Donald looks down on O'Malley, the two men set. He moves in to bowl.' David saw where he'd land it, in a footmark. Saw the change of direction. He bowled, and really got some spin on it, the ball whirring in the air outside leg stump. O'Malley came forward, bat and pad close together, ready to drop the ball, even though it was so wide. The ball hit the edge of the roughed area and spun. It spun a lot. It spun back towards the stumps and behind O'Malley's bat, crashing into leg stump.

'Oh my goodness,' said the other English batsman, Dorrington.

'Indeed,' said Mr Wisden, standing next to him. 'Hit a crack, I'd say.'

O'Malley was walking off, shaking his head.

The Australian players were approaching David, but slowly.

Baker said, 'That's the furthest I've ever seen a ball spin

in my whole life.'

Maud McLeod patted him on the shoulder. 'Did you fellas hear the noise—like bees.'

Calligan said, 'Well Babe, more milk for you tonight.'

Tanner nodded, clapping from a distance. Hall was shaking his head, but not looking at David.

Ten Ton finally reached them from his boundary position. 'Who's shellin' these peas?' He clapped David on the back, sending him spinning, before Baker caught him and set him upright again.

'Easy, Ten Ton. Let's not kill the golden goose just yet.'

'So,' said Richardson, with an eyebrow raised, 'what do you and your grandfather have in store for Mr Longford?'

Longford was an elegant back-foot player. He liked to stand tall, giving himself a good look, and often cutting to the off side. David's grandfather thought he was always a possibility for a slips catch, if you could get a ball to rear up higher or lower as he was attempting to cut late. But David wanted to get him leg before wicket.

Dorrington was down the other end dabbing at the footmark where David had landed his previous ball, looking for the crack.

David and Richardson set the field, with three slips, a prominent mid-on and Hall at short fine leg. Longford was paying special attention to Hall. David felt that he needed to do another ball like the one that had got O'Malley. It was what Uncle Mike had said when he was trying out for the team. He could make Longford and Dorrington, and therefore the rest of the team, think he could bowl those any time he liked, even though, with his finger, he probably only had a few in him. It would put Longford's mind in that frame too, while David tried the real get out ball.

David stood at his mark.

Longford stood tall, and nodded to David. 'Morning, Mr Donald.'

'Good morning, Mr Longford,' called David.

'All very bloody pip-pip here then,' called Hall.

Longford took his guard.

David whispered, 'And it's the moment we've been waiting for. Donald to Longford.' David saw the arc, saw the spin. He stepped in and bowled. The ball arced with nice height, and landed just on the edge of the footmark, where David had intended. Longford took no risks however. He stayed back, waiting. The ball hit the pitch, but didn't spin as much as the previous delivery. David's finger hadn't let him rip it. Longford came at the ball with bat and pad, but was a little surprised by the bounce, still managing to drop it to the ground. It went between Baker and Hall, and Hall had to lumber after it. Longford ran two runs.

David was glad he'd scored two, and was facing again, so he could keep setting his trap. Longford would look at you, David, his grandad had said, as he's careful and values his wicket. While he's looking, that would be the time to get him.

David stood at the top of his mark. He looked towards slips, then out to point. It was important, for this trap, to not move point yet. He needed to show Longford his stock ball. 'Donald eyes the pitch. Longford is ready, easy in his stance.' David stepped in and flighted another high one, landing it straighter this time. Longford started forward, but then stepped back, his bat lifted, as the ball spun away towards the slips. Longford had his bat covering it the whole way. He probably could have cut it as it bounced at a useful height. David watched him nod, and practise a cut.

David yelled, 'Mr McLeod, a little straighter please.'

Longford watched McLeod move to cut off some future cut. Longford eyed the gap between McLeod and extra cover. David would do it now. He stood watching where he'd land it and imagining the ball. 'Donald is waiting. Longford eyes the field.' David moved in and bowled. The ball was a little lower than the previous delivery, but looked similar and Longford went back. But this ball dipped a little, which made Longford adjust his cut shot, as he waited for the spin. It didn't come. David bowled his arm ball and the ball held its line going straight for the stumps. Longford tried to get his bat back towards it, but couldn't move in time. The ball hit Longford's pads right in front of the wicket.

The Australian team went up in appeal. Richardson started running forward from second slip. Mr Wisden was shaking his head.

David turned. 'Lbw,' he shouted.

'Not out,' said Wisden from behind his stumps.

'It was going to hit the stumps!'

'David, that's enough,' called Richardson still advancing down the wicket.

'But it was the arm ball. It was out leg before wicket.'

'David. Silence!'

Richardson took David by the shoulder. 'The umpire's decision is final. That's it. Bowl your next ball.'

'But it was out, Mr Richardson.'

'Lad, I think so too, but the umpire must have had doubts. So, according to the rules of cricket, Longford isn't out. Lucky him.'

'That's unfair. I set the trap.'

'Set it again. Get on with it. Or get off this field,' said Richardson sharply, as he turned and walked back to slip.

David blew the air from his lungs as he tried to calm himself. He became aware of the crowd. They were complaining too. David wiped his forehead and felt sweat there. It was another hot day with no wind. He looked to Longford, who was watching him with interest. He walked back to his mark. Jackson threw him the ball, calling, 'This time, Babe.'

David hated that nickname. He should have had Longford, just as his grandad and he had planned. What must he be thinking now, if he was listening on the radio? David stepped in and bowled, and Longford stepped forward two good steps and hit the ball way over David's head. Six. The crowd groaned, but then clapped.

'Nice shot,' called Dorrington.

David bowled too flat next ball and Longford hit him past a diving McLeod for four. Ten runs he didn't deserve already. David should grab his cap from the umpire at the end of the over, as he'd heard some disgruntled bowlers had done on occasion, only he didn't have one. The team hadn't even given him a cap. As he waited for Hampton to get the ball from the gutter, he wondered should he ask Richardson about getting a cap. All the other Australian players had green caps with the Australian coat of arms on them.

David tried for the rough again, but missed the spot and Longford hooked him for four more. He blocked the last delivery and David started to walk away with one for fourteen off his first over when Richardson called, 'David, go and stand with Chalkie. Stand next to him for the entire over.'

McLeod came on to bowl, and David went to Mr Johnson. 'Why do I have to come and stand with you?'

'I'm not sure. Are we both in trouble, do you think?'

David felt stupid, standing right next to Mr Johnson, but Dorrington blocked the first couple of McLeod's medium pacers.

'I've taken a wicket. I should have had two.'

'And I've scored some runs,' said Mr Johnson, watching the wicket as he talked, 'Hundreds and hundreds.'

Dorrington stepped in to McLeod's third delivery and hit it towards the mid-wicket boundary. Hall gave chase.

'Just not now?' suggested David.

'That's what I'm wondering. Why did you bowl so many bad balls after bowling so many good?'

David thought about that during the rest of the over. Even when Longford hit a single and Mr Johnson ran after it, and David ran after him, causing the crowd to laugh. He kept thinking about what had gone wrong. Then he knew. He had not done anything right. He had not thought about what he was going to do, and had not done it well. He'd bowled nothing balls, because he'd thought nothing.

'But it was out, Mr Johnson.'

'I didn't think so. I thought it was going to spin like your other deliveries and miss off stump.'

'It was my arm ball.'

'I didn't know you had an arm ball.'

'I do.' But David settled down again. 'I have to get the umpires to understand.'

'No.'

'What then?'

'I think you should think about the next ball, not what happened to the last.' He gestured towards the surrounding crowd. 'They can think about what's already happened, and we can too if we want, but later. After. While we're playing we must always be in the now and in the next and not in the was.'

David nodded when Mr Johnson looked at him, but couldn't make his team mate's words stick in his head. He understood the meaning of each word, but the way Mr Johnson was putting them together made it add up to something else that David couldn't untangle.

'The was,' said David hopefully.

'Yes. Mr Richardson is possibly suggesting that I'm also thinking about what's happened and not about simply dealing with the next ball myself.'

'The next ball?'

'He's clever, but I don't think he's that clever. I think he just wanted me to settle you down. Go and bowl like you have been before you got all angry and silly.'

'Yes, sir.'

It was David's next over. He was bowling to Dorrington, the stylish opener. He and Grandad had worked out a plan. Dorrington was a left-hander, and so offered many more options. The footmarks would allow David to spin the ball in to his wickets.

Dorrington suddenly called, 'Do your worst, baby!'

'Oi,' yelled Hall, 'go make up your own nickname.'

David concentrated. His finger felt pretty good. He'd be patient with Dorrington, but would have to open up mid-off to encourage the drive. David asked for a fly slip as well, because Dorrington liked to sweep and was likely to catch a top edge with David's extra bounce. He asked for a short third man. He imagined the ball. 'Donald to Dorrington. No love lost there. Dorrington eyes mid wicket.' David stepped in and bowled a flatter, faster leg break. He'd intended it to be a set-up delivery, with not much on it, so that he'd get a catch later in the over by giving him a topspinner. But for some reason Dorrington flashed at the ball awkwardly and too early. The ball popped up and Hall took the easiest of catches at gully.

The players ran up, including Hall this time. 'Nice nut, Babe.'

'I didn't mean it,' said David.

'Don't tell them that,' said Baker.

'It wasn't a good ball.'

'They're getting scared of ya,' said McLeod.

'Yep,' said Bardsley, 'He's been standing up the other end watching all these mystery balls and he's ...'

'Shit himself,' laughed Hall.

'Hmm, quite,' said Richardson, more seriously. 'So, same field as before for Windsor.'

'He'll try to dominate me,' said David.

Windsor did not. Longford and he had a long discussion when he came to the wicket, and whether it was that, or another plan, David was unsure. Windsor refused to play at most of David's deliveries. He stepped towards the pitch of the ball, as though ready to crash them to the boundary, but merely watched them spin towards slips. When David tried his arm ball, Windsor blocked it. When David bowled from the rough, he merely padded the ball away, keeping his bat high and out of the way.

'Careful there, Eddie, you might have got a run,' muttered Jack Tanner, as the over finished.

Longford went after McLeod. He hit a four then a three. Next ball Windsor lashed out, hitting McLeod on the up towards the extra cover boundary, where Ten Ton stood and took a catch just before the pickets. He spun to face the crowd, quite daintily, in order not to overbalance. Windsor was out for a duck, bowled McLeod, caught Hampton.

Everyone ran to McLeod.

'Mopsey. Gutsy ball.'

'Gotta keep flyin' the flag for us country boys.'

'Call ya Babe Senior soon.'

'Get stuffed.'

Bishop was coming out. England were three for sixty-five. They were still in a comfortable position to win the game, but as shaky a start as they'd had for some years.

Bishop and Longford both played carefully. Bishop blocked and prodded, even when David came on for his next over. When he edged a single, it was the first ball he'd tried to hit, rather than defend.

David got prepared for Longford, setting his field and clearing his mind. Longford stepped back and cracked the first ball past point for four. When David tried his arm ball, Longford picked it, and drove hard and straight for another boundary.

David saw a chance. He saw the ball that might do it. He bowled with good flight and height bringing Longford forward for another drive, but this was a good loopy. It hit the pitch and suddenly took extra speed and extra force. Longford tried to check the shot, but the ball kept rising at his bat and all he did was pop the ball up towards David. He grabbed at it, but the ball hit the hard part of his left hand below the thumb. It bounced out and up. It was still there in the air in front of him. Only David couldn't seem to move his feet. He watched it drop ever so slowly all the way to the ground. There was an enormous groan from everywhere.

Tanner called, 'You might be wanting to buy a lottery

ticket, Henry.'

'Some days make up for the other days, don't they?' Richardson said with a wise smile.

David was looking at the ball on the ground. All the planning and a good ball too, and still it hadn't worked. Even he should have caught that. He looked at his hands open in front of his nose. His finger was slightly swollen, coming up again. He shook it, thinking he didn't have long before he couldn't bowl that day.

Mr Johnson was there. He'd run in a long way to pick up the ball and hand it to David. 'So, David, lucky that's in the past, eh?'

'Yes, sir.'

He felt a pat on his back.

'While you're there Chalkie, come in to extra cover. Maud, silly point. Ned, leg gully.'

David turned. Mr Richardson was taking over the field. David was about to protest, but stopped. Richardson was dragging in the field. He was crowding them around Longford, close in. David thought about this. Longford had been given two lives. Had just given a return catch. He must be feeling the pressure. But this was Longford. The man had ice water in his veins, they said. What would he do?

'All right with you, David?' called Richardson, going to second slip himself, next to Bardsley at first.

David went back to his mark, nodding. David looked down the wicket, whispering, 'Donald to Longford. The field are in, waiting for a pop-up catch. Longford can defend here. Or he can attack.' David would guess. He saw the delivery he'd bowl. He saw what he hoped Longford would do. He stepped in, glimpsed Longford starting to move early. No. David changed to bowl flat and fast, still spinning. Longford came down at it in two big bounds, but the extra speed beat him and the ball spun past his swiping bat. Baker took it in his gloves and swept the stumps. The team jumped. Longford stumped Baker, bowled Donald.

Players ran at David. Chests and stomachs and big thumps on the back that made him cough. The crowd was a distant tumult of excitement. He'd got Longford.

Richardson was talking, 'Clever ball that one. Three moves ahead.'

Maud McLeod grabbed David's cheeks quite hard and yelled into his face, 'You little beauty.'

Jack Tanner came forward and patted him on the chest. 'Good ball, Mr Donald.'

'It isn't over, boys,' said Richardson. 'Lots more wickets to take and not many runs to play with.'

'Well, laddie,' said Ernie Morgan, the English wicket-keeper, when he came to the crease, 'you're starting to look like a bolt of lightning out of the blue.'

David thought he'd said it not unkindly. Morgan edged him through slips for a single.

Richardson brought Calligan back next over and trapped Morgan leg before wicket. Ostler scored off his first ball, then he and Bishop rotated the strike with ones and twos.

When David came back for his next over it was against Bishop and, as in the first innings, David had no ideas. The new English batsman would not keep still on the crease. Even when David was stepping in, he was still moving sideways or forwards or adjusting. It put David's placement out. Bishop edged David's first ball well over slips for four. On the next delivery, he danced down the wicket and drove along the ground. David put his hand out, and it cracked into his right hand. He dropped to the ground. The pain left his hand in a hot numbness and seemed to travel up his arm and then down into his stomach.

He heard Bishop say, 'Well that's taken care of that.'

David rolled on the ground panting, not sure whether to grab for his hand or his guts. His head throbbed. The men's faces appeared in the sky above him, and he heard himself groaning.

'I'm sorry,' he called. 'Sorry.' He was sorry, because he knew he was crying and he shouldn't be. He pushed his thumb into the palm of his hand and it eased the hurt.

Scully was there. He and Don Bidman helped him off, before Bidman, the local twelfth man, took his place in the field.

In the rooms, Scully put his hand in ice water, in a bowl on the table at the big window so he could still look out at the game. Scully muttered, 'Shouldn't be out there, 'cept you're so damned good.' His finger stopped hurting in the tearing way not long after it got in the water. Then it just ached. Scully came back with an aspirin, unfolding the paper to let the powder fall into a glass of water. 'Know what your figures are?'

'Um, three?'

'Three for twenty-four. Even better figures if you consider it's this team, and you got their top three.'

By lunch England had steadied a little. They were five for eighty-eight. Over shepherd's pie, Ten Ton promised to get Bishop for David. And in the fifth over after lunch he did, having him caught behind. He had Ostler, who had been on the march, caught at mid wicket half an hour later. England were now seven for one hundred and nineteen and in some trouble. Darby and Dwyer then settled in to take England to a slow but dangerous seven for one hundred and sixty-one at tea. Some of it had been at the cost of Bardsley who'd come on to try to bowl his part-time leggies.

David had been working his hand. He could not bowl leg breaks. He felt he could bowl off breaks. 'I can get Mr Darby out, Mr Richardson.'

Richardson looked to Scully, 'How's his hand?'

'I can bowl with the off-break grip. See, using mostly my first two fingers.'

'His finger needs rest, but it's bruised, not broken. I reckon he's still got the other injury under the bruise.'

'Naw, he's tough. Let him bowl,' said Hall, clapping him on the shoulder. 'We can win this.'

Richardson looked to Johnson who was sitting further along the window in his usual spot.

Mr Johnson looked worried, but shrugged. 'He can come off again if he can't bowl.'

'Yeah,' laughed McLeod, 'we got all of forty runs to play with.'

'I can do more, John,' said Calligan.

'Yeah, I know mate. Maybe not firing today,' replied the captain.

The crowd cheered when David went out with them after lunch. The ground seemed full. You couldn't see a spare seat or piece of grass anywhere around the outer. There was just one cloud in the sky; a white snail of fluff off in the east.

Calligan and Ten Ton bowled fast, but Darby and Dwyer seemed set. The wicket was giving the fast bowlers little. There was even bounce and it wasn't high. The English had some luck too. Dwyer edged Ten Ton for four that both Baker and Bardsley left for each other to catch.

At seven for one hundred and seventy-seven, Richardson called David in. David had asked Richardson to wait until Darby was facing, but he had Dwyer.

'I don't have a plan for Dwyer.'

'Well I can't wait. They only need twenty-three runs to win.'

David went to his mark, and held the ball in his usual grip, even though it was excruciating. He felt he had to because of his plan for Darby. He stepped and bowled and the ball came out badly. It never got the chance to spin one way or the other because it reached Dwyer on the full and he lofted it into long on. The batsmen ran three. Now Darby was facing.

'Very well,' said Darby loudly, 'let's see what all the fuss is about.'

David set a traditional leg-spin field, favouring the off side with a ring of fieldsmen. The English spinner played forward with a long stride, his other foot camped in the crease, so he wouldn't be stumped. David hid the ball in his hand, so that Darby wouldn't see the change of grip. He hoped Darby would assume leg breaks.

He stood at the top of his mark, with his left hand covering his right, but also trying to disguise that his finger hurt. He saw the ball he'd bowl. 'It's Donald to Darby, one spinner to another.' He stepped in and bowled. The different action did surprise Darby, but he was good enough to adjust to where it pitched, but he was still expecting it to spin away. Instead, it was a fast off break, spinning back towards off stump which it clipped. One bail fell.

Darby looked down at the pitch before walking off. He came close to David and said, 'That was poor batting, not good bowling.'

The team came in to David, but they didn't cheer. They just touched him, on his head and back and shoulders, but not as hard as usual. Just a touch each. Then everyone stood back to watch Tudor coming.

David said, 'I can get Tudor.'

'Right then,' said Jack Tanner.

'That's the plan,' said Richardson.

The men went to their fielding positions.

Tudor came out and took his guard. No one said hello.

Dwyer broke the mood. 'Only twenty to get there, Douglas.'

David stood at the top of his mark. He brought Maud McLeod into the silly mid-off. This was only to crowd Tudor. David felt he'd get him out caught behind. He saw the ball hitting the pitch and spinning back towards the wicket. He saw Tudor flashing. David bowled, but the ball did not land where he wanted it to. He bowled a long hop, and Tudor couldn't believe his luck. He had time to step forward and hit. David turned, as did everyone in the Adelaide Oval and watched the ball keep going up and out. It went way back. The crowd groaned, and David remembered their existence for the first time in hours. Mr Fitzmorris had both arms up. Tudor had hit a six, and David wasn't sure whether it had been hit out of the ground, until someone tossed it back over the fence.

David worked the base of his sore finger nervously. He did know how to get Tudor out. He wasn't sure he could carry out the plan. He thought of the same ball as he had imagined before. He stepped forward, but again it didn't land in quite the right place. It landed in line with off stump and spun down leg side. Baker had to dive to his left, to save a run. David tried again, but the ball came out just as it had the ball before. This time Tudor got some bat to it and they ran a single. Dwyer faced.

Richardson hurried up. 'Just keep him there, David. You don't have to take a wicket every ball. Just no runs. Got that?'

'Yes, sir.'

Richardson spread the field, putting more players on off side to protect David's leg breaks. Dwyer cut David down to third man for two. He did it again next ball. Richardson brought Calligan up closer, and Dwyer played exactly the same shot to the same ball but for a single.

They only needed eight runs to win and had two wickets in hand. David had one ball at Tudor. He signalled for Maud to come in. He had Bardsley and Richardson in slips, Hall in leg slip. Tudor looked confident. David started to step in. He stopped himself. Went back to the start of his run-up. He imagined the ball he wanted to bowl. 'Donald to Tudor. The Test may hang in the balance.' David bowled. He bowled an off break, but really flicked his fingers on release. It pitched just outside off stump and came in fast. Tudor brought his bat back to defend, but the ball climbed faster. It clipped his gloves and went through to Baker, who held it up. The slips fieldsmen jumped.

David yelled, 'How's that?'

Fitzmorris raised his finger. Tudor walked off.

David jumped up this time. Yes. He'd got Tudor.

The team gathered around him and there were more pats on the shoulders. They talked more quietly than before.

'Nice one David.'

'Can't call yer Babe. Baby gorilla more like,' said Maud.

'So,' said Richardson to Johnson, 'who bowls the other end?'

'I can do it, Captain,' said Calligan.

'Ten Ton's been loafin' all day,' said Tanner.

Richardson gave Hampton the ball saying, 'No loose ones. Hold down this end, and we'll bring David back for one more.'

Richardson set a defensive field to save the single. Dwyer blocked the first two, but hit the third ball cleanly past point. Calligan was coming at the ball, moving fast like he was a train. He picked the ball up with one hand and, without slowing, threw off one step. Dwyer was already turning, assuming it was an easy two runs, but then saw Calligan.

'No,' he yelled to Proctor, who turned like a tractor in a foot of mud. He seemed to take three little steps before he could take a big one sideways, and only then face back towards Baker. Baker caught the ball on the bounce and swept the bails, as Proctor finally lunged.

They all turned to Mr Fitzmorris at square leg. His finger was raised. Proctor run out, Calligan.

England all out for one hundred and ninety-five. Australia had won the third Test.

CHAPTER FOURTEEN

The people stared, all of them. A man with a sly smile only looked at David with one eye, bending in half to look up at him. A woman with a fox fur ruffled his head too hard, the fox's dead eyes looking nowhere. Soon David started to look only at their teeth, so he wouldn't have to look at their eyes. Some white ones, others missing ones. There were crowded teeth like a bent fence near a creek. There were wet tongues like huge blue leeches waiting to come out for a taste of him.

The mouths said the same things, which was to suggest that they were all being tricked in some way.

'Is this really David Donald?'

'The David Donald? The bowler.'

Uncle Mike would say, 'The very one.'

'That's him!'

'One and the same.'

'Don't shake his hand. It's sore.'

Uncle Mike got sillier as the evening went on, as more people bought David drinks, which Uncle Mike drank on his behalf. 'His royal specialness, yes.'

'Yes, the wonder that is Davey boy.'

'No, this is his brother,' he said once, but then went quiet for a while after that.

They had come into Melbourne late in the afternoon in a green motor car that Michael had bought, insisting that he was sick of trains and they'd find the team when they got in. David spent most of the drive thinking about the cricket game, never tiring of remembering as many moments as he could and turning them over and over to find some extra pleasure in each new angle of the reliving.

When Calligan had helped run out Proctor, all the men ran to the tall man. Hall had got there first, and tackled him like an Aussie Rules footballer, pushing Legal to the ground. They were both laughing. Everyone ran in and jumped on top of the stack, trying to pat Calligan for running out the last English batsman and winning the Test.

The crowd were waving and calling. Feet were stamping in grandstands. Others beat metal cups or plates with spoons. There was such a din that you couldn't hear any one thing through all the different callings and laughing and banging. As they neared the gate, a wave of 'Waltzing Matilda' washed out over them, and away.

Inside the change rooms Scully was dancing around excitedly and rushing backwards and forwards with bottles of beer. He'd run out to the card room and open another bottle with the bottle opener tied to the cupboard there, and then run back into the change room and hand it to another player.

'You bloody beauty,' yelled Maud.

Ten Ton grabbed Maud around the neck in a headlock and shook him, saying, 'Mopsey, you champion.'

'Yessss,' yelled Richardson at the top of his voice, as Tanner came out of the showers in just a towel, and started slapping his hairy chest with his open palms and howling like a dog left on its chain. Hall stopped not a foot from

Tanner's face and yelled at the top of his voice, 'Two Bob!' And Tanner yelled 'Ned,' like a sheep bleat. And they put their elbows down and ran into each other's shoulders, like rams, spilling beer everywhere.

'How sweet it is,' yelled Mr Johnson.

'Chalkie!' called Bardsley from where he was sitting with Jackson.

Tanner and Hall suddenly ran up to Mr Richardson and grabbed him under the shoulders.

'Oi, no,' said Richardson gruffly as they started to drag him towards the showers. 'I mean it, you two. Leave off.'

Beardsly and McLeod put their beers down and ran to help drag and push the fully clothed captain towards the showers. He struggled hard.

'I'm ya bloody captain. No.'

They got him in, and turned on the cold water, but he held both Hall and Bardsley, so they got soaked too.

Richardson stepped out of the showers, dripping. 'Ya bastards.'

'Ya bastard,' laughed Bardsley.

'You're a bastard, Legal,' laughed Hall, suddenly pointing at Calligan.

'An' you're a right bastard with the bat, Ned,' said Calligan.

Mr Baker screamed, 'We won!'

And men cheered, and Ten Ton up-ended his beer bottle so beer poured over Mr Baker's head.

Mr Jackson sat in the corner shaking his head, as Scully ran in with more bottles of beer.

'Plenty more where that came from,' he yelled, then turned to David. He looked horrified. 'David?' Then he got an idea and brightened. 'I'll get lemonade. I'll get you lemonade, boy.'

David nodded and smiled and called, 'And a pie? Can I have a pie, Mr Scully?'

'I'll break down the pie stall to get it,' declared Scully.

David smiled and turned. The room had gone quiet.

The men's faces were suddenly serious. Grim. David thought he'd seen a funny look, but wasn't sure. They were all looking at him where he sat with his hand in a bucket of ice.

Ten Ton said, 'Now what are we going to do about him, Skipper?'

'Yeah, driving me to the insane asylum, and he hasn't even got a decent nickname,' said Richardson, seriously, scratching his chin.

'Babe suits,' said Bardsley, also seriously.

'Naw, O'Toole'd love that too much,' said Jackson.

'Goliath,' said Mr Johnson.

'The Kid,' said Tanner.

'Like Billy the Kid?' said McLeod.

'Billy!'

'Wonder Kid.'

'Not going to call him Wonder Kid,' said Hall. 'That's poncy.'

'Besides,' said Bardsley, seriously, 'he's not like a kid. Not really.'

'No. No normal kid.'

'The Old Man,' said Baker. 'We should call 'im The Old Man. I'll just ask The Old Man where he wants his field set.'

There was laughter, which David didn't enjoy. Nor did he enjoy them talking about him as though he wasn't there.

Richardson said, 'We should call him Sweet Bloody

Thankful Manna From Heaven, that's what we should call him.'

They all looked at David again, some shaking their heads in the way people did.

Mr Jackson made a signal with his right hand, like he was drawing a cross in the air.

Things grew silent and fitful, and David looked down, but he could feel them examining him too closely.

Then Mr Johnson said, 'Bit of a mouthful mind, Skip. And this is our spinner here, Sweet Bloody Thankful Manna From Heaven.'

The men laughed again, and started singing and drinking and calling each other bastards some more. Mr Scully came back with a bottle of lemonade and two pies and David ate and watched, feeling good again now they'd forgotten about him. Until Mr Scully told him his uncle was waiting outside to drive him to Melbourne.

Melbourne was big. It was much bigger than Perth or Adelaide but only had a skinny little river. They drove in lots of traffic, Michael sounding his car horn and dodging the trams. They had to wait for trains to go by before driving into narrower streets where the houses were all joined together. There were laneways down the back, where David could sometimes see kids playing cricket with a metal dustbin as wickets.

Michael had parked the car in one of the little streets in a place he said was Fitzroy. He went through a short wire gate and up some steps at one of the houses that were joined together. There was no answer to his knocking.

'Maybe she's at work,' said Michael over-brightly when he came back to the car.

So they'd come to this hotel. They wanted Michael to pay in advance until he explained who David was. David had become The David Donald like Grandad was once The George Baker.

In the hotel room Michael had emptied his pockets onto the bed. There was money in all of them: notes in his jacket pockets, shirt, trousers. Twos and ones and fives and even ten pound notes. He let the money fall, like leaves, onto the bed.

'To think that until recently I was a communist,' he giggled. 'There's more in the bag. Still that was the run, probably. For those few days, I was the only one who knew that you are the greatest spin bowler the world will ever see. Now I've lost my edge. Maybe we both have.'

David had looked from the money to his uncle, looking for the joke of it. Perhaps there wasn't one. His uncle wasn't smiling. He was looking down at the money as though it were a broken vase. Finally David had said, 'Is it wrong? What you're doing?'

'Well, I hope so. A little bit of wrong, so at least there's the extra fun of the spit in your eye. Davey boy, you've just won a Test playing for Australia. It doesn't have to be all sackcloth and ashes. That's your grandad. A stony-hearted Scottish Calvinist to the last. All hard work and misery until we die and go to heaven.'

'Don't.' David would not let his uncle say bad things about his grandfather, even if it seemed to be nonsense.

'Right you are.'

'Can we send him some?' David said pointing to the money. 'Send him some for the farm.'

'Sure. We said we would didn't we? We'll cable some in the morning. Now, how about you take a second to enjoy it all?'

'But I do. Playing.'

'Hmm. Can we eat? Or is that too self-indulgent too?'

They sat in the restaurant of the hotel and all the people came, to prod and grab and gawk and say mean things to him. Once they were convinced he was David Donald, they'd focus on his hands.

'Cor blimey, did you see his fingers?'

'Make bloody good sausages, those.'

'Like a frangipani.'

David started to put his hands on his lap below the level of the table.

Michael drank their drinks and insulted them back on David's behalf. 'Yeah, well you get to the table pretty fast by the look of you, love.'

'Have you had a gander in the mirror lately?'

'What do you call those things, matey? Witchety grubs?'

The food was good. David steered away from the seafood, settling on steak. But he wasn't getting much eaten, as he'd have to stop when someone came up.

Some of the English team was staying in the same hotel, and they nodded to David. David explained, 'That was Proctor and Tudor. Proctor was the one who didn't nod hello.'

Bill Baker came up to the table too, on his way back in. 'Ah, ya made it, Old Man.' David was glad to see him.

'Mr Baker, this is my uncle, Michael.'

Michael stood, swaying a little, and put out his hand. 'Pleased to meet you, Mr Baker. How're the knees holding up?'

Baker shook his uncle's hand. 'As well as an old wicketkeeper can expect. Especially keeping up to a spin bowler.' Baker looked back to David, adding, 'You look after that hand, all right?' He shot a look at Michael.

'As I live and breathe—it's David Donald. Australian spin sensation.' The newspaperman, O'Toole, was coming towards their table.

'Leave it be, O'Toole,' said Mr Baker.

'How's that cheek, Mr Baker, healing all right then?' asked O'Toole, somehow making the question sound like an insult.

'Leave him alone.' Uncle Mike stood up again, using the table for support.

'Now then, Michael. You got your money's worth, and I've turned my opinion around, if you read the papers.'

'What, did I miss an apology?'

'Between the lines. Sure.'

'Ah, see, my mistake was reading the words, not the white part between.'

'Ha, that's a good one,' laughed Baker, looking at Michael differently.

'I'm sorry, David, for what I wrote. Look, can we start over?' O'Toole spread his arms wide, smiling around the table, before looking back to David again. 'You are the youngest player to play for Australia by a good four years. That is a record that will never be beaten.'

David noticed that O'Toole's hands had come closer together, as if he were holding some invisible thing out towards him.

'Not only that, but your bowling figures were outstanding ... on debut. Two for twenty-four, then five for thirty-two in the second innings!' O'Toole kept stepping forward as he spoke. 'How do you feel about that?'

'Can I have your autograph?' It was a man in a brown suit

and a wide tie with a griffin pattern.

'I dunno,' David said to O'Toole.

'You don't know?' said the man in brown.

'I can't, sir. My hand.'

'What's wrong with your hand?' O'Toole peered.

So did the man in the suit.

'Leave him alone,' said Michael.

'Nothin' wrong with his hand. Small bruise,' said Baker quickly.

'Just an autograph?' said the man. He was getting angry, like others who David couldn't sign for.

'That's enough questions, O'Toole,' said Michael.

'Look mate, he can't right now. Right?' said Baker to the man in brown.

'Too bloody good for me, eh?'

'I'm asking you,' warned Baker darkly.

'Is your grandad proud?' asked O'Toole leaning over the table at David.

'I dunno. He hasn't cabled.'

Michael grabbed O'Toole's shoulder, but O'Toole shrugged him off.

'You told me he trained you up for all this. And you don't know how he feels.'

Michael pushed O'Toole in the side of the face. O'Toole staggered, but turned. Michael swayed.

'Steady as she goes there lads,' said Mr Baker, one hand up towards them.

'You're getting personal, and I said no.'

'I haven't even begun, mate. What about the story of how you bet on his play? How about I dig into your freebies around Adelaide? What about the rumour concerning Ashleigh Hobbs' hurt hand?'

Michael swung to punch O'Toole but the newsman grabbed his arm and they both crashed down onto the table, smashing glasses and crockery.

A lady gave a little cry. A man yelled, 'Oi!'

Michael and O'Toole wrestled on the table for a moment longer, mashing food into their coats and spilling glass and cutlery to the floor.

David remained sitting. It was like he couldn't move or take his eyes off the men who finally rolled onto the floor, up-ending the table with them.

O'Toole managed to get on top, and from there headbutted Michael. Men ran in, grabbing O'Toole, then Michael. The brown-suited man was one. Bill Baker was another. Mashed potato and gravy were stuck to the back of O'Toole's jacket.

David saw Bartholomew Livingston, the chairman of selectors, and the ACB treasurer Steven Biggins over near the lifts, where they stood watching with dark faces.

'Wait til I'm sober,' yelled Michael. His head was bleeding.

'Wait til I care enough to really fight,' said O'Toole, blood coming from his nose.

Michael shrugged the men off, even though some were saying, 'Are you all right, sir?'

A man in a red jacket came forward, pointing at O'Toole. 'You are not a guest. Out!'

'I'm getting out, ya pack of hyenas,' said Michael. He turned and lurched between tables towards the front doors of the hotel and out onto Spencer Street.

O'Toole was straightening his clothes. 'Gentlemen, please. I simply asked a few innocent questions. I was attacked. We have a right to know.'

David didn't stay. He ran around the broken things, and out-of-focus shapes of people to get outside so he could find his uncle.

Uncle Mike was already down the street, pushing past a group waiting to cross to the train station. When Michael went into a pub David stopped and looked back to their hotel. He considered whether he should wait in their room. To do that he would have to pass Mr Baker and Mr Livingston and Mr Biggins. Mr O'Toole was there too. All would need to be dealt with in some way he guessed. Some kind of trouble had been created, and David didn't know what to say about that. Back in Dungarin, when a man got out of line and was warned to stop, if he didn't the other fellow would give him a clip. Depending on the men, that might be the end of it, or there might be a fight. It wasn't pleasant, but what Uncle Mike had done seemed all fair and square as far as David could see. In fact, now he thought on it, O'Toole's trick of headbutting the pinned man seemed the thing that wasn't right. David felt certain that this matter wasn't over with, and the men would want to do something about Michael and maybe about David. He'd also have to pass through the strangers too. All the faces that knew he was the cricketing boy, and been part of the trouble. Maybe he could sneak around the back. He wasn't sure whether these big city hotels had backs. They seemed to be all front.

Out here, on Spencer Street, they didn't know him. A man held his hat down, grabbed the hand of a lady and they set out across the road to a tram that had stopped. Others went there too, the motor cars stopping to let them go. David was just a boy without a coat, standing in the street.

Uncle Mike was coming out of the pub with a bottle of brandy. David went to him. The wound on his forehead had been cleaned up a little. The blood had stopped flowing.

'Gidday, Uncle Mike.'

'What are you doing here?'

'I came after you.'

Michael seemed to consider that for a moment, weighing up its worth. Then he shrugged and said, 'Bloody O'Toole. He got me a beauty.'

'Is he going to make trouble?'

'I expect. It's his nature and his occupation.' His uncle took a swig from the brandy. 'But what are we going to do about that? What can we do? They all own you now.'

Michael started walking away from their hotel, but with a purposeful stride.

David caught up. 'Where are we going?'

'See Helen.'

'Who's Helen?'

'Helen.' He smiled, then looked sad, then smiled again. 'We went there. When we got here.'

'She wasn't home.'

'At work. At the hospital. She's a nurse.'

David nodded. 'Maybe she can fix your head.'

Michael started laughing without humour. Finally he said, 'Naw. She already tried.'

David looked up and realised he couldn't see any stars, even though it was night. There was a kind of mist up there. He sniffed the gritty smell of petrol and wood and coal and gas and whatever they burned all day in the city. David missed the farm sky.

Michael stopped at every street intersection to take another swallow of brandy. He had been through happy to merry to rude and angry already in the restaurant, and

David was not keen to see him return to the half-sleep he'd seen on the train from Perth. Apart from anything else David didn't think it would help them find their way to the nurse's house. He thought he might distract him a little as he did on the train trip with questions he would like the answers to.

'Do you like cricket, Uncle Mike?'

'What? What you think? Course I do. Stupid bloody question.'

'What do you like about cricket?'

'It's a sublime game from another era. A game that lasts days and days. That men dedicate their lives to. I like it because of its tricks. Its lies and its contradictions. That it seems so slow, but can change in an instant. I love all the games within the game. The little stories within the grander one.'

Michael led David along the city street, waving his brandy bottle as he spoke.

'A batsman nearly nicks the ball. Next delivery he just keeps it out. He looks terrible. He's having a bad day. That cricket ball seems the size of a pea. It's coming at him so fast, he's only seeing it as it's on him. He adjusts. He tries to move his feet. Survives the next delivery. He gets his head down. Tries to grit it out and last just one more ball. And the other team see that. A player moved here. Another there. Crowding in. But wait, what if he lashes out in desperation? Another player there. Let's not let him get off strike. Let's keep the pressure on, till it builds up inside his own head, and that pea gets smaller and smaller, faster and faster.'

Michael swayed as he talked, sometimes stopping to play an imaginary shot with his brandy bottle or to point in the field. The shops they walked past now were long closed. A tram buzzed and clacked, empty but for the driver.

'But then maybe this fellow, he lasts a few balls. Gets up the other end. Faces another bowler who isn't bowling so fast, so well. The pea starts looking like a cricket ball, and he gets a couple of runs off. Just a couple. He's patient. So is the fielding team. And the crowd. They know. They're watching to see each tiny little manoeuvre. They know this story, how it might go. How they hope it might. But still at any moment it can change again. He sees the ball like a pumpkin and hits it to the boundary. What! The fieldsman has run. He dives full length. A catch, just inside the boundary. It's over. Ha.'

'Ha,' repeated David in a kind of wonder of recognition, his head reeling from the way his uncle could make him see with all his words.

They had left the brightly lit parts of the city and were walking past business. Lots of the businesses had posters covering their windows. As they went, more of the buildings seemed empty.

'Oh, and I like its fairness. Its justness. Its hypocrisy. Its unassailable good name.'

David stepped away. Something ugly had slipped into his uncle's tone. He thought he could hear voices somewhere. A crowd, like near a cricket ground. It was late and dark here and he couldn't see anyone.

'I bet ya didn't know that cricket became the national sport of England by the end of the eighteenth century. And guess what? Betting was part of it. Rich bastards began forming their own "select elevens." In 1707 ... um. Something happened in 1707. Forget that. How about this one? You ever hear about the Sydney riot of 1879? I bet your grandad never told you about that. Moore Park, Sydney.

English team versus NSW. Crowd invaded the ground, after a dodgy umpiring decision. Beat up the players. Now don't tell me they didn't care.'

His uncle was standing under a gas lamp, half reaching towards the post, but not quite holding it. 'Mind you, rumour has it that the invasion of the pitch was a put-up job by gamblers in the pavilion. See, now you know that. I never knew that, when I was young and believed in—all the pip-pip, rah-rah bulldust.'

Just when David thought his uncle might smash the bottle to the ground in disgust at all the cheating, he drank, then used the bottle to point at David. 'But there's rules in cricket, and two men who uphold them. As do both teams. A whole series of self-regulating interlocked layers of fairness and appreciation.' He started to come across the deserted road. 'Like some perfect centre of a cyclone, where it's calm. I like that too, David Donald, son of Earnest. There's something about cricket and the whole idea of cricket that I find peaceful. Maybe even good. It's like some fairy story really, isn't it? Just so smashing and wonderful—and impossible.'

'Why are you so angry, Uncle Mike?' David hadn't really planned to ask. It simply popped out.

'Angry?' His uncle shook his head a moment as though he'd received a punch. He blinked then smiled. 'I'm not angry. I'm deliriously happy.' The smile turned mean. 'Maybe I'm trying to teach you something, boy. Something about cricket and the great world. Maybe you remind me too much of a stupid, happy cow chewing grass unaware of the approaching butcher's wagon. Maybe I'm trying to drip some worldy sense into you.'

'I haven't done anything wrong,' said David. He turned

and walked down a side street, towards a lighter area down the end, where the voices were coming from.

It was not his fault that he didn't know things. It didn't make him stupid, even though others thought that. He knew it didn't make him happy. That was not something it occurred to him to be. Or not be. But he was not a stupid cow. David stopped. He had the urge to go back up the street where his uncle was following and to hit him. It was an urge so sudden and so strong it made him pant. Then he remembered O'Toole headbutting his uncle and he smiled.

He heard the sound of a bat hitting a cricket ball.

He went away from his uncle and towards the sound.

At the end of the street men were playing cricket.

There were some bright lights, up high, behind a fence. There were ships back there. Some policemen stood the other side of a fence, with a fire in a drum. But in front of David were men with dark eyes and unshaven faces. There were big men with big shoulders. Italian-looking men. There were skinny men too. Some stood around big drums of fire, warming their hands, even though the night was not so cold.

But in the street, there were more men, and they were gathered round a man with a bat, using a fire drum for a wicket, while someone bowled a battered ball. The man hit the ball and it spun through legs as he ran. There was a groan shared by some. And men grabbed for the ball. Someone threw. They missed the drum. Another groan.

Michael came up behind him. 'Ah. Workers of the world, unite.'

'They're playing tip and run. In the middle of the road. In the middle of the night.'

'They're locked out of the docks.'

Michael pointed, and David saw the chains across the gates. Noticed that one of the policemen held a rifle.

Michael raised his voice as he spoke across the road, like he was a teacher reading to a class. 'And the fire of war shall not keep a man warm. The fires of war are cold, and leave all the men just so.'

Some of the men turned from where they were standing.

'Time for a bit of revolution, I reckon.' Michael raised his voice again, so other men began to turn towards them, standing across the street. 'Here's one, from a fellow named Lenin: "The Soviet of Workers' Deputies is an organisation of the workers."'

At the word 'workers,' a couple of men cheered in a tired kind of way, but this turned more men from watching the cricket game.

Michael called out, '"The embryo of a workers' government —"'

'Up the workers,' someone called back. More shouts.

Michael took his turn. '"The representative of the interests of the entire mass of the poor section of the population —"'

'Hear, hear.' Men were nodding, edging towards them. The cricket game had stopped.

'"I.e. of nine-tenths of the population, which is striving for peace —"'

'Yeah.'

'"Bread —"'

Big calls.

'"And freedom."'

The men applauded. Nodding to each other. They began to mutter. The police behind the gate were talking. One of the workers there was talking urgently to them.

A big man came up to Michael. 'Leave it out, sunshine.'

'Not interested in the poor?' called Michael, so everyone could hear.

'I am the bloody poor, mate, an' I don't need some tosser with a plum in his mouth making trouble.' The man then raised his voice too and spoke to everyone. 'These men just want jobs, not trouble. They're hungry and so are their kids. So put a cork in it, or I'll thump you.' The big man came to within a couple of yards of Michael, who looked at him and smiled.

David knew his uncle wanted to be hit. And even though a moment ago he himself had wanted to hit him, he didn't want it now. 'No. Uncle Mike. Don't.'

His uncle blinked. Then straightened. It was like a switch on an electric light. Click and he was different. He laughed and looked at the big man. 'A laugh. No harm mate.' He turned again to the men, who were still watching. 'Ladies and gentlemen. May I present, currently bowling for the Australian Cricket Team, Master David Donald.' He laid out his hand to indicate David.

'Pull the other one.'

'Thump him, Muzza.'

'He's just a drunk.'

They grumbled and swore, and started to turn away again.

The big man, Muzza, turned back to look at Michael, trying to guess his game now.

'It bloody is,' said a tiny man, stepping forward holding out a newspaper. 'Here's 'is photo. It's The Kid.'

Everything got noisy again as the men looked at David and talked amongst themselves rapidly.

'Well, what's 'e doin' up at this hour?' asked an older man, suddenly. 'It's nearly midnight.'

'And no coat. Get round this fire, son.'

'Ladies and germs,' said Michael, arms raised in surrender. 'This is part of our royal tour.' Michael reached into his pocket and brought out a pound note. 'Here's my plan. Cos Davey doesn't want me angry. An' to prove I'm not. The great David Donald bowls to ya. If you hit him, you get a pound.'

The men suddenly went quiet. Some licked their lips. Most had eyes on the pound.

Michael went serious. 'No laughing matter, I know. Here's more of my plan. We don't leave here until every last one of you has won his pound. Fair enough, Muzza?'

There was a cheer. Muzza was still doubtful.

David whispered, 'But what if they don't hit it?'

'Then it'll be a long night.'

'But I don't bowl like that. I bowl my best or not at all.'

'Then it'll be a very long night.'

'No.'

Michael bent down to him. 'David, they'll take the pound, and I've got plenty, and they'll give it to their wives and mothers and it'll be gone. But that one night they batted to you, they'll have all their lives. They'll bore their grandchildren witless. That's your gift.'

'I'll bat first,' said the little man, who'd found the newspaper photo.

There were cheers.

David looked at the men. Some seemed happy. Others still looked wary, but hopeful, like a dog looking for a pat. But their voices were lighter. Their shoulders seemed higher. Even the police, the other side of the fence, were craning forward, smiling.

Michael said, 'Do it.'

David wondered what his grandfather would say in this situation. He was fairly certain he would tell him not to bowl; to save the hand. 'My hand is not so good,' he said.

'Then it'll be a short and happy night,' said Michael, going to stand by one of the fires. He took a swig of his brandy, then handed the bottle round.

'I told you he was hurt on that last day,' said someone, low.

One of the big men came to David with their ball. 'Here ya go, lad.' David took it. 'Don't bowl too good, will ya.'

'How's that Proctor then?'

David didn't see who asked. 'He's pretty ferocious,' said David, and the men started to laugh.

'Ferocious. That's a good un.'

David went up the other end and held the ball. His fingers were cold. Numb. The little man held the battered bat, his eyes alive. 'I reckon I coulda played for Australia.'

There were guffaws.

'A pound to every man who can hit him,' yelled Michael.

'That's more than the Poms can do,' yelled Muzza, finally a believer.

'Hey, there's over forty men here!' called someone at the back.

'Got ya covered,' called Michael.

The men laughed.

David bowled. It was a long hop, with no spin at all. The little man let fly and missed it.

The men laughed more.

'My missus coulda hit that.'

David rubbed his fingers. Looked at his swollen hand. He probably couldn't bowl well, even if he wanted to.

'I don't know whether he can bowl easier than that,

mind,' called Michael, happy now.

'Here ya go, David,' said a Greek-looking man, with a big bushy moustache, and a slight accent. 'Good on ya, son.' The man reached up and squeezed David's ear. It was probably gentle, but it stung a bit in the cold. The man's eyes were weeping slightly, but he had a huge smile.

David bowled a medium-fast full toss and the little man hit the ball way back over the men and up the street. They roared with a cheer. There was clapping, as the little man jogged down the other end with the bat under his arm, like Windsor after he'd scored a hundred. Three men were racing up the street after the ball, bumping each other until they tripped and fell into a tangled heap.

Men were doubled over with laughter. A man clapped another on the back, because he sounded like he was choking.

'Well bowled,' yelled Michael.

'Yeah, well bowled,' went a chorus.

The little man shook David's left hand, gently. 'God bless, son.' Then he went over to Michael and got his pound and held it up. Another cheer.

A man with a wild beard and a Collingwood football beanie grabbed the bat from the little man. 'An' the next drop is Jim Williams. Lot a form this fellow.'

'Yeah, but not form with the bat.'

The men cheered this man in too. 'Onya Jimmy.'

Someone gave David the ball. Patted him on the back. He was feeling warm now. His hand didn't even hurt.

'An' coming in to bowl, to the great Jim Williams, is the Aussie demon, David Donald,' said the man with the bat, doing his own radio commentary, just like David always did. 'The bowler looks a bit worried here. He's heard of

Williams, standing on ninety-nine not out.'

David stood a moment, listening to the man talk about him as though he was famous. Jim Williams smiled, his bat raised and ready. Then David bowled, as badly as he knew how.

CHAPTER FIFTEEN

As the police paddy wagon pulled to a halt, a light came from the driver's cabin and lit up the prisoner's part for a moment. David looked across to his uncle who swayed on a bench, his face bruised from where O'Toole had headbutted him during dinner. He looked down at his bowling hand. It was swole up like a lump of lamb. The lock clicked on the back door of the van and it swung back to reveal two grinning policemen.

One of them clapped David on the shoulder as he climbed out. 'Thanks gents,' said Michael as he came down to the road. 'Look after that hand, David,' said the other policeman, and he winked before they both climbed back into the front of their van and drove off. It was dark, except at the far end of the street, where David could see a lantern, barely illuminating a milk cart. A dog barked, which started some more.

Michael felt his way up to a gate and along a small path to the front door of a semidetached house. He knocked.

Muzza and the police had got together to organise a ride to Helen's house. The police had eventually come out from behind their gate and had a bat themselves, which, after some nasty jokes, the dock workers had let them do, so long as they didn't get one of Uncle Mike's pound notes. They didn't seem to mind, so long as they had the chance to hit David for six. David had never bowled so badly as he did that night, nor to greater acclaim.

A light came on in a window, then in the hall, behind the door. 'Who is it?' It was a lady and she didn't sound too happy.

'Michael.'

The door opened, and the lady stood in her dressing gown with her hair all messed.

'Just passing by, and I thought I saw your light on.'

She stepped out and hugged him, with her head on his chest and her arms around him. Michael stood in the hug, with his hat knocked crooked, smiling. She pushed him back, holding both his arms and looked him up and down, as if for dirt. 'You've been in a fight.' She turned to look at David before Michael could answer. 'Hello.'

'David, this is Helen.'

'Hello, David. Pleased to meet you.'

She was smiling, but at the same time studying him through the smile.

'Hello, missus.'

'You can call me Helen.'

'You're too old. It'd be rude.'

'Hmm. Yes, wouldn't want to be rude. Well, call me Mrs O'Locklan.'

'Cos that's her name,' said Michael.

Mrs O'Locklan turned and went inside.

'Come on,' said Michael, 'it's bloody freezing out here.'

David and Michael followed Mrs O'Locklan up the passage. It had a worn runner going all the way down. David thought that she was not a floozy. She seemed too old and not beautiful enough. Her bottom was big and her dressing gown was plain and thick.

In the kitchen Mrs O'Locklan lit the stove.

Michael fiddled with a sugar jar on the kitchen table. 'You're out of sugar?'

'Must have run out.'

'I'll pick you up some tomorrow if you like.'

Mrs O'Locklan didn't say anything, but stopped lighting the fire for a moment. Finally she said, 'Very well.'

Michael went over to the fire. 'I'll get that.'

David watched as Michael moved to the fire, and Mrs O'Locklan moved away, and around the table, not looking at each other, but not bumping into each other either, like they were watching each other but only out of their elbows and shoulders.

'There's half a loaf in the bread box, and some fig preserve, if you men are hungry.'

Michael turned to David and winked.

David didn't know what the wink meant.

'Not hungry?' Mrs O'Locklan was looking at him too.

'He's always hungry.'

'Yes, please.'

Mrs O'Locklan went to the breadbox and unwrapped some bread.

'That cupboard there, David. Will you get the preserve?'

David went to a row of cupboards and found the jar of fig. It smelt strong and sweet as though it were not far from going off, which was just how David liked it. He brought it to her, and put it next to the breadboard, where she was cutting big slices of bread.

'Thank you.' Then she grabbed his hand. 'What have you done?'

'I hurt it on the train. And I keep hurting it again.'

'Tendon?'

'Ligament, Mr Scully said. Maybe.'

She held David's hand, with four fingers under it and her thumb resting in the middle of his palm. Her fingers were soft, but her grip was strong. She didn't smell of tobacco or sweat. She smelled of powder and old soap. David looked up at her face, just for a moment, but she was looking down at his hand. She turned it over and looked some more, then turned it back.

'Long fingers.' She said it matter of fact with no teasing in it.

'Like Grandad.'

'I'll take a look at it in the morning.'

Michael said, 'Helen's a nurse.'

David looked over to see his uncle at the table, rolling a cigarette. David realised that he'd forgotten he was there, and moved to sit at the table too.

'How did you hurt your hand?' asked Mrs O'Locklan.

'There was a crash. In the Nullarbor desert, there was a train crash. There was cattle, and ... some dynamite blew up ... and ...' David remembered his uncle in the desert and how he got sick, and thought better of telling any more about that night. 'But then it got better, a bit, when we got to Adelaide, so I pretended it was okay. To beat the Poms. In the Test match. That's two to one now, but I reckon we'll beat them in the next one. Here, in Melbourne. They played in Brisbane at the Exhibition Ground, then here in Melbourne and then in Adelaide. Now it's back in Melbourne and then the last one will be in Sydney.'

'What a motor mouth,' said Michael, teasing. 'Must be the promise of fig jam.'

Mrs O'Locklan brought the big piece of bread with fig

jam and put it in front of him. She turned to Michael. 'So a giant cricket-watching trip around Australia.'

'I'm watching. He's playing.'

David watched his uncle's eyes twinkle. He was playing with her and waiting for her to catch on, so he could see her surprise.

She saw that, but she didn't smile. 'And so you're in Melbourne. Lucky me.'

'Don't be like that, Hellie.'

She looked sad for a moment, and somewhere else, then got the tea and started to put it in the teapot.

'How long?'

She wasn't watching Michael but he was watching her.

'It's a week before the next Test, then the week of the Test I guess.'

She went to the kettle and brought it back to the teapot. David thought she seemed angry.

'I was wondering if we could stay here.'

David turned to his uncle. They had a hotel.

'Is that all right with you, Hellie?'

'Of course it's all right with me. Love to have you. Both. We can try to sort out David's finger and fatten him up a bit.'

'A bit of stability'd be good.'

'For you or him?'

Michael looked at her, sharpish, then yelped like a dog and suddenly fell off his chair. He just let himself fall sideways and bang to the floor. David stood to see if his uncle was all right. He lay on the floor with his eyes open and a crooked smile on his face.

'For Lord sakes, woman, not the nagging. I just got home from pit and you're naggin' me noggin all o'er the town.'

David wondered about his uncle's ability to be very drunk, then very sober, all by turns. It seemed like a talent. Sometimes David didn't know which one was pretend and which one real.

'Have you got any money?' She asked it gently, maybe too gently, which made David wonder again about all kinds of things they weren't saying, or were hiding in the things they were saying.

Michael got up from the floor. 'Lots and lots and lots.' He started pulling money out of his pockets and dropping it onto the kitchen table, just like he had in the hotel room. There were twenty pound notes and tens and fives.

David said, 'But no pound notes. They all went to the men down at the wharves.'

'What have you done?' She looked down at the money as though it were some strange animal with sharp teeth.

'There's some in my bags too, but they're at the hotel.' He started giggling, all drunk again. 'Look at all this stupid moolah.'

'Michael, what have you been doing?'

'Making money in the only way an honest man can in these straitened times, my dear. Betting on a sure thing. David is the greatest spin bowler the world has ever seen, and until now, I was the only person who knew it.'

'Talk sense.'

'Am. David Donald and I are boring it up 'em, in our own ways, and life is grand, and behold, the ripe fruit falls for the righteous to gather. And no toiling for lilies or swallows this week.'

'What's he saying, David?'

'I got O'Malley out with my first ball to him, and Uncle Mike bet I would and then I got five English batsmen out in the second innings, and Uncle Mike made some bets that I'd do that too.' David looked to his uncle to see if he'd got it right.

Michael nodded seriously. 'And at appropriately ridiculously prodigiously long odds too.'

She looked back at Michael, but shook her head in mild annoyance, before looking to David again. 'You are actually playing cricket for Australia?'

'Yes, Mrs O'Locklan.'

'Tell me it's not too crazy not to be true,' said his uncle.

Mrs O'Locklan looked back to all the money doubtfully, then pointed at David. 'Sleep.'

She led him to the sleep-out on the back veranda. There was a bed there already made up. 'My dad's,' she said, 'but he's dead.'

'Mine too,' said David. He looked up and caught her thinking, about him, he was sure. He looked away.

'Goodnight David.'

David woke late. He sat up suddenly, worried about how angry his grandad would be, and then blinked at the strange room. He saw his grandad sitting at the kitchen table in Dungarin, ready to eat tea. He was looking up, the way he did, as he waited for David to come in from his last chore. David watched his grandad's look, as he came through the door, and he realised that that look was as close to contentment as his grandfather ever got.

He lay back on the bed with an ache around his heart. He cried, silently at first, just letting the tears bleed out. There was no one here to stop him, so he let them keep coming cold down his cheeks, while he looked at his grandad watching him practise his bowling. He heard his grandad's voice say, 'Give it some air.' Then David saw his grandad not say goodbye, and send him from the farm, and David heard an awful cry, a wounded howl from somewhere in the house. He sat up and listened, but couldn't hear anything except his own panting. There was no one here, except him, he was sure.

He got out of bed and looked out through the louvres. He hurried down the steps into the tiny cement yard to the outhouse by the back gate. He sat on the toilet, feeling its walls. He felt a bit shaky, like when a horse gets away a bit, and gallops too fast, before being reined in. He took some deep breaths, comforted somehow by his own smell. He could hear flies starting to come. He looked to a hook on the wall, where there were apple papers. He smiled again. As everyone knew, apple papers were soft on the backside. 'That's a bit of luck,' said David.

David washed his hands in the laundry and went into the kitchen. It was clean and empty. David went into the hall. There was a bedroom with a big mirror, and on the dressing table there were brushes and lipsticks and powders. There was a little shiny box of dark wood with shiny brass hasps. He sneezed, then sneezed again. There were some flowers in a vase, but the smells were perfume. A cushion on the bed was embroidered with a picture in green and red stitching. David stepped closer to see that it was a lady under a tree, embroidering a cushion of a lady under a tree.

There were long thick curtains that were open, then lace ones under that let the light come in. David could see the window of another house only a few feet from this one. The houses must be nearly touching, but not quite. David went closer to the window, to see inside the other house, but the blinds there were pulled down.

On the wall by the door, there was a painting of a boy, holding up an apple to a white horse. It was in a forest with yellow light and dark trees. The boy was wearing blue shiny clothes with a bow round his neck from times past. It looked like the horse was sniffing the apple, or maybe just looking to see what it was.

'You've found my picture.'

Mrs O'Locklan was at the door, full string bags pulling her arms straight down.

'No one was here.'

'Your uncle has gone to see the cricket people to explain why you can't go to training.'

'I have to go to training.'

'Not till your hand is better, you won't.'

David looked at her, a little angry, but she stared back, neither harshly nor worried, just looking. David looked away from her. He'd see Michael. No point trying to reason with a woman.

'Nice isn't it? Do you think the boy is frightened and trying to be brave even though he's feeling a little afraid?'

David realised that she thought he'd been looking at the picture again.

'No. It's just a horse. It'll eat the apple. Horses love apples.'

'Then he'll ride him through the forest.'

David looked at her. He tried to be patient. 'No. It isn't his. Be mad to try to climb on a strange horse. Get yourself killed.'

'Ah, you must be from a farm.'

'Yes. Dungarin. My grandad an' me.'

'You'll have to tell me about it, once we're settled.' She left the room, calling back, 'Help me put this shopping away, then I'll start fixing your hand.'

When David reached the kitchen, Mrs O'Locklan was already pulling things out of the bags to put on the table.

'Do you like spaghetti?'

'I don't know.'

'Soon find out. How about lamb chops?'

'Yes.'

There were peas and potatoes and butter, wrapped in greaseproof paper.

David said, 'Where's your husband?'

'He died.'

'In the war?'

'Yes. Did Michael tell you?'

'No. Is this his house?'

'No, this is my family house. When my mother died, it was left to me.'

'Why aren't you at work?'

'I've taken my holidays.'

'To be with Uncle Mike.'

'And to help get your hand better.'

She had stopped unpacking and was looking at David. She didn't seem embarrassed. Nor impatient. She was just looking with a mild smile, waiting.

David wasn't sure whether he liked her or not.

She went back to her things on the table, taking a jar out of the bag. It had a chemist's label. 'This is to rub in your hand.' Then she took out a toothbrush. 'Here, go and use this now, before you grow potatoes in your mouth.'

David looked at the toothbrush.

'Go on. Freddy Feenie will be here with his motorbike soon.'

The toothbrush made David's gums bleed, and the

ointment, which she came out to rub into his hand and finger, stank like compost. They stood on the back veranda as Mrs O'Locklan worked the ointment into David's hand. Her fingers were strong, and worked the sore parts as expertly as Mr Scully.

Her face had flecks of red little veins all over, and her neck had lots of little wrinkles as though it had once been bigger, but was drying up now. Her breasts were hidden under her dress, but big and seemed to be breathing, each on their own, like sleeping animals. David looked away, out at the tiny yard again. The back fence was a solid wall of wooden pickets, with a gate in the middle. There was a lane, then more houses, every two joined together, all the same, as far as he could see.

'That's the neighbourhood,' she said.

'It's all squashed in.'

'Yes, nice and snug.'

An arm came over the top of the gate, and pushed the latch. The gate was pushed open and a little man with a huge moustache looked up at them on the veranda. He jumped on the spot, then waved, then did a kind of dance as he turned around and went out again, to come back moments later, pushing a motorbike.

'That's Mr Feenie. He's going to help fix your hand.'

Freddy Feenie looked up at them, and raised a hand as though they should watch. He jumped on the bike, and cranked it to life by jumping on a lever. It growled, coughed then rumbled. He nodded to them smiling. He raised his hand again: now watch. Then he pushed down a stand, and with another leap, pulled the bike back up on the stand. He jumped off the bike, and David thought he might bow. But he smiled, and waved his hand at the bike, as though he'd just made it appear out of nothing.

Mrs O'Locklan led David down to the grumbling motorbike. Freddy nodded and smiled. He nodded a lot. Mrs O'Locklan grabbed David's hand and put it on the back mudguard of the motorbike. It was shaking terribly and David tried to bring his hand away, but Mrs O'Locklan made him keep it there. She shouted, 'The shaking will make your finger heal faster.'

David looked at his hand on the bike mudguard, and finally crouched so his back wasn't all twisted. He looked at Mr Feenie, who stood next to the handlebars revving the motor occasionally. He nodded eagerly again to David, who nodded and smiled back.

David spent the afternoon with his hand variously on the mudguard, the seat and the petrol tank. Occasionally a neighbour or passer-by would put their head in through the back gate or over the side fence and have a look for a minute or so, then go away again. The fumes from the bike made David a little sleepy, but his hand was already feeling better, even if Freddy Feenie wouldn't stop looking at him and nodding each time David looked back.

At dinner time Mrs O'Locklan came out and gave Mr Feenie some money. 'For petrol,' she yelled.

He got on the bike and moved it back and forward so it was pointing towards the back gate.

'Again tomorrow?' yelled Mrs O'Locklan.

David yelled, 'Thank you, Mr Feenie.'

He nodded and nodded some more and smiled. David was relieved when the bike finally left. His ears were shaking as much as his hand.

'Can he talk?'

'Oh yeah. The leg off a chair. Did he bend your ear about

the cricket?'

'No. He never said a word.'

She shrugged. David could smell food. There was a big pot on the stove of tomato and meat and another of spaghetti. There was bread, cut thick with butter on it already.

Mrs O'Locklan made him put his hand in a bowl of warm, nasty smelling goop while she dished out their tea. David looked into the bowl and thought he could see bits of seaweed and stones amidst the greasy cream.

'Secret recipe from a Chinese man at the markets.'

Mrs O'Locklan put a bowl of spaghetti with the sauce on in front of David. She cut some funny smelling cheese onto the top.

'You'll have to eat it left-handed, unless you want me to shovel it in?'

David did the shovelling himself, but found it difficult. Large drips of the delicious sauce kept dribbling down. He looked up anxious, but Mrs O'Locklan laughed, as she sucked up a piece of spaghetti making it look like a snake going into a wood pile.

'Where's Uncle Mike?'

'Not here,' she said with a shrug.

David was trying to decide whether he should say something that was nice, like that Uncle Mike was probably on his way, or whether he should tell her the truth, like that he thought Uncle Mike was probably in a pub, which meant he wouldn't be here any time soon. Only Mrs O'Locklan spoke first.

'You don't get a cow, then complain about the milk.'

'Why would you,' said David. 'That's why you get a cow.'

'Hmm. Maybe not a good figure of speech. But what if you think you've bought a cow, but you find it's something else, when you get it home?'

'What? It'd be a cow. You mean like a barren one or a crook one?'

'Let's forget the cow. What I was trying to say is that ... I never met your uncle before ... the hospital, but by all accounts he was a different man. Anyhow, the one I met, all and all, is who he is.'

She took a drink of her sherry. David noticed the glass there for the first time. It was a tumbler rather than the tiny stemmed kind David had seen at the hotel dining room.

'You met Uncle Mike in the hospital?'

'During the war.'

'When your husband died?'

'Around then.'

'When he hurt his foot?'

'Yes.'

'Did you know my father?'

Mrs O'Locklan started coughing. She'd been sipping on the sherry, and was choking on some that had gone down the wrong way. David was about to try to go to slap her on the back but had his hand in the bowl, and by the time he'd looked from the bowl back to her, she seemed all right again.

'You need to wipe your mouth and chin, and possibly your neck, chest and stomach. I'm not sure you got much spaghetti sauce inside you.'

David took his napkin and wiped.

Mrs O'Locklan got up and put her plate in the sink. 'Would you like to go into the parlour and read a book or listen to the radiogram?'

Mrs O'Locklan held the bowl while David concentrated on keeping his hand in it, as she led him up the hall to the parlour at the front of the house. There was a lounge chair and a bookcase full of books, but no piano. Mrs O'Locklan put the bowl on a table next to the lounge, and David followed it.

She turned on the wireless, which was playing songs. 'I'll get us some cake after I finish the dishes.'

David started to listen to the song, but soon thought about Nell. It was still summer holidays, so she'd be up late. It'd be light and too hot to go to bed anyway. David saw Nell and himself outside her dad's smithy. They watched moths in the light coming out of the open workshop, while Mr Parker hammered and swore inside. There was a rhythm to the hammering, and to the swearing. The cars made Nell's dad angry in a way that horses never did. But as Nell explained, with great seriousness, the more he hated the cars, the more needed fixing and the more money people paid him. 'I never used to have skinned knuckles before automobiles.' David remembered the night he and Nell were sitting outside when Mr Parker hit his knuckles and swore the longest sentence of swearing ever, and Nell giggled, and David sat listening to Nell giggle and Mr Parker swearing like it was music on the wireless.

After one of the songs there was a news bulletin. Mrs O'Locklan came in with some fruitcake, and sipped her sherry while she listened to the news with David.

The drought was breaking a record for going so long. The men without jobs had big numbers too, all over the world. A big factory in Melbourne was closing, and the men down on the wharves were having a protest about the police. David was about to tell Mrs O'Locklan that he knew the wharf men and the police, when the man on the wireless talked about the cricket.

'The Australian and English teams arrived back in Melbourne yesterday, after Australia won the third Test in Adelaide. The English captain played down the future impact of child bowling prodigy, David Donald. Henry Longford: "It was a surprise. No doubt. However, one is rarely surprised in the same way twice, it being of the nature of surprise, not to be expecting it."' There was muffled laughter coming from the wireless, which must have been the people listening to Mr Longford standing at a microphone somewhere. '"Seriously though, we will be treating young Donald with respect in the next Test, but also as an adult."'

The newsman spoke again. 'John Richardson, Australian captain: "He's a very gifted bowler. We don't have an age bar in the Australian team. He's in, and I'm hearing that as many people have enjoyed seeing him as are complaining. Mind you, I know the English players aren't very supportive."' There was laughter, but Richardson spoke over it. '"Let's not forget, our victory was a team effort and we will have to play just as well to match the English team in the fourth Test."'

It was like the commenting and descriptions he did in his head, but just in a different voice. David looked at his hand in the bowl. It had gone down quite a lot, but was still sore. He wiggled his fingers in the witch's brew in the bowl. There was an orchestra playing on the radio now and David wondered if he'd heard the radio report or whether he'd just dreamed of hearing it. He turned and there was Mrs O'Locklan in her chair looking at him.

'Bloody hell, eh,' she said.

It made David giggle.

Mrs O'Locklan made him wash the goop off his hand and

brush his teeth again before bed.

'Do you want a story?' she asked after he was in bed.

'A story?'

'A story in bed, or would you rather read?'

'No ma'am. I'm in bed. I'm gunna sleep.'

'Oh,' she said, rather sadly. 'I always had a story before bed when I was little. I still have some of those books.'

'I'm not little,' said David, angry with her again. He turned over in the bed, away from her. She could make him feel good then bad by equal turns. She made him do things instead of letting him be. And she hadn't answered about his father. They'd been interrupted. David thought he'd ask her about his dad again. But when he turned back to say, she'd gone.

David woke in the night. There was music and light coming out from the house. When he got up, he saw his bags by the bed. There were boxes of food and bottles of grog on the kitchen table. The music was coming from the parlour. Flapper music. Shadows rippled on the wall in the hall. He went to the door, and there were Uncle Mike and Mrs O'Locklan, hugging and swaying to the music. Although the music was lively, their swaying was slow, her head resting on Uncle Mike's chest. His uncle had his eyes closed as he swayed, like he was asleep. He looked happy.

In the morning David got the fire going in the kitchen and boiled the kettle. He ate his breakfast then put away the shopping, but decided not to clean up the parlour. The lamp had been knocked over and lay with the box and paper from the new gramophone. There were empty beer bottles and glasses and records out of their covers. It seemed like a lot of mess for two people to have made.

When Mrs O'Locklan got up, her face was puffy, her

make-up smeared. Her hair was bunched up at the back, like a mass of weed but she seemed very happy as she busied herself making a pot of tea.

'Where's my uncle?'

'Having a lie in.'

'When will I go to training?'

'When your hand is better.'

'It's better now.'

She came and sat on the chair near David and took up his hand. Her eyes were red and the skin under them was puffed and bunched. She pressed his hand quite far from the finger, first in the flesh under the thumb, working her way around. David realised that his eyes were closed as he felt her feeling his hand, like Jess getting a pat, he reckoned, feeling the feeling of it.

'Uh,' he said, his eyes opening. It had hurt.

'You're not ready yet. Not by a long stretch.'

'I can bowl.'

'Maybe, but if you're completely recovered wouldn't you bowl better?'

David shrugged, angry with her again. 'I want to talk to Grandad.'

'Does he have a telephone?'

David got up from the table and went out the back. There was just the little dirt yard with the outhouse and a washing line and fences and roofs as far as he could see. On the farm, when he felt like he did now, he'd walk. If he accidentally hit his thumb with the hammer, which he often did, possibly on account of his fingers always getting in his way, he'd simply drop it to the dirt and walk in a straight line doing nothing but walking until the feeling went. Then David would find himself looking at a tree or a bird or post, or often be down near the dam, like waking up somewhere else, but he'd no longer be thinking about his thumb. He'd be better, and he'd just go back to whatever it was he'd been doing before he got angry. But here, in the city, there was nowhere to walk because there was too much in the way.

He went back inside, where Mrs O'Locklan was still sitting at the kitchen table looking a little ill.

'I want to cable Grandad. And Nell too.'

'Very well. Good.'

'I want to send Grandad some of the money, like Uncle Mike promised.'

She nodded, looking towards the bedroom.

'And I want to practise bowling.'

'Not until your hand is better.'

He looked at her. She just sat there, looking back, with no anger, but with no weakness, just like a man not going to change his mind. Finally, David looked down at the table. Her short and chubby fingers touched the tea cup sitting in the saucer.

'Very well,' he said finally.

They went to the post office as soon as Mrs O'Locklan got dressed and ready, which seemed to take quite some time. When her hair was brushed and her make-up on, she didn't look so old. Uncle Mike's motor car was parked out the front.

In the next street were some railway tracks. There were two men in little huts at the road crossing. Mrs O'Locklan explained that their job was to pull across the gates to stop people and cars when the trains went past. When David had looked at the whole apparatus curiously, Mrs O'Locklan let them stay and wait. Sure enough, at some secret signal, the men came out and dragged the white gates from across the tracks so that they cut off the roadway. They rang bells to stop the people walking through and soon a train came whooshing past in a sooty storm lasting only seconds. Then the men looked up and down the track and pushed the gates back across the track and blew a whistle, like a train guard's, and the cars and wagons and people who'd lined up waiting all went on their way.

'Good job,' said David.

'Not that many going around,' said Mrs O'Locklan.

There were more closed shops on the high street, and lots of men sitting and standing about, like they were waiting for the train to come and pick up the wheat after harvest, only without the wheat or the train.

In the post office Mrs O'Locklan took two telegram forms and they went to a writing counter, where she handed him a pencil.

'Will you write it?'

'It's your telegram. You should. Try to use few words.'

'I'm not much good with the writing.'

'Now is a good time for practice.'

'Did you used to be a teacher?'

'No, I'm just naturally bossy.'

David laughed. He couldn't help it. It just came out in a couple of quick snorts. He put his hand to his mouth, embarrassed, but she started laughing too, until they saw stern looks about them, and they shushed.

David printed *Hello Grandad, I got 5 for with my sore hand.* He was about to write of Ten Ton, but realised he wanted to tell his grandad about all the team. How Ten Ton was bonzer, and Mr Richardson was a great leader and how he shouldn't think too unkindly about Mr Johnson, because he was just having a run of bad luck. Then he thought of Proctor and Windsor and wanted to tell him they were mean, but Longford was a gentleman, and ... it would take too long to write. Mrs O'Locklan was leaning in with another pencil and turning his l's and r's around on what he had written.

'They always go the wrong way round.'

'What else do you want to say?'

'Not much.'

'Love from David?'

'No! A girl would say that.'

'Oh dear. Can't have that. So what kinds of things do you say to your grandad when you're off to school?'

'Bye, sir.'

'What about when you're off to sleep?'

'Night, sir.'

'What does your grandad say about if you do something really good ... when you bowl well?'

David thought about this. He saw his grandad standing by the lamp flicking at mossies. His grandad looked at where the ball had pitched and then at the wicket. He nodded. Then he said ... David said it, as he heard it, 'All right. That'll do.'

'Hmm. Could you put "wish you were here"?'

David thought about that. It was true. He did wish that, even if he knew his grandad couldn't leave the farm. He nodded and Mrs O'Locklan wrote that on the cable form.

'Now who is this Nell?'

'She's my mate.'

'But she's a girl.'

'No she's not. Not like that. She's good.'

'Well, at least there's one of us out there somewhere.'

'One what?' asked David.

'Never mind.'

And they composed one to Nell together, and Mrs O'Locklan wrote this one out asking David some more about if the letters seemed the wrong way around on lots of words, but he had to explain that he only saw them differently sometimes, so he wasn't sure which way was the right way and when.

They went to the counter, and Mrs O'Locklan fished in her handbag and brought out a roll of twenty pound notes.

'I'd also like to cable two hundred pounds with that cable thank you.'

The man behind the counter looked up at her sharply. 'Two hundred pounds?'

'Is that not possible?'

The man looked at her, then at David, and made a note.

'We might be sending some more later, if my investments continue to thrive, so I would like to know that there is no problem.'

David looked at her. She was smiling, but her eyes were not.

'No problem, Mrs O'Locklan.'

Outside the post office she looked at her receipt and laughed. 'Thought I'd nicked it, he did.'

'You got it from Uncle Mike though.'

'Yes. Just have to tell him when he wakes up.' She looked at David, to share the joke, and in spite of David being unsure about the wickedness of what she'd done, he joined her smiling.

Finally David said, 'He promised.'

'And now he's kept his word.'

Michael was gone when they got back to the house and still not back when Mr Feenie came again with his motorbike. David put the goop on his hand, and Mr Feenie did his elaborate show of turning on and setting up the motorbike. David put his hand on the back mudguard, feeling it shudder and shake under his fingers. Mr Feenie said nothing, until Mrs O'Locklan went back inside.

Then he yelled, over the motorbike noise. 'So this uncle? Does 'e hit yer?'

David shook his head, unsure what Mr Feenie was getting at.

'Well, if 'e does, you let me know.'

'He never has,' yelled David.

Mr Feenie looked hard, didn't believe him, and tapped his nose. 'If 'e does, I'll sort 'im.' He nodded many times then, and seemed to growl a bit for a while, but David couldn't hear much above the bike engine.

A little later, when David was crouched down with his hand resting on the side of the motorbike, Mr Feenie's face appeared over the seat.

'Often are ya?'

'Often?' yelled David back.

'Or-phan. No mum 'n' dad.'

'Yes,' yelled David back, nodding and hoping Mr Feenie would stop.

Later, Mr Feenie yelled, 'Yer poppy's right tho'.' Mr Feenie nodded eagerly. 'Yer poppy.'

David supposed that the motorbike was making his eyes go poppy, so he scrunched them closed a moment.

'Taught yer like yer tricks,' Mr Feenie went on, nodding some more.

David stood up, and Mr Feenie stepped back, as though he thought David might strike him. David couldn't think what he was talking about and just nodded, putting his hand back on the mudguard.

Mr Feenie faced away from him again, looking at the house for some time, but then looked back from the corner of his eye. 'Five for thirty-two. With a busted hand.' He laughed and shook his head, and then slapped his thigh, and then looked back at David, winking. 'With that hand.'

David was quite glad when Freddy Feenie left, and asked Mrs O'Locklan. 'Have you told Mr Feenie about me being an orphan?'

'No, David. I wouldn't do that. What has he said?'

'It's true and so ... but I just didn't know he knew things like that.'

'The papers, David. There are stories in the papers and they are asking who you are and where you're from and why are you so good at bowling.'

'Oh,' said David, surprised, but then when he remembered what he'd done and where he was, he nodded. 'Like a famous person.'

'Yes,' she laughed. 'Just like one.'

Uncle Mike came home in the afternoon in a new suit. 'Get dressed. We're going to a party.'

David wasn't keen, nor Mrs O'Locklan.

'You say I never take you anywhere.'

Uncle Mike put the gramophone on loud while David got dressed. He was acting strangely, even for Uncle Mike, tapping his fingers on the mantle as though they were drums. Then he'd pace, and then dance two steps, then pace back to the mantle. David watched him lean in towards the mantle mirror as though he'd seen something in his own eye. He pushed his hat forward, nearly covering his eyes, and squinted at himself, looking mean. He turned suddenly to look at David and said, 'Gangsters,' and burst out laughing.

'It's a private party,' said his uncle as they parked his car next to a grandstand at Moonee Valley Racecourse. There were some other cars: new ones, with running boards and some without roofs. Two men in uniforms waited with the cars. One doffed his cap at Mrs O'Locklan as they passed.

Near the steps a blond man stepped in front of them. He had a jagged scar under one eye.

'Squinty invited us,' said Michael to him.

The man looked at Michael a moment like he didn't believe him. David could see that some of his ear was missing. He turned to David suddenly. 'What's wrong with your hand?'

David pulled his hand behind him.

The blond man sneered.

'Settle down, Blackie.'

There was a big man with a fat neck at the top of the steps. One eye was puffed with a droopy eyelid that made him look like he'd just woken up. He flicked both eyes towards David. 'You've brought the little miracle man.' He smiled like he was hungry and about to eat his lunch.

'Gidday Squinty,' nodded Uncle Michael.

Squinty nodded and said, 'Excuse Blackie Cutmore. He's from Sydney and so doesn't know any better.' He glared.

Blackie turned and looked back a moment with no smile or anything at all. He shrugged and said without apology, 'Just what the papers are saying.'

'Come on up and have a drink,' said Squinty.

Blackie seemed to step aside reluctantly, and was still trying to get a look at David's hand as he went past.

David wanted to call out to his uncle. He wanted to say, 'Let's go back to Mrs O'Locklan's, Uncle Mike. Please.' But he didn't say anything.

Inside, there was a room with tables, like a restaurant, but with a stage up one end. You could see the track out enormous windows, just like the cricket. Some men and ladies were at two tables dragged together, eating. The men wore loose day suits, but the ladies wore shiny dresses that were just flat material, leaving their arms and legs not covered. They had long beads around their necks and small hats with little feathers.

Michael was talking loudly. 'Well, this looks nice. All we need is a bit of music and we got it made.' Michael walked across the hall towards the tables.

David felt Mrs O'Locklan stop, and he stopped too.

'Jock, get some more champagne and some beers,' said Squinty to a man at another table. 'Oi, you girls move up. David Donald is here.' The ladies in the shiny little dresses moved up the end of the table, while the other men looked over towards David.

'Oh my,' whispered Mrs O'Locklan, 'That's Jack West there. And Mr Scallin, the member for Yarra. Squinty has to be Squinty Tyler.'

'Who?' said David.

'The criminal. These people run Melbourne.'

'David, come here,' called Michael.

Everyone was staring now with the tasting look that David had come to dread. They would be ready with their questions that would all be the same and their peering at his hand and their comments on what he did wrong.

David looked to Mrs O'Locklan. She seemed unhappy too.

'David, come and meet these fellas.'

'Toilet,' said David suddenly. 'I gotta go to the toilet.'

David went down the steps and to the track. The men in uniforms were talking by the cars with Blackie Cutmore. He looked up and stared at David.

David went towards the track. He didn't need a toilet but he didn't want to talk. He realised that he didn't mind being at Mrs O'Locklan's house. He could listen to the radiogram and sit on the back step in the sun, listening to kids play somewhere out in the back lane.

There was a sprinkler clacking on the short straight. The grass looked thick.

David looked up to the huge window overlooking the straight. He thought he saw Squinty standing there, but when he looked away a moment and back, the window was empty.

There were some stables near the track. David thought he'd like to touch a horse, if there were any about. Even if there weren't, he'd like to smell the animal smells that would be in there.

The stables were big and open but had no horses. They'd been mucked out and there was fresh straw. The troughs held water, but the feed drums were clean and empty. David heard the sound of what he thought was a scraping shoe, but when he looked around he couldn't see anyone. The gates to each stall were open, but darkish. A mouse ran across from one empty stall to another.

David saw something in the dirt and bent to get it. It was a horseshoe nail, bent and a little rusty. He held it and turned it, like it was a cable from home with good news.

In the middle of the stalls was an alleyway that led to large gate at the edge of the track. David threw the horseshoe nail down and moved towards the green grass and sunlight.

His fingers felt good, he realised. He stretched them and made a fist, then loosened and wriggled. He looked at his hand. There was no swelling. He flicked his wrist, gently, then sudden and hard. He looked at his open palm and realised that he wanted a cricket ball, wanted to feel his fingers around it, to heft its weight.

David rested his palm on the wooden railing that ran along the racetrack straight, pushing gently against the edge, testing beneath. A sharp pain made him snatch his hand back from the rail. It wasn't his injury, but a splinter. A big one, stuck in his palm. Blood was seeping out around the piece of wood.

'What's that?'

Blackie was behind him. He grabbed David's hand, and pulled, spinning David around.

'Let go,' said David.

'Hang on. Hurt does it?'

Blackie held his wrist, and put his other hand on David's arm, so he couldn't pull away.

'God, you are a freak. These fingers are longer than bloody octopus tentacles.'

'Just a splinter,' said David, trying to pull his hand back again. 'Let go.'

'Hold still.' He twisted David's hand until his wrist was being twisted too. David tightened his wrist, so the man couldn't keep twisting. Blackie stopped and looked at him. Then he sneered, meanly and started to twist again. As he kept twisting, David had to kneel down to stop the pain.

'See, this hand is worth a bit. Good or bad, it's worth something either way.' The man reached into his jacket pocket with his now free hand.

'I'll call out,' said David, kneeling in the dirt by the racetrack.

Blackie's hand came out of his pocket holding a razor. 'If you do, I'll cut yer.' He flicked the razor outwards, and the blade flashed out from its hinged protector. 'The thing about a razor cut is how much it hurts, even when it's not deep.'

David looked at the razor blade raised above his hand. He was helpless, held still by his wrist. All he could do was try to spread his fingers so the splinter didn't dig deeper.

Blackie looked down at David and smiled at something he saw in David's eyes that he liked the look of. He looked back to David's hand. 'How about I just take one finger off, how'd you like that?'

David looked at the razor blade, then at a movement behind Blackie. 'How about we don't?' There was the double click of a gun hammer cocking. Squinty Tyler stood just behind Blackie with a revolver pointing at the blond man's head. 'Tell me why I shouldn't put a bullet in your head.'

David's hand was free. He pulled it back, grabbing himself around the wrist.

'Relax, Squinty. Kid's got a splinter.'

'Is that right?' said Squinty, his drooping eyelid aimed down at David. He pushed his pistol until it touched Blackie's head, just under where the piece of his ear was missing.

David could see the revolver load, a bullet in each chamber.

'Look Squinty, sorry for putting the wind up Little Lord Frontenroy here. No harm.'

David tested his wrist. It felt stiff.

'If you've damaged the ...'

'If I've damaged the merchandise then at least you know, for sure.' Blackie turned with difficulty, turning through where the pistol was pointing until he was looking at Squinty past the barrel, which was now pushing into his scarred cheek.

Squinty seemed to be deciding whether he'd shoot him.

'Nothing like betting on a sure thing,' said Blackie, as though there were not a gun pointing into his face.

David got up and ran.

'Hey, stay here,' ordered Squinty.

David didn't turn around. Still holding his wrist, he ran around the pavilion and up the steps. His uncle was coming out the door as he reached the top.

'Thought you got lost.'

'I want to go home,' panted David.

'Not yet mate. Got these blokes for you to meet.'

'Now.'

'What's wrong with your hand?' said Mrs O'Locklan coming out too.

'I got a splinter.' David didn't know why he didn't tell them what had just happened. He wanted to be away from here, but he didn't want to say anything. Not here. 'We have to go now,' he said, looking at Mrs O'Locklan.

She put her hand up on David's shoulder, and said, 'Very well. Let's go then, David.'

'We're just getting started,' said Michael.

'Let me see,' she said.

David held his hand. She peered and reached towards the splinter. Her nails weren't long, and weren't painted either. They touched the edge of the wood and for a moment he felt the start of the sharp wood digging deeper, but then it left. She was turning it in the air, so he could see. 'Wow, that's a beauty. About an inch,' she said.

'We still have to go.'

'We gotta meet these people. It's all set up.'

'We'll walk,' said Mrs O'Locklan, heading down the stairs. 'Don't know why we drove in the first place, it's so close.'

David followed her, looking out for Blackie and Squinty. The drivers watched them but not with much interest. The sprinkler spat its water on the straight.

'All right.' Michael had come after them. 'Not a problem. Let's get outta here.'

David nursed his hand as they drove out of the racecourse. There was a big old building across a park and a cricket ground.

'I want to go to training.'

'I thought you wanted to go home,' said his uncle dully, without turning round.

'I want to train.'

'How's your hand?' said Mrs O'Locklan. She was having trouble turning round in the front seat.

'That man Blackie. He had a razor and said he'd cut one of my fingers off.'

The car slewed sideways, scaring a fellow on a bicycle, before coming back to the left of the road, and stopping. Mrs O'Locklan had been flung back towards the windshield, Uncle Mike shooting out his arm in time to hold her.

'Blackie Cutmore?'

'The blond man with half his ear gone.'

'Bitten off,' said his uncle.

Mrs O'Locklan looked at him. 'Gangsters and shylocks.'

'Mr Squinty stopped him by pointing a gun at him. A black pistol.'

'Were they joking?'

'They didn't smile and wink or ...'

'For goodness sake, Michael! They're killers and drug dealers and ... You had no business putting us in with them.'

'They wanted to meet David. They —'

'They give you hop.'

'Yeah, well they don't sell that at the grog shop.'

'It isn't always about you.' Mrs O'Locklan grabbed Michael by the chin, her fingers squeezing so hard he couldn't speak. 'Is David safe?'

His uncle mumbled nonsense, making a joke of her squeezing his mouth. She let him go, not laughing. 'What do they want?'

Michael turned to David. 'What did Blackie say?'

David had trouble thinking what was said. He had been too busy with his twisted wrist and the cut-throat razor. Finally he said, 'My hand is worth something. Either way. And then about a sure thing.'

'All right. Good.' Michael put the car in gear again and pulled back out onto the road. After they'd gone a little way, his uncle asked, 'How *is* your hand?'

'I don't know.'

'You don't know?'

'He needs another week to be sure,' said Mrs O'Locklan, watching Michael.

'The Blackie man twisted my wrist.'

'Not forgetting the splinter too! That hand's a bit of a lightning rod isn't it?'

David had to smile at that. His hand was held in his other, palm up. There was a little hole in the centre now where the splinter had been. Since that train accident in the desert all kinds of things had been happening to his hand. It was true.

Michael pulled up outside Mrs O'Locklan's house. Some kids were playing cricket with a dustbin further up. Mothers were talking over fences. There were men too, mostly solitary and on verandas, home too early from no work. They were all watching the car.

'I'll have a chat to Squinty. Sort it out. All very sensible and proper, and then ... we can get back to having some fun eh?' David's uncle sounded flat, in spite of his words.

Mrs O'Locklan got out of the car and went in without looking back. David squeezed past the front seat. His uncle said, 'Rest your hand. The next Test starts the day after tomorrow.'

'What?'

'When'd you think?'

'But we just finished the last one.'

'It's been over a week.'

The car pulled away, scattering kids from their cricket game. The car horn seemed to give a jaunty kind of beep that for some reason made David wonder how safe his uncle would be 'reasoning' with Blackie and Squinty.

A man yelled, 'Good on yer, David. Bore it up those Poms!'

David looked around the street. There was movement, like water coming down the river in a rush, grabbing up all the summer branches and leaves and lifting them, only this time it was the people in the street, as they started moving out of their yards and coming towards him. The kids, who'd been playing cricket ran ahead, and reached him first.

'David Donald, aren't ya?' said a boy with black clumps of

hair jutting all over his head.

'Yeah,' said David.

'You gunna get them Poms?' said a lady in a floral dress that looked like it was holding pillows.

'Um, I hope so missus. If my hand's all right.'

'So, it's true,' said a man, 'what Freddy said.'

'Yes sir. Mrs O'Locklan's been getting it right.'

'And Freddy,' said a thin lady in a cloth hat.

'Yes, missus.'

David turned to see Mrs O'Locklan, but she'd gone inside.

'Ya gunna bowl a googly?' asked a little girl with skinned knees.

'Course he's gunna bowl a googly. Get Windsor with that,' said a male voice.

'Naw, off break and catch. Like the first innings,' came another.

'O'Malley's his bunny though. No one else can touch 'im, 'cept The Kid.'

'Have ya got a cap?' asked a boy.

'Not yet,' said David.

'You didn't have a hat in that last Test.'

'Naw, I forgot.'

They laughed, but David didn't mind.

'Play cricket with us,' said the girl with the skinned knees.

'Oi,' said a man. 'Leave him alone.'

'He's got a Test coming, love,' said a lady who had a bowl of peas in her hand.

David looked back to Mrs O'Locklan's house for a moment.

Some kids were already dragging the rubbish bin up,

scraping it along the road. Two boys were wrestling over the bat.

A boy came up, 'Show us yer big fingers.'

'Hush Billy!'

'Naw, it's all right,' said David. 'Big as sausages some reckon.'

More laughter.

'That's why I keep getten 'em caught up in things.'

Someone gave him the ball. It was a well-worn tennis ball. He looked at it, not sure he could do much, but a man in a singlet pushed through. 'Here. It's a real one from my club.'

'Thanks, mister,' said David.

They laughed again. All of them. But then they went quiet, stepping back and waiting. David looked to the rubbish bin, down a corridor of people. An old man edged up, and said, 'Well, is he as good as Grimmet? Eh?'

David stepped up and he bowled. He bowled leggies and offies and shooters and skidders and loopies. He played with flight and he sorted through some gentle spin and some that he really ripped. He played with line and length, dropping some short and pushing others through to hit the rubbish bin. No one laid bat on ball that afternoon, and everyone in the street, and many more from connecting streets turned up to have a go at David Donald. No one seemed to mind. In fact, thought David later, it became increasingly important to all, including David, that he be absolutely invincible that afternoon.

It only ended when Mrs O'Locklan yelled, 'Time to come home for dinner, David.'

And it was like David waking, to see it was twilight and dim, and to hear their voices again. 'Good luck, David.'

'Um thanks,' said David. And he turned to go to Mrs O'Locklan's.

They started clapping. It was silly really, clapping like that in the street, thought David as he kept going to Mrs O'Locklan's house. But when he opened the gate, he looked and the people were gathered there, and they stopped clapping when they saw him look, and when he got to the veranda he turned and they were still there and he couldn't think what to do, so he waved, and all of them, the men and the kids and ... they all gave a wave back.

David's hand had swollen again and Mrs O'Locklan put it into the bowl of her magic goop.

'I don't think its swole up nearly as much as before,' said David.

'Does it hurt?' They were eating lamb chops with vegies. Mrs O'Locklan had said he was allowed to eat the chops with his hand as he only had one free. He could feel the fat running down his chin.

'Not as much.'

'How about where you got the splinter?'

'It was nothing. Will you read the cables again?' He gestured to the telegrams in front of him. There had been two, waiting for him inside. Grandad and Nell.

'You should practise your reading.'

'Yes, ma'am.'

She picked up the cables ignoring what she'd told him, letting him get away with it. She looked at the cable and back at him before she read. 'No more offies STOP Bowl leggies STOP Use your field STOP Grandad.'

David nodded. He was right, but didn't understand about his hurt hand. 'He doesn't know they won't always put the field where I want.'

She read the other. 'Master David Donald comma bonzer stuff stop Best wishes stop Nell Parker.'

'She doesn't talk like that,' said David a little embarrassed because he wanted Mrs O'Locklan to think well of Nell.

'It's telegram talk.'

'She doesn't talk that much. You know. She's more a doing person. But no airs and graces.' David put down his chop bone and picked up his fork again. It was greasy from his hand. He pushed at the peas. 'But she talks about cricket and droughts and peas and has a laugh. She's cheeky about the Pringles, but not so they hear.'

'Who are the Pringles?'

'Just people ... in Dungarin.'

David looked up. Mrs O'Locklan wasn't listening, he thought. She had her glass of wine in front of her and the bottle out on the table. She still had her make-up on, but her cheeks were puffy and her eyes a little runny. He wondered how his uncle would go with the gangsters.

He went to bed and Mrs O'Locklan came in to say goodnight, as she liked to do. David said, 'Tell me about my dad.'

'I don't know anything.'

'You do. You've said.'

She looked at him, then turned and left the room. David thought he might follow her and demand something, but Mrs O'Locklan came back with her glass of wine.

'I met your uncle that night for the first time, when he carried your father in. I had been moved up to the field hospital, to help tend the wounded while we moved them back from the front.' Mrs O'Locklan spoke dreamily like a teacher reading on a hot day. 'He was very popular apparently, which was very difficult on the line, being a captain and popular, especially in the 51ˢᵗ, as many of them had been to Gallipoli. Your uncle's battalion was the 16ᵗʰ I think, and so they finally met up around Amiens. That's a town in France. The most haunting church there I have ever seen, bombed but still standing like it was made out of giant fish bones. Your mother ... do you know what your mother did?'

She looked at him and he whispered, 'My mother?'

'Apparently, she sailed to England, which was a very dangerous thing to do, so she could see your father when he was sent up from Gallipoli.'

'They got married in England,' said David.

'Ah,' said Mrs O'Locklan. 'Then she must have gone ... come back to Australia. Anyway, this was before Amiens. What was I saying?'

'My father was a captain.'

'Yes, and Michael was a ... private again, I think. His cheeky mouth had him demoted as frequently as his bravery had him promoted.'

'Brave?'

'Yes, both of them. Fearless. They looked similar. Your dad's hair was darker. But your father, Captain Donald, was very brave.'

She turned and looked at David, then came forward and sat next to him on the bed. She looked away again and said, 'I'm going to tell you how he died, David.'

David felt like he'd suddenly burst out of the bush onto a ridge by the river, trying to balance and not fall in.

She was still staring at him, like asking.

'Tell me.'

She didn't for a moment, but then continued. 'Michael had sneaked up the line from his battalion to see Ernie … your dad. There was a bit of a to-do that night with shelling and forays; the big run hadn't happened yet. However, they and some other soldiers were mostly ignoring it and having a cup of tea. A grenade—one of those German stick grenades—came out of the dark and landed in their trench.

'Michael yelled, "Fire in the hole!" which was the warning, and everyone dived for cover. Except Earnest. Michael thinks he could see there was no cover, and they probably would have all gone. He jumped up and grabbed the grenade and tried to throw it out of the trench. But he wasn't fast enough.

'Michael grabbed him up with both hands around his arms to stop the bleeding. Pulled him up over his shoulders and ran him along the trench and up onto one of the duckboards back to the hospital tent. He died on the way. Michael's foot was injured. A piece of shrapnel from a bombardment shell had torn off his toe while he was running. He lost a fair amount of blood himself. No one could have got your father back in time. His injuries were too bad. But he had time to tell Michael to give his love to your mum and to look after the baby. His last thoughts were you.'

David felt sick and winded at the same time. He tried to get out of bed, but could hear choking, like gasps coming from some sick creature. Mrs O'Locklan was grabbing at him. He tried to push her away but he couldn't see properly, nor manage any strength. It must be her, he thought, wailing like a child. She was hugging him, his face pressed into her chest. She was warm and soft and he was being squashed to her.

'I'm sorry,' she said.

David imagined his father, looking like a dark-haired Michael in a captain's uniform, seeing the grenade and rushing to it. He saw it happen again, but this time his father tossed the grenade out over the top of the trench and was safe.

David pushed Mrs O'Locklan back, out of the hug. He could see properly again. Her glass had spilled on the edge of the bed. She had tears in her eyes, searching his face looking for something or trying to give something, he wasn't sure.

David picked up the glass and gave it to her and said, 'Thank you, Mrs O'Locklan. Thank you for telling me. I'm going to go to sleep now.'

She didn't say anything, and David turned away from her, wondering if she might pat him or hug him again. He saw this man see the grenade and saw the man decide to throw it back out. No secret. Just a brave thing that didn't come off. He sighed, and the air felt good coming in, and so he sucked it in deep and held it in his lungs until his chest felt tingly.

David woke to find Michael shaking him. The light was on.

'We gotta go.' His uncle's face was bleeding.

'Come on kid, O'Toole's got wind of where you're staying. It'll be in the papers tomorrow, which is soon.' He dragged David out of the bed. 'Get dressed. I've put Squinty and Mr West off, but I reckon Blackie will be right onto it if he reads the paper.'

David started dressing, as his uncle stuffed clothes

and cricket gear into their bags. 'Bloody O'Toole. Like a vendetta against you. He's hunting down your grandad for his story.'

'Did you fight him?'

Michael wiped at the blood. 'Naw. Him I can take any time. There's been a bit of a falling out between Squinty and Blackie. Come on. Do up your boots in the car.'

'Where's Mrs O'Locklan?'

'Asleep.'

They went through the kitchen, Michael carrying the bags.

'I wanna say goodbye.'

'Well you can't. She's as pissed as a newt.'

David looked at her closed door.

'Later, David. We have to go.'

It was black outside, and David could barely see the car from the light spilling from the hallway. Michael pushed their bags in the back, and cranked the engine, turning on its headlights. He ran back in and closed the front door. Then he ran to the metal dustbin that was still on the pathway and kicked it hard, making it bang and roll and clatter into the fence.

'Bloody bastard!' he yelled. 'You've seen the last of me, bloody woman,' he yelled more loudly.

A light came on next door. He jumped back in the seat and revved the engine. More lights came on. He turned to David and said, 'So they know we've left, mate.' He pushed the gearstick and it clunked and started driving fast.

'Where are we going?' asked David.

'Hotel'd be the best, in spite of the bastards. You got a cricket match tomorrow.'

'Tomorrow?'

The car took the corner too fast, its tyres squealing as it slid a little.

'Did you have to fight Mr Squinty?'

'No bloody way. Wouldn't be here if I tried that.'

David looked at his uncle in the reflected light in the car. His face was bruised and puffed and bloody. One eye was half shut, peering out into the streets, as the car drove slower now. David imagined him with darker hair and in a captain's uniform. He realised then that until Mrs O'Lockan told him, he'd started to wonder if Michael were really his father, and whether that was the secret.

Michael caught him watching. He smiled at him, lit only a moment as they passed a street lamp. 'I've been thinking, Davey boy. Time for a new trick. Bore it up 'em all again?'

'What do you mean?'

'What if you do it like we did for the wharfies? You know, for a bit of a laugh, and keep everyone guessing.'

'What?'

His uncle's voice came out of the dark, 'In this Test, don't take any wickets at all. How'd that be for a laugh?'

CHAPTER SIXTEEN

David's hand was only a little swollen. It was his shoulder that hurt. The aeroplane wall shuddered against his back, even though he was wearing two coats on account of the awful cold. He supposed this air travel would not catch on if it were to be so uncomfortable, except in emergencies such as this. There was one consolation, thought David. The noise of the engines prevented Mr O'Toole from talking to him. He'd tried yelling his questions for a while, but had finally given up.

Mr O'Toole was huddled on the other side of the plane nursing a whisky bottle. Mr Biggins, who the Australian Cricket Board had sent as chaperone, seemed even more miserable as he sat amongst the sacks of mail and petrol tanks. He was further disturbed, periodically, when Mr Ulm came back from the cockpit to up-end one of the petrol containers into a funnel through to the fuel tank of the Fokker called the *Southern Cross*. It was in this way they could attempt to fly non-stop from Point Cook to Perth, Mr Ulm had explained when they'd loaded up the plane. Mr Kingsford Smith had said they planned to try to fly from America to Australia the following year, and thought they'd have a go at flying to New Zealand after that. 'If we don't stack it on this one,' quipped Mr Ulm. They both seemed quite cheerful at the 'stacking it' and 'buying it' and 'dropping it in the drink,' which only made Mr O'Toole and Mr Biggins even more grumpy. Not being allowed to smoke, on account of all the fuel, had not improved matters.

The Prime Minister, Mr Stanley Bruce, had insisted on getting David across to Dungarin, once everyone heard that Grandad was sick, and Mr Kingsford Smith and Mr Ulm had volunteered to move up their record attempt. 'May as well get in on the record-breaking act,' Mr Ulm had said at the airstrip as the newspaper men took photographs to record the event. 'With the Wonder Kid's luck, we'll probably get there by yesterday,' Mr Kingsford Smith grinned. Mr O'Toole claimed, 'Nothing is too good for David Donald. The entire nation rallies.' There was some coughing at that point, and one press man said, 'Steady on, Charlie. We'll write our own headlines if you don't mind.'

David felt his sore shoulder, and then had another go at reading the newspaper. Even without the shaking of the plane, the words were difficult to make out, but he had many hours to practise his reading.

THE FOURTH TEST MATCH
VICTORY FOR AUSTRALIA —ALREADY!

Donald Astonishes

The fourth Test of the current series of the Ashes began and concluded yesterday when England was bowled out for a total of 1 run. Australia, by virtue of scoring 2 runs in the first innings, has consequently won the Test. The entire Test match lasted less than three hours.

The wicket was affected by the lack of water, yet this is clearly the most astonishing bowling feat of the modern or any era. Young bowling prodigy David Donald took all wickets, finishing with the incomprehensible figures of ten for 0 and ten for 1.

THE PLAY

MELBOURNE, JANUARY 27— Words seem as inadequate as an English bat in attempting to capture the tumult of today's play, however these reporters will endeavour to record the day as if it were an ordinary game of cricket.

Anticipation turned to the first of many surprising pieces of play when Richardson tossed young Donald the ball to open the bowling. Muttering could be heard around the ground, as this move was dissected by the crowd, some assuming the kind of gamesmanship Australia was accused of using during the third Test in Adelaide.

William O'Malley, who had already become somewhat Donald's 'bunny' in the third Test was safely at the other end, and it appeared Dorrington was attempting to curb his natural aggression by defensive play. From the beginning he did not seem comfortable. The first he edged onto his pads.

The second delivery went to ground short of a diving Hall, at silly point. The third ball seemed exactly like the second, however, it caught the bat high and managed to hold in the air long enough for Hall to take a fairly simple catch. England were one down for none, and Australia were cockahoop, no one imagining what was to come.

Succession

In what was to become a succession of wickets in which the walk to and from the wicket took longer than the batsman's innings, ample time was allowed for the crowd and cricket reporter to dissect the bowling. This discussion was essential as it is doubtful whether anyone other than David Donald and perhaps umpires Bosanquet and Wisden had specific knowledge of any of the types of balls bowled by Donald today.

Indeed, this will be a matter for later analysis, requiring intense interrogation of fielders and batsmen to achieve any intelligence of the issue. Donald's combination of flight, dip, trick balls and massive spin seem to defy descriptions of stock spin bowling. Put more simply, the ball is doing too much to read from the press box. Clearly the English bats felt the same way.

Longford appeared to greet Donald with a friendly nod. The ball he received was far from that. It reared up off the pitch and climbed sharply. The English captain began a simple block, however the ball caught an edge and was claimed by Baker, keeping up to the stumps. Longford nodded his appreciation of the delivery to an unmoved Donald.

Edward Windsor strode to the wicket, imperious as ever. Making no concession *to the circumstances, he charged Donald, who appeared to alter his line such that the next delivery passed the swinging bat, only to spin back into Baker's gloves where he made an easy stumping. Windsor did not adjust his stride to continue back to the pavilion.*

At three down for no score, young Timothy Bishop, who had caused Donald some problems in the third Test, came to the crease. There appeared to be a conference between Donald, Richardson and Jack Tanner at this point, with much pointing from Tanner and Richardson and much nodding from Donald.

The field came in, and Bishop wandered and darted about on the crease as if to dance the foxtrot. A man less nimble would not have managed to evade the ball so delicately as Bishop did today. Bowled middle stump.

England four for none. At this point, delirium broke out around the ground.

Not on the field however, where matters remained concentrated. Donald still had one ball left of his first over. He used it to bowl an attentive Morgan. The ball pitched well outside the left-hander's off stump. There have been reports since the game that there was a kind of whirring sound, "like a tiny car engine." The English wicketkeeper was determined not to get an edge, as the ball changed direction and headed inexorably towards the top of off stump. Morgan watched the ball all the way behind his legs to its final destination. England five wickets down for 0 runs.

The Second Over

The jubilation of the first over soon gave way to new interest. Relieved of Donald's total domination, what would the English do? The answer was predictable, as it turned out, in a most unpredictable day. O'Malley, who had been secure up the other end, did what O'Malley always does. He did not play any ball that he did not have to and he blocked those that he did. Let us be clear. Calligan bowled very well. On any other day in any other Test he would be lauded. He probably might have got a wicket. But on this day, he bowled a tight, spirited line just on and outside off stump. He took no wicket. O'Malley scored no run.

Over Number Three

Ostler, having watched O'Malley play tight defensive cricket for an over, appeared to decide he'd have none of that. As Donald came in to bowl his first ball, Ostler stepped back and forward and swung lustily. More importantly he connected with the ball. It travelled in the air halfway to Bardsley at a kind of deep backward point. Whether Ostler was so surprised at his feat, or whether O'Malley was too fearful to leave 'the shallow end of the pool,' both batsmen paused sufficiently for Bardsley to gather the ball on the bounce and fire it back to the wicketkeeper. On any other day in any other Test, it was surely an easy single.

Ostler attempted a similar shot next ball, but it appeared to hold up on him, and he mis-hit. Still, on another day it may have been four. McLeod, at extra cover, leapt high and to his left. The ball bobbed from his outstretched left hand, only to be gathered in by both before he hit the ground, to take a corker of a brilliant catch.

Darby, perhaps employing spinner's tactics to a spinner, swept his first delivery to square leg, but sent a catch to short fine leg when he attempted the same shot to the similar-looking next delivery. It is illustrative of the game that Johnson was brought into the short fine leg position for that very ball.

The remaining batsmen did not trouble the scorers and should little trouble this account. Dwyer was caught in first slip by Richardson. Tudor was bowled middle stump, trying to get his pad to the ball outside the line. Finally, and next ball, Proctor did not offer a shot and was pronounced leg before wicket. Four balls for four wickets.

I confess I remain giddy reporting the day's play. It is as though I have stood too hurriedly and lack sufficient blood to the brain. I can't quite recall exactly what happened next, and I have asked many people. There was no cheering.

As Australia came off, and allowed Donald first egress, the crowd stood and they clapped, in a rather restrained manner. Perhaps they knew what was to come.

Australia's Very Astonishing Innings
(More on this issue by another columnist—Ed.) Douglas Tudor seemed particularly fired up for his opening over, and struck Johnson with the second and third ball. When, after five balls of Proctor's opening over, Johnson nicked one down to fine leg, Bardsley charged down the pitch, Johnson turning for a second on the throw and just making his ground for a chancy two runs.

As though on an arranged signal, the Australian batsmen looked immediately *to the pavilion. It took all those at the ground quite some time to work out what had gone on. They had been called in. Australia was declaring the innings closed—for just 2 runs! It seemed an insane decision at the time, throwing away all the advantage of Donald's glorious work with the ball.*

There were mutters and booing from the crowd, and no little consternation in the press box. A bewildered English team tarried on the oval, but had broken up into a number of smaller groups in earnest conversation as they retired from the field.

Second Innings Begins at 1.30

Donald was given the new ball again, but employed different tactics at the beginning of the British second innings. Richardson and Donald crowded an outrageous number of fielders around the bat. Only two fielders (not counting Donald) were further than two yards from the batsman, one being Hall at extra cover and Bardsley at short fine leg. England had changed tactics also, O'Malley facing.

It was a brute of a delivery which bowled O'Malley first ball. It was especially damaging not only to him but to the whole English side, I believe, given O'Malley's renowned defensive abilities. When the ball pitched, it seemed as though it would very nearly be called a wide, but was already drifting in. It spun viciously, both more briskly and more sharply than this reporter has ever witnessed. But it also kept low. And it didn't appear to be finger spin. O'Malley was simply too late to get his bat into position.

This ball did not just get O'Malley out. It did much more than that. This ball, The O'Malley Ball, may signal the necessity of a structural change to the game of cricket. O'Malley in his normal stance, ready to face all comers, at least expects them to come from the front. This ball seemed to come from the side, and O'Malley was not in a position to cope with it. The ball that bowled O'Malley at the start of the second innings in Melbourne today is the greatest ball I have ever seen, not least because it seemed to defy the laws of physics. It was impossible and outrageous and unplayable. O'Malley stood, as we all did, shaking his head like a big man who has been punched hard by

a bantamweight. Or like Goliath on that day.

Longford did not come in next. This may have been a ploy to save the left-handers, although everyone was now vulnerable to Donald, if he could switch from unplayable leggies to right-angle googlies/arm-balls at will. Whatever the reason, the batting order was changed and Windsor strode out, I suggest, a little less manfully than before. Windsor swept the first ball beautifully. His left leg went forward early, and he was down on his knee hitting cleanly across the spin. Only a miraculous dive by Hampton sent the ball ricocheting towards Donald at the bowler's end. Dorrington only just made his ground to prevent a run-out, although it must be admitted that Donald fumbled the ball. Even with all the miracles of today, Donald cannot field or bat.

Attempting the same sweep shot next ball, Windsor took a top edge, which, being hit with some force, flew over Baker's head. Tanner at second slip dived backwards and at full stretch to take the catch magnificently. The crowd cheered again when Windsor threw his bat away when he was halfway to the rooms. (We are sure to hear more of that matter.)

Bishop was next. He danced around the wicket again, and again failed to achieve congress of bat on ball, being hit below the roll of his pad, dead in front. Umpire Bosanquet denied an enormous appeal, and not just from the players. It appeared plum. The next ball was equally straight, but lower, some suggesting it was Donald's famous skidder. This one was given: Bishop out lbw for none, and no longer Donald's nemesis.

The crowd became more restive at this point. So did the press box. It began to dawn on all of us watching today that the special thing we were witnessing could turn into something miraculous. It was now three wickets down for no runs in the second innings. Would England even score a run? Even the contemplation of such a thing was surely impossible.

Dwyer, elevated in the batting, flailed at a slow googly that landed and spun so far it evaded his bat but took the top of his leg stump. He actually grinned at Donald before shouldering arms. Proctor was also caught in slips, but by another superb catch to Tanner, this time diving to his left and grasping it just before it hit the ground. Both batsmen had attempted defensive shots, which proved a disastrous strategy against the rampant Donald. (And another hat-trick — Ed.)

England were now six for 0. Another odd thing had begun in this second innings. No one had rushed to Tanner to congratulate the brilliant fielding. No one had so much as patted Donald on the back during the entire second innings. There was a workmanlike silence out in the middle, with the occasional word here and there from the captain.

Hampton's Heroics

It was only now that Longford walked to the crease, and he alone seemed immune to the gait of condemned men that had accompanied the preceding batsmen. He nodded to the Australians, and chatted to Dorrington, surely as Nelson must have done on those burning decks. But Longford was not facing. And the ball was given not to Calligan but to big Paul Hampton.

Richardson set a conventional off side field to the left-handed opening batsman. Only McLeod and Calligan patrolled the on side. Hampton bowled three perfect balls that rose sharply and temptingly outside off stump. Dorrington was having none of it, appropriately ignoring what was still 'the new ball.' Longford came down and there was a mid-field conference. It was clear what his captain's directions had been. Longford wanted a run. Clearly Hampton had guessed too, for his next delivery was a yorker, which Dorrington only just managed to dig out.

Mistakes, Divine Intervention or Sacrifice?

The next two balls may be discussed for just as long as all of Donald's deliveries put together. Only Tanner and Hampton will ever know. Dorrington flashed at Hampton's next delivery just *outside off stump. It was too quick and too wide and there was an audible snick. The ball flew straight to Tanner at second slip. And he put it down. My suggestion is that it must have taken quick thinking and concentration to not fulfil the years of training and instinct that Tanner possesses in order to drop such a regulation catch. The cheer that erupted from the crowd was greater than any for a catch actually taken.*

The next piece of play was more transparent. Perhaps there was panic. Perhaps. Hampton bowled another yorker, and Dorrington squeezed it out. Longford was backing up and the ball went straight to Hampton who picked it up, as Longford turned. All Hampton had to do was touch the stumps not two feet away. He seemed to look at Longford who actually stopped running. Then Hampton turned and threw down to the other end,

as Dorrington scrambled back to only just make his ground. He needn't have worried. The ball was well wide.

Another cheer from the crowd. The mythical perfect game was still in the offing, even though the Australians were clearly doing all they could to collude.

Donald Versus Longford
The field set for Longford was nothing like that set in the first innings. After much discussion between Richardson and Donald, a copybook leg-spin field placing was used, although there were two slips, point, cover point, extra cover, mid-off, mid-on, mid wicket and a short fine leg. There were no easy singles, but there were gaps in the field, especially out on the on side. The first ball had good height and drifted in, seeming to pitch in line with off stump, before it spun away to be

taken towards slips by Baker. Longford watched it all the way, his bat remaining between the ball and his wicket. The crowd, spoiled as they had been that day, groaned.

Richardson trotted from slip and called McLeod and Calligan from mid-off and mid-on respectively. The crowding of the bat was beginning, but with no protection at all straight down the ground. Donald's next ball looked like it was going to be his famous skidder but this one sped up. Longford, seemingly inclined to play back and watching for a low slowing ball, was caught by surprise. Up on his toes, he seemed frozen as the ball kept on coming, just like the ball that dismissed him in the first innings. Only this time he managed to drop his gloves out of the way at the last second. The ball passed over the stumps and into Baker's eager gloves.

Through my field glasses I clearly saw Longford smile as he nodded, but prodded the pitch where the ball had pitched as though suggesting the ball had hit a sweet spot on the dry grass. Donald held his position at the top of his run, only six steps really, and stood staring at Longford a moment, before bowling his next delivery. Longford went late, but went with a rush. Clearly deciding that a ball that does not hit the pitch cannot spin, Longford danced down the wicket. Donald either saw him coming, or was expecting the bait to be taken. He speared the ball shorter still, at Longford's feet. Longford went through with the shot, edging the ball out past Hall into mid-off. There was a very loud call of 'Yes' as Hall turned and scrambled for the ball and Dorrington ran through to make what really should be called an easy single. The crowd groaned. The perfect game was gone.

History

Dorrington was out lbw the next ball. He had seemed ready to play his shots, but the topspinner, I believe, was too straight and too early for him to get bat to ball. It did not appear to be a difficult umpiring decision. The crowd was more relaxed now, finding their voice once more.

Ostler was bowled off stump, uncharacteristically hanging his bat out towards the ball as if it might burn him. The left-handed Morgan changed his stance significantly, seeming to position his left leg outside the line of his off stump. The ball was a brute. It spun hugely and quite high. It would seem to this reporter that if one cannot find the ball with the bat, then thrusting a leg is compromised. The ball seemed to catch Morgan's back leg, and off that, find its way to the stumps. It could have gone anywhere, but on this day, there could be only one answer. And yet another hat-trick.

Tudor, who has never been a crowd favourite, trudged to the centre for the last ball of Donald's over. There were so many men around the bat that, should he edge, it had to fall in someone's hands. Longford may have suggested he let it go. He seemed to try, but the ball bounced in line with the middle and even the worst batsman must place his bat between ball and wicket. The ball spun, taking a faint edge, and Tudor was caught by Richardson in a copy of the first innings dismissal, although this one came to Richardson at a more comfortable height.
It was over. England all out for 1 run. Australia 2 runs, declared. Australia win the fourth Test by twenty wickets and 1 run.

Richardson Explains 2-Run Declaration

'It was matter of momentum. The moment was there to be seized. Young David was clearly bowling like a magician, and I felt our fielding performance was rising to meet his challenge. Certainly McLeod's catch at mid-on in the first innings, and many pieces of work by Tanner all through the match, were special efforts. So, momentum and self-belief were a factor.

'I also believed, as did my team mates, that the English were a little shell-shocked, if you'll forgive that phrase. I did not wish to give them time to regroup, nor to have time to rethink their approach. I actually only wanted one run, so as it turned out, getting two was exactly what was needed. I concede it was a gamble, but cricket is sometimes that, and life is always that.

'Can I also say,' he said in closing, 'and I don't have any perspective at all on this thing that has just happened, that I thank God for granting me the privilege to have been on this field of play today.'

Balls Checked Again

Umpires Wisden and Bosanquet have stated that the balls used in the Test are not in any way faulty. They examined the ball carefully at the end of the first outrageously destructive over. Indeed, Longford examined it on arrival at the wicket in the first innings. It was changed for the Australian innings and changed again for the next English innings, albeit with a great deal of shine still left.

Further tests were done at close of play, with a representative from the English team present for bowling and batting tests in the middle. [They continued for the afternoon. Many of the crowd, perhaps feeling they had paid to see a day's cricket, remained to observe the testing procedures].

Whirring Sound a Fright

The ball tests may confirm a theory concerning the mysterious whirring sound reported by players during Donald's bowling. Opposing wicketkeepers agreed that the noise was caused by the speed at which Donald was spinning the ball. Mr Baker reported hearing that kind of noise every now and again when a spin bowler managed to elicit a particularly large amount of spin on the ball. Likewise Mr Morgan had also heard such sound on occasion, but certainly never on every delivery.

The theory is that the whirr comes from the stitching catching in the air like some whining piece of war ordinance. The effect on the English batsmen was equivalent. Minds seemed focused and then alarmed and befuddled. In the end the sound seemed to evoke sheer terror.

Off Their Heads

BY VISITING BRITISH NOVELIST BERNARD CHESHIRE—

Delight. Then astonishment. Then a kind of glee, just as one imagines the rising expectation as the carts brought in the aristocracy to be guillotined, and as the inevitable next wicket fell, like some coiffed head tumbling into a basket, so too the next roar of approval. The executions were despatched so swiftly that scorers and crowds-people could barely take in the moment, let alone the whole occasion. 'Was that a googly?' 'Was he stumped or caught?'

Let me share a confidence. Where normally somnulating hacks take our moment in the sun and catch up with a little reading and correspondence, a new thing began to dawn out here today: enormous tension. Would they score even one run? We'd entered a new kind of world, some drunken night in April, some Shakespearean midsummer, where top is bottom and Alice rules our world. Somehow, we knew quite early the wickets were gone. It was that one run that was in doubt.

And I therefore declare victory. Longford got the run. The English captain stood tall today and rained on the Australian parade, denying Donald his perfect game. The king is not dead yet. Long live the king. I am still not sure whether I completely dreamed this.

David's Grandfather Ill

David Donald's grandfather is gravely ill. George Baker, West Australian cricket coach and farmer, has looked after David since an early age, and trained him in the art of spin. WA is gripped by the worst drought in twenty years and it is understood that the family farm is mired in debt. It is to be hoped that young David's exploits on the cricket field may rally his grandfather.

The official attendance was 87,446.

CHAPTER SEVENTEEN

The aeroplane landed on the playing fields of the Esplanade in Perth between the town and the river just after dawn. A thin group of office workers, idlers and government officials had shown up with a band playing 'God Save the King'.

'Might want to play that a few times an' all,' muttered Mr O'Toole, rather drunkenly.

Mr Biggins hissed, 'That will be enough of your dark wit, thank you, O'Toole. I for one care very deeply about the King's health.'

Mr Kingsford Smith gave some speeches, but proceedings were interrupted, as a car had been arranged by the Western Australian Cricket Association to take David to Toodyay, where they were holding up the train to Dungarin. The dashing pilots had tried to arrange for some fuel to be taken to Dungarin so they could take David all the way, but there had not been time.

David tried to thank both men but couldn't reach them through the crowd. People were patting David on the shoulder and ruffling his hair and generally not letting him through. When Mr Biggins dragged him towards the car, David saw the crowd doing the same thing to Kingsford Smith, who took it with good grace and a very untired smile. David wondered at Mr Kingsford Smith's ability to draw energy from his feat and from the crowd like a kerosene lamp being turned up. David found it draining. He slept in the car, woke for some breakfast in Toodyay, and slept again on the train back home.

It was just after lunch when they came into Dungarin. Even though David had only been gone for some months, the town seemed to have pulled back on itself, like a puddle drying in the heat. What had seemed a limitless world appeared no more than a siding to David now, even before O'Toole spoke. 'Well kid, maybe it's not the arse end of the world, but how about its armpit?' For once, Mr Biggins seemed to agree.

David had been watching Mr Biggins and still could not decide on him. He was a neat man who wasted few words or movements. So, while he was of average height, he seemed shorter. According to what Mr O'Toole had got out of him, he had once been a solicitor but was now the treasurer of the Australian Cricket Board, but also, suggested O'Toole, a bit of a 'fixer.' David doubted from the way he said it that this meant he was good with machinery. Mr Biggins' eyes never smiled, and never gave any hint at what was going on behind them.

On the other hand, there was Mr O'Toole, who never left you in any doubt whatsoever concerning every single thought, feeling, opinion and bodily condition that made up each minute of each hour of the day. He'd finally got to David about half an hour out of Dungarin, plopping himself on the seat next to him on the train while Mr Biggins was off fixing something. David opened an eye, and closed it again, pretending to sleep. O'Toole smelt of tobacco and stale milk.

'So, where's your uncle?'

'I don't know,' said David, and he didn't. His Uncle Mike
had delivered him to the hotel that night, and Mr Biggins
and Scully had come and got him a few hours later to go to
the cricket ground.

'So he's just abandoned you, has he?'

David said nothing. He couldn't think of a way to answer
the question that didn't come out badly.

'How about your grandad?'

'He's good.'

'I thought he was sick. I thought that's what I found out
for you, and that's why we are going to see him.'

David looked at him. O'Toole was smiling his loose
dribbly smile. His face was pink, like he was lifting
something heavy.

'You do know you wouldn't be getting back to see him
if I didn't write those articles about you and him and the
shared plight of our nation, and being mired in debt?'

David shrugged. He wasn't sure if that was true. He'd
only read the article in the one paper on the plane.

'So you don't care about your grandad?'

'I do.'

'Man who raised you single-handed out on the farm.
Taught you everything you know.'

'Stop it.'

'Do you love him?'

David looked away, like he was looking out the window,
even though he was not looking at anything except his
own angry feeling.

'Doesn't matter, David. They call you Billy like in Billy
the Kid, but they also nicknamed you The Old Man. Is that
after him?'

'No. Mr Baker said I had like an old head on young

shoulders. At cricket. Nothing else.'

O'Toole started laughing. It was like a low rumble of thunder down a mine. 'Yeah, well we'll keep that one from them won't we? That's called projection that is. Projection onto a pretty clean canvas.' He nodded to himself, satisfied with his joke.

David started to get up. 'I got to go.'

'Where? We're on a train.'

'Toilet.' David just wanted to be away from him.

'Okay, tell me about that ball you got O'Malley with in the second innings?'

'Yeah, that was a good un,' said David with a smile.

'You know they're calling it the greatest ball ever bowled?'

'Ever?'

'And it wasn't even leg spin was it? It wasn't your googly. It was a different grip, like you used in the third Test.'

It was true. David had intended to keep bowling leg spin. They were coming out exactly as he wanted and with good control. But Mr Johnson had been watching him bowl a couple of very good offies in the corridor that morning, and thought a good off-spin delivery at the start of the second innings would confuse and panic the English even further. It sure did that, although at the time David was not thinking about the collective minds of the other team. He was concentrating on nothing more than getting as much spin into his off break as he possibly could. He put everything into that ball and it sure did change direction off the pitch. He'd actually erred in putting it too far out to the leg side. If it had not drifted in a little, it might have been called a wide. The greatest ball they all talked about was a whisker from a mistake and nearly another run.

'Anyone home?' O'Toole was watching him. 'What kind of ball was it?'

'I can't tell you. You'll put it in the paper, and then the Poms will read it.'

'Who told you that? Richardson?'

David nodded, sure he'd got O'Toole back.

'Well, sure. But we can put a little bit of truth on some and then we can put a little bit of misdirection in there too. A bit of spin of our own.' He smiled, his eyes closing like a cat in front of a fire, sharing his secret.

David said, 'I'm sure you could. But I won't.' David prodded him with his knee to be let out.

O'Toole winced, but did heave himself up out of the seat, so that David could pass. 'I don't need your cooperation for the story, Old Man. You are the story, but where that goes is up to me.'

David didn't sit again on the train to Dungarin.

David was adamant that Mr O'Toole not come out to the farm when the oldest Mr Pringle offered to take them in his car. There had been a welcoming committee of sorts at the little station. Nell wasn't there. All three Mr Pringles and their wives were dressed up. David smiled at the Mrs Pringle who had been his mother's friend, and she smiled back with no sign of sadness at all, although the morning sun lit her face hard, and David realised that she might be as old as Mrs O'Locklan. Her husband, as mayor, offered a speech concerning returning sons who had done great things, which in this case was not a dead soldier but David. The other Pringles tipped their heads forward as though listening, but they were really allowing the hat brims to shade their eyes. Bob Pringle and Jimmy Clarke leaned up against the steps, yawning. Bob had a white shirt, and David supposed he must be working in the bank now. He whispered something to Jimmy who laughed out loud until he saw a Mr Pringle glaring. Old Jack came over from the pub, and he looked David up and down, before shaking his head and going away. Apparently there was to be a town dance that night. There was some clapping, but when O'Toole yelled, 'And we can declare a fundraiser to save the Donald farm,' it stopped abruptly.

Eventually they all turned to David and it was evident it was his turn to speak. He said, 'Can I go see Grandad now?'

There was a splutter of a laugh from Bob, but everyone else seemed as relieved as David that the welcome was over.

Mr Pringle, the banker, explained the financial side to Mr Biggins while he drove them to the farm. He may have forgotten David was in the back, as he made no attempt to be polite. But then David considered that this was how Mr Pringle had always dealt with him.

'It's not a recent debt. It has accumulated with the interest and every now and then, when it gets out of hand, we buy up some of the land, so we can square things.'

'Foreclose, you mean,' said Mr Biggins, nodding.

'Yes. Most of the farmers have been finding it hard. Fourth straight year of the drought. Old Baker held out better than most on account of his pumps and pipes contraption from the river.'

'Irrigation?' Mr Biggins turned to David then, and nodded appreciation, which David felt his grandad deserved.

'Yeah. Good land by the river, usually,' said Mr Pringle, looking out at the dusty paddocks and bush.

'And how much of that is now ... the bank's?'

'I'd have to look at the map and the deeds and surveyors reports to be sure.'

'You don't know?'

'Been a long drought, Mr Biggins. Not much decent rain before that. You reckon we want dead land? Not worth anything if you can't grow wheat on it. Always bin too dry to run much sheep.'

Mr Biggins nodded as though he'd been chastised.

Mr Pringle looked over at him, and nodded once himself. 'Old George is a pretty stubborn old coot.'

'He is not,' said David.

Mr Pringle looked back for just a moment, but then away. 'Anyway, he won't hire anyone. Only been him and the boy, so they haven't been doing much work. And now he's ...'

'Thank you, Mr Pringle. Most interesting. Of course, when the drought breaks, the river land would appreciate quite considerably, wouldn't it?'

Mr Pringle looked at Mr Biggins, who looked back. Neither man let his feelings show, like a good batsman looking at a good bowler.

'We worked really hard. Both of us,' David said finally, but it didn't make David feel any better about what he'd heard.

It looked dry, even for February, and the easterly was kicking up dust down by the river line, which was not a good sign. Jess barked as they drove into the yard. There was dust thick on the kitchen window and some leaves over the doormat.

David scrambled out of the car and started for the door, but Jess kept jumping in his way, and he yelled, 'Git out of it dog,' and she slunk down so he could go inside.

'Grandad?'

There were some dishes in the sink and flies there. He went into the bedroom, where his grandad was lying on the bed in his clothes.

'Grandad.'

The man opened his eyes. 'David.' He struggled to sit up. 'Having a nap.' His face was pale, a whiteness having somehow insinuated itself into his tanned face. His lips looked bluish and his eyes yellow. He'd lost a lot of weight, also from his face. The dog came in and sat just inside the door. His grandfather didn't order her away. He was looking at David. 'You done the watering?'

'No, sir. Not yet.'

He looked at the window. 'What time is it?'

'After two, I guess. You want some lunch?'

'I must have dozed off.' Then he looked at David again, as though for the first time. 'David.'

'Yes, sir.'

Then he must have seen the men, because he squinted, and yelled, 'Get out Pringle. I'm not bloody dead yet.' His grandfather's voice seemed as strong as ever. It was his eyes that had gone soft.

'Steady on, George. Just brought the boy out. Trying to help.' Mr Pringle raised his eyebrows at Mr Biggins, but the little man was already backing out of the kitchen.

His grandad watched the doorway a moment longer before he said, 'There's some pay books and other papers hidden in a biscuit tin under the rain tank.'

'Yes, sir,' David said, and checked to see that Pringle had gone out too.

'When I'm gone, you take them to someone ... not a Pringle,

and you get them to sort it out. Maybe the blacksmith.'

'Nell's dad. Yes, sir. But Grandad, you'll be all right.'

He looked at David again, and again it was like he had forgotten he was there. His skin had gone tighter around his cheeks. Some of the hundreds of lines that had crossed the old man's face had evaporated. His lips were moving, and David leaned to hear, but he wasn't speaking. He was working up a smile. The smile passed like the thin shadow of a cloud. Then his grandfather's face set hard.

'Are you all right?' David said, feeling fearful for the first time.

'Why are you here boy?'

'You're sick.'

'Why aren't you with the team?'

'Grandad?'

'Why aren't you with him?'

'But Grandad, you're sick.'

'Get out.'

'Grandad?'

'Get out of this room now. I don't want you here.'

David stood, and turned to go, but turned back nearly as fast. He didn't look at his grandad, but he sat back down. He wasn't afraid. Finally he said, 'I reckon if you're too sick to kick me out of this room, Grandad, then I'll just stay sitting awhile.'

'Are you disobeying me?'

'Yes, sir, respectfully, I reckon I am.'

He tried to glare at David, tried to get that steel in his eye that David was afraid of, but couldn't manage it, and realising he couldn't, he closed his eyes. David thought he was about to sleep, but he said, 'She never disobeyed me a single day in her life, and then when she met him, she never obeyed me again. Off to dances, off to wed, off to England in the middle of the bloody war. Off forever.' Then the corners of his mouth turned up into a gossamer of a smile as he seemed to recall other things, and he lay there smiling again. David couldn't recall so many smiles in a year being on his grandfather's lips.

David waited until he was sure his grandfather was asleep before he went out to the men at the car.

'I'm going to stay here, Mr Biggins,' he explained as he got his bag.

'Are you going to be all right out here?'

'It's my home, sir.'

'But your grandad?'

'He's got cancer David,' said Mr Pringle.

David looked to Mr Biggins.

'He's had a doctor apparently. Is there someone?'

'We look after our own out here, Mr Biggins,' said Mr Pringle.

David said, 'Nell'd be good. Nell Parker, the blacksmith's daughter. But ...' David shrugged. There was no one else.

'You will be at the dance,' said Mr Pringle.

David didn't want to go. He couldn't. Not leave Grandad now he'd made it back.

Mr Biggins patted his shoulder and said, 'No, no. We'll take care of all that.'

'It's in his honour!' insisted Pringle.

'I will find Nell Parker and bring back some groceries,' said Mr Biggins as though he had decided on what he'd have for dinner. He pushed his homburg tightly onto his head and went to sit in the passenger seat of the car.

'A lot of trouble for this. And no guest of honour.' Mr Pringle only looked at David a moment before turning to go.

David went back in without waiting for the car to leave. Jess lay in the kitchen with her head in the bedroom door. His grandfather lay sleeping on his side on the bed. David found a jug of water under a fly net in the kitchen. He poured a cup and took it into the bedroom and put it there on the night stand.

He went outside to the rain tank next to the house. It was empty; the clump of mint that had grown under it was just black stalks. The chooks had water and he chased off some mice and topped up their barley and pollard. He looked in their nesting, but only found one egg. He went to check on the horses, but the barn was empty. His grandfather might have sold them he reckoned, but might have agisted them somewhere too. There was a bore out the back of the stables and, in that yard, water was still in a trough. Four pretty scrawny sheep fought for the shade under the eave off the shed. David got a hay bale and broke it open on the top fence rail, letting half fall into the yard. They came for it straight away.

He went over to the shed. The tank had a trickle and he filled an earthen bottle. There were little wrigglers in it. He'd have to boil it up. David lit the fire in the stove and put the water on to boil. Then he went out and got some firewood and checked the vegie garden. He got some spuds and a couple of scrawny carrots. The parsley looked good. He could make a soup later.

Jess whined at his grandad's door, but the old man did not stir. David watched the way he breathed, taking two good slow breaths and then holding for some seconds before taking the next two breaths. David did not know what cancer was, but had seen enough death on the farm to know it was in his grandfather.

He found his hat on its peg by the door. It had a new band. He turned it, letting the sunlight catch the mesh of dugite snakeskin that his grandad must have skinned and cured and sewn into the new band. He ran his finger along the oiliness of the band. It was a mighty flash snakeskin hatband.

David went out on the farm. He went to the dam, only it wasn't a dam any more. The mud at the bottom was hard cracked clay, its sides wind blown smooth. When there had been water, who was to say what may or may not have been hidden beneath. Now it was obvious. There was nothing hidden. His mother wasn't here. It was just a big gravel hole with no magic.

David pulled his hat down a little, feeling the hug of the new band tight around his head. He looked at the dam again and he conjured up the water in which his mother had drowned. He imagined it there, full and black. He saw how it turned golden as the sun went down. He stood with his eyes open and dreamed of the midgies dancing as the light faded. Then it was just an empty hole in the clay again under a biting sun, but he laughed out loud that he could pull off this trick of just thinking of other times and making them so.

Jess found him and they went off together to the river, where David found all the pipes and taps lying hot on the dead land. Tic-tics screamed all around. The earth was hot dust and the brightness of the sun made him squint even when looking down, until he got into the trees of the river line and found some shade. The pump was still there, but the river was a dry trench of sand. You could dig in the river bed at some spots and probably find water and drink it through your hat if you needed to, but there would be no crops this year.

On the way back to the house he came upon his practice wicket by the shed. He looked over the metal wickets towards the bowler's end. He went up to that end and picked a ball from the bucket and spun it, no wrist, just his fingers. They felt good. He noticed the lantern that he'd practised by was already covered in spider web, even though he'd only been gone a little while. David couldn't recall how long he'd been gone. Then he realised he couldn't recall the boy who'd practised here on this cement wicket, either. It was not just a different time, but a different person, only to be guessed at, like all the other people he found in the world.

He took the ball inside and put it on the kitchen table while he chopped the vegetables. There was some iffy chicken meat in the meat safe, and he put some of that in the pot too, giving the carcass to Jess. His grandfather coughed and he went in to him.

'Chicken soup,' said the old man, wriggling himself up a little on his bed.

'I guess,' said David.

'You guess? Did you close your eyes while making it?'

'No, sir. I put some chicken in it, so I'm hoping that's what it tastes like when it's finished, is all.'

His grandad nodded.

'Be ready in a bit. There's some water.'

David pointed to the bed stand, but his grandad had trouble getting up to it, so he grabbed him under the shoulders and lifted. It was easy. There was nothing to him any more. He was not much heavier than Jess. He settled him half-sitting on the couple of pillows.

'Under the bed is some brandy.'

David got the bottle which was half full and went and got

another cup and poured in a good couple of nips, and held it up to his grandfather's mouth.

He gulped at it, like his Uncle Mike. Like Mrs O'Locklan.

His grandad caught him looking, and said, 'I got cancer.'

'Yes, sir.'

'Eats up your insides. Like rust.'

'Oh.'

'Hurts too.' He didn't look at David while he said this, but into himself where the ache must have been. 'Like you never tasted, this one.' His eyes snapped back up, looking a little clearer than they had before.

'You need to get back to the team.'

'I will, sir. With an aeroplane, you can go across the whole country in a day or so.'

His grandfather looked at him dubiously.

David shrugged. 'I don't know about all that, but it's true. Weeks by train and a day and a night by flying, sir. If the old crate doesn't end in the drink.'

His grandad thought on that a moment.

David asked, 'Did you hear about the cricket?'

'Yeah. Little Nell came out and told us. Brought some stuff. And that teacher of yours.'

'Mr Wallace?'

'Yeah. Funny bloke. What did he do to you?'

'Um, nothing. He's good.'

'Kept apologising for not understanding your greatness. Silly bugger.' He was quiet again.

David thought about this. It felt good. Mr Wallace thinking he was great.

'Broke some records, huh?' said the man.

'Yes sir. They're talking about you too about that.'

'Room for improvement?'

'Yes sir. I'll have to come up with some new things, I reckon. And I'll have to come up with some new ideas about Mr Longford. He got that run, and I never got him out in the second innings. They'll play me different now. I brought the paper. Can I read it to you?'

'You been practising your reading?'

'Trying, sir.'

David went and stirred the soup and got a chair from the kitchen and put it near the bedroom window where the afternoon light was best. Then he got the paper from his bag. It was creased and screwed up now, and some of the print had smudged from his handling of it.

'I never could figure why you can't read, son.'

'No, sir. Letters keep turning around, Mrs O'Locklan reckons. She's a lady I met in Melbourne. You'd like her, sir.'

'I mean, you're not stupid.'

'No, sir. I hope not. Not just some dumb cow that's for sure.'

'You're not, but David, you got to bloody think. Use your noggin.'

'Yes, sir. Sorry, sir.'

'Your uncle, is he looking after you?'

'Yes, sir,' David lied. Then he wondered if it were a lie, because he didn't know the real answer to the question. He knew it would take too long to explain all that, while he was still trying to understand it himself. He thought about the night his uncle had come and about his leaving.

'Did you know you were sick when Uncle Mike came and took me away?'

He didn't speak straight away. In fact, David assumed he'd gone to sleep when he finally said, 'Yes.'

'Oh.' David settled some in his chair while he turned his grandfather's answer over and over and held it against some of the things that had happened to him. This new fact was like a lantern he could shine on that morning and now see things that had been dark and misunderstood.

David sighed, relieved. 'Did Uncle Mike know you were sick?'

'No. The king still sick?'

'Sir?' David looked up, and his grandfather indicated the newspaper.

'The king, he better, worse or dead?'

'Um, getting better, sir.'

'You making his team look stupid won't improve his mood.'

David felt alarmed that he should cause the king concern, but then realised his grandfather was joking. He looked at him a while wondering how many jokes he might have been making all this time without David knowing. Had his uncle or someone taught him jokes while he was away? Or was his grandfather loosening his too-tight grip on what he had set against the world?

David looked down at the paper. During the game he had not thought of the king. Or his grandad, or his uncle or even his father. The crowd had not existed. He couldn't even particularly recall his team mates. There was only each batsman and the field set around them. He remembered voices. Tanner's and Mr Richardson suggesting strengths and weaknesses. But it wasn't like that either. It was more like a clock with its back off, or an arithmetic problem at school that you just suddenly see all of it at once laid out in the air. That morning, he imagined the ball he'd bowl and he saw what the batsman would do. And mostly, that's exactly how it happened. He was surprised sometimes. When that ball moved so far from the offbreak, or when Windsor didn't step forward to loft him and dominate, but went back … and out.

The three balls to Longford in the second innings had been the best. Like a dance. Mr Longford had countered and David then too, and Mr Longford again to score the run. David clapped Mr Longford, but realised he was the only one at the whole ground who seemed to be doing so. Those three balls were a thing in themselves. But the rest was somehow simple and clear and done. Nothing else had existed except those batsmen and the field placements and bowling the ball, like on top of a hill looking at forever.

Early on the morning of the fourth Test, Mr Richardson had asked David to prove whether his hand had healed. In the hall outside the change rooms of the Melbourne Cricket Ground, with Mr Johnson facing and Mr Baker keeping, and the rest of the team bobbing heads out of doorways, David had been able to really let the ball sing. In fact the first two were in line with Mr Baker's knees but spun off to hit the wall before passing Mr Johnson. That's when they first heard the whirring sound. Mr Baker called it fizz — like your homemade ginger beer going off. Mr Johnson said it reminded him of the electric wires in Sydney when it rains on them.

'That happens when I get some really good spin going,' explained David. 'When I give it a rip.'

'Meaning of course that you haven't been on song until now, like, eh lad?' said Mr Jackson's voice from a room somewhere. There were guffaws.

'What you think?' Mr Richardson asked.

Mr Baker said, 'He's got a new nut and he's turning it on ice, Cap.'

'I couldn't touch it, John,' said Mr Johnson looking only at the captain.

'Show 'em your googly, Little Man,' called Ten Ton.

Mr Richardson took the ball and bent down to David, pushing it into his hands. 'Show me your googly.'

David bowled and Mr Johnson, ready as he was, still had trouble with it. 'Now do a leg break,' said Mr Johnson, tossing the ball back to Mr Richardson.

David did. The leg break turned away, but bounced higher than the googly, forcing a catch to Mr Baker.

Mr Johnson laughed.

Maud McLeod called out, 'Yeah, well that don't prove much, an' all.'

'Get knotted, Mopsey,' said Mr Johnson.

'How 'bout the one that stands up?' It was Mr Calligan.

Mr Johnson nodded.

David bowled a loopy, and Mr Johnson only just kept it down. Mr Johnson said, 'You can make that ball hit the bat faster, can't you David?'

'Yes sir, with the shooter. Hard off the lino though.'

'Hard off the lino though.' It was Ned Hall, guffawing.

David could hear Maud laughing with him. 'Bit hard with an egg, Cap'n, but I'll see if I can make it go round his ears. Oh, I can.'

They all had the giggles.

Mr Richardson got David's attention and asked him to bowl some more.

He made the ball hit the bat harder and shoot forward, then bowled another topspinner that climbed higher. Then he put in his skidder, which didn't really grip on the linoleum but still kept low.

'So what about Bishop?' asked Ten Ton.

'I don't know,' said David, 'he won't stay still so I don't know how I'm going to set him up.'

'I do,' said Mr Richardson. 'David, if you can do exactly the kind of ball you want, then we should be able to let you know what we think might do the trick.'

'I got some ideas about Dwyer on that,' said Legal.

'Yep,' said Chalkie.

Mr Tanner came out of another doorway. 'What about the charge?'

'Easy,' said David.

Hall and McLeod started laughing again. Even Mr Johnson and Mr Richardson were grinning.

'Easy,' said David again, not smiling.

Mr Tanner took the bat from Mr Johnson and spat on his hands. 'See that window.' Tanner pointed to the window at the far end of the hall. 'Fifty pounds that it goes in a couple of balls.'

'You're on,' said Ken Hall stepping out of the dressing room.

'I'm out of here,' said Morgan as he and others cleared the hall behind David, like it was on fire.

Mr Richardson stayed standing just in front of David. 'You understand, Jack, that if you injure David in any way, I will have to kill you.'

'Yeah, I'll bloody kill ya too after he's finished,' yelled Ten Ton.

'Sounds fair,' said Tanner.

Mr Hall stayed too, a little up the hall.

As David reached the top of his run-up, Mr Hall whispered, 'He's not going to charge.' David thought about

Two Bob, and knew it was true. He bowled him a topspinner, and Jack Tanner was forced to fend it off and onto a wall.

'Bloody Mopsey an' Beardie woulda caught that. You're out.'

'No they wouldn't. There's a wall in the way,' said Tanner.

At the top of David's mark Mr Hall whispered, 'Swotting it.'

And sure enough, Mr Tanner stepped down the wicket. Only David had a nicely singing ball bounce in front and spin away, catching the edge of the bat and smashing through the ceiling.

There was more laughter.

'Window in what country?' yelled Maud.

'That one's coming off the moon,' said Hall.

Baker replied, 'And into my gloves I reckon.'

'The charge,' whispered Mr Hall, tossing David a new ball.

David sent it at Jack's feet as he jumped down the hall.

'How's that?' said Mr Baker catching the ball.

Mr Tanner insisted on another and David whispered to Mr Hall, 'He's going to charge again, isn't he?'

'I think you've made him mad, Billy Boy.'

David tried to bowl a slow off break so that it would evade the bat, but spin in towards Mr Baker. There wasn't enough room in the hall, and the ball hit the wall on the full. It evaded Jack's swinging bat, hit the other wall and ricocheted into Mr Baker's hands.

'Hey, no fair,' yelled Jack.

There was laughter and cheering.

Jack Tanner stood glowering at David, who swallowed and made himself step forward towards the big man.

Mr Richardson said, 'You've been out four times in four balls, Two Bob. Give Ned his fifty pounds and let's get into the Poms.'

Mr Tanner glared at David for a moment, then shrugged, and said, 'Yeah, fair enough,' and went to give Mr Hall his money without another word to David.

Mr Hall, however, said loudly, 'I owe you a seriously large pot of lemonade, Ol' Man.'

David felt a wave of warmth. He smiled.

Mr Richardson patted him on the shoulder.

Mr Johnson did too. 'Fine bowling, Billy.'

Ten Ton finally found him in the change rooms, while he was putting on his bowling shoes. 'How you going, little man?'

David felt good. Looking at his hand and turning it, he felt strong too.

He said, 'Ten Ton, I feel … perfect.'

Jess barked and David opened his eyes. The newspaper had dropped out of his hands and onto the floor. His grandfather was sleeping, propped up, half sitting on the pillows. There was noise in the kitchen and David went out to find Nell stirring the soup.

'This isn't much of a soup,' she said not looking at him.

'Wasn't much here to put in.'

'I've brought some bacon and peas from that Mr Biggins,' she said indicating a package on the table. She flicked her hair back as she looked into the soup again. Her fringe was a bit long, and David realised she always did that, flicking her whole head back so the hair flared back up onto her head for the barest time before it tumbled down and straight forward into her eyes again.

'How's your grandad?'

'Sleeping.'

David came to the table and started to pull open the package. He saw two horses out in the yard, one of them his grandad's.

'I brought one of them back, so you can get around and go to the dance tonight.'

'I'm not going.'

'Give me that.' She came and took the package from him. She opened the paper carefully and put it aside, then got the cutting board and started cutting up bacon into bits.

'I don't want to leave Grandad.'

She nodded. Seemed satisfied. 'Peggy Pringle will be disappointed.'

'Peggy. Why?'

'She was going to dance with you.'

'She hates me.'

'Not now you're famous.'

'I'm not famous.'

Nell stopped cutting. 'David, of course you're famous. You're in all the papers and all the radio and there's people all over the country giving money to pay off the farm. They're having a Relief kind of thing and the Prime Minister of Australia might even have something for all the farmers too. The David Donald Drought something or other.'

David looked back to the bedroom. He wasn't sure how his grandad would take that. He wouldn't want the charity.

'There's a news reporter in town too, asking all kinds of questions about you and you growing up and your family and the farm too.'

'That's O'Toole. He hates me.'

'Lot of people hate you all of a sudden.'

'Yeah,' said David sitting down at the table. 'Well Peggy always hated me. But how come you do?'

'What?'

'How come you're mad at me?'

'I'm not.'

'How come you weren't at the station?'

'School. Remember. That's a place we unfamous folk have to go.'

'Oh, I didn't think of that. Did you get my cable?'

'Yes. Otherwise how could I reply?' She did smile then, but turned and went to the stove and scraped the bacon into the soup. 'Well, are you gunna tell me what it was like or what?'

'Yeah.' He wanted to more than anything. So while she shelled peas, he told her.

'Nell, it was nothing like the paper. It was nothing like anything. It was like ... just practice. Instead of Grandad saying spin it further, spin it less, make it jump, it was Mr Richardson and Mr Johnson and Mr Hall whispering what to do. Sometimes Mr Richardson, like when Mr Longford played my first ball to him so carefully, he said, "David, I'm going to take those fieldsmen from long mid-on and long mid-off to try to get him to drive. What you think?" And I knew why and what I should do, and I just nodded. It was like I could see what I would do, so doing it was no different. But then Mr Tanner came in and said to Mr Richardson and me that he thought Mr Longford wouldn't go for it straight away nor maybe at all unless I scared him into it, and so why don't I let him think he's getting set up for that drive, but try to get him with the same ball as the first innings while he was thinking about Mr Richardson leaving all that juicy space out there straight up the wicket.

Least ways, that is what he would think, in this situation, if he was facing. And Mr Richardson said that's a plan. He always says that. And that's what I did and we all thought Mr Longford would go for it the next ball. But he got a bit of an edge to get that scratchy run. He moved his bat so fast.'

'Wow, David, you sure got a lot more words now you're famous.'

'I'm just telling it,' he said, but then he said, 'You are right though. When you're famous they take you to this special place, in Canberra, and you do these famous people classes.'

Nell looked like she might be half believing him, and he put all his effort into keeping his face serious and his eyes not blinking but couldn't do it for long.

'No,' he said, laughing, and she looked like she might go sulky again, so he used one of his uncle's tricks which was to say something else straight away. 'There was a train crash in the middle of the desert and we had to have Christmas out there, and I couldn't get into the team, and my uncle kept betting people what I'd do, and we won all this money, and there were these wharf workers who I let hit me every time. In Melbourne there is this nice lady named Mrs O'Locklan and she's got this picture of a boy with a horse. Nell, she told me about my dad.'

Nell stopped shelling the peas and looked up. 'Yeah?'

'She was a nurse. My dad was throwing a grenade out of the trench to save people and it blew up.'

'Stupid war.'

'Yeah. Oh and all the cricketers have nicknames.'

'Yeah? What?' Nell came around the table and sat in Grandad's chair, while David explained.

'There's Ten Ton cos he's so big, and Two Bob is Jack

Tanner cos he's always dressed up like he's going out and what a tanner is too. Richo—'

'Is Richardson.'

'Yeah, easy. Chalkie? That's Mr Johnson. He's a teacher, but he's having a rough trot right now. Beardie is Bardsley, but I'm not sure why that's his nickname. He's young. Um, Mopsey is Maud. He didn't used to like me much.'

'Another one!' She leaned her face forward and made her eyes pop and drawing out the last word and somehow smiling at the same time.

David went quiet. Nell had freckles. Not a lot, but just a couple on her cheeks. David said, 'Your freckles are like little bits of jewels under your eyes.'

It was like he'd slapped her. She blinked and went red a moment, and then she punched him in the arm.

'Ow,' he said, and meant it. She had punched him really hard.

She looked at him, and he wasn't sure whether she was going to punch him again, but she looked to the soup and went over and put the peas in there.

'Who else doesn't like you?' she said finally.

'Um, well Mr McLeod didn't but maybe does now, and Mr Hall only started liking me in the hallway the morning of the last Test, I reckon. I don't think Mr Tanner does, or will ... but I think that's on account of my uncle. Mr O'Toole, there's another one. Oh, there was this gangster named Blackie Cutmore, in Melbourne. He didn't like me at all.'

She was looking at him again.

'I'm pretty sure I was hated just as much before I got famous, but I just never noticed.'

'Well I don't hate you.'

'I know. You're ...' He'd been going to say she was his mate, but that wasn't quite right. She had been, but something had changed. He blushed now, and it seemed to please Nell that he did, maybe that they were even.

Nell washed the dishes and cleaned the kitchen while David told her more stories about what they'd been up to on his trip. He kept a little back, mostly to do with his Uncle Mike, because he didn't want to worry her. At dusk, she had to go, so she could ride home before dark, but she went to the bedroom door one more time and looked at David's grandfather.

Outside, by her horse, she said, 'He's gunna die, isn't he?'

'Yep.'

She suddenly kissed him on his cheek, and he couldn't move. He was like a tree stump there in the yard, while she got up on the horse and said, 'See ya, David Donald.'

He couldn't say anything, just watch her ride off at a gallop.

After a while, when he finally worked out that the speck off towards the road must be a tree and not Nell riding, he went in and lit the kerosene lamp in the kitchen.

'Who's that?'

'It's me. David.'

'Oh.'

David went into the bedroom and lit that lamp too.

His grandad lay back down on the bed, pale in the yellow light of the lamp. His eyes were closed again, and he breathed shallowly, like panting.

'I made some soup, Grandad.'

'It hurts.' The old man still wouldn't open his eyes.

David got the brandy bottle again and poured a half a cup. 'I got the brandy.'

He wouldn't lift his head and when David tried to pour

a sip into the corner of his mouth, he coughed and choked some. The convulsion of the coughing must have twisted his body in the cancer part because he whimpered.

'It's all right. It's all right,' David whispered, patting his grandfather's shoulder.

David got a singlet out of the bureau and dipped it in the cup of brandy and let one of the shoulder straps of that hang and drip the brandy into the old man's mouth. He sipped that way, from the makeshift brandy teat, until he settled. His skin still had a tinge of brown tan, but his cheeks were gone, fallen away under the flaking skin. David ran his fingers gently across the hair at his temple, brushing back.

The old man smiled and said, 'Mary.'

'It's David, Grandad.'

'David,' he said and nodded a little.

David stroked his skin some more. It had become as soft as a dog's tummy. 'Did you think I was ... my mum?'

'No.'

'Do you wanna talk about her?'

His grandad grimaced, and David fed him some more brandy drips into his mouth. As the old man settled, David saw the newspaper where he'd left it by the chair, and decided to read aloud, just for something to fill the night. 'I'll read you a bit, Grandad. From the paper. They talk about you. You wanna hear that?'

'Yes,' he said, without opening his eyes.

David had intended to read the section concerning the great George Baker being gravely ill, but decided it sounded too sad. Instead he found a column he hadn't read on the aeroplane that had George Baker mentioned down the bottom. He folded the paper yet again and angled it towards the lamp and tackled the reading with patience.

'What Makes Donald So Very ... spec. Splec. Special. What Makes David Donald So Very Special. This one is by Mr O'Toole. Physically Donald is of average height and weight for a normal, thin twelve year old. However, his fingers are extra-ornery long. Twice as long as normal. This means he has an extra-ornery ability to grip the ball all over. His right wrist is thick and powerful. His shoulder and elbow agile. This enables him to extract huge amounts of spin, but also bounce.'

David grew bored with it, the listing of it all, the picking it apart. He looked outside at the darkness.

'Would you tell me something about my mother, Grandad?'

The old man's eyes were closed although he seemed to be listening.

'What was she doing in the dam? What was she doing there to get drowned?'

Bright light suddenly swept the room.

'Huh,' yelped David, dropping the paper and standing. He was sure the ghost of his mother was about to leap in at him from the dark. But it was a car.

David met Mr Biggins at the front door.

'Hello David,' said the neat man seriously. 'How is he?'

David shrugged, but stepped back to let Mr Biggins in.

He took off his hat and edged into the kitchen, turning it around the brim.

'I still can't go to the dance, Mr Biggins.'

'Oh, no. No need son. That finished an hour ago.' He checked his fob watch and said, 'It's after midnight.'

David smelt the soup for the first time and knew how hungry he was. 'Do you want some soup?'

'No thank you. Go ahead. I just wanted to make sure it

was all right here. The fifth Test starts soon, and ...' He shook himself and sat down at the table, slipping his homburg onto his knee. 'But don't worry about that. We have had some success in raising money for the farm.'

David ladled some soup into a bowl and came back to the table. Two moths were thwocking into the kerosene lamp glass then chasing each other off before they did it again.

'What if we set you up in a nice house in Sydney, David?'

'A house?'

'We could work out something, with school and what not ... housekeeper, eventually a trade.'

'But I want to live here.'

'These people, the town ... I met many of them at the dance.' Mr Biggins seemed to be having difficulty choosing his words, sorting through them and throwing some out like overripe grapes in a bunch. 'Without your grandfather, is this really ...'

'Yes, sir. This is where I want to live.'

Mr Biggins sighed, then nodded just once. 'Very well.' He looked around the kitchen as though taking inventory, and said, 'There aren't any ledgers or receipts or important papers are there? A desk where your grandfather does his business work?'

'No, sir. We're a farm. We don't do business.'

Mr Biggins gave a little smile, but then turned serious again. 'The bank manager is making it difficult for me to access records you see, so it's more difficult to assess the ... problem.'

Then David remembered the biscuit tin his grandfather had mentioned hidden under the rain tank. David looked at him, not sure whether to trust the fixer that the Australian Cricket Board had sent. 'I'll just ask Grandad if it's okay.'

'So there is a file?'

'I'll just ask Grandad.'

David went into his grandfather's room, but the old man wasn't breathing any more.

CHAPTER EIGHTEEN

They flew out early from Adelaide on their way to Sydney. David was getting used to the sudden surge of speed as the plane hurtled along the flat landing field before it took off. He was even starting to get used to the drop in his stomach as it lifted up into the air. He wasn't used to the flying though: not the up in the air like a bird-ness of that. One thousand yards above the earth was not a place he wished to be.

They'd flown from Geraldton to Perth and from Perth to Adelaide, landing in different towns every four hours or so. They'd slept the night in a place called Forrest which seemed to be just an airfield with a small hostel next to it. Mr Biggins had organised it all on behalf of the Australian Cricket Board so that David could reach Sydney in time to play the fifth Test. Mr Biggins had organised everything, including the funeral and the farm and even the leaving behind of the reporter O'Toole. Yet, coming out of Adelaide, David was glad of the cotton wool used to block out the sound of the airplane engines. He did not want Mr Biggins to be able to talk to him any more.

They had held a funeral for Grandad on the farm the day after he'd died. David had insisted on burying his grandfather on his own land. Mr Bonner, the minister from the church, and Old Jack from the pub, of all people, came out early in the morning and showed David what to do with tidying up his grandad's face, closing his mouth and dressing him in his best clothes.

'Yer best duds are for your wedding and for yer funeral,' said Old Jack seriously.

'And a few visits to church in between maybe, Jack,' said the minister.

Old Jack ducked his head a few times like he was dodging blows.

'Grandad didn't go to church, Mr Bonner,' explained David.

Mr Bonner looked David square in the face, like a man. 'He didn't lately, David, but he used to. Then, during the war, some things happened, which I guess you know, and George fell out with God and stopped speaking with him, least ways in public. Well, I reckon God never took the same approach to that argument that George had running, otherwise he wouldn't have made you, would he?' Mr Bonner set about adjusting the dead man's collar. 'I'm hoping you'll forgive God on your grandfather's behalf.'

David nodded even as he tried to contemplate God and his grandfather arguing. He reckoned they were probably pretty well matched. He tried to conjure some light with this piece of information about his grandad, and to shine it on the man he knew, but nothing would come. George Baker never spoke of God. He was a fair man, but not a particularly friendly or forgiving one. Then David considered the war. People talked of before the war and during the war and after the war. Things and people changed. Out of the swirling empty mist of his mind came the idea of his father, smiling over a cup of tea, just before the grenade landed.

Mrs Doolan and two other old ladies had also come, and they cleaned the kitchen and set out food and made big pots of tea. They kept trying to pat him so he took refuge in the bedroom with Jess and his grandfather, waving off the flies.

The old man had lost his wife during the birth of David's mother Mary, and he'd lost Mary during the war when David was little. Bit by bit, he'd been losing the farm. But he'd got up every day and worked the farm and taught David cricket and looked after him. In spite of the old man's hardness and the silence and the rules, David thought he had been glad of David, and that George Baker's life had been a good one, with some satisfactions along with the disappointments. He had lived long enough to hear about David's wondrous piece of bowling in Melbourne and surely would have taken that with some kind of pleasure.

David wondered whether he should have some regrets himself but he couldn't think of any. Maybe if his mother and father had not died then his grandfather would have been softer on himself. Maybe not. Maybe if David's mother and father had not died the whole town might have been softer on David but he suspected not.

The man had lived and he was now dead. David was used to death and used to the idea of it. Everything dies, even the biggest tree, eventually. David would miss him. He would not forget.

Anyway, that's the kind of thing he might have said over his grandfather's grave if he had the talent, but instead he just thought it. Nell's dad, Mr Parker, had brought out a wooden coffin and they'd fitted him in by forcing his knees a bit sideways. It seemed important to David that they kept the old man's neck straight.

'I damn forgot to bring the bloody hammer and nails,' said Mr Parker angrily. 'Sorry, David.'

David didn't mind and went and got some from the work shed. He helped hold the lid straight while Mr Parker hammered in the nails, occasionally giving out a mild string of swear words if one didn't go in just right.

Mr Fowler from across the river and Mr Clarke from the next property helped Mr Parker and David carry the coffin up to the hole that they'd all dug on the hill overlooking the dam. David was again surprised at just how light his grandfather had become, as though whatever it was that had kept him going was made of some kind of rock. They put ropes under the coffin and inched it over the hole and lowered it down.

Words were said. The minister said prayers. Others said things about his grandad. Mr Parker made a joke about George driving a hard bargain and denying the invention of the motor car. Others said he was tough and strong. Mr Biggins talked about his contribution to local cricket and not just David.

David tried to concentrate, but someone had tied Jess up back at the house and she kept barking. 'Will you look after Jess until I get back?' he whispered to Nell.

The Pringles nodded but left quite early, although the nice Mrs Pringle came and hugged David, just like Mrs O'Locklan, and David let her and felt her breasts push into him like the clean soft pillows they had in hotels.

He said, 'It's all right, Mrs Pringle. Don't be sad about everything.'

She looked at him, kind of surprised, but then nodded, trying not to let David see that she was starting to cry at what he'd said, before she hurried off.

Mr Biggins found him amidst the condolences and cups of tea to say, 'The farm is back in your hands again, Master Donald. The contents of the biscuit tin and the donations have assured that.' He tapped his nose and gave what must have been a smile, before slipping off again amongst people holding plates of cake.

Before Mr Biggins had left, the night his grandfather died, David had taken the lamp out and dug up the biscuit tin from under the water tank. Inside, Mr Biggins had found receipts and what he called a payment schedule. While David ate another bowl of soup, Mr Biggins had gone over the papers at the kitchen table, tapping a pencil on his teeth and saying every now and then, 'Ah,' and 'I see,' and, 'Hmm.' There was evidence in the biscuit tin that George Baker owned much more of his farm than had been thought.

Mr O'Toole had been at the funeral and, though he mostly kept away, David couldn't help noticing his satisfied smile as he stood near the back of the people smoking and looking at the dam.

While Mr Biggins was pouring petrol into the car Mr Parker had loaned them to take them back to the plane in Geraldton, O'Toole came up.

'Well son, the money's pouring in. From around the country. All for you and the farm. A national outpouring of gratitude and consolation. They're rallying for you.'

This news did not make David feel happy. He guessed it was because he was taking money that other people probably needed just as much as he.

'Oh come on, David. Bygones? I have actually helped Biggins save your farm for you.'

'Thank you, Mr O'Toole.'

'You're the biggest thing in the country. Maybe the whole world. You bowled out a whole team twice for just a run. No one has even come close to that before. No one ever will. It is monstrously improbable and miraculously manifest. You did it. And they got a right to hear about your exploits and your tribulations. Don't you think? For them. To give them a little ... hope and cheer in these dark times?'

'I guess,' said David, but not sure.

'Then why don't we start over. No more misunder-standings.' O'Toole smiled. Sweat was dribbling down from under his hat and trickling by his ear and down his neck. He held his hand out, and David shook it.

'Your hand's bigger than mine.'

'I suppose.'

David tried to take his hand back, but O'Toole wouldn't let go. He looked round, seeing Mr Biggins coming.

'Why'd you bury your grandad near the dam there?'

'He liked that spot.'

'The dam's special, isn't it?'

David pulled his hand back.

Biggins was getting into the driver's side of the car, dragging on his thin leather driving gloves. Nell and her dad were coming round.

He had time to say, 'It's private, Mr O'Toole,' before they edged the reporter away.

Now David was flying above Adelaide, looking down at the river, with cotton wool in his ears, flying towards Sydney and the final and deciding Test match, and he was thinking about the dam once more. 'Of course the dam is important,' he said.

David turned from the window to find Mr Biggins looking

at him. The ACB treasurer nodded, taking a piece of cotton wool from his own ear. David looked away. He still wasn't ready to talk to Mr Biggins.

When they'd stopped in Adelaide, they took a hotel close to the plane for Sydney. David had remembered Mrs O'Locklan's address and he'd got a telegram form and had spent some time working over it, trying to keep the word numbers low and the letters the right way round. *Dear Mrs O'Lokolan comma Grandad is dead stop farm good stop how are you stop where is uncol mike stop love David.*

It took him some time to decide to sign it 'love David,' but he knew she'd like that on account of their discussion about his telegram to Grandad. He thought he should have put in about their two hundred pounds helping save the farm, but that would have to wait to be in his first ever letter maybe.

The hotel man had corrected some spelling and Mr Biggins had paid for it, frowning a little when he took a peek.

The reason for the frown came while they ate dinner in the hotel.

'Your uncle.'

'Yes?' David looked up from his roast chicken.

'In Melbourne, he tried to negotiate a different contract for you.'

'I don't understand.'

'A special contract with a higher rate of pay than the other players.'

'Oh.'

'You can tell him, David, that we might agree to that.'

David nodded.

'But we would need some guarantees.'

David chewed his chicken.

'Do you understand the message?'

'I think so Mr Biggins, but I don't want that. I don't think it's fair if I get more money. I mean Ten Ton has a family. He needs more.'

'That is not the basis of this arrangement. It's about providing enough so that you can concentrate on your cricket, and also ...' Mr Biggins searched the floor, before going on, 'it allows your uncle sufficient funds ...' another little search, 'such that he would undertake not to wager on the game.'

'Oh.'

'He'd also have to stay away from the other players and the ground during the games.'

'Oh.'

'I'm sorry, David. We would run over these things with him, but ... we don't know where he is either.'

'Yes, sir.'

'Will you convey these things?'

David noticed how Mr Biggins wasn't quite looking at him again. For a little while at the farm he'd been looking and talking to David. But now he was once again looking at an imaginary person just past David's left ear. 'I'll tell him, Mr Biggins.'

'Good.'

'But ... my uncle is a bit of a worry sometimes. I'll have to talk to him about it.'

'Certainly. Talk. We can discuss the details.' Mr Biggins shrugged a little shrug and turned back to his fish, rather unhappily, David thought.

David excused himself early and went out and practised bowling in one of the big sheds that they had built for the aeroplanes to rest in. The flooring was hard and they had big lights up near the roof. David had brought a couple of old balls from the farm, and he bowled them at a strut on the wall of the shed.

Mr Biggins appeared again in the big open doorway. He stood a moment, his hat centred on his head and his full-length coat done up against the night, even though it was pretty warm.

David landed a ball to the right of the strut, spinning it only slightly so it just grazed the metal. He landed the next far to the left, with his new off-break grip, and bowled that back the other way into the strut. There was no pain in his fingers. None at all.

Mr Biggins came in to get the balls for David, his leather shoes making a clop clop on the floor. When he got to David he didn't offer the balls.

'I have a problem and I've been looking for the right time to talk about it with you.' Mr Biggins looked sadly around the shed at the planes.

'What?'

Mr Biggins sucked on his bottom lip a moment. David had often seen him choose how to say something, but never take this long. Finally he said, 'Can you bowl better than you did in Melbourne?'

'Yes. On some balls. I can get Mr Longford out. But they'll play different this time, don't you reckon.'

'Possibly,' said Mr Biggins to David's ear. 'Let me tell you my problem and maybe you can help me.'

'Yes sir, if I can.'

'The Australian Cricket Board takes a share of the gate receipts from each ground where the Test is held. From those receipts we make player payments, salaries and contributions to tours and the like. We try to keep the gate costs down so the public can afford to come. It's a delicate balance between revenue and doing the most good.'

David nodded, keeping all the information clear in his head, but not seeing the problem.

'In Adelaide, the receipts were quite outstanding, starting low, but as word of Australia's fightback and your curious and then amazing inclusion filtered out, we achieved full ground capacity. In Melbourne, the ground was sold out. By lunchtime, they broke down a fence and poured in. The official attendance was eighty-seven thousand. Some estimate that there were a hundred and twenty thousand people in the MCG to witness the ... miracle.'

Mr Biggins giggled. It was a strange sound coming from him. He looked up suddenly. 'It was truly amazing, David. I was there. So ... exquisitely beautiful, like a piece of music. Extraordinarily ... pure.' He looked at the scuffed cricket balls in his hands and smiled. 'But also like some crazy comic thing too. You know, people who weren't there still won't believe that it happened.'

His face went serious again. Sad again. 'But the receipts, you see. Eighty-seven thousand, yes, but no day two. No day three or four or five. Do you see?'

'No, sir.'

'The greatest day of cricket in the history of the game has cost us a fortune. By my calculation, given your current age and, barring injuries, we have possibly thirty years of monetary losses ahead of us. Massive losses.'

David blinked. It was a completely different way of seeing. It ... well it was like flying really. Or like Uncle Mike suggesting no one should own a horse so that everyone can have them.

'Can you get a loan?' said David, brightening.

'Hmm.' Mr Biggins looked into David's eyes. 'Can you bowl less well? Just a little.'

So, David was glad of the cotton wool in his ears. He could tell Mr Biggins felt very bad about what he'd asked, but David did not want to talk about it. Mr Biggins had not been the first to ask, but the answer remained the same. It would be disrespectful to cricket. It was completely against everything his grandfather had taught. But, even over those things, David knew it was against everything he did and the way he did it and who he was.

David sat in the plane, trying to imagine bowling below his best and every time he got near the idea he found his whole body tensing, every muscle tightening, and all the while, he could hear his grandfather's voice, deeply disappointed with him. Finally, in another plane approaching Sydney, he'd started vomiting in some bags they had for just that. He only stopped when he could see the huge city of Sydney below, with its two big bridge ends ready and waiting for a bridge to be built across the harbour.

As David came out of the plane in Sydney, Mr Biggins said, 'Listen, David. I've upset you. I'm very sorry. Forget that idea, will you? It was a mistake on my part. You just play well tomorrow.'

David nodded, and the man patted him on the shoulder. 'Good man. I'll get our bags. There should be a car.'

He hurried off amid the baggage and bags of mail and sheds.

'David.'

David turned to see a lady dressed up in furs and jewels smiling at him.

'Your Uncle Michael has a car. Round here.'

'Where is he?'

'In the car, darling. He's had a skinful.' She laughed, but it was quiet. She wore lipstick so pale pink that it was nearly white, and a green colour on her eyelids.

David followed her. There were wooden sheds and buildings mostly painted green. A trolley of parcels and bags of mail were being stacked outside one shed.

'Hurry up or they'll turf us out of here.'

She wore a short skirt and it showed her knees, which were skinny. He'd have to talk to his uncle about her. She might be nice, but David needed rest to prepare for the Test match, not his uncle's parties. He wondered if Mrs O'Locklan would approve and thought not. If he could get his uncle to promise to behave, which he had done sometimes, he could get Mr Biggins to let him come to the games too.

The car was a big Dodge with four windows in the back. A driver in a loose suit had a back door open and the lady clattered on her heels to it. Then she stepped back so David could get to his uncle. Only it wasn't his uncle. It was Blackie Cutmore.

David tried to step back but the other man was behind him, pushing. Blackie grabbed David's wrist and pulled him in, as the driver slammed the car door behind.

'Gidday, Billy.'

David was pushed back into his seat, as the car took off. The driver was driving them fast. The lady was walking away past the mailbags. David turned to look at Blackie, his smile twisted like the scar on his cheek.

'Where's my uncle?'

Blackie had a little bottle of liquid. He started tipping it into a handkerchief.

'You cost everybody a shitload of money, kid.'

Before David could answer, Blackie pushed the hand-kerchief up at David's face. It smelled like a nasty medicine, and David tried to get away from it, but felt his head being pushed back into the seat and then his head felt like it was being pushed through the seat and through air like he was tumbling out of an aeroplane and through the clouds.

Black. Nothing.

He was lying on something like a pallet in a dark room. His head ached and he felt like his arms were asleep. There were men's voices muttering somewhere below and the scuttling of rats somewhere above. He held his breath a moment and could make out someone snoring nearby, but the ache in his head grew sharper and he had to breathe again.

It was day. He could tell because a little light came in from behind some hessian bags hung over a high window. Brick showed through broken plaster on the walls. Across the bare boards David could see someone else, lying on another dirty pallet. It could be his uncle, judging from the clothes and from the back of his head, but David couldn't be sure. He tried to speak but his mouth wouldn't say words. He heard a door open and footsteps, boots on bare wood, then crunching on fallen plaster too. He made out a radio somewhere.

'… fine start by Australia, even without Donald. Perhaps he will show, but with England three down for forty-four, this is a promising start.'

The footsteps were right there. 'Not too much,' said Blackie's voice. 'Don't want to kill 'im.' The handkerchief was there, stinking of the chemical.

'Not yet, anyways,' said some other man.

Black.

When David woke fully again he was drinking warm water from a jug. He gulped and gulped but couldn't make his thirst go. He guessed he must have crawled over here while half asleep. He must have smelled the water. His head hurt like he'd been kicked, like the kicking was still going. It was early on another day judging by the light and the cold. He was on the floor next to his uncle, who still snored. There was a smell of piss and shit. There were six empty brandy bottles on the floor and one full one. David got up at once and nearly fell. He went to the glassless window, holding onto the bars. He vomited in the corner.

When he was done, he went back to his uncle and pushed his shoulder roughly. 'Uncle Mike,' he whispered. 'Michael, wake up.'

His uncle's face was bruised, his lip split. There was blood all over his shirt and jacket.

'Wake up.'

'David.'

'We have to get out of here.'

David went back to the window and pulled open the hessian sack to peer through the bars into the dawn light. There was a lane or street down a floor, but it was filled with sandstone bricks and corrugated iron. The houses had no roofs, half their walls had tumbled into piles of bricks.

'Where?'

'The Rocks, I reckon,' said his uncle with a pretty clear voice, even though he remained laying on his back with his eyes closed. 'Hear those horns?'

David realised he did. Had.

'The ferries.'

'Fairies?'

'Ferry boats in Sydney harbour. They've taken up the

houses down in The Rocks so they can build a bridge across the water. We're in one of those houses. Might be Katie, the Queen of the Underworld, is my guess. Don't think Blackie works for himself.'

'That was the man at the racetrack. The one who was going to cut off my finger.'

Michael pushed himself up, his back resting on the shattered plaster. He pulled a cork out of the full bottle of brandy with his teeth, but winced then felt with his tongue to where one was missing.

David went to try to drink more water. The stink from urine, their sweat and David's vomit made him gag again. There were big cockroaches moving about on the wall, like leaves drifting on water.

Michael took a big gulp of brandy. 'They don't want you playing the Test.'

'I heard it. On a radio.'

'Not doing bad without you. Least to start with. Even Johnson made thirty.'

'What day is it?'

'No idea.'

'We have to get out of here, Uncle Mike.'

'Can't be done. They drug you, and ... me too.' He indicated the empty bottles on the floor. Then he smiled. 'Will you throw this Test if they let you out?'

'No.'

'Good for you. Their original plan was for me to persuade you to throw it. They mistakenly believed O'Toole's little Fagan articles about me leading you astray. I disagreed. I never thought they'd kidnap you.'

Michael closed his eyes again, clearly ready to return to the kind of long, half-drunk half-sleep he had on the train.

David put on his brightest voice. 'Then we should play a great trick on them and get out of here and get back to the team and win the game and cost them a packet. What a lark.'

Michael opened his eyes and smiled brightly at him, pointing a finger and nodding. 'Spoken like a master, David. You have learned well, my son.'

David suddenly recalled his grandfather lying just so, waiting to die. He felt weak and had to sit, his back against the wall under the window. His head hurt, but he was trying to think past that, to form a plan. He looked to the door.

'Hey,' said his uncle, 'I haven't seen you since Melbourne. That Test was magnificent. It was like time stood still. Like something that seemed only theoretical—discovered and made real and concrete and clear. It defies description.' He gulped his brandy.

'We have to go, Uncle Mike.'

'Made a lot of people angry with me down in Melbourne, Davey. When I promised no wickets and you did what you did. So bad, then so wonderful all in an instant. Like a big bomb.'

'They'll kill me, Uncle Mike.'

'No, I'll talk to them. We'll be right. Little chat.'

'They'll kill me because I won't do what they say and it'll be no good for them ever, if it's no good now.'

'We'll sort something out.'

David tried to get up. His legs were too wobbly and he couldn't. He crawled through the broken bricks and plaster to the door. It was locked. One of its wooden boards was missing and David tried to see through, but there was just a landing and some stairs.

Michael drank deeply from his bottle.

David knew that he would soon be dozing, happily useless in his brandy-drink half-sleep.

'Grandad died.'

'I heard. I'm sorry.'

'You didn't like him.'

'True, but not. I didn't like that he didn't like me, but he didn't like me for very good reason. And our present circumstances rather bear out his low opinion of my character.'

'Why don't you shut up. You're not being clever. You just say things cos you like the sound of them, but they don't mean anything.'

Michael finally blinked. Maybe he was listening.

'He knew he was sick. That's why he let you take me.'

'Ah. Yes. I didn't think he cared about my broken promise to Ernie.' Michael grinned, but sadly.

David sensed there was more on offer. He wasn't so fearful of the knowledge now. 'What promise?'

'No. Not a patch on Earnest James. Better man all round. Believer. Got the girl. Kept whispering in my ear you see. 'Promise to do this and promise to do that ... I couldn't even run ... kept slipping in the mud and my blood and his blood. Blood everywhere. Open front of my boot kept catching on things. He's on my back and in my ear, whispering. "Love you. Love them." Love. Promise. A bloody dance on a broken bridge. I don't even know when he stopped whispering.'

Michael gulped at his drink.

David thought about what Mrs O'Locklan had said. Was that it? His uncle's wound. David got himself up onto all fours ready to crawl back to Michael.

'It wasn't your fault, Uncle Mike.'

'What?'

'It wasn't your fault he died.'

'I know that. You think it's that? That simple?' His uncle had his nasty edge, the nasty edge of his drunk self. 'Even though I met her first, she fell in love with him and made the better bargain. No hard feelings. Cross my heart.'

David waited on hands and knees still near the window.

Michael kept on, quiet and bitter as though talking to himself. 'What happened is he got blown up, but that's not what happened. What happened was I promised, you see. What happened was I was supposed to come back ... to you and her — the big piggyback promise — and I was supposed to look after her. But I didn't. I didn't answer the call and she killed herself. That's what happened.'

'What?'

'True. You know it.'

'No, don't say.' It was David's voice that David heard, little and frightened. Her. It was about her. David hadn't been ready for this.

'And if you don't know it, you'll read it if you ever get out of here, because O'Toole has it plastered all over the newspaper. Blackie showed me.'

David vomited again, on the floor where he was, then tried to crawl from it. His ears buzzed. It was true. He did know it. The whole town knew it. His mother. The nice Mrs Pringle nearly saying. David realised that he had known for some time and had somehow kept the secret from himself.

'In the dam,' said David, his head now against the wall.

'I didn't know where until you told me at the farm.'

'She must have been so sad.' David saw a beautiful young woman standing by the dam. He felt how she felt. A hopelessness. It was a sadness that was as cold and deep and black as the water in front of her.

'That's what I did. That's the thing.' Michael was talking to himself, not David. 'O'Toole finally told a truth. Not all of it, of course. There are layers in your brain, says Freud, and the layers can lie to each other to protect other layers ... you can go a little bit mad so you don't go really mad. That's the theory. And that is also what I did wrong. I went a little bit mad.'

David was back against the chipped wall watching his uncle smile. He was like an actor on the movie screen, changing his voice to become a teacher, then a storyteller and then a sad old drunk, all by turns and sometimes within a sentence. It was like his uncle wasn't even out there, but inside David's head, imagined. Like the lady David also watched as she started walking into the water of the dam, her loose white dress spreading out on the surface of the water.

'I promised your father I'd look after you and your mother ... only my foot developed an infection. Big flap of skin full of mud and bits of other men. Helen was looking after me. Her husband had just died. Solace. Soul-less? That's the thing I did wrong. That's the broken thing, there. I bludged. I stayed in hospital for longer than I needed to. As long as I could. I stayed back from the front and in a warm place where I slept and slept on dry sheets under warm blankets. I fed. Caressed. Slept.'

Michael looked at David, suddenly real again and open and raw. 'She killed herself. I had time to get back to help her and I didn't and she killed herself.' He closed again, and with a lazy smile went back to making a story of it. 'She couldn't take the loss of him. She died of a broken heart.

I had promised him I would ... and I didn't. The news of her death came by cable. That is the moment. Then, not before. I did go mad.

'Insanity. It is enticing. Like drink. You can give yourself to it. It's like sleep. No pains. No chores. It's like falling, falling up. Hellie joined me, and we went mad together and shut everything out except what we felt with our skin and tongues. Wine and cheese and skin. They found us of course, not at Stonehenge, but in a cellar. I was discharged. Not honourably, but my missing toe misled folk. I was and am a coward but not in the way they all think. I stand falsely accused of a couple of crimes and guilty of the ones left uncharged. It's all fake. All chaos and random and meaningless. There, my whole confession.' Michael drank more brandy.

David said, 'I don't believe you.' He leaned his shoulder into the wall and tried to push himself up.

'Don't believe?'

'I don't believe it's meaningless.'

'It'll be true whether you believe it or not. Wake up.'

David stood, leaning against the wall to stay up. 'I don't believe you. I won't believe you or any of your story.' David took some steps towards his uncle. 'You. You're the stupid cow just waiting to die. We're going to get out of here and we're going to help Australia win. And we're going to be all right.'

David was shouting. The shouting brought the men.

Blackie and the other man crunched into the room with their bottle of sleeping stuff.

David ignored them. He shouted again at his ugly, drunken uncle. 'I don't want to die. I want to live.'

His uncle said nothing and did nothing except look

emptily at David as the men grabbed him and held him down while they pushed the rag of horrid smelling stuff into David's face.

Black.

CHAPTER NINETEEN

I didn't drink much that day and not much during the night either. I pretended to drink. I'm good at that, both drinking and pretending. I pretended to drink but would tip most of it out, so they'd think I was as drugged in my own way as David was with the chloroform. I had to hope they didn't overdo the chloroform, while I dried out enough to be able to manage some glorious, doomed, limping attempt at rescue. Perhaps I'd have more success than the last time I tried such a thing.

Me. Had you guessed? Yes, it's me doing the telling. Michael. And not as you'd imagine, not sitting in the front bar getting free drinks while I spin a tale, and maybe auction a few old cricket balls with dubious D.D. signatures, which I confess, I have done. Not then, but later, the survivor yet again who is fated/feted to look back and set out the exploits of his betters. I'm telling David's story for him, trying to get it in his words, from his point of view. You must admit, I was uniquely placed.

By the way, and for this record, I was not magically changed in the wee hours of the morning by my confessions to David about the various ways I had let down every person who mattered to me. I wasn't cured, after lying on that straw-filled couch in the abandoned house in The Rocks, pouring out my brain pus to my twelve year old analyst. No.

But even I, the ugly, drunken uncle, saw they would kill the kid. As I'm sure you will have noted, repeatedly perhaps, I do not believe the world is just or fair. It is a Dickensian melodrama with a fair measure of Thomas Hardy thrown in. It is, of course, much worse than that, if we take out the irony. Even so, I felt David deserved the chance to live. Maybe it was the crack about me being the stupid cow, thrown back in my face. You gotta admit The Kid had pluck. So, fuck Blackie and fuck them all. It was worth a crack.

I tried to wake him in the last moments of night. This appeared to be when the anaesthetic was closest to wearing off, and also when Blackie and his offsider, Wally Timlinson, were at their least vigilant. I couldn't rouse him.

As David has observed, or at least me through him, the door had been locked, but increasingly less so as the Test match progressed and we behaved more like sleepers than escapees. I grabbed him under the arms and draped him over my shoulder, holding his arms with my left hand to keep him secure, but leaving my right arm free, in what was to become known as the fireman's lift.

The bedroom door was not locked. It was merely latched, and only took a perfunctory bump of my shoulder to click and swing inwards. I moved carefully onto the landing. There was a window there, unbarred, and mostly unglassed. I got over the ledge and found a small portico-like roof of corrugated iron. It bent and groaned under our weight, and I had to lean into the post of the next building's upstairs veranda in order to lessen our downward pressure. While I leaned there, with David on my back, I had time to look at the new day sky. Dark clouds were gathering off towards dawn, like an army pregnant with intent.

The Rocks had had a long and inglorious harbour history, even back then, and had developed into a pretty ramshackle and condensed inner city suburb of long ill-repute. However, the old was making way for the new as they had started to build an impossibly long bridge across the whole of Sydney Harbour. They had torn down houses and moved on the poor, to make way for the big towers that would hold their bridge. The Rocks, that I looked down on, holding the post grimly, had all the look of a mildly bombed village in France.

I managed to keep hold of the post and inch us to the rotted wood of the next veranda. By leaning my left shoulder into that post to prop us both there, I was able to pull away the rotted rail enough to allow me to step across. Even so, it was a little dicey swinging us around the post, hoping it would hold, and hoping I wouldn't drop the dead weight of David. He was still breathing. And easier to hold than Earnest had been.

Ernie never had any arms to hold him on by. Both of them had been blown off at the elbow, when for once in his life his timing was off and he misjudged that grenade. Even though I got the tourniquets on, to stop the great gush of his blood, it still ran out all over my chest in a constant drizzle of his life. I'd tried to push his shoulders down onto mine and I'd tried to bend enough to carry him, but my foot kept catching and slipping on the duck-walk boards. Half my boot hung down like a the mouth of a dopey dog. For a long while he whispered demands for promises and declarations of love. I should have told him that I loved him back and I never did. Not a thing to occur to a lesser man. The whispering stopped before I made it to the field hospital, but I'm not sure when. Or if it ever has.

I put David down when I reached the veranda. He had long skinny arms that kept on going to these fingers that kept on going too. If he hadn't had such long skinny legs, then his fingers would have dragged on the ground behind like some primate. I touched his cheek, finding it warm. He was alive. I thought of some mild endearments, but couldn't make them come aloud. Funny the few things that I can't say.

I took his arms and swung him up onto my back again, then kicked in the piece of corrugated iron that was nailed into the doorway of this veranda. It made an awful din, but gave easily. I ran with him down the stairs and out the back.

I headed uphill, away from the giant pillar that was part of the new bridge. It looked like a huge cenotaph that morning and I was looking for some living part of the city. I must have made more racket than I thought, because as I neared the end of the lane I heard Blackie shout and turned to see him coming out from where we'd been imprisoned.

I reached the corner, but there was Wally tracking us along another road, so I turned up the nearest gap between houses away from both of them. Blackie Cutmore, of the self-fulfilling surname, was later to shoot Squinty down in Melbourne. No honour amongst thieves either, it seems. Wally Timlinson was to later become Katie's lover. Katie was one of the two Queens of the Underworld of Sydney. Then Wally got shot in some other altercation over some other patch. But those pieces of colourful historic trivia had not yet come to pass. This day they were two fit young thugs steadily gaining on David and me.

There was a vacant block with neatly piled old bricks

and a parked lorry. I went the other side of the lorry and
stepped magically into a normal street. Cars were parked on
the road and milk bottles parked on front verandas. Smoke
climbed from cooking breakfasts. It was as though we had
spun from one time into another out of an H.G. Wells' time
machine.

Across the way at the next corner was the Hero of
Waterloo, a pub, illegally open at five or six in the morning. I
kept running, trying to sense whether there was a heartbeat
in the lad I was carrying on my shoulders.

There are small mercies in the world if you can just time
your run to come upon them as they pass. For instance,
although they hadn't yet brought in the concealed weapons
laws that drove some of the more avid crims of Sydney to
start carrying razors instead of pistols, neither Blackie nor
Wally seemed to be 'packing,' as the Americans say.

The second dubious mercy was the open pub. In an era
when early closing was a major issue, and sly grog the
beginning of many a dynasty including Katie's and Tilly's,
it seemed that The Rocks continued to follow its own legal
system, an independent principality in Campbell's Cove.

I ran into the bar where the men reacted instantly. A navy
type pulled out a knife. A man near the back jumped up,
knocking four beers from the table, his mates yelling their
anger at him and me. The barman pulled out a big piece of
well-worn wood, suitable for splitting a skull or two.

'I gotta get this kid to hospital,' I yelled, still moving
towards the back, looking for other doors that might lead
out and not into the dead end of a dunny.

'What's wrong with 'im?' someone eventually asked.

Before I could answer, Blackie and Wally came through
the door. They looked straight at me, but then nodded

around the room, smiling. They knew a lot more men in here than I.

'Phew, mate you stink,' yelled someone else, and I knew it to be true. I was rank and stinking and unshaven. As a potential saviour I presented badly.

'This is David Donald and I'm trying to get him to the cricket.'

'It bloody is,' said an old soak, peering at David's face.

'It's the last day today,' said someone.

'An' Australia are batting. We're three down for forty-nine. Got no chance.'

'England have batted twice?' I asked.

'Where you bin?'

I kept watching Blackie. He was the dangerous one. Although for David it might have been his scarred face and missing ear, he gave no credit to Blackie's eyes. Blackie always watched you like he was deciding what you tasted like. His eyes had not the least ounce of sympathy or spark of humanity. On the other hand, Wally was quite handsome. His face was unmarked, least of all by many thoughts. He looked very much the happy grocer.

'I'm his uncle,' I said to the bar. 'I'm trying to get him to the cricket.'

'You killed his father.'

'What?'

'Says in the paper. Over in France.'

'Nonsense,' I said, with perhaps too little conviction.

Most of the men in the bar seemed to be standing now: ten men in this illegal opening before breakfast.

Blackie had his razor out. He flicked it so the blade swung free from its protective sleeve and flashed nicely as it caught light. 'I read that. Me 'n' me mate are tryin' to rescue the kid, see. From this bastard.' He smiled around the room.

Wally nodded. It was as clumsy a piece of lying as I have seen.

'Blackie, you don't need him any more. Didn't you hear? Australia are batting. They've already bowled twice, right? He can't bowl. It's over. He's not going to be able to bowl.'

I could tell I had Wally, because he kept trying to glance at Blackie to see what he thought.

'Gentlemen, please. If you don't believe an old digger like me, fine. But get this lad to hospital.'

'That's not my orders, Donald,' said Blackie, advancing.

I swung David onto the bar, where he lay like a roo carcass waiting to be butchered.

'David Donald! You blokes are gunna let Blackie Cutmore and Wally Timlinson kill David Donald? Are you bloody drongos?' I looked Blackie in the eye. 'Oh, golly gosh. I mentioned your names. A lot of witnesses to whatever you're going to do.'

They were thinking. So was everyone in the bar now. 'Just get the kid to hospital,' I yelled as I ran at the crims, screaming like a banshee.

Wally must have been very busy thinking about the points I'd raised, because he wasn't paying much attention to me. I caught him a beauty right on the jaw with my first swing.

But Blackie was already slashing downwards, slicing through the jacket and shirt and into my left forearm. I grabbed him in a bear hug, stepping forward and trying to smash my forehead into his, as O'Toole had done to me. I could feel light cuts on my back as we fell, and I opened my mouth to bite his nose. He pulled his head back just in time, banging it hard into the floor. I swear, I would have done anything. But, there was the crack of something woody hitting my own skull.

Black. But not nothing.

You may have noticed an awful lot of waking and sleeping in David's story. Such a lot dozing, and semi-consciousness. It made me wonder. Is he lying in the Dungarin road after falling off his bike? Is he lying in hospital there, dreaming the whole impossible thing? Or is it me? Am I lying in France, my brother dead, having a crazy guilty adventure, delirious and off my head? Am I dreaming David or is he dreaming me? Or both or neither.

I get up from my typewriter all these years later and I go to my bookshelf. I could choose from many cricket books, but pick a favourite that opens to a well-worn page. 'D. Donald. Twenty wickets for one run. Melbourne ...' I touch the print as though it is him. Then I know the truth again, beyond doubt.

He woke to find Mr Scully looking down at him, his face too big and craggy. David closed his eyes.

He heard Mr Scully say, 'He's back.' He heard another voice which sounded like Mr Richardson's, but he couldn't make out the words.

When David woke again he saw more men. He was lying on a bench in a change room and Richo and Chalkie and Beardie and Tinker were all around.

'He's awake,' called Mr Scully.

Mr Biggins came in, but before he could talk, Ten Ton pushed through the group.

'Davey!' he said, coming forward in his batting pads.

David tried to sit up as the big fast bowler reached out for a hug, but his head suddenly hurt and he fell back groaning.

Mr Scully pushed some water at him.

'Get the doctor again,' said the Australian captain.

There was a huge groan from the crowd outside and Mr Jackson came to the door. 'They've donged Maudy and he's been caught at mid-off.'

Mr Richardson looked alarmed. 'I better have a word to Legal then.'

'He's already on his way out there, Cap.'

Ten Ton knelt down next to David's bench. 'I just gotta go get my eyes ready in the light, Davey. Then we'll talk, okay?'

David said, 'You must have bowled well.'

'Yeah. Got more in the first innings when they were still a bit frightened you might suddenly appear from the change rooms. Bit harder work in the second. Buggers got over four hundred.'

'Mostly Longford and Windsor. Windsor loves batting when you're not around, Ol' Man,' said the young opener, Beardsley.

David watched Ten Ton leave. He suddenly remembered the dark room that smelled. 'How did I get here?'

Mr Johnson said, 'Apparently some questionable types brought you in. One of them knew a bloke at a gate, who knew a sheila at a pie stall, and in they crept, bearing you like the ark of the covenant. Apparently.'

'He said apparently because Chalkie was out in the middle so long, he missed that action.'

Someone patted him on the back, and Mr Johnson nodded grimly. 'Finally.'

'A tough little century.'

'No century is little,' shot back Mr Johnson.

'What's the score?' asked David, still trying to think

clearly enough to know who he was and where.

'Seven down for a hundred and forty odd.'

'How much do we need?'

'Another fortyish,' said Ken Hall, looking closely at his captain.

The men shuffled.

'An' there's some clouds over east,' said Mr Jackson.

Maud McLeod came in bleeding from the nose. The big red drops that covered his cricket shirt were already turning brown. 'Bloody bastards.' He threw his bat the length of the room and it crashed into the wardrobe there.

David looked more closely at the team as they turned to look at Mr Richardson. Ned Hall had a big bruise on his cheek. Beardie had a cut over his eye.

'Two all and a draw is pretty good, considering where we were a few Tests ago,' said Mr Jackson.

'I'm not too sure we can keep 'em out that long,' said Maud McLeod mopping at his nose.

Mr Biggins came back with the doctor.

The doctor shook his head. 'Like a field hospital down here.'

Just then there was another groan from the crowd in the stand above the change rooms. Ten Ton yelled, 'He's not out, but he's down.'

'I'll be right back,' said the doctor hurrying out, followed by most of the team.

Mr Richardson headed out calling, 'Tanner or Calligan?'

'Welcome back, Billy,' said Maud.

'Yeah, Kid, sorry we're lettin' ya down,' said Ned Hall.

'You're not,' said David.

David noticed Mr Biggins still standing in the doorway. He had his hat in both hands where he was turning it round and round.

David said, 'My uncle was a prisoner in this room with bars, Mr Biggins.'

'I want you to know I had nothing to do with that.'

'Of course not. You wouldn't!'

Mr Biggins nodded. 'Thank you. I'll see if I can find out where he is.' He turned to go, but said as he went, 'Welcome back, David.'

David closed his eyes to the pain in his head, but made himself open them straight away. He didn't want to sleep any more. The world had a habit of moving on rather quickly when he wasn't there to watch it. He stood, and felt like vomiting again. He grabbed on to the jarrah cupboard only to see his name on it. David Donald.

His cricket gear was inside. On top of his creams and shoes was a brand new Australian cap. It was dark green with the emu and kangaroo on the front. He took the cap and fitted it firmly on his head. He dressed, fighting off his headache, but once he had one of the batting gloves on, he stopped dressing, overcome with how huge his hands seemed. He looked to his left hand. Ungloved, it was immense. 'My hands are so big,' he said with wonder.

'Yeah an' my nose might have been broke a few times an' all.' It was Mr Scully, coming into the change rooms with a little bottle. 'Tell me something I don't know.'

'Mr Scully, I can't put my other glove on.'

'How many times I gotta tell you not to put your right glove on first? How you going to do your other hand? Can't you remember anything?'

'No, sir. Not about batting.'

'No, sir. And that's the truth. What are you getting into those things for anyway? You can't go out there.'

'But just if we need the runs. If everyone else gets out.'

'And you think you'll be any help?'

David sat down on the bench. He supposed not. He wasn't very good at batting. He wasn't any good at all at batting. Only bowling and he'd missed that.

'Anyway, take a big sniff of this.'

David looked at the tiny bottle that was thrust towards him.

'Will it fix my headache?'

'No. I'll go see if I can find some aspirin. Clear your head a little from all that stuff they had you on.'

'My head feels like it's got an axe stuck in it.'

'Let's see then.'

Mr Scully turned David's head and looked at the back.

'Yep. A dirty great axe stuck in there.'

David giggled. 'Do you think it might put their bowlers off? Me batting with an axe in my head?'

'Probably not the way they're bowling. Just give 'em more to aim at. Anyway, you'll not be going out there, so you an' your axe can sit here and get better.'

Mr Scully pushed the bottle at David again and he sniffed the nasty smelling salts. They made his eyes feel big and clear, like he'd jumped in the river.

'What happened to me?' asked David.

'You were kidnapped. Then rescued.'

'My uncle?'

'Don't know about that.'

'He was there. What happened to him?'

'I'll go get the skipper. He can tell you what's what. Or not. Up to him.' Mr Scully hastened out, muttering like a new harvesting machine.

David was aware of the crowd above. They seemed

clearer than before. Instead of the general murmur and noise, there was more one voice. A groan. A cheer. There was a lot of silence.

David took his right-hand glove off and put on his cricket pads, buckling the ankles first, then under his knees. He dragged the left glove on first, then the right with more difficulty, wriggling his fingers and dragging the glove up using his teeth. He looked at his enormous fingers once again with a new wonder. Had they grown even more?

Uncle Mike ... Michael had said some things. The crowd gasped as one and David was thankful for it. He stood and fished his bat from the back of his cupboard and set out to watch the rest of the Test match.

Outside the players' rooms, it was like a white sheet on the clothes line with the sun shining behind. David just stood inside the door waiting for the whiteness to clear. He saw them out there. The whole team were sitting forward on their seats looking out. They seemed frozen.

David noticed heavy clouds over the far pavilion, the big flags flapping.

Another crowd groan and David looked out to the centre of the oval. Legal must have ducked under a ball. He was straightening himself and loosening his arms, like he was putting on invisible suspenders.

The field setting looked odd. It was unbalanced. There was only one player on the off side. The rest were either in slips or crowded around the on side.

Tudor walked back to the top of his long run.

The scoreboard showed Australia eight wickets down for one hundred and forty-seven. David did the numbering and figured they only needed another thirty-four to win.

Tanner was on thirty-five.

Tudor ran in and bowled.

David couldn't see the ball, but did see Mr Calligan lean back, pushing his bat at what must have been a sharply rising delivery. There was a groan from the crowd.

Someone dived from silly mid-on. Everyone went quiet.

But Mr Calligan straightened himself again and David heard Ned Hall yell, 'Naw, didn't carry.'

The crowd began its quiet murmur again, as someone tossed Tudor the ball, and he turned to go back to the top of his run, ready for the next delivery.

Mr Tanner went some steps down the wicket and said something to Mr Calligan, who nodded. Mr Calligan put on his invisible suspenders again, and waggled his head around as though his neck hurt.

The clouds looked dark, like they might have some rain. David could remember that far back, before the drought, when such darkness filled the sky and fell in great sheets you could see coming across the paddocks. The noise on the farmhouse roof would make you have to shout, and the dogs would be miserable and smell damp, and water would shoot off things in hundreds of mini waterfalls, making holes in the ground where they scrambled into the hungry earth. The paddocks would turn to thick mud. Grandad would hitch up the horses and break open the grain and get to planting. And thousands of slivers of water, like silver snakes, would rush down the sides of the dam where his mother had drowned and it would fill once again.

The crowd gasped and David saw Mr Calligan walking away from the wickets, batless, rubbing his chest. He bent over, hands on knees, gathering himself a moment. An English player patted him on the back.

Maud said, 'Don't bloody offer consolation and then do it again, ya mongrel.' There were some boos up in the stands, agreeing with Maudy it seemed.

Ned Hall turned to Maudy and yelled, 'How 'bout we get Tudor by the cars at the back of the pub and sort him out once and for all?'

Mr Richardson said, 'Oi, not in public, boys. Everything they're doing is within the rules.'

Mr Johnson said, 'But hardly cricket.'

'Well, I'll be,' said Mr Baker.

They turned and were all looking at David, who'd edged out into the players' seats.

David couldn't account for why, but he put his bat forward and grounded it, leaning it away slightly at the top, and looked out over it as he had seen Windsor do. Maybe it was something his uncle would do, for the joke. Then he grinned and turned to them.

'Not on your life, David. No chance at all,' said Mr Richardson.

'I told him, Gov,' said Scully.

'But just in case,' said David coming towards them.

'Donald.'

'David.'

'The Kid.'

'David Donald.'

'It's David.'

His team mates stopped and looked up and around.

David saw that the crowd in the Members were looking. And people in the stands above. They were all saying his name. It was like wind coming across the paddocks. You could see it moving around the ground slowly, both ways, a ripple of wheat in the breeze.

'David Donald.'

'David.' Then they started clapping.

Out in the middle, the cricketers stopped playing. They stood and looked back towards the pavilion.

And the people stood, all of them. They stood and they started clapping.

Then Ten Ton stood, still in his pads and he started clapping too, and Mr Johnson followed and Bardsley and Richardson and Hall and Baker and McLeod all standing and clapping towards David.

Just past his team mates, David saw the English batsman Timothy Bishop, who had run out from the middle to see what was going on. He smiled in a strange way, like someone who sees a batsman nearly play on, but instead French cut a four. Bishop turned and ran back out to the middle.

Mr Richardson made sitting gestures with both hands towards the crowd.

David tried to sit, but his bat got caught up in his pads and he fell on the bench, managing to jam the bat handle into his side as he did so. 'Ow.'

'Enter the third ballerina, riding on an elephant,' said Mr Baker.

Mr Johnson came over saying, 'You know why you can't bat, don't you, David?'

David got his bat untangled from his pads, and his feet onto the ground before replying, 'Because I have no technique and no eye for the ball?'

'No, not generally can't bat. I mean why you can't go out there today.'

David looked out. There had been a change of over during all the cheering and clapping, and Mr Tanner was facing Proctor, again to the strange field setting.

Mr Johnson continued, 'They're bowling at the batsman. At the batsman's chest and head. If the batsman does the natural, instinctive thing and uses his bat to protect himself, the ball has a very good chance of being caught by one of all those fieldsmen gathered around.'

David watched Tanner get up on his toes and hit a ball out to the on side and run for three. The crowd roared its approval.

Ten Ton yelled, 'Maybe we got our lucky charm back.'

David said, 'But you got a hundred, Mr Johnson.'

'They didn't start doing it until I was set. It also plays to a strength of mine. I'm a good hooker. When I remember to move my feet, that is. I was able to move early and get inside the line of the rising delivery and help it to the boundary.'

'Then that's what I'll do.'

Mr Johnson shook his head.

Proctor bowled to Legal. The ball reared up and Calligan raised his bat. O'Malley, fielding in a fly slip, ran back and caught him over his head. The crowd moaned.

David looked up at the scoreboard. Apart from Mr Johnson's one hundred and six, only Jack Tanner was making runs. Bardsley, Hall and now Calligan were all out for a duck. Only Richardson had made double figures and he was out for eleven.

Ten Ton said, 'You think if I stop to retie my shoelace, that rain'll save us?'

Baker said, 'There's a plan.'

Mr Richardson said, 'Just hang around for a bit, Ten Ton. Let Two Bob take most of the strike. Tell him to farm it and go for the draw.'

'Right, Cap.' He nodded.

Other players were nodding. A draw seemed possible.

Honourable even.

Mr Calligan was coming back, dejected, but receiving polite applause.

'Cometh the hour, cometh the man, Ten Ton,' called Johnson.

Maudy yelled back, 'I thought it was cometh the hour, cometh the barmaid.'

They laughed loudly, but as soon as Ten Ton turned to go, their faces turned serious again.

'So David, you got away from those kidnappers, huh?'

David turned to see the reporter Charlie O'Toole, pushing his stomach up against the small fence next to the players' area, only a few yards away. Sweat bubbled all over his face like a squeezed sponge.

'Not now, O'Toole,' said Mr Johnson.

'Nice hundred there, Mr Johnson. Might be too little too late to save your spot in the team, of course.'

'Not now please.'

'David, tell me about the kidnappers. They snatched you at the airport? Did they have help?'

'Don't answer, David.'

'Was it Sydney criminals or was your uncle in on the act?'

'He wasn't.'

'You two didn't cook it up to make some more betting money?'

'Scully!' called Mr Johnson, 'Can you get this chap out of here?'

'David, did you read my story about your uncle being there when your dad died?'

'No.'

'Could your uncle be involved?'

Mr Richardson came to their seats pointing a finger at O'Toole across the little wooden fence. 'That'll be enough of that, Charlie.'

'Just doing my job here, John. You do yours and I'll do mine. Public is interested and has a right. They did buy the kid his farm back.'

'My uncle tried to save my father.'

'Hey, leave the kid alone.' It was a man in a grey suit, near O'Toole in the Members Stand.

'Did your mother commit suicide?'

'Enough,' said Richardson.

'Was she caught between the two men?'

'No,' said David.

Another man from the Members was trying to take O'Toole by the shoulder. 'Have some decency, man.'

Maud McLeod was sliding between the bench seat in front, moving towards the reporter. 'How'd you like to meet Mr Thumb and his four sons?'

'David,' shouted O'Toole, 'Everyone is dead. You're an orphan.'

A policeman moved down through the members' area towards O'Toole.

Maud was climbing over the fence towards him too.

'Enough, you nasty creature,' said Mr Johnson, also standing.

O'Toole yelled, 'If your uncle is dead, then who do you have?'

Maud threw the first punch, and O'Toole the second, but then the two men in the Members were joined by the policeman and others in pushing and prodding O'Toole. Mr Richardson, Mr Johnson and the others were also crowding up to the fence.

'A lifetime ban, O'Toole. I'll be pushing for it.'

No one seemed to have noticed the cricket game. Ten Ton was at the gate, dejectedly pushing it open.

David was going the other way, looking at the scoreboard. Mr Tanner had sixteen more runs. Ten Ton had only got one before being caught by Windsor in slips off Tudor. Eighteen more runs seemed a lot as David headed towards the wicket. The sky was getting dark. Perhaps they'd call off the game due to bad light.

David thought about his mother and about how everyone said she had killed herself in the dam. Uncle Mike, O'Toole, everyone was so adamant. He guessed that his mother's death must have had something to do with his grandad's quarrel with God.

But how did they know? If someone was there, they would have stopped her. So no one was. Well, what if she slipped? What if there was a lamb or a butterfly even that she was trying to save and she just slipped and it was all an accident. Maybe it wasn't, thought David, but no one could know that she meant to.

The crowd noise, as far as David could work it out, had not reached any agreement. There was some cheering, but it seemed half-hearted. David could make out groans. He was after all a very bad batsman. His Test average might be zero he thought. Had he scored a run? He'd only faced three balls that he could recall.

Mr Tanner came to meet him, looming up with the dark clouds behind, just like always. 'Where have you been?'

'Um, I was kidnapped.'

'Kidnapped! You mean those stories were true?'

'Yes. If they said I was kidnapped.'

'But they let you go, once we'd finished bowling?'

'Escaped.'

Mr Tanner looked at him seriously, looking over his face. Finally he said, 'Well, now it's back to the drudgery of everyday life then. You have to face just one ball from Tudor. All right. Then I'll try and keep the strike until the rain comes.' Tanner led David towards the wicket, saying, 'I must admit I'm surprised you're out here. Thought Richo would say no.'

'He did.'

Tanner stopped and turned back to David.

'He did say I shouldn't, but there was a fight and I don't think they noticed me come out.'

Tanner looked back towards the pavilion and then round the ground. 'I think they've noticed now.'

David said, 'But if I didn't come out, the Poms will win the game.'

'Well, they probably will anyway, but yeah. The captain'll come out and wave us in or something I suppose. Might get hung, drawn and quartered by this crowd if he tries, mind you. Come on. Let's draw the bloody thing.'

Mr Bosanquet was heading towards square leg and Mr Wisden was moving down to the bowler's end. Mr Wisden said, 'Let's move along gentlemen, before this rain comes.'

Henry Longford, the English captain, waited at silly mid-on. 'Good afternoon, Mr Donald.'

'Good afternoon, Mr Longford.'

'Nice of you to join us.'

'Yes, I'm sorry I couldn't bowl to you.'

'I'm sorry too. I think I've worked you out.'

David stopped, mouth open. Then he smiled.

Windsor said, 'Let's hurry, Henry, before the rain, and bedtime.'

'Quite right, Edward.' Then Longford raised his voice, so both umpires and Tanner could also hear what he said. 'Now there has been some discussion about whether you have a right to bat, David, given that you have not fielded for any of the last five days.'

Tanner stepped towards him. 'And you can thank your lucky stars that didn't happen.'

Longford raised his arm, palm open. 'And it has been decided that, rather than get the lawyers and match referee out here, we will waive that challenge, in the interests of a result.'

'Very well then,' said Tanner.

'But you should know,' went on Longford, 'you have entered a man's game, David, and we will bowl and field to the utmost of our abilities and the laws of the game of cricket in order to get you out. I personally believe that you should not be out here. That you are endangering yourself by being here.'

Tanner said, 'Especially if you bowl at the batsman.' Tanner looked at Longford with a steady dark gaze.

Longford ignored him. 'Last chance, David. Mr Wisden?'

Mr Wisden shook his head sadly. 'There's a lot of things going on today, Henry, that I don't agree with, but I can only deal with the rules of the game.'

Mr Longford looked for a moment as though he agreed, but then his face closed as he turned back to David.

David said quietly, 'You sound a lot more like Mr Windsor than yourself today, Mr Longford.'

Mr Morgan the wicketkeeper said, 'Hmm,' in a way that sounded like he might agree, but Longford simply nodded, and clapped his hands once. 'Very well. Let's get one of these fellows out.'

Tudor had been standing at the top of his run-up the whole time throwing the ball into the air and catching it again.

David took his guard.

The umpire dropped his arm to signal that Tudor could bowl.

David considered once again just how bad a batter he was. He would get out. Or worse. He'd get sconed by a beamer and be knocked out of cricket forever. And for what? To draw a game. People like Mr Biggins didn't even want him to play well. How could you care about a game when in real life people died? O'Toole was right. David was an orphan. He was alone, standing in the middle of a huge, empty piece of grass, with one of the most fearsome bowlers in the world ... Tudor was letting go of the ball.

David saw him at the last instant and flung himself to the ground, as the ball hit halfway up the pitch and climbed well over him and his wickets.

Tanner yelled, 'Get back in your crease!'

David got up on all fours and turned in time to see Morgan pull back his right gloved hand ready to throw. David scrambled back behind the line just before the ball hit the wickets. He was safe.

Tanner yelled, 'You concentrate, Donald.' Then he turned to Mr Wisden. 'It's getting pretty dark out here, Jock. I can barely see the hatred in their eyes.'

Mr Bosanquet and Mr Morgan set about righting the stumps, as a grey-coated groundsman came out carrying a bucket. He knelt on the wicket and proceeded to fill the little foot holes created by the bowlers running in with sawdust from the bucket.

Proctor yelled, 'I didn't ask for this, Mr Longford.'

David was reminded of something about the grounds-man's walk that made him pay attention. There had been a slight limp. He looked down as the groundsman raised his head. Past the wide hat brim David could see his Uncle Mike trying to wink at him.

'Gidday comrade.' His two front teeth were missing. His eyes were red, surrounded by swollen purple-coloured sockets. He must have seen David's shock because he instantly bent away to continue putting out the sawdust.

'I just thought I'd let you know that I'd got out too. So you wouldn't worry. So no one could tell you lies about what might or might not happen to me if you did or didn't do whatever it was that the whole world does or doesn't want.'

'Pardon?'

His uncle stood with difficulty. He was holding his left arm against his side. It appeared to be bandaged. He tried to smile again, but just made dribble come over his fat lips.

'Uncle Mike.'

'What the devil?' Mr Tanner had come up. 'What are you trying to do now, Donald?'

'Just wishing the lad luck, Jack.' He kept looking at David. 'Few folk are angry with me right now, David. Which makes me very happy, by the way. But I have to stay low.'

'In front of a crowd of sixty thousand people you mean,' said Tanner.

Michael's eyes never left David. 'Bore it up 'em, okay.'

Mr Bosanquet was there. 'You're not the groundsman.'

'Just filling in, ma lud.' Uncle Mike started to go.

Mr Longford said, 'Is this an Australian ploy? To delay the game?'

Michael began to shuffle off, the brim of his hat tilted to hide his face.

Tanner started back to his crease. 'I'm ready to go, Mr Longford. What about your team?'

'Uncle Mike.' David went after his uncle. Caught up in a couple of strides. 'Uncle Mike.'

His uncle looked at him. David could feel the look. It was like ... it was like ... a full belly.

'Thanks for coming.'

Mr Longford called loudly, 'Mr Wisden and Mr Bosanquet, I must protest. I am officially protesting this clear attempt to waste time and delay the game. This is a poor form of gamesmanship bordering on cheating.'

'See ya later, mate.' His uncle turned and limped towards a gate on the far side of the ground, attempting a tuneless whistle as he went.

'Mr Donald, please take your place, or you will be given out.'

David went to the bowler's end.

Anthony Dorrington called out, 'Get a single, Tanner, so we can dong this little blighter.'

'Yes,' called Windsor, 'stop being such a snotty little cheat, Donald.'

Two Bob had taken his stance, the fieldsmen on the leg side again, but not all of them. Some had been sent out near the boundary now on the on side. They were offering Tanner the single, in order to get David on strike.

David looked to see if Uncle Michael was still in sight, but he had gone. He took a deep breath and concentrated.

Proctor came in and bowled a short delivery at Jack Tanner, who weaved under it.

Proctor glared at Tanner.

Ernie Morgan, the wicketkeeper, called, 'He's afraid to hit it, Thomas.'

Tanner leaned on his bat casually. 'Sure is getting dark, Mr Wisden.'

Tanner dropped the next at his feet. He hit the next one a short distance out onto the on side, but when David started to run, he called no, and sent David back. He came down the pitch. 'David, you know how farming the strike works, don't you?'

'Um, yes.'

'Well, it means we only score twos or fours until the last ball of the over. Then you run like hell when I call yes. But be ready on the second last ball too.'

'Yes.'

And so Tanner blocked or didn't play the next three balls. On the second last ball Longford called fieldsmen in so that they would no longer give away an easy single. Proctor bowled a fast yorker next ball, and Tanner could only jam down and keep it from bowling him.

'Ready, David?'

'Yes,' said David.

Tanner took guard.

Proctor bowled fast and slightly down the leg side.

Two Bob tried to get some bat on it, but must have missed.

David didn't see or hear the bat hit the ball because he was already running. He dimly heard Tanner call, 'No,' and then he heard Tanner say, 'Oh shit,' and then he was sliding his bat in as the English wicketkeeper looked up in shock and threw the ball in his gloves towards the wickets.

'Other end,' someone else had yelled, but it was too late.

'How is that?' yelled Morgan towards Mr Bosanquet.

David looked over to the square leg umpire who stood immobile. His finger stayed down. David must have made his ground before Morgan threw his wickets down.

Tanner called from the other end, 'So, no don't run is not an option?'

'You said I had to run. And now we only need sixteen to win.' David sucked in air. He could hear the crowd settling their excitement now. The whole sky was completely filled with the clouds. They seemed to hang low, as though too full of water to remain any higher.

'Look at those batting gloves. Had to have them specially made for your fingers did you?' It was Windsor. He was standing close to David's end, while Tudor went to his bowling mark and the players hurried to their spots. The umpires were talking together and looking at the sky. 'Your hands are positively deformed, Donald. You're a monster, a freak. You should never have come back. You stupid little deformed thing.'

David laughed. He looked at Windsor and he laughed. It was like school. In Dungarin one of the Pringle boys used to say things like this. About his hands. And his ears too. David looked at Windsor and he said, 'What happened to your chin? How come you don't have a chin?'

Windsor turned away. And David said, 'I'm sorry Mr Windsor. I didn't ...'

'Shut up. You freak.'

Mr Bosanquet and Mr Wisden walked to the centre of the pitch. Mr Wisden said, 'It really is getting too dark to bat against such spirited bowling.'

'No,' yelled Longford.

'I'd like to offer you the light, Mr Tanner.'

Tanner started to nod. The crowd started to cheer.

David yelled, 'No!' He ran down to Jack Tanner.

'We've been offered the light. We've got the draw!'

'Let's not.'

'What?'

'It's only sixteen runs Jack. You can get sixteen runs easy.'

'David, we have the draw.'

'We can win.'

'Or lose. We can't last out here.'

'We can. Let's win.'

Tanner looked towards the players' area. He gestured towards the wicket.

David joined the mime show. He ran to his end and showed he was ready to keep playing.

The English players said nothing. They stayed very still. The crowd went silent.

John Richardson did not raise his arm to call them in. He sat down ... and he left it to the batsmen.

Jack Tanner looked around. Then he yelled, 'Up to the West Aussies, I reckon.' He went back to his crease and the people around the oval gave out a huge cheer, although it had the sound of bravado rather than triumph.

David yelled, 'Let's bore it up 'em.'

'Come on, briskly,' called Longford. 'Before the rain.'

Windsor gave a nasty beat-you smile.

Tudor ran in and bowled a full toss straight at Tanner's head. Jack raised his bat, horizontal, and the ball seemed to just skim it and then it kept going and rising and going.

David turned to see Mr Wisden raise his arms to signal six runs.

Tanner stepped towards Tudor and said, 'You do that again and I'll smash your face in.'

Tudor glared.

David called, 'We only need ten to win now.'
Tanner took guard again. Tudor sent down a half-pitched
delivery that climbed rapidly. Tanner did not raise his
bat to meet the ball and protect himself. He dropped his
hands and took the bat away from the path of the ball and
he let it hit him high on his left shoulder. David heard him
gasp. There was a louder gasp, as though an echo from the
crowd.

David went down to see him. 'Are you all right?'

'No.'

'Does it hurt?'

'No. My arm is numb.' Tanner undid a button on his shirt
and David could see a number of round purple bruises on
his chest and other round red ones that had not yet turned
blue.

'Oh.'

'Better go down swinging. I can barely see it anyway.'

David returned to the bowler's end, while Tanner took
guard. His stance looked a little off.

Tudor bowled another short-pitched delivery and Jack
swung early and a little blindly. The ball caught the top of
the bat and flew high and behind. Tanner screamed, 'Run.'

David ran. He could see Proctor way down on the
boundary running in. He was aware of Windsor running
back.

'Yes, another,' screamed Tanner.

David was running through and had to skid to a halt and
turn around.

Tanner was already nearly down his end. David wanted
to see where the ball was. If it had been a catch.

'Run,' screamed Tanner in his ear.

David ran down the other end and was there easily before the ball was returned. It had apparently dropped safely between the two fieldsmen. David panted and felt at his forehead. Blood? It was rain. A big wet drop splashed on his cheek.

Tanner was ready.

Tudor ran in. It was exactly the same ball that Tudor had bowled the previous two times.

Jack stepped forward and hit early and sweetly. You could hear the wood clap like thunder. The ball drove through the on side along the ground all the way to crash into the pickets with another loud woody thud for four runs.

'Shot,' yelled David. The crowd cheered and clapped.

Wisden put his arm out and round, signalling four.

Jack Tanner stood resting on his bat, looking at Tudor, comfortable with the world.

David realised that Tudor had panicked.

Longford called to the umpire. 'This rain, Mr Wisden. My players could slip and fall. Shouldn't we go in?'

Jack was on forty-seven. They only needed a four to win.

The rain was steady, but light. The flags on the clock pavilion had stopped swirling. They hung, sodden. It would not be long.

Mr Wisden called, 'A little longer, gentlemen.'

Jack Tanner swung his left arm and winced. He took his guard.

Longford changed his field. He put a couple of players out on the boundary. Then he brought some others in. He was wasting time while he looked at the sky.

Tudor bowled a yorker. Tanner stepped forward, saw it late, and jammed the bat down even later. He missed the ball, but the ball just missed the stumps. David could not see how it had missed.

On the next ball, Tanner played back, but Tudor had bowled a perfectly placed outswinger that drew Jack's bat to a nick. The ball flew to Windsor in second slip. His hands came up to meet the ball, but not quickly enough. The ball hit his wrist and came forward. He reached again, too slow. The ball hit the ground. The crowd gasped.

Morgan and Longford groaned too.

Windsor yelled, 'The ball is wet and I couldn't see it properly. We shouldn't be playing in these conditions.'

Two Bob wiped the rain out of his eyes and took his guard once more.

Tudor came steaming in and bowled another yorker. Jack caught it low and hit another drive out towards the boundary. There were no fieldsmen out that way. He yelled, 'Run four.'

David ran. He got to the wicketkeeper's end and turned.

The rain was slowing the ball down to stop inside the boundary. Ostler was still running around to it.

David ran again, Tanner already nearly down his end again.

'Again, David,' yelled Jack.

'Bowler's end,' yelled Morgan.

Jack had caught up to David. 'Run!'

David ran back to the wicketkeeper's end for the third run and he turned for the fourth to see Jack stopped at the bowler's end.

'No,' yelled Tanner, and David turned to ground his bat across the crease.

The powerful throw from Ostler came in on the bounce and Morgan caught it over the wickets. They'd only made three. Tudor had one more ball left, and the scores were now tied.

While Tudor caught and dried the ball and stalked off to the top of his run, Longford brought the field in to surround David.

Windsor said, 'I've seen a player die from being hit on the head with a cricket ball.'

Longford said, 'That's enough.'

'What did you say?' asked Windsor, angrily.

'I said enough. I think he's being quite brave.'

'Might I remind you, Henry, the board has suggested a failure to win today will cost you your job.'

'And so it's already gone then, mathematically, wouldn't you say, old chap.'

Windsor smiled. 'The king is dead, long live the king.'

Wisden called, 'David, this light is awful. Can I offer you the light?'

Morgan called, 'It is within your power to do more than offer, Mr Wisden.'

'Within my power but not my inclination,' replied the umpire.

Jack called down, 'We can take the tie, David. Even better than a draw. They'll talk about it for years.'

'I'm ready,' said David. He wasn't. He realised how dark it was. Rain kept getting in his eyes. His bat was slippery. He waited, hitting the base of the bat against the ground, trying to open up his eyes in order to see everything more clearly. He kept his mind on the bowler.

Tudor was running in. His arm came over.

David swung his bat at the same time. He heard his elbow shatter before he felt the pain. It was intense for a single moment, like being stabbed with a burning stick. A bright light burst inside his head, then passed. His bat was flying in the air, doing a slow arc down the wicket towards the bowler. He felt faint, but made himself take a huge lungful of air, and turn and step back into his crease. He would not faint. He would not go to sleep. There would be no blackness. He would stay awake.

And then the pain went. It didn't hurt. There was a lot of booing coming from the distance. Maybe it was thunder.

The Englishmen were around him. 'Are you all right?'

'Shouldn't have been out here.'

'None of us.'

'Oh dear. Look at his arm.'

'This is your fault, Tanner.'

'You fucking bastard, Tudor.' It was Jack.

David looked up. 'I'm fine, really I am.'

Mr Bosanquet said, 'No you're not.'

Longford said, 'You need to go off.'

'Call a stretcher.'

'The doctor. There's blood.'

'No,' yelled David.

Mr Wisden said, 'It's broken David. Bone is sticking out!'

David felt cold. His arm was starting to ache, deep inside, from a place he'd never felt pain before.

David said, 'Let's finish the game. I'm not out.'

Jack Tanner said, 'David. It's only a game. There'll be others.'

'No.'

'Quite right, Mr Donald. Very well. Let's do this. And let's do it correctly.' It was Longford who was taking charge. 'Allegro, Jack, before we can't see a single thing. Windsor, first slip. Dorrington second. I want a ring of slips fieldsmen. Ostler, fly slip. Tudor and Proctor, both of you down at the boundary behind Morgan.'

Proctor said, 'But who's going to bowl, then?'

'I am,' said Longford.

Windsor said, 'What? You're mad.'

Other players nodded. Some grumbled. But Jack Tanner nodded and went down the batter's end. Longford ran back a couple of steps.

David could see all the English players behind Tanner.

Ernie Morgan yelled, 'Hear hear, Henry.'

Henry Longford took two steps and bowled a slow looping delivery outside off stump. Jack didn't hit it hard. He didn't need to. He hit the ball to the vacant mid field. 'Run, David.'

David could not run. He didn't even have his bat. He held his right arm at the wrist, feeling blood or rain dribbling from his elbow, as he walked down the pitch towards the Englishmen. Only Windsor had turned his back. People were already coming over the fences and running towards the middle. Thousands of people seemed to be running towards David as he walked towards them.

'Come on, son,' yelled Darby.

David walked across the crease.

Jack Tanner got his fifty.

Australia won the Test series three games to two.

It rained for a week, even in Dungarin.

David Donald did not bowl in the fifth Test, nor did he score any runs with the bat. He did not bowl or bat for Australia again. His elbow did not heal properly and this meant he could never again completely straighten his right arm. Nor could he turn his right wrist without a little pain. Doctors agreed that there were probably drifting bone fragments.

Cricket went on without him. Young Dan Bidman was about to enter the Australian team and become the greatest batsman who ever lived. Western Australia joined the Sheffield Shield and played cricket against the other states. Other British colonies besides Australia produced their own champions. The West Indies were unbeatable, until the next great team. And still things changed. Six-ball overs replaced eight. Five-day games replaced ten. A version of cricket was invented in which each team only batted for a mad dash of fifty overs as the world got faster, and found new ways to sell more of itself for less.

David went back to his grandfather's farm, which was now his. The rain soaked the ground and the river flowed high. He used the irrigation system to put in new fruit trees and even tried a stand of olives. He didn't go down to Perth, nor attend a hundred dinners they tried to organise in his honour. It wasn't him, he said, who did all that, but someone else. He planted wheat and ran sheep and kept a couple of Jess's litter. The girls spoilt the dogs for working, but David didn't have the heart to stop them. He found that the strength of purpose and character that had helped turn him into a great bowler and national hero seemed to have deserted him utterly when confronting his own wife and children. It was an abject failure he never regretted.

David married Nell Parker and had four girls, none of them cursed or blessed with especially long fingers. Frances, the youngest, was good at piano. Jill became a pretty good swimmer. Samantha and Bronwyn would go to university, Bronwyn becoming a historian. They all played netball, including Nell, just for the fun of it.

Occasionally one of the team would visit, 'just passing by like,' even though it's hard to be passing by Dungarin, as it's not on the way to anywhere. Bigger, better cars on bigger, better roads made that easier. Ten Ton visited with his whole family, and Two Bob came up quite a lot, strange as it may seem. He'd sit on the front veranda and have a cup of tea while he told David about Australia and the world, and they'd remind each other of the little things about each other that got up each other's nose that particular summer.

There are some myths around all sports and no less with cricket. Bidman was reported to have practised his impeccable timing by using a cricket stump to hit a golf ball up against a corrugated iron water tank. A lovely story, but a little too neatly crafted, I always thought.

Rumour had it that the lost cricket ball from that

final over in Sydney was souvenired by none other than Henry Longford himself. He had fielded it and tucked it immediately into his pocket, making sure there was no possibility of a run-out. According to this version, Longford keeps it in his office in Leicester and calls it his Redemption Ball. Longford never played cricket for his country again. He retired from the international circuit, but captained Leicester for the next fifteen years, establishing a team noted for its sense of fair play and sportsmanship.

Others declare that Longford can't have the ball, as many distinctly recall one of the groundsmen limping out to retrieve it almost as soon as Jack Tanner had hit it. Apparently this groundsman then managed to get young Donald to sign the ball, left-handed, as he was carried on the stretcher to hospital. Hitting hard times, the distraught groundsman had had to sell the ball in a pub raffle. Many people from all around Australia have personally sworn to this version of events, an improbable number also offering to produce the ball.

There are myths, and then there are facts and then there are the real people. Ten Ton retired from cricket, and opened a pub in Fitzroy. Freddie Turner, the injured spinner, returned to the team following David's injury, proving every cloud has a silver lining. John Richardson captained the team for another five years. He became a major in the Second World War, in which Andrew Bardsley and Maud McLeod were killed. Jack Tanner served with bravery and returned to sell television sets before entering parliament. O'Toole fell under a tram and was killed, but not before he published a very successful book called *The Kid* based on David's life story. It was full of lies and controversy, and Geoffrey Calligan teamed with Steven Biggins to sue

O'Toole for the slander. David used the money to build a health clinic in Dungarin.

He tried to entice Helen O'Locklan to work there, but she would never leave Melbourne.

I tried Dungarin. At first, I'd wander in like a stray tomcat with a chunk out of me and get a feed and a couple of pounds before heading off again to spread the communist revolution and assorted cricket paraphernalia. With Nell's help, I taught David to read a bit better. It turned out that he had a medical condition called dyslexia. They got me a job in the Dungarin school, and that seemed to be working fine for the town and myself, until I complicated things a little too much with a brief dalliance with one of the Mrs Pringles. Lovely girl, but that was the end of Dungarin for me.

I'm writing this account in Melbourne now, between teaching in a public high school near Helen O'Locklan's house. We continue to share a drink and some laughs and our various injuries with a lurching contentment. Sometimes, in the evening, reading a letter from David, we share him too. Occasionally, I'll go in a pub and tell David's story and sell one of those old cricket balls he'd practised with, just to keep my hand in, so to speak.

There are myths around sport and cricket and around David. People forget the facts or ignore the truth pretty soon, and believe the things that suit them. With every passing year, it becomes harder to affirm David's brilliance. He remains so damn unlikely. He bowled a whole cricket team out, not just once but twice, and for only one run. It is impossible. The cricket records make it seem even less real. He only bowled in two Test matches and the decision to bat that dark Sydney afternoon leaves you wondering what might have been. Many talked in the press and in some books about the tragedy of David Donald ... that the cricket world had been robbed of twenty or thirty years of brilliance. It was as though the world had only just been given this bright hint of potential, to have it ripped away again ... a beautiful bird glimpsed amongst the trees and gone. Like the men and women gone to war.

David did not regard any of it as a tragedy. He was happy with what had happened. He brought back some good memories from his adventures away from the farm. He was also happy about the person he had become while he was away. Somehow the pressure had re-clicked some things inside his heart and he was less anxious and less afraid. He'd opened up to the possibilities in other human beings, and this had allowed greater complexities within himself. It allowed him to love.

'What are you going to do now that you've got no one?' O'Toole had yelled that day, and David had his answer. He did have people. But he also had who he had always had. David was content with his own company, with his own thoughts and feelings and memories and his reflection on the world. He was at peace.

David liked the size of Dungarin. You can know all of a small town. Where it ends. What its parts are. You can know each of the people who live there and who they are and what they've done and even pretty regularly predict what they might do. A small town is a thing that is of human size, at least of the size that David's mind could encompass.

It got too small for David's girls and they left. Dungarin foundered and failed, as the nearer towns thrived. One, then all, of the Pringles moved into cities large enough to hold them. The railways closed down, then the school. Even the highway moved east.

David liked his town, and he loved the space that was his farm. He liked working it: digging and planting and harvesting. He liked fixing it. He liked the seasons and how they needed to be stepped into and worked with. David liked the pre-dawn and eating breakfast with Nell. He liked being out there, anywhere on his land, when the sun came up.

And at dusk, he liked to be on the hill overlooking the dam. From there, he could see the lights of the house. His favourite time was still just before sunset, when all the midgies came out to dance in the last gold the sun put out. They danced around the golden liquid of the dam, turning from grey to silver and then golden themselves. And for those fifteen minutes they turned into orange and yellow fairies and wraiths and whatever else that was filled with magic, and you could remember or imagine being anything in the world, absolutely anything you wanted.

ADDENDUM

I came into possession of this manuscript while helping my mother order my father's affairs, following his death in 2008. It would appear that the manuscript was sent to my father following my Uncle Michael's death in 1986. It is characteristic of David Donald that he did not mention it to the other members of his family. I'm not even certain that he read it. He was never a great reader, nor a great talker for that matter. He was a wonderful father.

I have been persuaded to share these writings with a wider public. It is, after all, a very different version of matters, but one I think of which my father would have approved, most certainly in the abundant mischief of the thing.

I have not changed any of the text, but I have added some accompaniments that should help readers who, like myself, are not particularly deep students of cricket.

The diagram depicting fielding positions is courtesy of *Learning Cricket: Rules and Strategy* by J.M. Lawler and R.S. Trumper (Oxford: Olive Press, 1984) and is provided in an effort to explicate some of the fielding changes and positions mentioned in the manuscript.

I have also provided a very brief glossary of cricketing terms courtesy of www.action8cricket.com, added to and amended by Tom Hampton, who is the son of bowler Paul and a personal friend. Again, this is aimed at the non-cricketer and therefore quite likely not to be nuanced or complex.

Finally, and perhaps most controversially, I have written the briefest of biographical lists. There seemed to me on my first readings of the manuscript to be such a profusion of historical and minor figures with such a varied use of surname, first name, nickname and position that some kind of guide would be useful, much like the ones provided in recent printings of the Russian novels of the Napoleonic era (and contemporary television fan websites for that matter).

However, I did not want to spoil the immediacy of the time and events my uncle conjures. Therefore I have not used the fuller biographies currently available in the many fine extant cricket and general historical works. I have attempted to provide biographical sketches of the participants as at the time depicted. In this regard, I have chosen to 'freeze' or snapshot the participants at the time of the Adelaide Test, as this is the moment that David Donald emerged upon an unsuspecting world.

So, for instance, the captain of the time is not the sage and urbane silver fox who became the well-known television cricket commentator of the eighties, Sir John Richardson. Rather, he is described as he was at the time, as lean and athletic, a neat batsman with a growing flair for leadership and risk taking.

I am sure my choices in the biographical area will be contested. Please accept the apologies of an academic playing well out of her area of specialisation. I mean no offence.

Dr Bronwyn Elliott (nee Donald), 2010

THE AUSTRALIAN TEAM

(Batting order for Adelaide, Melbourne, Sydney Tests)

Terry Johnson (Chalkie) New South Wales. Right-handed, opening batsman. Good defence. Slow to start, then fast scorer. Mathematics teacher. Thirty-two years old. Fifty-five Tests for Australia.

Andrew Bardsley (Beardie) Victoria. Left-handed, opening bat. Free scoring. Sales assistant. Twenty-one years old. Debuted in the first Melbourne Test.

John Richardson (Richo, Skip, Gov, Cap) New South Wales. Right-handed batsman. Dashing. Australian Captain. Bank manager. Thirty years old. Fifty-one Tests.

Jack Tanner (Two Bob) Western Australia. Right-handed batsman. Big hitter. Farm machinery salesman. Twenty-five years old. Debuted in Adelaide Test match.

Ken Hall (Ned) Queensland. Left-handed batsman. Bludgeoning hitter. Excellent fieldsman. Refrigeration mechanic. Twenty-five years old. Twenty-two Tests.

George Jackson Victoria. Left-handed batsman. Worker of the ball. Professional cricketer. Thirty-four. Five Test matches. Recalled to the Australian team after three years away.

Maud McLeod (Mopsey) South Australia. All-rounder. Medium-fast swing bowler. Right-handed batsman. Good close infieldsman. Farm labourer. Twenty-two years old. Ten Test matches.

Bill Baker (Tinker) New South Wales. Wicketkeeper. Right-handed batsman. Primary school teacher. Thirty years old. Eighty-seven Test matches.

Geoffrey Calligan (Legal) Melbourne. Fast bowler. Tight line and length bowler. Lawyer. Twenty-seven years old. Twenty-seven Tests.

Paul Hampton (Ten Ton) New South Wales. Fast bowler. Very fast. Brewery worker. Twenty-four years old. Fifteen Tests.

David Donald (Old Man, Billy, Kid, Nipper, Babe, The Kid) Western Australia. Spin bowler (wrist and finger). School student. Twelve years old. Debuted in Adelaide Test match.

Dan Bidman South Australia (born in NSW). Right-handed batsman. Promising. Nineteen years old. Twelfth man in Adelaide.

AUSTRALIAN CRICKET BOARD

(I have not included the whole board, but merely those two members who were instrumental in the events of the time.)

Sir Bartholomew Livingston Chairman of the Australian Cricket Board. Chairman of a number of industries. Knighted for services to industry. Played grade cricket at university. Also played rugby for NSW in his youth.

Steven Biggins Treasurer of the ACB. Lawyer. Member of the Liberal Party of Australia. Engaged to Lucinda Pucker, daughter of newspaper publisher Robert.

THE ENGLISH TEAM

(Although the batting order was to change, and the team
for Sydney, I have used the Adelaide order.)

Anthony Dorrington Kent. Left-handed opening bat.
Free scoring. Professional cricketer. Twenty-eight years.
Sixty Tests.

William O'Malley Middlesex. Right-handed opening bat.
Tight defence. Slow scoring. Soldier. Thirty-two years old.
Seventy-two Tests.

Edward Windsor Somerset. Right-handed batsman.
Front-foot and elegant player. Fast scorer. Landholder.
Twenty-five years. Forty-two Tests.

Henry Longford Surrey. Right-handed batsman. Elegant
back-foot player. Tight defence. English Captain. Banker.
Thirty years old. Sixty-four Tests.

Timothy Bishop Somerset. Right-handed bat. Reportedly
a dasher. University student. Twenty-two years old. Two
Tests. Debuted in the Brisbane Test.

Peter Ostler Surrey. Bowling all-rounder. Fast-medium. Big hitter. Professional cricketer. Twenty-four years old. Thirty-eight Tests.

Earnest Morgan Yorkshire. Wicketkeeper. Left-handed batsman, although not a prolific scorer. Professional cricketer. Thiry-five years old. Eighty-nine Test matches.

Lesley Darby Kent. Spin bowler. Poor batsman. Groundsman. Twenty-nine years old. Fifty-two Test matches.

Albert Dwyer Worcestershire. Medium-paced swing bowler. Devastating in damp conditions. Professional cricketer. Twenty-six years old. Thirty-five Tests.

Douglas Tudor Somerset. Fast bowler. Great speed but also exceptional bounce off the pitch. Accurate. Accountant. Twenty-three years old. Twenty Tests.

Hugh Proctor Hampshire. Fast bowler. Very fast. Farm worker. Twenty-six years old. Thirty-eight Test matches.

CRICKET FIELDING POSITIONS
(for right-handed batsmen)

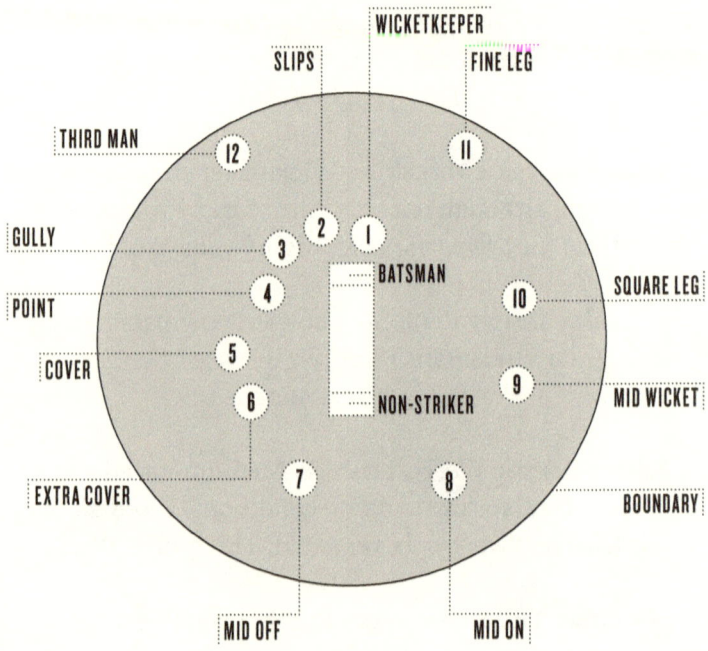

Source: Learning Cricket: Rules and Strategy *by J.M. Lawler and R.S. Trumper (Oxford: Olive Press, 1984).*

GLOSSARY OF CRICKET TERMS

This is an edited and amended version of the glossary provided online by action8cricket.com. Additional definitions and amendments have been kindly added by Tom Hampton.

Agricultural shot A batting stroke that is anything and everything other than standard or copybook. Inelegant.

All-rounder A player who is good at both batting and bowling.

Appeal A request made to the umpire by the fielding side that a batsman be adjudicated out. This request is sometimes loud.

Arm ball A ball delivered by an off-spin or left-arm spin bowler which does not have much turn. The arm rather than the fingers plays the larger role. It drifts a little more in the air and skids rather than spins.

Attack Refers to the variety of available bowlers at the disposal of the fielding captain. It also refers to an approach to scoring and to preserving one's wicket, as opposed to defence.

Average The total figure reached by computation of a batsman's run-scoring performance measured against the number of times dismissed, or a bowler's performance measured by the number of runs conceded when compared to the number of wickets taken.

Away swinger Also known as the outswinger. A ball moving from the line of the stumps at the bowler's end, towards the slips area, but through the air.

Bad light The umpires can suspend play for the day or for a period of time if it is adjudged that the light is too dim for the batsman to fairly see the ball or it may endanger the batsman. Rain can also cause a delay or suspension of play.

Back foot Refers to the movement of the batsman who has placed his centre of gravity onto the back foot. Generally a defensive batting technique, but occasionally used to attack the ball in shots such as the cut, pull or hook shot. (There is a back-foot drive.)

Back up Refers to the batsman at the bowling end who leaves his crease after the bowler has released the ball in preparation for making a run.

Bails The two small pieces of moulded timber which sit atop the stumps. Their placement is an aid in determining more precisely when the stumps have been disturbed. Stumps are often disturbed and never serene, even though they can be untouched, unmoved and unaffected.

Bat The 'handle' is the thin end of the bat held by the batsman. The 'shoulder' is the point at which the bat widens. Bats are sometimes referred to as 'the willow' after the wood they were traditionally made from. The very bottom edge of the bat is the 'toe.'

Bat pad Refers to a close infieldsman placed for a catch for a ball that, after striking the edge of the bat, goes on to strike the pad and rise into the air. A very specific position.

Batsman A player who uses a bat to hit, edge, snick or guide the ball after it has been bowled, usually with the intent of scoring runs or defending his wicket during a match or game, but often also to practise the art and skills of batting.

Batting The process of using a cricket bat for the making of runs or defending the wicket.

Beamer A bowling delivery aimed at the head of the batsman. If not a mistake, then poor form.

Beaten When a batsman attempts to strike the ball with the bat and fails to make contact. He is said to have been 'beaten' by either the pace or skill of the delivery.

Bite The amount of turn a spin bowler can obtain from the surface of the pitch.

Block A defensive batting stroke in which the ball is hit only a little way and usually not in the air. A block suggests no intent to score a run, but rather to concentrate on defence.

Bouncer A bowling delivery of fast pace and pitched short with the purpose of rising to around chest height when arriving at the batsman. Difficult to play most attacking and front-foot shots to this kind of delivery.

Boundary Indicates the outer limit of the playing area. Also used to describe a stroke by the batsman that immediately results in four (over the boundary along the ground or after bouncing) or six (all the way in the air) runs. See fielding diagram.

Bowl To deliver the ball in a manner determined to be legal by the umpire interpreting the rules of cricket.

Bowler Refers to a player who primarily excels at delivering a ball to a batsman or a player in the process of delivering the ball.

Bowler's mark The bowler makes a mark at the 'top' or start of their run-up for bowling each ball. The bowler's mark allows the bowler to keep the same stride each time they run in to bowl. A fast bowler's mark is necessarily further away than a spin bowler's because they use a longer run-up in order to help generate their speed.

Break A delivery that spins to either side of the pitch after leaving the surface. Also used to denote a short halt in play. There is a lunch break and a tea break. There are also a number of drinks breaks. There are also breaks for weather and injury.

Bump ball A ball that hits the ground immediately after leaving the bat and, to the appearance of some fieldsmen and spectators, looks to have come directly off the bat. Once the ball touches the ground after being hit, it should not be given out, caught, and it is up to the umpire to decide whether it was a catch or merely a bump ball.

Bye A run scored through any means other than being struck by the bat.

Call Either a confirmation or refusal that a run should be taken by a batsman in order to alert his partner. Usually shouted as a 'Yes,' 'No' or 'Wait.' Shouting 'Run' is not generally used as a call beyond the junior levels. Calling correctly and the consequent understanding between batsmen is one of the skills of batting in cricket. Judging the run entails judging the fieldsman involved as well as the abilities of the paired batsman. It often also involves estimates on the bowling and the state of the game.

Cap The peaked headdress normally worn by a team member and showing the colours and/or team logo.

Caught behind A ball caught by the wicketkeeper after being struck by the batsman.

Cherry Refers to a new ball because of its bright red, cherry-coloured appearance.

Clean bowled When a batsman is beaten by a ball and subsequently dismissed through the stumps being disturbed or broken (hit by the bowled ball).

Close Refers to a declaration by the batting team of a closure to an innings or the end of the day's play.

Cover drive An attacking batting stroke, usually off the front foot, directed towards the covers area between mid-off and point.

Crease The lines drawn across the wicket to denote the 'safe' area for a batsman. The batsmen usually play in and run between the two crease lines drawn approximately a yard in front of each wicket. If the bat is not grounded after a shot and the batsman is out of his crease he can be stumped. If the bat is not grounded and he is 'out of his ground' while attempting a run, he will be run out. The bowler must bowl the ball from behind the bowling crease.

Crumble Refers to the state of the pitch, usually late in a game after experiencing considerable wear but also because the green grass dries. A crumbling pitch is often favoured by a spin bowler, as it will allow the ball more 'bite' and turn.

Cut Refers to a batting stroke played to the off side between the covers area and the wicketkeeper. In bowling, refers to the deviation of a delivery, caused by a non-spin-bowler imparting varying types of spin on the ball. These types of deliveries are referred to as 'cutters'; either leg-cutter or off-cutter.

Dead bat A form of defensive shot in which the ball is blocked from the wicket and dropped harmlessly to the ground by the batsman attempting to remove all force from the shot and therefore from the power of the balls rebound from the bat.

Deep Refers to the outfield. A fieldsman 'in the deep,' is either at or near the point boundary.

Declare Usually a batting side's innings is 'closed' or ended when ten wickets fall. However, the batting team can 'declare' its innings closed at any time before. This is a most important strategic decision when 'going for a win.'

Delivery Bowling the ball or a ball bowled.

Dig in The act of a batsman concentrating on remaining at the crease for a long period, usually involving defence at all costs rather than risking his wicket by attempting to score frequent runs.

Draw The Test match is declared a draw if the side batting last does not pass the other side's aggregate score, yet has 'wickets in hand,' that is, batsmen not yet out. This is a quite common result of Test matches, even of five days. See also Tie.

Drawing the stumps The physical act by an umpire of withdrawing the stumps from the pitch to signal the close of the day's play.

Drift The sideways movement in the flight of the ball after being bowled by a spin bowler. A side breeze can affect the amount of drift, as can the amount of 'air' given in 'flighting' the ball.

Drive A drive is a straight-batted shot, played by swinging the bat in a vertical arc through the line of the ball, hitting the ball in front of the batsman along the ground. It is usually off the front foot (but not always) and includes the off drive, straight drive, on drive and square drive. See fielding diagram.

Duck A score of zero. Someone, somewhere, thought the numeral zero looked like a duck's egg. One would hope the real derivation was more complicated.

Edge The outermost perimeter of the bat. Also refers to a ball only just struck by the edge of the bat. Sometimes called a 'snick.'

Feather A very faint edge of a ball by the batsman.

Field The ground or oval on which a match is played. Also refers to the placement of fieldsmen within the playing area.

Fieldsman Sometimes referred to as fielder. A player strategically placed within the field of play, with the object

of stopping the batting team from scoring runs and/or taking a catch to get them out. The teams take turns. The fieldsmen play against a series of batsmen.
See fielding diagram.

Fiery A particularly fast-paced bowler. Often referring to a bowler who bowls a succession of short-pitched deliveries.

Finger spin A method used by a bowler to deliver a ball that will spin off the surface of a pitch. The spin on the ball is imparted with the use of a finger or the fingers (as opposed to a wrist action).

Flat Generally refers to the condition of a pitch with an even surface and not much bounce. Batsmen prefer 'flat tracks' because it makes predicting the bounce and direction of the delivery more predictable.

Flight The loop in the path of the ball after being bowled. Flight refers to vertical variation in the trajectory of the bowled ball.

Flipper Leg-spin ball that uses backspin (rather than overspin or side spin). The ball tends to be flatter than the normal leg break and keeps lower. David Donald referred to this ball as a skidder, possibly referring to the way the ball seems to skid low and straight. If he had been among more experienced cricketers, they would have explained the correct term for this kind of delivery (although the category is general and therefore does not quite do justice to the variations he was able to achieve).

Follow-on The option by the fielding captain for the batting team to immediately bat again if a team is dismissed during its first innings for two hundred runs less than the opposition. To put this complicated matter in a different way, should the team batting first amass a sufficiently high score, and the team batting second manage a sufficiently low score, the first team can demand (enforce) the second team bat again, taking advantage of the possibility that the second team may again achieve a low enough score such that the sum of both scores will still not be enough to force the first team to have to bat twice, or that, even if the first team has to bat again, and if there is a sufficiently low score to overtake, then any deteriorating pitch conditions will still give the first team sufficient numerical advantage to win the game more easily.

Footmarks During the course of a game the bowlers wear footmarks into the pitch where their feet repeatedly land on their 'follow through' after releasing the ball in the bowling action. There are laws governing running on the pitch, but footmarks inevitably develop and deepen as a match goes on. They offer significant aid to a spin bowler.

French cut Mis-hit shot in which the ball takes the inside edge of the bat and changes direction such that it passes behind the batsman, but in front of the stumps (and often away to the boundary, which only deepens the irony of the ball missing the wickets).

Front foot Refers to the movement of the batsman who has placed his centre of gravity onto the front foot. The movement forward, rather than back, can be used for defensive shots, but is usually used to play such attacking shots as the drive(s), the sweep shot and the leg-glance. Getting to the pitch of the ball is often a key to this shot, as well as timing.

Full-blooded A batting stroke played with the full physical power of the batsman.

Full toss A bowling delivery that reaches the batsman without first having struck or bounced off the pitch. On the full.

Gardening The act of a batsman patting down, with the tip of his bat, either loose areas of pitch or pieces of the playing surface that have come apart.

Good eye The ability of a batsman to assess and sight a delivery much quicker than would normally occur.

Good length A bowling delivery that pitches in such a position, it will confuse the batsman as to whether the ball should be played off the front or back foot. A good length is usually about one to two yards in front of the batsman. Advancing batsmen try to alter the length of the ball, as do batsmen who play back.

Googly This is a delivery by a right-arm leg-spin bowler which, to a right-handed batsman, appears as if it will spin from leg to off, however, spins towards the wicket. A legspinner's 'wrong-un.' Like most spin deliveries, this is easier to show via a diagram, but suffice it to say, this spins the opposite way to the bowler's 'stock' or usually spinning deliveries.

Groundsman The person who prepares and maintains the pitch and playing field.

Guard The batsmen 'takes guard' when in his prepared neutral stance as he waits for the ball to be bowled. He is guarding his wicket, but also in a position where he can move onto the front foot or the back or move sideways in order to score runs.

Half-volley A bowling delivery which pitches in such a position that the batsman is able to strike the ball almost immediately it leaves the surface of the pitch. In terms of a good length, this ball may be slightly over-pitched or the batsman might have moved his own position such that it favours the bat.

Hat-trick When a bowler is able to achieve three dismissals from three consecutive deliveries in the same match.

Hit wicket To strike and subsequently 'break' the stumps with the bat during the execution of a shot. This results in the batsman's dismissal.

Hook (shot) A batting stroke played to the on side where the ball is hit over the batsman's shoulder, often as a result of a short-pitched delivery from the bowler.

Innings The period of time spent batting by a team or individual. Each team has a maximum of two innings each in a Test match. A batsman's innings takes place until he is out or retires. If a batsman has not been dismissed, Not Out is listed before his score.

Inswinger A bowling delivery that deviates in the air, to a right-handed batsmen, from the off side to the leg side (or in towards the batsman and stumps).

Knock A term used to describe the batting innings of an individual player, but most often when the batsman has scored some runs. For instance, a batsman might have a good knock, or a patchy knock or a tough knock, but never a knock of nil runs.

Lbw, leg before wicket This is a method of dismissal where the batsmen is adjudged out should the ball have hit the wickets if not for the pads being in the way. Only the bat can be used to stop the ball hitting the wickets.

Leg, leg side The part of the field that is to the left of the batsman when he faces the bowler when batting. Also known as the on side.

Leg break A delivery from a spin bowler which turns off the surface of the wicket from the leg side to the off side, away from the right-handed batsman (and towards slips).

Leg cutter A delivery from a pace bowler which deviates from the leg side to the off side after leaving the surface of the pitch.

Leggie Spin bowler whose 'stock' or usual ball is a leg break.

Length Used to describe the part of the pitch where the ball either struck or would have struck prior to reaching the batsman.

Lofted, lofted shot A delivery struck in such a way it travels high in the air for some distance.

Loopy Looping. See Top spin and Overspin.

Maiden When applied to a bowler, describes an over where no runs have been scored by the batsman from any delivery. For a batsman, it refers to a maiden innings or maiden century, both being the very first occasion of each.

Men A great deal of the terminology of cricket involves batsmen and fieldsmen. Many of these terms have evolved along with the rest of society to become more gender neutral, such as batter, bowler and fielder. Maids are recorded playing a game of cricket in Surrey in 1745 (according to Bronwyn) and it must be clearly recognised that women's cricket continues to flourish around the world and is played by the same rules.

Middle order Refers to the batting positions or batsmen numbered between five and seven.

Nets Generally applied to any area where cricket is practised. Netting, therefore leading to the term nets, normally surrounds these areas.

New ball Simply, a completely new ball yet to be used in play, or one that has not been used for many overs.

Non-striker A term used to describe the batsman waiting at the bowler's end.

Off (side) The area immediately to the front right of the batsman when waiting for the bowler to deliver a ball.

Off spin Spin bowling in which the ball is 'turned' so it spins towards the stumps of a right-handed batsman. The ball is turned the opposite way to a leg spinner.

Offie Bowling off spin or an off-spin bowler.

On(side) The area immediately to the front left of the batsman when waiting for the bowler to bowl.

Outfield The part of the playing surface of the arena closest to the boundary.

Over The set number of balls bowled by a bowler. An over now consists of six balls. The term 'over' is also called by the umpire when the bowler has completed his six balls. The six-ball over was adopted around the world after 1976. Prior to this there were eight-ball overs. In the 1800s there were four-ball overs.

Overspin, top spin The ball rotates forwards. David Donald used a variety of these sharply rising deliveries, calling it a 'loopy.'

Over the wicket Used to describe the bowling action of the bowler when the delivery arm follows through on the side closest to the stumps. The opposite term is 'around the wicket,' which describes the bowling action of a bowler when the delivery arm follows through on the side furthest from the stumps.

Overthrow Describes the extra runs scored when a ball is missed by the fieldsman or wicketkeeper when returned to the stumps by a fieldsman.

Pace bowling, bowler Describes all types of bowling other than spin bowling. Can vary from medium to fast pace.

Pad A protective device used to protect the legs of both batsmen and wicketkeepers from being struck by the ball. Can also describe the manner in which a batsman may deflect the ball away from the stumps by thrusting the leg and striking the ball, sometimes called 'padding up or padding away.'

Partnership Refers to the batting performance by two particular batsmen whilst batting together during any particular innings. Or to the cumulative score made by two partnering batsmen.

Pick In batting, refers to the ability of the batsman to visually observe the type of delivery about to be bowled by a bowler. In confronting spin bowlers, this also refers to the batsman's ability to know which way the ball is going to spin. In confronting exceptionally good spin bowlers, picking which way it will spin is no small thing and picking how far it will spin is even more problematic.

Pitch A term also used to describe the wicket where the batting and bowling is performed. Wickets must be twenty-two yards in length to comply with the Laws of Cricket. Sometimes called 'the wicket.'

Plumb When a batsman is standing directly in the line of the stumps and the ball hits his pads. The batsman should be given out, leg before wicket. This matter is decided by the umpire standing at the bowler's end.

Quickie A term used to describe a bowler of fast pace, and nothing to do with floozies.

Raised finger The umpire raises one index finger on the right hand to signal that the batsman is out. The umpires adjudge whether the bowler is caught, lbw, run out, hit wicket, stumped or bowled. Being bowled is usually self-evident as the wickets are disturbed or a bail is dislodged. However, there are many factors in deciding whether a batsman is out in other circumstances, including whether they have 'made their ground,' that is, are behind the crease. Judging if the ball would have hit the wickets if it had not struck the pads first (lbw) can be particularly difficult.

Retired hurt When a batsman is injured or ill they may temporarily leave the ground. They are not out, and therefore, if well enough, may return to resume their batting innings if they can do so before the end of that team's innings.

Return The throw by a fieldsman of the ball to either the wicketkeeper or the non-striker's end.

Run The method of scoring during a game of cricket. Also a single unit of score. Runs are scored by hitting the bowled delivery. Batsmen may then run as many times up and down the wicket as they judge possible before the ball is thrown back at the stumps (if they are short of their ground they are run out). They may also receive automatic runs if the ball crosses the boundary on the full—six runs, or crosses the boundary, but not on the full—four runs.

Run-out A method of dismissing the batsman by disturbing the stumps before the batsman has made his ground and is within the batting crease.

Seam bowler, bowling Refers to a bowler who can cause a ball to strike the pitch on the seam of the ball, thereby causing it to deviate in its delivery path prior to reaching the batsman.

Selectors A group of officials appointed for the purpose of picking the players to represent a cricket team.

Session Refers to a period of play during a cricket match. There is a morning session until lunch. And two afternoon sessions: from lunch until tea and then from tea until close of play.

Shooter A variant of leg spin, the ball is most like a flipper or skidder except that it speeds up off the pitch rather than holding up. Hurries onto the batsman, but does not climb high like a topspinner (or David Donald loopy).

Sightscreen A screen placed near the boundary behind the line of the bowler's arm in order to aid the batsman's sighting of the ball when bowled.

Silly Refers to any fielding position that is located very close to the batsman, which consequently holds extra danger. The fact that the word silly is enshrined at all levels of the game is a testament to cricket's forefathers.

Sitter Refers to a very easy catch.

Skidder Delivery using backspin such that the ball slows and keeps low. See Flipper.

Skipper The captain of a cricket team.

Slips Fielding position behind the facing batter and next to the wicketkeeper. Position is designed to catch the ball knicked or edged by the batsmen. A fast bowler, bowling the new ball will often have 'a number of slips' waiting for a slips catch. See fielding diagram.

Slow wicket Describes the attributes of a pitch that offers little advantage to a pace bowler, however, a considerable advantage to a spin bowler. Usually a pitch is at its hardest and fastest on the first day when it is well grassed and rolled. It then usually settles down to give some advantage to the batsmen before starting to wear such that it finally offers advantages to spin on the last day. There is, of course, infinite variation within the norm.

Sticky wicket Describes a pitch which, although dry on the surface, has underlying soft patches. This type of wicket is generally a difficult playing surface for batsmen as it can cause a ball to behave unpredictably.

Strike, striker The name given to the batsman who is facing the bowler. The batsman is said to be 'on strike.'

Stumps The three upright timber sticks at each end of the pitch. Sitting atop each set of stumps are two bails. A term also used to describe the end of a day's play.

Sundries Refers to any run scored by any means other than from the bat.

Sweep shot A sweep is a cross-batted front-foot shot played to a low bouncing ball, usually from a slow bowler, by kneeling on one knee, bringing the head down in line with the ball and swinging the bat around in a horizonal arc near the pitch as the ball arrives, sweeping it around to the leg side, typically towards square leg or fine leg.

Tail Generally refers to the last four batsman on the batting side who are usually in the side for their bowling ability, and thus not expected to be very good batsmen. When the 'tail enders' do score some runs, then the tail is said to have 'wagged.'

Test A cricket match of international standard of two innings for each side. While Tests are now scheduled for five days, they were once 'timeless,' lasting as long as it took for a result.

Tie A tie is a much rarer event than a draw (see also Draw), in which the last batsman is out when both teams aggregate scores are exactly the same.

Top spin Spin ball in which the seam rotates in a clockwise direction and towards the batsman. Sometimes known as 'overspin.'

Toss The toss of a coin is used to determine whether a particular team will initially bat or bowl to open a match. The winner of the toss can decide whether to send the opposition in, or bat first.

Twelfth man An extra player chosen for a team to act as a substitute fieldsman in the event one is called for. The twelfth man is not permitted to bat or bowl.

Walk Generally used by a batsman to indicate his acceptance of a dismissal without waiting for the decision of an umpire. The physical act of walking away from the stumps. It was once usual practice, but is now very uncommon.

Wicket This term has many different uses. It can refer to the batting and bowling area, a dismissal by a bowler, or the stumps.

Wicket, maiden An over in which the bowler has taken a wicket without a batsman scoring runs. When a bowler bowls a whole over with no runs being scored, it is said, rather jauntily, that he has bowled a maiden over, which is the desire of many a young cricketer.

Wrist spinner Wrist spin is bowled by releasing the ball from the back of the hand, so that it passes over the little finger (causing spin). This imparts an anticlockwise rotation on the ball (from the bowler's perspective).

Yorker A bowling delivery that generally passes under the bat near to a batsman's toes. Presumably an invention claimed by a Yorkshireman.

Adapted from www.action8cricket.com.

ACKNOWLEDGEMENTS

All of the characters depicted in this novel are fictitious, even the real ones. The novel is set at a time of my choosing traversing and conflating the late 1920s and early 1930s. If David were to do the things he does, he would likely have met some of the kinds of known and unknown folk constructed for this story. I researched the time, the war and the cricket, then used what suited me, changing what did not. As much is drawn from Australian fiction and film as from non-fiction sources. The history, like the cricket, is not to be fully trusted. I hope it feels real.

I would like to thank the people who read my early drafts and provided extremely important feedback. Thank you Michelle, Jill, Les, Samantha, Leonie, Callum and Jeff Z.

I'd also like to thank Driftwood Manuscripts for their invaluable reader service. Special thanks to my editor, Georgia Richter, for a wonderful working relationship, to the Fremantle Press team, and to the proofreader, Deb Fitzpatrick.

Curtin University allowed time during my final preparation for publishing this novel. I thank Curtin for this and for the place of creative arts within the humanities.

Lastly, to Dennis Lillee, Alan Border, Greg Chappell, Steve Waugh, Ian Botham, Dougie Walters, David Gower,

Derrick Randall, Merv Hughes, Richie Benaud, the other West Aussies, the other Australians, the English, the Kiwis, the West Indians, the Indians, the South Africans, the Pakistanis and Sri Lankans. Even though I have never met any of them, I have derived great pleasure over many years following the strange game of Test cricket. And finally to Shane Warne and that ball he bowled to Mike Gatting. I think that was the moment when I started to daydream about a twelve year old boy, who ... well, what if —

Michael alludes to a number of literary works and makes up a few. However he also directly quotes from Shakespeare's *Macbeth*, a version of the Homeric *Hymn to Delian Apollo*, Wilfred Owen's 'Strange Meeting' and V.I. Lenin's lecture entitled 'The Tasks of the Russian Social-Democratic Labour Party in the Russian Revolution'. I have attempted, without success, to contact and ask permission of action8cricket for the adaptation of their online glossary of terms.

First published 2010 by
FREMANTLE PRESS
25 Quarry Street, Fremantle
(PO Box 158, North Fremantle 6159)
Western Australia
www.fremantlepress.com.au

Consultant editor Georgia Richter
Cover design Allyson Crimp
Cover images © Mirrorpix and istockphoto

 A catalogue record for this
book is available from the
NATIONAL
LIBRARY National Library of Australia
OF AUSTRALIA

ISBN 9781921361937 (paperback)
ISBN 9781921696428 (ebook)

Fremantle Press is supported by the Western Australian State
Government through the Department of Cultural Industries, Tourism
and Sport.

www.ingramcontent.com/pod-product-compliance
Lightning Source LLC
Chambersburg PA
CBHW031026030726
47497CB00004B/1023